After Whorl
Donning Double Cloaks

Celtic Fervour Series
Book Three

Nancy Jardine

Ocelot Press

Second Edition Nancy Jardine with Ocelot Press 2018

*"As in her earlier novels, Nancy Jardine brings to life the
culture and lifestyle of the Celtic Britons, embodied in the
lives of people the reader can empathise with. Donning
Double Cloaks also gives us a vivid and compelling picture of
the developments leading up to the great battle of Mons
Graupius (Beinn na Ciche) and the battle itself. The lives of
the characters are skilfully woven around these historical
events, resulting in another very satisfying novel in this
excellent series."* Tim Taylor, Historical Author

Find Nancy Jardine online: www.nancyjardineauthor.com
Join Nancy Jardine on Facebook
https://www.facebook.com/NancyJardinewrites
Follow Nancy Jardine's blog: https://nancyjardine.blogspot.co.uk/
Nancy loves to hear from her readers and can be contacted at
nan_jar@btinternet.com or via her blog and website.

Dedication

Making journeys is a central theme in this novel as my main characters, Celtic and Roman, travel northwards. Brennus of Garrigill journeys to the far reaches of the island of Britannia, till he is successful in finding the one charismatic Celt to lead them all in battle, against the forces of Rome. Unlike today, any knowledge of the Late Iron Age peoples he meets along the way has to be acquired by word of mouth. Likewise, my Roman legions move northwards into what is relatively unfamiliar and potentially hostile territory (only the advance scouts having walked the paths before them). My characters cannot pick up a guide book, or map, to give the information they seek, yet they stride onwards.

Today, some people travel the world for pleasure, liking the idea of journeying to far flung places to experience new cultures—many of my family members are very good at this. Other people are launched into a life of travel for professional reasons: sometimes enjoying the lifestyle; though at other times they may tolerate it as a necessary evil, balanced by the rewards of their career. My husband, Alan, travelled from home to far flung parts of the world as part of his job. In his case, it was easy for him to read in advance about the territory he was about to experience, and the lifestyle of the people he was about to work with. All good information, yet it could never diminish the fact that every new place was initially foreign territory, and it took him away from hearth and home.

I dedicate this book to Alan; to the many people who choose to work away from home; and to those who follow orders and accept a life on the hoof. May their travelling life be fruitful!

Acknowledgements

I give hearty thanks to the many people who have given me advice during the preparation of this latest edition of After Whorl: Donning Double Cloaks, especially to those associated with Ocelot Press.

As with Books 1 & 2 of my *Celtic Fervour Series*, my sincere thanks go to friends who helped me with Scottish Gaelic phrases—Leanne Ferguson and Seumas Gallacher.

A very special thank you goes to my brilliant editor, Sue Barnard, whose corrections are spot-on!

Nominations:

After Whorl: Bran Reborn, Book 2 of the Celtic Fervour Series, was accepted for THE WALTER SCOTT PRIZE FOR HISTORICAL FICTION 2014.
The Taexali Game, a time travel novel set in Roman 'Aberdeenshire' AD 210 achieved Second Place for Best Self Published Book in the SCOTTISH ASSOCIATION OF WRITERS—Barbara Hammond Competition 2017. It achieved an *indieBRAG* Medallion status, January 2018.
Topaz Eyes, an ancestral based mystery thriller, was a Finalist for THE PEOPLE'S BOOK PRIZE FICTION 2014

Books in the *Celtic Fervour Series* have Discovered Diamond Status from https://discoveringdiamonds.blogspot.co.uk/

About the author

Nancy Jardine's life-long interest in all historical periods continues, but the era of the Ancient Roman invasion of northern Britain is a particular obsession. Those barbarians (according to the Romans) who lived beyond the Roman Empire's boundaries left secrets that have still to be unravelled.

When not researching, or engaged in various writing tasks, Nancy is a fair weather gardener and a regular grandchild minder. The 'castle' country of Aberdeenshire, Scotland, is a fabulous place to live—there are thousands of years of history on the doorstep.

As a member of an Aberdeenshire Crafters group, she regularly visits local venues where signed paperback versions of her novels are available for purchase. This direct contact is also a great way to gain bookings for author presentations across Aberdeenshire.

After retiring from primary teaching in 2011, seven novels have been published, and an eighth is due 2018.

Nancy is a member of the Historical Novel Society; The Romantic Novelists Association; The Scottish Association of Writers and The Federation of Writers Scotland.

After Whorl:
Donning Double Cloaks

Characters in After Whorl: Donning Double Cloaks

A—Aeonghus (slave spy at Dunpendyr); Agricola (Gnaeus Iulius, Legate of the XX Legion); Antonius Pulis (Praefectus Castrorum at Viroconium Cornoviorum/ Wroxeter); Arun (warrior who exonerates Ineda of spying for the Romans)

B—Balbithan (chief of Balbithan Hillfort); Beathan (son of Lorcan and Nara); Benignus (Roman Brennus delivered wood to at fort); Brennus of Garrigill—Bran of Witton

C—Calgach (The swordsman/Calgacus); Callan (Nara's father); Cartimandua (Queen of the Brigantes); Cerialis (Governor of Britannia AD 71-74); Ciaran (Venicones); Creidne (Gabrond's second daughter)

D—Dairmid (old friend to Brennus at Garrigill); Dermatt (warrior who exonerates Ineda of spying for the Romans); Dubv (son of Ineda and Gaius); Dulius (2nd in charge of supplies at Nidd Roman Fort)

E—Egidius (Decanus contubernium leader); Enya (Gabrond's eldest daughter); Eolus (centurion's scribe); Esk (warrior of Tarras)

F—Fergal (red-haired smith at Crannogs of Gyptus); Fionnah (Gabrond's wife); Frontinus (Governor of Britannia AD 74-78); Fulvia (Gaius's dead cousin);

G—Gabrond (Brennus' brother); Gaius Livanus Valerius (Ineda's captor); Glaucius (soldier in Gaius' personal guard); Grond (of the Crannogs of Gyptus)

H—Hermanus (Praefectus Castrorum at Deva)

I— Ineda of Marske; Iohan (chief of Scortin)

K—Kaideigh (Brennus and Lleia's daughter); Kilmahog (Calasraid Caledon chief)

L—Lara (Iohan of Scortin's wife); Lipanus (goods contact at Quernium); Lleia (sister of Grond and Brennus' hand fasted wife); Lorcan of Garrigill

M—Madeg (Ineda's lover); Marsali (old woman of Balbithan); Meaghan; Mheadhain (chief of Baile Mheadhain settlement); Moran (Brennus and Lleia's son)

N—Nara of the Selgovae, Nith (warrior of Tarras)

O – Onesiphorus (in charge of goods); Orchil (herbs wife at Wroxeter)
P—Pomponius (Gaius' secutore); Publius (aide of Dulius)
R—Ruarke (Ineda's father); Rubrius (chief surgeon at Deva); Ruoridh (Gabrond's eldest son)
S—Seonaigh (Kaydeigh's friend at Dunpendyr Hillfort)
Sorcha (Brennus' lover at Witton); Sorn (Brennus' contact with Venutius)
T—Trune (Venicones High Chief); Tuathal (druid);
U—Uallas (Ineda and Gaius' second son)
V—Varius (scribe to Dulius); Velius (tironis); Venutius (Brigante King)
Z—Zosimus (tironis guard to Ineda)

Gods and Goddesses mentioned:
Celtic: Taranis; Rhianna,
Roman: Juno; Jupiter; Fortuna; Etain (Celtic form also Epona, horse goddess)

Tribal Map AD 74-84
Northern Britannia

Vacomagi

Caledons

Taexali

Venicones

Epidii

Votadini

Damnonii

Selgovae

Novantae

Carvetii

Brigantes

Setantii

Deceangli

Ordovices

Cornovii

AD 74-84
Locations in After Whorl: Donning Double Cloaks

BEINH NA CICHE
MORAN DHUIRN
TULLOS
BAILE MHEADHAIN
CEANN DRUIMIN
BALBITHAN
OBAR DHEATHAIN
MONYMUSK

GREAT SEA LOCH
LUNAN LOCHS
PINNATA CASTRA
TRUNE'S HILLFORT

BERTHA
GLEN OF THE EAGLES
FENDOCH
CALASRAID
AN DUN
UISGE FOR

DAMNONII
HIGH CHIEF'S
SETTLEMENT
DUNPENDYR

EASG
CORSTOPITUM

TARRAS
CRANNOGS OF GYPEUS
LUGUVALLIUM
GARRIGILL

BREMETENNACUM
MARSKE
EBORACUM
WITTON

DEVA
VIROCONIUM
CORNOVIORUM
LINDUM

Chapter One

"Who are you?"

The warrior's eyes lit up in shock, even a little fear, as he took in the sight of the man who approached the tall wooden gates of the hillfort at Garrigill.

"The man you think I am, and yet not that same man. Though I am not a dead warrior either." Brennus could not have wished for a better guard to be at the entrance to his old home.

"We thought you gone from us after the battles at Whorl. Grond was sure you must be dead."

"I know you all must think that, but I lived in spite of my injuries."

Relief spread when his old friend began to smile, acceptance creeping across his familiar features. He grinned at the hearty laugh which bellowed into his ear, Dairmid's clasp across the shoulders the warmest greeting he had had for many a day.

"The face may different, but the voice is unchanged!" Dairmid's inspection was acute as he continued to slap his palms lightly at Brennus' upper arms in cheery fashion, still amazed by his arrival.

"Brennus I am, but not quite the same person you used to call friend. I am also now named Bran of Witton."

"Welcome then, Brennus or Bran. There is surely a story to hear about that. We have long missed your drawn-out tales ringing out around our hearthsides!"

Dairmid stood back and took stock of him. His old friend's keen gaze at his ravaged face no longer bothered him. He appreciated Dairmid's next words as much as the genuine welcome in the man's grin.

"What's a scar or two to a tribal warrior? We all have them somewhere. But come and tell your brother, the chief of Garrigill, where you have been. Your arrival will be such a surprise."

Brennus was certain it would be an immense shock, though he hoped a pleasant one. A long time had passed since he had seen his brother wend his way to the Brigante Tribes' dealings with Cerialis, the Roman Governor of Britannia. And it was an even longer time since Lorcan had set eyes on him.

"Garrigill is quiet, Dairmid." He deliberately kept any censure from his tone, but from what he had seen on the approach to the huge hillfort of Garrigill, there was a poor guard force at its gates.

"Quiet?" His old friend paused before he latched on to the meaning. "We have a large area to patrol, and few able warriors to do it."

Having come up through the series of defence ditches that surrounded the settlement, Brennus assessed in his usual fashion, his gaze a swift move to both right and left. People ambled around, but not in the numbers he would have seen before he left for the battle at Whorl.

"We have even fewer able warriors now, Bre...Bran. Whoever you wish to be named. The defeat at Stanwick left us with many dead, male and female."

"My brothers, Lorcan and Gabrond?"

"Both still live. Gabrond fretted as any warrior would, but he never recovered enough after Whorl to go to battle with King Venutius. He remained in charge here at Garrigill, though Lorcan will tell you all. You have much to catch up on."

They had reached what had been his father Tully's roundhouse, but was now the hearth of his brother.

"Lorcan?"

Dairmid's call brought a small child running out through the entryway of the roundhouse: a little boy who stopped short at Brennus' feet and then tumbled over in a heap alongside.

2

"Slowly, little one. Learn to walk properly before you run." Brennus picked the child up in his arms, certain he knew who the child belonged to. The eyes and facial features were exactly like his brother Lorcan, the hair a slightly lighter bronze than what he remembered of Nara. The little one had to be his nephew.

"Beathan!"

Nara's cry came as she flew out the entrance tunnel after the bairn. Brennus watched her stop short at the sight before her. Her stare went from sheer astonishment, to doubt, and on to utter delight, as he felt her blue eyes slide from the top of his head right down to his feet. Only after the tiniest hesitation did she rush forward, almost knocking him to his knees, her hug encompassing her squirming son.

"Brennus! You are alive. I am overwhelmed. Where have you been?"

He watched his brother exit the roundhouse in pursuit of the commotion, the movements slow and steady. That was not like the Lorcan of old. Since the last time Brennus had set eyes on his brother it looked as though he had not fared so well in the battles at Stanwick; those battles where King Venutius of the Brigantes had fallen under the might of the Roman Empire. An ugly gash marred Lorcan's brow, and his gait was stiff and awkward.

"By Taranis! Can this be? My little brother!"

Lorcan's stare was even more incredulous than Nara's had been. Brennus only hoped the happiness he was reading in his brother's expression truly was so.

"Aye! I still live."

He was so relieved to find that the hug he received had not changed. Although Lorcan was almost a head shorter than him, his grip had ever been tight and welcoming.

"Come! Come and tell us where you have been. We have thought you long dead!"

Beathan fell asleep across his father's lap while the story of his recovery was told, food a-plenty at his elbow, and he was well-watered with Nara's best small beer. The fire at the central hearth was low-burning, emitting a dull red glow, less smoke than usual spiralling up to the conical ceiling beams. His tale was easily told, no coughing induced by choking fumes to interrupt it.

He knew what Lorcan's look of censure meant.

"You would not come sooner because Nara and I had the blessing of our father, Tully, on our marriage."

There was no point in dissembling.

"Aye, to a point. But remember I told you it was a long while before I was able to even consider returning. Like you my brother, my bone breaks took time to heal, and then, at the settlement of Witton, the Romans were ever vigilant over their forced labour."

Lorcan's bone fracture had not healed well. Regardless of Nara's expert tending, the movement at Lorcan's ankle remained limited, his foot permanently askew. Brennus sympathised with his brother's loss of full movement.

Nara looked only a little concerned. "But what makes you come now?"

"Many moons have come and gone, Nara. I can see no need to especially inform your father that I still live. He must have learned to accept your marriage long ago."

"Callan remains indifferent to whatever Nara may do. We informed him of your death – as we thought had happened – and told him that Nara and I had had the marriage rites performed. He was angered to find I would not go to live at Tarras, though he had no way of enforcing it. That part of the bargain had been made with you. So, although you have delayed your return to Garrigill, there was no need to do so."

"Are relations cordial with your father, Nara?"

Nara's laugh rumbled around the roundhouse, her look scathing. "Cordial with Callan? Nay, Brennus, they will never be affable between my father and me. We do trade useful information, though. Since before the battles at Whorl, that exchange of information with the Celts who dwell over the high hills has continued."

That was excellent to know. Brennus knew he would need leaders like Callan of the Selgovae if his vow to Tuathal were to be fulfilled.

4

"I have more to relate to you, Lorcan, of my recent purpose. I have been aiding our king, Venutius, in different ways, and with different people. If you have a mind to listen, I will tell you everything."

A short time later Lorcan's laughter surprised him, the hearty clap at the shoulders a welcome thump. "You were never just mere brawn, my little brother. You may have been the Garrigill champion at hand to hand combat for a while, but there always was more to you. I am delighted to hear of your task. Whether others name you Bran of Witton or Brennus of Garrigill matters little to me, you will always be my brother Brennus even though you are not the same man who left for the Whorl battlefields."

Nara's words were tentative. "Do you believe your work is at opposite purposes to what Lorcan and I have been doing with the Roman Empire?"

"Nay!" Brennus was quick to reassure. "The treaties you have made with Cerialis have also given stability to our mid and southern Brigantes. I have lived amongst them. The Roman Army camps at their village doors, and breathes on their necks by day, but those tribespeople no longer live in such fear that the Roman *gladius* will kill them while they lie in their beds."

"But they must pay the price we have negotiated for that." Lorcan sounded pessimistic. "We of the northernmost areas have escaped their oppressive presence."

"Garrigill will not remain free of Roman occupation, Lorcan. Times are changing again for the northernmost Brigantes."

"Aye. After the newest treaties were made last summer, half a *cohort* constantly patrolled our northern reaches, ensuring no tribespeople raised arms. Of course, that only continued till the cold weather set in." Nara's contempt of the Roman scourge was clear as she tossed on a couple of logs to revive the dying embers. "Then, most of them retreated to their southern wood-walled garrisons to overwinter in greater comfort, only leaving small patrols in encampments spread around."

5

Nodding his head, Brennus agreed that was usual practice as far as he had learned. "Their lines of communication are secure enough for them to be confident of monitoring the Brigantes."

"You mean the signal posts that mar our skyline?" Lorcan's spit into the fire was accurate. "*Ceigean Ròmanach!* Those Roman turds appear in the blink of an eye at the top of those posts."

Brennus laughed at the look of dismay on Nara's face as she stared at his near-blind eye. Shaking his head he assured them talk of his infirmities no longer bothered him, though they had soon after the battles at Whorl.

"Pay no heed to my lack of sight, Nara. I have learned to accommodate it. In answer to you, Brother, the Romans are as skilled at building those towers as they are at making ditches for an overnight encampment."

Nara's scowl was deep. "You sound as though you approve of their ability."

"Never. But I have seen those soldiers work swiftly and effectively. They know exactly how to achieve the swift erection of their towers and camps, and they carry all the tools necessary on their back."

Lorcan nodded into the fire as though watching the Romans at work. "It is true that each soldier carries a heavy burden and is fit and ready for those tasks. I have witnessed their marching."

Nara intervened, rising to fill a pot with water from the large wooden tub which sat at the entrance to the roundhouse. "I know this is so, Lorcan. But if they do the work themselves, then why do they need physical toil payment from some Brigantes?"

"Around Witton it was a way of demonstrating their dominance. My work at hewing wood for them in the forest was intended to humiliate and suppress resistance. For many tribespeople, like those of Witton, they now accept the usurpers in their midst. Soon, for them, it will be as it is in the far south – they will no longer see the Romans as brutal conquerors. The tribes of the far south have embraced the

Roman ways for more than half of a man's lifetime, and have adopted much of the Roman culture."

Nara took the empty cup from him and refilled it from the beer container near the doorway. "Did you consider remaining at Witton?"

"Nay! I needed time to properly recover from the aftermath of Whorl and to come to terms with my new character, but I never intended to remain there. My vow to my old nurse, Meaghan, about thwarting the Roman infiltration of northern Britannia, remains firm. My friend Tuathal, the druid, gave me the necessary tools to wander amongst the tribes to collect information about any insurrection in northern areas. Someone was needed to organise the information now that our former King Venutius is no longer the pivot of news, and I have become that someone. Though I manage that exchange of information, I do it in a quiet way as Bran of Witton. However, I no longer need to be based at Witton. My chain of messengers will now find me wherever I move to."

"You do not allow your blindness to affect your purpose?"

Lorcan looked closely at him. He made sure his one-eyed stare showed no offence at his brother's keen inspection.

"I still have one good seeing eye, Lorcan, but I can never ever trust my right eye ever again. Though there is no clarity, I am aware of darkness and light, which gives me some warning. I have learned to live with my infirmities, as I believe you must also have had to do, after the battles at Stanwick."

Nara patted Lorcan's leg.

Brennus thought her words meant to reassure when she laughed and said, "Your limp is of no matter, Lorcan"

"The constant ache makes a difference to me!" Lorcan nudged her with his toe, his elbow not free since it cradled Beathan.

He laughed along with Lorcan. "Aye, indeed. Some injuries heal well, and others like to remind you of them regularly. It is like that with my back and leg injuries, but I allow the pain no quarter. It will never hold me back from my purpose."

7

For a while they discussed who the conveyors of information were, in the northern areas.

"Then you see a way that I can fulfil my vow, and also aid you without any compromise to your task as negotiators with the Roman Empire?" Brennus asked Lorcan. Having reunited with his brother, he had no wish to set up any form of alienation.

Lorcan's nods were conclusive. "The treaties made after the defeat of King Venutius remain firm, and we have no intentions to alter that status. At present the tribes of Brigantia accept the restrictions put upon us by the Romans, but small skirmishes happen regularly in our northerly areas. I do not negotiate out of any love for our Roman oppressors, but seek to find a compromise that allows us some measure of normal living."

Brennus did not doubt it. Lorcan had always been a peacekeeper of sorts, even amongst Brigante tribes in dispute.

Lorcan continued, "Occasionally a Roman loses his life, but mostly the heavy death toll is of our tribal warriors. But if they continue to engage in small skirmishes when the Romans take over their land, then all will perish. I know it is our nature to repel any usurpers of our soil, but our race must not die out under the hand of a Roman *gladius*. However, I cannot be seen to negotiate these treaties and also give support to someone who will rally a multitude of Celts to fight our oppressors, though that can certainly be your task. Especially as Bran of Witton."

"The Selgovae will never accept the yoke of Rome, not while Callan is alive to prevent it." Nara sounded sure of it.

Having had dealings with her father, Brennus believed her statement. "Aye. My task is set. The Brigantes will not halt Roman expansion, though the Selgovae may be able to do so."

"The high hills are a natural barrier, yet they will not stop a legion. The Roman Army will find their way across if they choose to." Lorcan tossed another log onto the fire, sending orange red sparks to fly around.

Nara sounded fatalistic. "Apart from a few larger settlements, like Tarras, my Selgovae tribespeople live the

8

simple life of the farmer. They will fight for their own land, but I do not see them massing together to block a Roman surge across the high hills."

"Would Selgovae neighbours act in similar fashion?" He was fairly sure it would be so, but needed Nara's knowledge of them.

"The Novantae of the western shores will resist as much as the Selgovae. The Votadini of the east I am less certain of, yet their villages are larger and perhaps even more vulnerable."

Brennus talked long and hard about the way he had gathered information for King Venutius of the Brigantes before the battles at Stanwick.

"No Brigante chief wishes to take on the mantle of kingship now," confirmed Lorcan, adding that the situation did not look likely to change.

Nara's vehemence was high when Lorcan stopped talking. "Our lines of communication must not falter. Links must not be lost, and it is crucial that they are extended beyond the high hills."

He told them his method of sending on messages via Sorn, and of the links in the chain beyond him.

"And this woman, Ineda? She also forwarded information to Venutius?"

Brennus found speaking of Ineda gut-wrenching, her lively nature still so very much missed.

"Aye," he said. "At least, she thought she did, though her messenger was one of my contact's minions. When she sent word on, it was relayed to Sorn, who was my immediate connection; though Ineda thought she was conveying her information directly to the king."

"You allowed her to think she was passing on vital information and kept your role a secret?" Nara's words rebuked enough to bring back his focus which had strayed to the empty rafters.

Only a little guilt bothered him. His intention had been to keep Ineda safe at all times: Ineda, the woman who had meant so much more to him than as a foster-sister. Yet his keeping her safe had clearly failed.

As was becoming habitual, his fingers strayed to the silver band that hung at his chest – the band which had belonged to old Meaghan and which Ineda, as Meaghan's granddaughter, should have inherited. Moreover, as the woman he had been in love with, Ineda had qualified for the gift according to old Meaghan's wishes. It was well past too late for Ineda to receive it. Instead, Brennus continued to wear the band as a reminder of his lost love. He knew he should be anticipating feeling hopeful that another woman would gain his heartfelt affection, but he was not convinced that would ever be possible.

"The attack on you by the auxiliaries of Agricola's *Legio XX* was not due to any miscarriage of information via this woman Ineda?"

Lorcan's question shocked him. The idea that someone could think Ineda a traitor sickened him to the very gut. If it had not been his brother he might have brought his fists into play, even though one of those fists – now missing two part-fingers – made a less effective impact than it had before Whorl.

"Nay! It was no fault of Ineda. Agricola's troops were moving north. Their orders were to search all areas and root out any movement which could be under suspicion. They attacked us and dragged Ineda off before establishing why we journeyed so close to Quernium."

"You said you could find no trace of this woman?" Nara's keen gaze seemed to see into his heart, much as he tried to appear unaffected.

"None. Many people from Witton looked for her, but we could find no sign. Not of where she might be, and no evidence of her passing to the otherworld either."

"I believe our god, Taranis, must favour you, my brother, if you were found."

It was easier to look at the weapons stand near the entryway than face his brother. Less than half full of spears it looked bereft, like his heart. The words were hard to find. "A young warrior, Madeg, was looking for Ineda. Though he perhaps did not want it, he found me instead."

Nara's too-keen inquiry seemed to understand what he did not say, sending a silent sympathy. Ineda's fate at the hands of the Roman Empire still plagued him after so many long, long moons. His life without her had much meaning, was purposeful... but had no love, no enjoyment. Ineda had been a bright spark in his existence before she had been mown down by the Roman scum, and nothing of his new purpose replaced her glow.

He ignored the assessing looks Nara sent him. He maybe had protested a bit too vehemently, but Nara had absolutely no idea of Ineda's hatred of the Roman scourge, and neither had Lorcan.

"Then your future is set, my brother." Lorcan sounded convinced. "At Garrigill you will always be known as my brother Brennus, but as the messenger of our northern tribes I believe you must continue in your role as Bran of Witton. At least, until some situation alters that need."

Brennus agreed.

Chapter Two

AD *74 After Beltane – Viroconium Cornoviorum, Cornovii Territory*

Something had altered the tribune's mood. Ineda had no idea what, but she was determined to find out.

"You new orders please you, Tribune Valerius?"

He was deep in thought during the evening meal they shared in his quarters, fairly unusual since they normally ate in her tiny cell. It was a time when they conversed about mundane topics, but he had been silent. The smile that came her way startled her; it was such a rare occurrence for him to show any feelings, apart from displeasure or anger.

"My new orders?"

"Your grin must mean something pleases you."

It was unexpected when he reached forward and took her hand into his own. He never made any contact with her body, except during the night dark.

"Something does please me very much, Ineda, but it has nothing to do with any new orders. Why would you think that?"

She had no idea what to answer. He knew she was always interested in what was happening around the fortress, though he was always close-mouthed about relating any important developments. Anything new happening she gleaned from his secretary, Pomponius. In no way did she want him to be suspicious of her motives, or to curtail the small advantages she had obtained as his slave since he had started to make love to her. "Only that such smiles are rare."

He continued to grin as he pulled her to her feet and led her to his resting couch.

"It is long past time for you to call me Gaius."

Ineda was not so certain of that. She had resisted thinking of him as anything other than her hated captor, although time and his proximity were making her understand more of the man who had taken her prisoner and used her as his personal bed slave.

The following morning Ineda met Pomponius at the doorway to the tribune's quarters as she headed back to her own room. A sneer was her greeting as the man squeezed past her, not withholding the bitterness in his gaze.

"The tribune will be in a good mood this morning?"

She would not allow the odious man to annoy her, or spoil what had been an eventful night. "I believe you will find him, so, Pomponius."

"His disposition should be excellent, after a night with his personal whore, though whether his father will think so is another matter."

Ineda had no idea what the man referred to, but realised it could not be good. Pomponius may think of her as a whore, but he rarely voiced that word in her presence. Her inquiring silence set the man chattering.

"How can the tribune possibly smile, when he has just learned about the death of his betrothed? It is beyond my understanding."

Pretending to know what the man talked about, she hid her dismay. Tribune Gaius Livanus Valerius had used her last night as a remedy, having learned that his intended wife was dead? It was certainly true that he had shown no remorse of any kind. Teasing and playful for the first time with her, after moons of functional coupling, she had reluctantly found herself hating him less than before. She had almost begun to think of him as Gaius, though she had no intention of naming him thus to his face.

Pomponius was not quite done. Hearing the tribune calling him from within, he hissed, "His father will be greatly displeased by the dispatch I just sent him. Tribune Valerius has written that he will never honour any agreement his father makes to get him another betrothed wife in Rome. He has no intentions of returning to his father's estates. But he will never

13

ever take a whore like you as his wife either!" Strutting off, the odious man never looked back.

Ineda watched him greet Tribune Valerius as though no nasty conversation had occurred with her. As she wended her way to her tiny cell, her thoughts whirled. What did Tribune Valerius' new circumstances mean for her? Had he truly been happy to hear of the death of the woman who had waited for him in Rome?

He did not love her, but it seemed clear his betrothed back in Rome had held none of his love either, and that made him seem such a callous unfeeling man. Till the previous night she would have agreed with such a supposition. Not now.

The night they had just passed had been quite baffling. Tribune Valerius had been tender in his loving; he had even encouraged her to show some of her own feelings for the first time after eleven moons of captivity.

The most momentous part of it all was that after all those moons of avoidance, Tribune Valerius had deliberately shed his seed while still inside her. She knew the consequences to her had changed, but what of him? The remark made some time ago by Glaucius, one of the legionaries assigned to the tribune's personal guard, no longer made sense.

Did Tribune Valerius now want a babe in her womb?

AD 74 Before Lughnasadh – Crannogs of Gyptus, Brigantes Territory

"Atha math dhut!"

Brennus' 'Good day to you' greeting seemed to have no effect as he approached the crannog dwellings of Gyptus. He did not know if Grond had renamed the village after himself since the old chief had died during the past winter. Arriving unexpectedly, Brennus timed his visit to coincide with the festival of Lughnasadh, the beginning of the harvest of the earliest crops.

A chuckle escaped him as memories flooded in. The last time he had visited, three springs past, he had had Nara of the Selgovae in tow, and she had been such a reluctant visitor. Her

14

attempts to escape from Lorcan and the band of warriors were amusing memories which may yet become legendary around the fireside. He could easily see himself making a good tale out of it.

"Declare yourself!"

As was usual in the area, he was accosted on the narrow reed walkway by four of Grond's guards. Though they were striplings they were thorough in their duties, their spears at the ready. It pleased him to see that there were enough able warriors to assume the task, and made no demur as they encased him on the narrow strip of man-built pathway on the lake shore.

"I come to see Grond. Tell him Brennus of Garrigill did not die, and that Bran of Witton has come to pay his dues."

The sentry who answered was unknown to him, and clearly suspicious. It was as he should be over the oddly-phrased statement.

"Dismount."

No conversation was shared till they reached the smithy area, a roundhouse that was set apart from the crannog village of Gyptus.

"Wait here!"

The command was firm but polite enough, as the reins on his horse were removed from his grasp and the beast tethered to the overhang which sheltered a couple of other horses at the edge of the clearing. Two of the guards remained; the other two sped off in the direction of Gyptus' crannog dwelling.

The area was familiar, a rhythmic ring-ting-ing coming from the smithy. Cloying black smoke billowed free from the forge, but the smith was a different man from his former visit, a much younger man. The sweating face lifted from a serious study of the iron that was being beaten, and looked in his direction.

"By Taranis! Brennus? Son of Tully of Garrigill? At first I thought you dead, but recently there has been a rumour that you lived!" The tongs were haphazardly tossed down as the young smith approached. "By Taranis, twice over. Grond will be so pleased to see you."

The man's red hair was a tangled bird's nest around his brawny shoulders and scratched at Brennus' face as Brennus felt the man's squeezing grip at his upper arms. The claps at his back were in hearty fashion when the huge meaty fists slid around.

"That old healer woman managed to keep you alive, then! All the gods and goddesses must favour you, since you were so near death."

The hearty chuckle was encouraging as the smith propelled him along the pathway between the reeds, a firm hand at his shoulder.

"Our guard is good, Brennus, but they are too young to know who you are. Come. Grond will be so pleased to see you."

Though the smith was shorter in height, his girth was far greater. Brennus ignored the mixed odours of the forge and natural sweat, realising he owed the man much gratitude.

"You are the red-haired warrior who helped Grond get me to Meaghan the healer?"

Again, a genial laugh almost deafened him.

"Aye! But it was more that we came upon the old woman by chance. We were directionless after the battle, and though we did not know it were heading south instead of north."

"I now know that Meaghan's village was far from the battle grounds at Whorl. How did you come to be so far away from it in such a short time?"

They reached the log causeway leading to what he knew of as the crannog dwelling of Gyptus, the roundhouse set out on a platform above the waters of the lake. The guards erupted out of the entranceway in pursuit of an even faster warrior.

"It is you, Brennus! Taranis be thanked! This is a happy, happy day!"

Grond's welcome was almost as effusive as the smith's had been, the backslapping so welcome. Although Grond was his brother Lorcan's foster-brother, he knew the man quite well.

"Come in and tell me all." Grond caught the arm of one of the young guards as they made to head back to their patrol area. "See to the forge. Fergal will stay a while with us."

16

A comely young woman stood at the doorway.

"Lleia?" Brennus was slightly hesitant. Grond's sister Lleia had grown into beauty since he last saw her. "You look well."

"I am well, Brennus of Garrigill. Come in and be welcome to my brother's hearth. He has no hearth-wife, so I do the duty for him."

It always amazed him how quickly the women of the crannogs rallied round and produced plentiful fare to eat and drink at short notice. Grond's roundhouse filled with the elders of the small community, all eager to share in his story, but also keen to hear the latest news of northern Brigantia.

Around a mouthful of fish he told of Meaghan and what came afterwards. The arm ring beneath his tunic drew his fingers; painful memories of Ineda needed to be suppressed.

"Aye! We managed to transport you in a makeshift wheeled litter for a long while after the battle at Whorl. But, though we did not know it at the time, we were forced south by the marauding Roman patrols, and the sky being shrouded in thick cloud we had lost our bearings. We had travelled far in the wrong direction before it became clear to us. Then the axle of one wheel snapped, and we had to fashion a carrying litter for you from the cart bed. It was by chance that the old woman came upon us."

"Was that near her village of Marske?" Brennus was keen to hear Grond's answer.

Grond looked to Fergal before he answered, as though to remember. "Aye! After she declared herself, we carried you into her roundhouse and got you on to her cot. The old woman had only just tended to you when we heard the thumping feet of a Roman patrol approaching the village."

Fergal sounded apologetic. "We had no choice. We had to leave you; the Romans were after our blood. We were lucky to find a place to hide fairly quickly, and avoided that fate."

He looked to the two men to whom he owed so much. "I am deeply in your debt, both of you. You may ask of me what you will."

"Another day!" Grond laughed off his statement, but accepted the gesture in time-honoured fashion. "Now tell us of recent Roman developments, and of what you do now that you are come back to the north."

They talked long and hard, Brennus establishing that he could count on Grond to ensure contacts in his area would forward information of any Roman activity.

"As happened before the battles at Whorl, we do take note of Roman scouts in the area. They come and they go, but so far they have been small patrols."

"Aye! They will be relaying information back to the main *agrimensors*."

Brennus explained what he knew of the Roman engineers who built the small forts, using the information given to them by the scouts who assessed the land for the best sources of water, and the best layout for either a temporary marching camp or a more permanent fort.

"This Roman Empire is a thoroughly organised force?"

"Aye!" He could not keep a hint of reluctant admiration from his tone. "They work together in ways our brother Celts have never even dreamed of."

Well into the evening, he made plans with Grond to extend his network of contacts, and shared his experience of Roman dominance. He also did a bit of entertaining, something he had not done before at the hearth of the former crannog chief.

Three days later, Brennus stood at the shoreline, a short stretch from the crannogs, with Lleia at his side. He had shared the Lughnasadh festival with Grond, but it was now time to leave. He had many villages to visit before the days turned too short and before the poorer weather set in.

"Where will you go, Brennus?" Lleia sounded reflective.

He named a list of the places he would next go to. "And then back to Garrigill for the festival of Samhain."

"Will you spend all of your days being messenger to Lorcan?"

Shaking his head, he pulled back a drooping branch that was in the way, to allow her to pass without harm. "Nay, only some days will be spent conveying information between the villages of the north. But Lorcan will not see me idle!"

Lleia's cheery laughter rang out over the loch side. He chuckled in response, realising it felt good to laugh again. Laughter with a woman had not passed his lips since the last time Ineda had amused him. As was becoming a habit, his fingers strayed to the arm ring near his heart, though he sensed from Lleia's wistful expression he was not the only sad one.

"As chief of Garrigill, I am sure Lorcan would have no idle warriors, brother or not!"

The twinkle in her eyes was good to see, banishing the unhappiness that tended to lurk there. He remembered how much Lleia had admired his brother Lorcan when Lorcan had fostered with old Gyptus, knew she would have been Lorcan's hearth-wife in a heartbeat had his brother been of similar mind. He also remembered how devastated she had been when Nara had been captured by Lorcan, and that Lleia had seen the love his brother had showed for the Selgovae captive.

However, after that first calf-love for Lorcan, Grond had told him Lleia had found her true soulmate. The young man she had hand-fasted with before the battles at Stanwick, according to Grond, had been her match in every way. The pair had been inseparable, their love unmistakable. Her lover had perished on the battlefield, leaving Lleia a sad and sorry survivor whose silent mourning touched all who looked upon her. Yet Brennus knew that with her unassuming quiet ways she would make a pleasant, acquiescent mate for someone who demanded little of her.

Maintaining an answering smile to her question, his heart was less joyful. He now owed as much debt to Grond and Fergal for saving his life as he owed to Meaghan's family for her nursing of him. His hand rubbed at his chest, his palm circling the silver ring. Grond had hinted that Lleia would do him well for wife, and that he should consider her – though Grond had not claimed it as his price for removing him from the battlefield. Brennus found it painful to think of being at a hearth with any woman who was not Ineda, yet he felt unable to deny Grond.

Lleia's words made his wandering thoughts return. "Lorcan will find a use for you, Brennus."

"He already has. After our Samhain festival I will resume my task of overseeing the training of the younger warriors, even though Lorcan knows I will never wield a sword with my left arm as I did my right. He insists I can still be useful in schooling our striplings. They may never be asked to bear arms as we have had to, the treaties made with the Roman Empire enforcing our laying down of mass weapons, but our young warriors must still learn to ply a sword."

"The sons of Tully of Garrigill are all adept at overcoming their infirmities." Lleia's smile was convincing, her words even more so since she had known his father.

Another guffaw from him, still slightly lopsided, broke free. "Aye! With Tully as our example, we can do no less."

Lleia stooped to pick up a pebble before rolling it in her palm, her small fingers feeling its smoothness. Before throwing it high into the air and then across the lake, she appeared to be sending a plea to the lake goddess. Turning back to him her smile was confident. "Your sons and daughters will grow up with the same qualities that you share with your brothers."

It was his turn to overlook the rippling water of the lake, twinkling blue in the sunlight. He had difficulty thinking of siring children, yet he had to live a hearth life of some sort. The guilt of losing Ineda was heavy; guilt that through his neglect of her she had been denied the opportunity to become a mother.

Lleia's soft voice brought him back from his thoughts of a small woman of spelt-bright fair hair. "I have enjoyed getting to know you again, Brennus. We have few visitors here."

Lleia was a pretty woman, but she had no spark as she made full eye contact with him, yet she was unafraid to face him. Feeling compelled to be kind to her, his tongue rambled.

"Perhaps if Grond can spare you, you could return to Garrigill with me after my next visit and get to know Nara?" He had no idea why he asked the question, since he had no notion of when that might be.

Her returned smile was a treat. "I would like that."

Chapter Three

*AD 74 After Lughnasadh – Viroconium Cornoviorum,
Cornovii Territory*

"It is a fine day, is it not?"

As expected, Ineda received a scant nod but no conversation from the legionary officer as she passed him by. Though she persisted in greeting people, she was still regarded with suspicion, perhaps even derision, but she had learned to bear the treatment and did not let it sour her.

She looked around her as she walked to the market area, her latest *tironis* guard at her heels, Zosimus having been replaced when his novice period as a first level recruit was over. Whether or not Zosimus had made the next rank of *militis*, she did not care about. His lugubrious presence was gone, though the irony of his name had to be borne out. 'One likely to survive' was what he had said when asked about its meaning. Holding back her laughter had been a trial, since the lad had been fairly witless.

She had not bothered yet to ask her second *tironis* keeper what his name meant, but this newest one was a young man of different sorts. He had only been her guard for a few days, and already she was not sure she trusted him. Only just come to the huge garrison fortress of Viroconium Cornoviorum, she was surprised at how many people he knew already, his attitude vastly different from his forebear.

She had a feeling he was answering to more than just the tribune.

"Velius?"

She was not surprised when he jumped into step alongside her, since his orders were clearly to walk behind her, unless required for some task. His fervency to duty, as much as his

21

presence beside her, put her on edge. Just short of a lascivious look, his eyes admired too much when he had the opportunity to look her directly in the face. But she put any doubts aside, and probed. His readiness to answer was of possible use to her, though how she had not yet worked out.

"What would you have me do, Ineda?"

Not earning the title of lady did not trouble her. Her status as a slave hardly merited anything like that, though she often wanted her name to appear less familiar to all who spoke to her.

"Where did you come from? I mean, before you came to Britannia, and were sent here to this garrison?"

His light grey eyes twinkled, the quirk to his mouth one she had become used to even in such a short time. "You would not have heard of it."

"How would you know such a thing?"

Though she guessed she was younger than him by a few seasons, he was a confident young man for his age. Her answer must have been firm enough, since he replied, even though it was as though she asked a very foolish question.

"My people are of the Chauci."

Ineda grinned. "The Chauci? Let me see..."

Lately, she and Tribune Valerius had come to an accommodation whereby he shared general information about the Roman Empire with her when they dined together. She listened to him, and even sometimes commented on it. He improved her knowledge of Latin every day, and she explained the Brigantian Celt he had difficulty with. Their conversations had become more...sociable. Not convivial, but easier, the turning point having been after Tribune Valerius had learned about the death of his betrothed. She still deeply resented her captive status, but found that searing hatred was difficult to maintain day after day.

She had begun to dislike herself, had felt the cloying detestation was changing her personality. Snapping and harping at everyone just was not her nature. She had come to a decision that even though she could do nothing about her captivity, she would not allow it to destroy her spirit. Since she had made that judgment, she had forced herself to enjoy some aspects of her life.

Meaghan's words made more sense now. She wore the bratt of acquiescence in Tribune Valerius' presence, and about the fortress, but underneath it still vowed to find a way to thwart Roman domination.

"What do I know about the Chauci?" She toyed with the guard who now strode alongside, all the while thinking of a recent conversation. Tribune Valerius had told her about a friend of his, who conducted a similar role as tribune with a legion in the lands Velius spoke of.

"Your native language is of the northern Germanic tribes?"

Velius did not conceal his surprise, and was extremely vocal about it when she went on to talk about the northern place where his family still lived.

"You will be no stranger to our cold damp weather, then? Tribune Valerius tells me the lands you come from are far colder in the winter than we have it here, and that you live close to sea access?"

Velius was delighted to tell her about his homeland, even confiding that his becoming an auxiliary soldier of Rome was not his own choice. There were many young conscripts from his tribe attached to the legions, the human tithe payment to the Roman coffers. Treaty agreements demanded their conscription.

Ineda sighed. His fate was really no different from many of the Celts of Britannia.

"I thought at first you must come from a Roman Family. Is Velius not a Roman name?"

He shrugged as though unconcerned, but she had an inkling he truly thought otherwise when his answer came after they had passed an oncoming group of soldiers. "It is the name that has been given to me by the legion."

"What does Velius mean?"

A full blow grin showed his many strong teeth, large and predatory. "I have been told it means a concealing one."

A laugh leaked out. Ineda thought it appropriate. "Would you rather I call you by your Chauci name?"

Velius' head shook, his returning gaze gone flat and lifeless. "I am not that boy any more. Drastic changes make you someone else."

Though she said nothing, Ineda heartily agreed with him. She was not the same girl who had journeyed with Bran, not the same person who had vowed to be a Celtic messenger for her king. It crossed her mind that someone in Velius' position might be useful to local Celtic insurgence. Someone, yes, but probably not Velius. What she needed was to find a contact who could guard his tongue.

"My body debt to Rome has barely started, but already I am stronger."

Velius sounded proud, and that confused her. A deep sadness crept over her. She too paid a different kind of body debt to Rome, though she desperately hoped her term of allegiance would not be as long as Velius'.

"Five-and-twenty winters is a usual term, is it not? Engaged to fight against all the enemies of Rome?"

His short nod was sufficient: she already knew the answer.

Much had changed around the fort since Tribune Valerius had taken her to Viroconium Cornoviorum the previous summer. His unease before the last festival of Samhain had eventually become clear to her, his irritability back then almost a daily simmer. It had seemed to her that he should have been exultant. Her former King Venutius and his Celtic warriors had suffered a great defeat at Stanwick, any surviving and still rebellious Celts scattered further north. A worn-out, beaten force. But Tribune Valerius had remained livid.

She had learned why only after he had made a short journey to an encampment near Deva, some gentle persuasion on her part leading to her finding out. Harsh winter snows, and biting storms, had prevented him from going on further north to the encampments at sites planned for new smaller forts and guard towers, in northern Brigantia. He had wanted to brave the inhospitable conditions, but his orders had been clear. He had to wait till the winter had abated and the local tribes properly subdued. And meanwhile, he had to get on with all the other new aspects of his job.

She needed to know more of the latest fort-building which had restarted well before the Beltane rites, those rites that she had recently missed celebrating. It was building work which had continued whenever the weather was clement enough. The burning question she wanted answers to was: how far north in Brigantia had they settled upon?

"Have you served at any other garrison, Velius?"

His snort alongside her sounded less affable than before. He made his experience sound more glorious than it possibly could be. "Of course. In Britannia, I have served at Eboracum."

She knew he could not have been there long, since he was still of *tironis* status. "Ah! Eboracum? That is now developed quite importantly. That must mean you have not personally been to any of the new smaller forts around these parts?"

Her questioning was not subtle, but as they ambled along she wormed more information from the *tironis*. Tribune Valerius never told her anything of importance; therefore she had to find out from others. She stored away even the tiniest detail. And where Velius' allegiance lay, was important to know.

As well as Tribune Valerius' commission to organise the best sources of iron and copper, she had found out that he had an additional task. The loyalty of members of the *Legio XX* was questionable, and had apparently been in doubt for a long time. Incidents and disruptions had increased, especially amongst the different tribes who formed the auxiliary *cohorts*. She had learned that even some of the legionaries, those who considered themselves full Roman, were feuding with one another, former emperor loyalties resurging to the fore. Though some four winters had passed and gone since the unrest time of the four Roman emperors of quick succession, old enmities still lingered. Soldiers contracted for twenty-five summers had long memories when it came to allegiances.

That the Romans were not such a loyal force had delighted her. Any dissent amongst the ranks sounded favourable, and something any resisting Celts of the north could exploit, but since she had no one pass her information to, it was a constant

25

frustration. She had no idea who might still be repelling the forces of Rome, though she had tried well enough to find out.

"Ineda. Good day to you!"

The veteran centurion who now walked towards her was one that Tribune Valerius greatly mistrusted. She halted by the cloth trader, hoping to avoid the man, but it was not to be as his bellowed greeting was followed with the opening of a conversation. The soldier's manner was as imperative as his haughty bearing.

"You conduct business for Tribune Valerius?"

There was no reason for the question; she would not be at the garrison produce stalls otherwise. She kept a smile in place as though interested in his conversation.

"I do."

She may be prepared to be polite, but she would give no details. The centurion was a man she could not read well. He was too garrulous at times, yet sometimes greeted her with repressed anger. A danger to someone in her slave status. She avoided offending the man, knowing that Tribune Valerius barely tolerated him. Tribune Valerius favoured Emperor Vespasian's policies, but she had heard the centurion was reactionary, was inclined to cling to the past, and a previous emperor had had his allegiance. A previous emperor whose policies were different from those of the current Roman Emperor – Vespasian. Sadly, his position of centurion meant the man held considerable influence over the troops under his command.

"Tribune Valerius is in good health. I have just seen him at drill with his *cohort*." The man's information was something she could have worked out for herself, if she had chosen to.

His raised eyebrows, and eyes lit with some unkind fervour, did not bode well. Her smile was meant to be gracious, though she was not sure how successful it had been. Ineda knew what the snide comment referred to. Gaius Livanus Valerius did not need to exercise his fighting skills with his men, but he liked to. The centurion's jibe indicated his view of the tribune's tactics, knowing it was one of the best ways for a tribune to learn the current mood of the troops under his direct command. Any flare of dissent could be suppressed quickly if discovered, while directly interacting with his soldiers.

Her answer was circumspect. "Tribune Valerius is very fit indeed."

As *legate* of the *Legio XX,* Gnaeus Iulius Agricola had been a commander who had kept a firm hand on such unrest, allowing little straining of the leash, but as soon as Agricola's recall to Rome had been announced before the previous Samhain, the *Legio XX* had become a fermenting ale-barrel ready to brim over. It had been left to Tribune Valerius, and the other tribune who remained at the garrison, to dampen down the building resentment, to pacify the quarrelling troops, and to wipe up the mess from some actual internal bloodshed at Viroconium Cornoviorum. The task for Tribune Valerius had been arduous over the past winter moons, a time of restlessness during the traditional overwintering period at the garrison. Tempers had easily flared, and the whole situation of turbulence was not helped by the arrival of the new *legate*, who did not exercise the same control as Agricola had.

The centurion's voice barked on as she moved around the stall, fingering the cloth displayed. "Tribune Valerius will be pleased with progress made to our new small fort building, since the first thaws after winter? I'm told the men work together at their tasks much more amiably. Their petty bickering is now over." The centurion's repulsive smile was accompanied by a slight nod of the head, the compliment insincere to the point of insolence.

Her rebellious self relished that not all Romans respected each other, but Tribune Valerius did not deserve the slights this man proffered. Not responding to the man's taunts took a lot of her control as she focused on the wares displayed, heartily wishing the man gone.

"Does the tribune head to Nidd for another visit soon?"

Why the man persisted, she had no idea. He must think she was in Tribune Valerius' confidence, but she was not. She never had any inkling of his movements, except when he told her whether or not to expect him that evening at her room.

Sarcasm was hard to bite down, her temper rising with every new question.

"You must ask the tribune yourself; I am sure he will give you his exact movements if you request them." She was certain Tribune Valerius would do no such thing – save if directly ordered by his superiors.

It was only well after the event when she had heard that Tribune Valerius had headed to Nidd for just such a purpose during one of his absences. The troops there had been conducting paltry squabbles which had escalated into more important ones. On hearing where he had gone, she had been furious that he had made no mention of where he was journeying. He had merely told her he would be gone for some days. His absence had been more than a half-moon, and during that time she had been guarded even more zealously. He had known that if he had taken her with him, she would have done her utmost to escape.

Sometimes her guarding came from less obvious sources, like the centurion presently in front of her. The veteran was too keen to find her at fault. His intense regard, as she fingered some fine-weave whitened cloth, was extremely annoying. He was a danger to her that she had not quite worked out. The man might desire her as a woman, but his attention was more than that. It was more as if the centurion waited for an occasion to cause mischief, which would damage the tribune as well as her.

"Tribune Valerius has some hurt you need to attend to?"

She would not rise to the man's taunts. "Not that I know of, but this cloth would do well to aid the stiffness at your knees, if used in a firm binding. Perhaps you might try using it, sometime?"

She did not require healing knowledge to see the way the centurion hid his aging infirmity as he attempted to stomp off, having bid a terse farewell.

"*Diùdhah*!" She cursed the Roman scum all the way over to another stall. Her idle life was so stifling. She needed some better occupation, or she feared her head would burst open with frustration.

Some days she could walk around the fortress and barely see anyone she recognised. This, however, was not one of those occasions. The centurion was not a man she could gain information from, but she knew others who were almost reliable in their consistency. Burying another groan, she prepared a smile for the man who acknowledged the departing centurion with a nod, the seniority a marginal yet volatile thing.

She had learned something of the levels of power in the legion. The centurion officially outranked the man who walked towards her, but the one who wore minimal armour did not think so. Tribune Valerius was rarely inclined to share any useful information with her, but his *secutore*, Pomponius, was a blabbermouth when in a bad mood. She had learned how to extract useful information from the man, even though no one outside the garrison could yet transport messages for her. She merely bided her time, till she could do something about her lack of resources. Living in a fortress inhabited by more than five thousand soldiers did not make her task easy, but she had not given up.

Greeting Pomponius, she prepared to quiz the man, the expression on his face indicating great displeasure. That was good, in that he was more inclined to divulge useful information when he was disgruntled. It was also bad, because she always bore the brunt of his temper.

Pomponius constantly bemoaned the fact that any triumph of Tribune Valerius reflected on the rate of his own progress, and the lack of triumph on the part of his superior did the opposite. The *secutore* was ambitious, and the tribune's recent lack of advancement was a bone of contention.

"Good day, Ineda. You are here to purchase something for Tribune Valerius?"

There was no point in dissembling with Pomponius. He dealt with all the traders on the tribune's behalf, and regularly paid the accounts Tribune Valerius agreed to.

"Yes. I need to acquire cloth for his bathing."

The short nod from Pomponius put a stamp of agreement on the purchase, though she would have argued otherwise.

29

"Tribune Valerius is fair in his dealings to all, Ineda. I do hope you appreciate that?"

She ignored the veiled threat, and accepted the cut cloth from the trader.

Pomponius bristled further. "I very much enjoy my task working for Gaius Livanus Valerius, I will have you know that, but there are times when the tribune can be very exasperating."

Ineda suppressed a smirk. Pomponius was indeed annoyed by some recent decision by Gaius. It was the perfect time to probe. "I am not certain of your meaning, Pomponius."

The huff of displeasure went along with serious squeezing of his eyebrows. "Tribune Valerius could be back in Rome by now, in a lucrative senior post. He has earned the transfer, yet chooses to remain in Britannia."

Tribune Valerius never shared such details with her. She knew full well that Pomponius was disgruntled, because relocation for the tribune might mean his own transfer to Rome.

"Tell me again about these terms that tribunes serve?"

Pomponius exhaled and stared at her as though she was a child lacking learning, though his words explained in measured tones as they journeyed back to Tribune Valerius' quarters.

"Your not being Roman will mean it is difficult to comprehend, but I shall try to depict it for you."

A nod was sufficient, since Pomponius liked to hear himself talk.

"Tribunes generally come from equestrian rank – that is men not from the top echelons of Roman society – but good nonetheless, if they have gold to pave the way for success."

Another nod kept him talking.

"Tribunes enter service in a junior administrative role at first, since they are usually young men. After a first term of service, of some three or four summers, with an auxiliary or legionary unit, they may progress to a second post in higher administrative service with a legion. Then after more time, they may move on to be in charge of an *ala*, an equestrian unit

– sometimes small, though at other times with as many as five hundred mounted men."

She watched the tense working of Pomponius' jaw, phrasing her words carefully. "Has Tribune Valerius served with a mounted force?"

Gaius Livanus Valerius' obeisance to the goddess, Etain, meant some link to an equestrian force was likely.

"He has. Tribune Valerius' first post was as an adjunct to an *ala* where he gained his initial military experience, though that was not in Britannia. His first posting in Britannia was to the *Legio II Augusta,* based in the far south as second-in-command to the *tribune militum*, and then he moved here as a tribune." Pomponius huffed and strutted. "Tribune Valerius prefers to continue at his current level, since he has refused to allow his father to pay his way into higher service with the Army in Rome."

"He has refused elevation of rank?" Ineda was amazed by that concept since Gaius was so dedicated to his position.

"Twice he has asked to be transferred to new fortresses, with the proviso that he continue in the same rank as before, and do much the same tasks. The only difference here at Viroconium Cornoviorum is that he is dealing with a legionary fortress, and not an auxiliary one."

"Is that why the tribune is older than his fellow officers?" She had wondered about that.

Pomponius rifled his thinning hair and looked askance. "I do not understand the man."

Neither did she, but she was not going to say it. "Tribune Valerius is a dedicated worker. What would have earned him a passage to Rome?"

"His conduct during the defeat of King Venutius of the Brigantes was more than sufficient."

That was even more confusing. Gaius Livanus Valerius had been nowhere near Stanwick during the fall of her king, as only some of Agricola's men had been marched further north. He had been left out of that first advance, though had left for the north some days after Agricola's departure. She, naturally, had been left under guard at Viroconium Cornoviorum. When

31

he had returned some moons later, he had not seemed at all happy to have been left in charge of the troops around Quernium.

"I thought Tribune Valerius was elsewhere when the battle occurred?"

Pomponius crowed at her, clearly in one of his nasty ill-tempers. "Tribune Valerius was not actually at the battlegrounds, but he did arrive at Quernium in time to be extremely instrumental to Rome's success. Do not misunderstand me. Tribune Valerius wanted very much to engage in the battle to defeat the Brigantes, but Agricola's orders were clear."

"What could be more important than he took part?" The question sickened her, since it meant the annihilation of warriors of the Brigantes, but she had to know what he had done instead of fighting.

"Tribune Valerius was instrumental in rallying the auxiliaries of the *Legio IX* and the *Legio II Adiutrix* as one unit. It was his firm command that dampened down their lack of discipline, and brought them back up to scratch."

"But Tribune Valerius is not a centurion. How could he do that?"

Again Pomponius treated her like a child. "Force through orders is not the only way to bring about unity. It takes an installation of pride and remembrance of dedication to duty. Some men are able to engender that without brutality. Tribune Valerius is that kind of man."

She believed it.

"Harsher men like Agricola also have that charisma, but they rise more effectively through the ranks."

Censure dripped from the man's tongue. Comparing Gaius to Agricola was unfair, and she could not let his words pass without some intervention.

She glared at Pomponius when she stopped at the door to Tribune Valerius' quarters. "Tribune Valerius has chosen to remain in Britannia for his own reasons, Pomponius. We must accept that." She had no idea why he had made that choice, but Pomponius' expression made her wonder. The secretary seemed to really hate her. The words spat at her as his face came right up close, so close that the sight of his rotting back teeth were obnoxious to her.

"Tribune Valerius refused a transfer back to Rome last winter. That was after he brought you to Viroconium Cornoviorum, after the defeat of Venutius – but more importantly after the death of his betrothed. And now he has fully installed you in his own accommodation as his private whore, instead of the store room you started your slavery in. I do not know what he intends with that measure. His unpopularity is rife, but he chooses not to acknowledge it!"

His evil words delivered, Pomponius turned on his heels and walked away.

The man shocked her, but Tribune Valerius refusing to return to Rome explained some of Pomponius' frustration.

When Agricola had surged northwards, and then Tribune Valerius had also departed, she had been kept in isolation from the bloodshed and annihilation at Stanwick, and when her master returned he had told her nothing about his role.

Though her heart was not in the least bit engaged, she wondered just how much Tribune Valerius valued her. Perhaps it was a lot more than he ever showed, if he chose her over his own esteem within the legion.

Chapter Four

AD 75 Before Imbolc – Garrigill, Brigantes Territory

"Are you certain this is what you wish to do, Brennus?"

Nara's tentative question was a difficult one to answer. He was not sure it was the correct thing to do, but he was lonely. Ineda's absence left him feeling hollow, even though life had settled into a pattern at Garrigill. He ensured his line of contact was sound amongst the northern Brigantes, although he worked most of his days at the training ground, along with another of the most skilled warriors. He enjoyed what he was still able to do there, though in his heart he knew that he was not really preparing them for battle with their Roman oppressors. He instructed them in simple ways to help defend each other, but the Celtic way was not to drill warriors like the Roman fighting wall.

"Lleia is a beautiful woman. She will tend you well." Nara persisted, her gaze still enquiring.

"She will." His attempt at enthusiasm failed. Nara's expression registered her doubt. He knew those doubts were not about Lleia, but more about his reasoning.

"Brennus is well capable of choosing his own woman, Nara, without your many questions." Lorcan's words sounded sharp, although Brennus had never known Nara to take his words in bad humour.

"My decision is made." Brennus stood firm. He knew exactly why his brother and Nara showed concern. Their love was still so deep; they wanted the same for everyone else. He had long since told them of his love for Ineda, on a night when the small beer had been particularly strong and plentiful. "Many unions are made without a great bond of love, and you know that well."

"We will likely have no druid, brother, but that is no reason not to feast your hand-fasting. Nara will bless your union as best she can."

Nara's acolyte learning at the priestess nemeton had been used well by all at Garrigill for many seasons. Her broad smile showed wholehearted pleasure, with no doubt about it. "Gladly, Brennus. You will bring her back with you?"

He was journeying to Grond's crannog dwellings, having not visited since the previous Samhain when he had talked to Lleia. He had left with the understanding that if she made no change of mind over the winter months, then they would make hearth together after the festival of Imbolc.

"Imbolc comes in less than a se'nnight. Will Lleia be prepared to come to Garrigill so soon?"

"Aye, Nara. Rest easy. If Lleia had changed her mind before now, she was set to send me a message. I have had no such message. All will be well."

As he travelled to the lakeside crannog dwellings of Lleia's brother Grond, later that day, he wondered if all truly would be well. The new Roman Governor, Frontinus, had made no massive push into the lands of the northernmost Brigantes, and was honouring the treaties that Lorcan, Nara and the Brigante delegation had recently renewed with Rome. The line of forts established by Cerialis at the Brigantes mid and southern borders, along with the few fortlets built in the north, seemed to be all Rome desired to man at present – so long as those tribespeople to the north made no attacks on those defences.

Garrigill had no heavy Roman presence in its immediate environs though patrolling Romans were, at times, seen around the area. An almost false security pervaded amongst the survivors of the battles at Stanwick. Mostly the villages and settlements of the north just wanted to rebuild their communities, and get on with their life on the land, free of any political struggle.

Though he desperately wanted peace, too, and some form of hearth life, Brennus could not put aside the task set him by Venutius and Tuathal. He had no intentions of halting his quest to keep people informed of Roman movements, and was still placed to be aware of who in the Brigantes federation of tribes was inclined to a show of resistance. His contacts were well-established; information regularly came to him. If the new Governor Frontinus changed the recent dealings, then continued travel from the very hearth he wanted to establish with Lleia was likely to be inevitable.

"Brennus? I would have you know something first." As ever Lleia was beautiful, calm and almost unnaturally serene as they walked along the lakeside, a repeat of many moons ago. He had been feasted by Grond, and had taken leave to speak with Lleia alone.

"You do not love me?"

The tiniest flicker in her expression showed she had not expected his answer.

"Lleia, it is of no matter. I cannot say I love you either, but I do respect you, and will be proud to look to your needs. I will not demand that your heart loves me, but will hope you can take me as a lover who likes you very well."

The soft smile of acceptance was sufficient.

"We will neither of us be lonely then. Whenever my brother agrees, we will leave."

He took her into his arms. It was not the first time he had made love to her, since she had given him her body the previous summer. As before, they came together happily enough but with no spark.

"You are an attractive woman, Lleia." His words were interspersed with slow kisses, while he removed her dress and laid her down on his bratt.

Lleia had been with men before, knew how to gain some enjoyment from the act of loving, and gave his body the release it needed. He was not entirely sure how much pleasure she really had from him, though. What Lleia said in her quiet way, and what she really felt, he was sure were two different things.

They hand-fasted at Grond's crannog, surrounded by her own people, and then they left the following morning.

"You will become used to me being a man of two names, Lleia?" asked Brennus.

They had been discussing his role as messenger of the Celts as they rode to Garrigill.

"Your name will make no difference. If you wish me to always call you Bran from now on I can do that, though in my head you will be the Brennus of Garrigill who used to visit my crannog." Lleia's smile was confident.

"I prefer you to call me Brennus, but there may come a day when I will need to be more recognisable as Bran."

"Then let us work that out when the time comes."

It was a quality he respected in Lleia: little seemed to bother her.

When they reached Garrigill, Nara organised another hand-fasting for their union. They had no druid to properly celebrate, but Nara made a fine substitute.

It made sense to live in Lorcan's large roundhouse, the one that had been his father's since Brennus would often be travelling. Lleia was happy to bide there, having made good friends with Nara.

AD 75 After Beltane – Deva, Cornovii Territory

It was not long before circumstances improved, and more to Ineda's liking. Escape was still as elusive, but her purpose changed when Tribune Valerius took her with him when he was posted to the encampment at Deva. Though the Cornovii tribe had largely been subdued for some time, the rebuilding and improvements to the earlier abandoned wooden fortress had been delayed till shortly before their arrival. The troops needed to build it had been deployed elsewhere for many seasons, but the present Governor Frontinus had decided the time had come to release sufficient soldiers from other legions, to build the new structure.

Having seen a little of the assembly of the fort at Nidd, and having lived for so long at Viroconium Cornoviorum, Ineda saw many similarities, though the Deva garrison fortress was much larger. Situated on a headland, the fort overlooked the river that meandered below it. It was also close to a natural harbour on the western coast, and would dominate any sea traffic in and out of the area. The position was ideal for containing the Brigantes, the Setantii and the Carvetii tribes to the north of it, and effectively kept the local natives to the south of it under control, with little unseen intermixing of the tribes.

The new walls of the fortress were in place before they arrived, but the construction of interior buildings was still underway. Manned mainly by auxiliaries, the noise behind the walls was deafening as building after building took shape. The whole interior was already so well laid down it was easy to walk around, the paved walkways being laid out in similar fashion to Viroconium Cornoviorum. Ineda could not help being reluctantly impressed by the whole organisation within the Roman Empire. The function Gaius currently performed in supplying the necessary iron to make construction nails, and other building supplies, was being mirrored across the empire.

Gaius. She now allowed herself to think of him as Gaius, and even named him so as well when directly speaking to him. His persistence that she should do so had eventually worn down her reticence.

A small measure of enjoyment was had as she learned more and more about Gaius' world, her natural curiosity fed. She became a woman of two parts as well as one who wore two bratts. Day after day she was drawn more and more into the life of a Roman, her former Celtic identity pushed into abeyance. It was only when some important insurgence happened that her Celtic loyalties came to the fore.

It was after a particularly troublesome incident, near the fort, that Ineda's life took a different turn.

"You have the white pus and swelling still under the wound, Gaius, and for full healing it must be drawn out. My grandmother would have made a paste of plantain and some other herbs, but I have none of these. Would anyone have such things at Deva? Already in a mixture, or the fresh growth of the plant?"

Gaius had just returned from a short journey to Cambodunum, to the site of a permanent encampment. Governor Frontinus had marked out the area as an excellent site for a small fort, and Gaius had started to send supplies. Unfortunately for him – though something which delighted Ineda – the supply wagons were often being intercepted by local Celtic warriors. The convoy he had personally accompanied had been attacked, but since the guard was heavy enough the Celtic assailants had fled after only a short skirmish.

"How should I know such a thing, Ineda? My dealings at present are about iron and copper supplies, not plantain, whatever that is!" Gaius was bitingly terse, obviously annoyed that the pain was sufficient to bother him, all evident in the grimace he darted her way. Brushing her aside, he clutched at the goblet of wine.

Quelling anger at his offhand attitude, she bit her tongue to keep from being just as rude. A deep breath taken, and after a deliberate turning away from his wincing features, she summoned control of her emotions. "You use herbs when you give prayers to your goddess Etain."

Only after drinking deeply from the cup did Gaius deign to answer, his gaze confrontational, his teeth crunched together, his lips pursed against the pain. "That is different from me knowing where they come from!" Quarrelling with him was not uncommon, but this incident was exacerbated even more by his hurting. "Why ask me? How should I know such things? Go from my sight, if you cannot help me."

She could tell that Gaius had noticed the fleeting hurt she was unable to hide from her expression, because he glared at her all the more. Having come to dislike him less, being treated badly hurt her ambivalent feelings.

"Ask Rubrius! He should know these things."

She had an idea who Rubrius was, was certain he was one of the superior surgeons, and was also fairly certain the surgeon would not spend time with her. But she did know one of his *militis*, a man friendly with one of Gaius' clerks.

Stomping off in high dudgeon over Gaius' harsh behaviour, her temper was still roiling when she reached the quarters of the senior *medicus*, and requested to speak to his *militis*.

"I am told that Rubrius used the services of a healing woman to acquire herbs for some of his unguents? Is this true?" That she was rude to the man did not trouble her, though it would have in her more temperate moments.

"Orchil?"

"I do not know her name! Tribune Valerius needs treatment for his wound. Where will I find this woman?"

"Does he need our immediate assistance?" The man looked bothered. "We have many wounded soldiers to deal with right now, but I will ask Rubrius to tend to the tribune."

She began to feel harassed when the *militis* glared, though her words were measured with care. "The wound needs to be treated, but given the proper unguent I have the skills to deal with it. All I need are the correct essentials to make the paste. If the woman has plantain, I can do what is necessary."

Though the man looked sceptical, he told her where to locate the woman named Orchil.

Ineda felt the blood surge around her body. Orchil lived outside the walls of the fortress! Was this her chance to escape, after being so long a prisoner behind the walls? Excitement mounted, her thoughts whirling.

"What is this I hear? I am extremely busy!"

Ineda roused quickly from her momentary distraction. The man striding towards her looked to be important and yet full of bluster as his words rattled on.

"I am Rubrius and you are Tribune Valerius' whore. I heard you say you wish to talk with Orchil, the herbs woman? And you say you can deal with the tribune's wound yourself?" His disdain dripped from every word, his sneer accompanied by a lascivious glare.

"With plantain I can. I have the other items I need to make a paste to draw out the white pus that is under the skin." When Rubrius continued to stare at her without saying more, she named a few other herbs she knew were available to her.

"Is that all that ails the tribune? I thought him to be much needier of my expert services. What you name should work well enough." Dismissing her, Rubrius turned and bawled at one of his underlings. "Fetch a guard and personally escort this slave to Orchil. See that she returns safely to the fortress. The tribune would be most upset if his personal woman ran off. He would not wish to be the butt of any ribald jokes when evening comes, though I dare say many of the soldiers within would make haste to recapture her. There are many of us who have to do without the services of a private whore."

Before striding of, the man's chin moved right down to her face. "Your beauty causes much resentment at this fortress!"

Something of Grandmother Meaghan's words of so long ago came back to her as she was marched to the dwelling of the old healer. Though she had no recollection of the actual phrase, she remembered Meaghan commenting that her healing skills would be needed after a long time of no use. She also remembered Meaghan saying something about always looking forward to the good and not to dwell on the bad. It was not the first time she had been referred to as the tribune's whore, and most likely not the last, but it hurt. Badly.

"Aye! I have what you need." The old woman cackled as she went about collecting the items Ineda requested. "So, the tribune is not immune to a Celtic sword? Sometimes our Celtic brothers strike back successfully. I would that more of them were successful against this Roman scum that floods our land!"

Stunned that Orchil would be so openly ridiculing, Ineda found herself lost for words. Gaius could have been killed, but she also rejoiced that there was still some resistance to Roman domination of Celtic territory. She was amazed that the old woman voiced her opinions so loudly, but at least the soldiers who accompanied her were outside the roundhouse.

Orchil grumbled ominously as she handed over the herbs. "Your whoredom status is known to all, Ineda of the Brigantes, but that need not mean you should be termed Roman. Those who refuse to accept the tyranny of Rome need the support of every Celtic heart. If your tribune had been killed, what would you do then?"

Ineda had no idea what to answer. Her confusion was total. Her mumbled words of thanks given she left quickly, in her agitation bumping against the wooden door post.

"Come back when you have something useful to tell me, so that I can pass it along, Ineda of the Brigantes! You are still of the Celtic people, and always will be. Remember that." Orchil's words rang out as Ineda sped away.

While returning to Gaius, she deliberately put the old woman's comments from her thoughts, thoughts that whirled her whole journey back. Orchil could not possibly mean what she was thinking? Maybe was even secretly hoping? Had the herbs woman indicated she could pass messages along to insurgent Brigantes? Orchil had also mentioned something troubling as well. What would be her fate if Gaius died? It seemed the dislike she felt from many of the soldiers that she encountered may not be because she was a Brigante slave, but more because Gaius had stirred resentment in keeping her as his personal woman, instead of sharing her like a camp prostitute.

During her absence Gaius had drunk more wine, the almost empty flagon a sure sign something was amiss. Soft snores greeted her when she tried to waken him, but he slept on. The salve was fully ready by the time he stirred.

"What is that mixture?" He winced in pain as he sat up, his arm jarring against the cot with his sluggish movements.

"The unguent you need to draw out the white matter that lies beneath the skin. This paste will draw it out and clean the wound."

Gaius seemed sceptical, though clearly interested in her movements as she used her stone pestle to transfer her mix from the mortar to a small pot. "How do you know this will work?"

Encouraged by his tone, she poured clean water from a jug into a small basin and then dipped in her wiping cloth. "My grandmother was the healer of our village. She taught me many things about tending ailments."

"We have skilled surgeons here at Deva who treat the wounds of our casualties."

Though his words could have been a rejection of her skills, his tone said otherwise. It held a question, maybe a doubt about her expertise, yet also held a trust in her.

"Aye! I know this. And they are very busy with other wounds just now. But if you prefer to wait for Rubrius, that is your choice." Though she would never divulge what had happened, she was not confident the surgeon would even look at Gaius' wound after what the man had said to her.

Gaius, holding out his wound, told her his intentions. The glint in his gaze was trusting... and even... affectionate.

"I trust you to heal me, Ineda. Over many long moons now you have had many opportunities to have poisoned me, yet you have not."

She did not know what to think as she cleaned the wound. Uncertainty flooded her, since she no longer knew where her loyalties lay. Gaius was her lover, and to all effects her hearth husband, even if no hand-fasting had occurred. But he was Roman.

He was also the father of the babe in her womb, though, as yet, he had no knowledge of that.

She resolved to put Orchil's taunts from her thoughts.

***

After Ineda had successfully tended Gaius' wound, he allowed her to help with healing the men of the garrison when the surgeons were overworked. At times, that was not because they were casualties of skirmishes with troublesome Celts, since disease and sickness were no stranger to the fortress. Some of the soldiers began to seek out her potions, which appeared to be as effective as those which the surgeons were supplying for minor ailments, though she was wise enough to not incur any rivalry.

As one new moon succeeded another, she learned not to look to Rubrius for any personal support. His dislike of her was still prevalent, but she worked out ways to ignore the unkind comments and jibes that came her way.

"Gaius?"

Though Gaius was always busy, some seven moons later she interrupted him at his desk, something she rarely dared to do.

43

"Ineda? What is amiss?" She felt his keen gaze on her face, on cheeks she felt must be reddened with embarrassment.

"I feel the child may be coming." Pains had been gripping her for some time.

She did not expect Gaius to jump from the stool and come around his work table to take her elbow. "Perhaps you should lie down?"

Her laugh sounded feeble in her ears. "The babe will not come immediately, but I need a woman to help me."

There had never been any discussion of her needs during the babe's coming, such talk not one Gaius would have been comfortable with. In the past, she had assisted her grandmother Meaghan attend a difficult labour, and knew what to expect when her time came, though she preferred not to be completely alone.

"Is there no woman you know to help you?"

Gaius' question was laughable. She had no friends, and after the words had been said the colour seeping across his cheeks showed her he realised just what the problem was. He had never allowed her the freedom to make friends, not that there were many women around the fort to choose from.

"There must be someone who does this kind of thing?"

"The only woman I know of would be Orchil, the herbs wife."

Gaius was bawling orders before he even got to his door.

During a labour that lasted for more than a day, Ineda learned that Orchil knew many Celts outside the fortress at Deva, the old woman's Brigantian babble ripping at her sensitive feelings. Insidious suggestions from Orchil seeped into her weakened head; hints that she had been betraying her fellow Celts flayed her ragged nerves. She could deny none of what Orchil said, for it was all true. She was doing nothing to support her fellow Brigantes.

Striding around to allay the strongest pains, she cursed the situation she was in. She prayed to her goddess, Rhianna, that it was not her fault her child was not Celtic – though she knew that to be only partly true. Resisting Gaius' sexual advances would have been possible, yet she had chosen otherwise and must now accept the consequences. She could have refused to eat, though had not done that either. And if she had been really determined to die, that could have also happened. She would have found a way.

Celtic emotions which had been buried deep resurfaced as she brought forth her Roman child, every pain-filled contraction of her womb accompanied by loud curses of evil against Rome.

"*Ceigean Ròmanach!* Rhianna, my goddess! Heed my pleas. Banish the whole morass of Roman turds from these shores!"

One last push and the baby slipped free. Mere moments later, a lusty squealing surpassed her own cries.

"You have a loud and hearty son, Ineda. Equally as noisy as you have been." Orchil's genuine smile was unexpected as she wiped mucus from the babe's mouth. Ineda had thought the old woman's disapproval of her too deep for such warmth. Accepting the squirming babe from the old crone, she gave her a weak smile. Her child was indeed hale and hearty, and was creating such a clamour.

"Give thanks to your goddess Brigantia, for your babe has had an easy path out to your nipple." Orchil turned the baby in her arms and helped the child to suckle before tending to the afterbirth. "You may even use my name to your goddess, if you wish, though believe me you could have brought forth the child on your own."

The meaning of Orchil was prayer. Ineda thought on the word. And what it meant to pray to, and be favoured by, Brigantia.

Chapter Five

AD 75 After Beltane – Deva, Cornovii Territory

Ineda's many prayers to Brigantia had been answered. She had wanted, so much, to be more than just the unacknowledged concubine of Tribune Gaius Livanus Valerius. She had yearned to regain her tribal-fervour and to do something useful to help her fellow-Brignates in their times of trouble. The goddess Brigantia had led her to Orchil.

As Ineda looked lovingly upon her already greedy son, she dwelt on the talk she had had with Orchil. Contact could be made with the Celts of the north.

But did she want it?

That question plagued her for a long while after little Dubv's birth. A friendship of sorts with Orchil had begun, and Gaius had not forbidden it. Ineda knew why. Gaius was truly proud of his son, and believed the old woman's skills had ensured both his son and Ineda had survived the birth – a time when many babes and mothers both perished.

Ineda was deeply troubled by the tussling of her conscience, and did not know what she wanted, what her aim was or her allegiance. She felt she was not even wearing one bratt, never mind bearing the mantle of two. Her son was essentially a Roman child, even though Gaius had never publicly declared him to be so. A light-hearted side to Gaius emerged when he dandled the baby on his knee, so it was unsurprising that her *tironis* guard was extremely vigilant after the birth of her son. Gaius very protective of his offspring.

Escape from the fortress was impossible.

Many times during the early moons of Dubv's life she pondered the possibility of Gaius returning to Rome, even though Pomponius had declared he had no intentions of doing so. Would he insist on taking Dubv with him? She was certain he would never take her, and dreaded what would happen if he decided to set her aside. If he freed her, she would rejoice in that, but the thought of him turning her out of his quarters to be at the mercy of the men of the garrison did not bear thinking on. She had allowed Gaius to use her body, but would rather die than let any other Roman touch her.

Many of the men she encountered still resented her. The snide comments continued, though never in earshot of Gaius. Pomponius was the most baffling of all. He doted on the baby, but continued his nasty jibing, his comments often directly demeaning – though naturally never in Gaius' company.

Since much of her time was taken up with nursing her son, her walking around the garrison was less frequent. Contrarily, being more tied to Gaius' quarters gave her a security she did not feel when outside them. If Gaius's attitude to her had become more loving, it would have balanced her vulnerability. But it had not, and Dubv's birth had made no difference to her slave status.

The idea of Dubv being taken from her made every day a dangerous one.

After many nights of lost sleep, she came to a momentous decision. Her son's wellbeing would always be paramount, but her life must have more purpose. The double cloak Meaghan had referred to, many long moons ago, must be donned. Her healing skills could work to her advantage, since she would be in a better position to find out important developments from more than Pomponius as the source, so long as she could withstand the resentment of many she would be in contact with. Like Rubrius.

Resurrecting herself as a messenger of the Celts became a reality.

At first, the information she sent on via Orchil was useful, but it was irregular and never anything crucial. Had Orchil not praised her efforts so well, or encouraged her to continue, she might have given up in despair. Old news did not seem to her, to have much import at all, but then, she received little back. Small insurgencies were happening constantly across northern

Brigantia, but they were localised and were immediately suppressed by the Romans.

Living within the might of Rome, Ineda could see exactly why it appeared northern Britannia had come totally under the thumb of the Emperor, having apparently acquiesced so effortlessly. Pacts had been signed and appeared largely to be honoured. Governor Frontinus seemed content with maintaining the peace in areas already settled by the Romans.

Season followed season, and more followed those. Gaius remained stationed at Deva, though was out of the fortress more often than in, ensuring copper, iron and lead stocks were flowing properly to the needed sites. Maintaining that shipments were unhampered by local attack, and petty pilfering, was a constant problem.

Some of those attacks could be laid at Ineda's door, since information about the movement of goods wagons was passed on to Orchil, though she was wise enough not to send such information too regularly. Detection could mean her death. Avoiding suspicion was daily worked at, yet Ineda found herself locked into a routine that was predictable and often tedious, while her son grew healthily from babyhood into the life of a typical toddler. Ineda was not sure if she was happy with the fact that no further bairns had been born to her.

Her slave status never changed, though after Dubv's birth she knew that the guard who still accompanied her on a daily basis was there for a different reason. She had learned to ward off the looks of disdain, of censure, and (from some factions) of downright hatred.

Gaius was her captor, but also the protector of her son.

The tedious equilibrium at the fortress, and even across Brigantia, altered for everyone with the change of Governor to Britannia. Frontinus had filled the post for four summers, about the usual time for a consulship, when he was recalled to Rome.

Ineda groaned when the news came.

Gnaeus Iulius Agricola, the man who had been the *Legate* of the *Legio XX* a few summers ago, was Britannia's new Governor.

AD 78 One Moon Before Lughnasadh – Garrigill,
Brigantes Territory

"Go with your father, Kaideigh. He goes to the training ground."

Lleia hustled the little girl out of the wattled entrance tunnel, muttering more instructions about behaving well. The excited squeals of the toddler broke up the conversation taking place outside between Brennus and his brother Gabrond. Bending to grab the little girl rushing at his legs, Brennus threw her up high into the air, deftly catching her, laughing along with her screams of delight.

"Horse ride? Horse ride?" Her entreaties were deafening, even comical, as she whooped and grinned right into his face.

"You will be a mighty warrior-woman, my little daughter, mayhap the mightiest of the Brigantes. Did you know Kaideigh means first-born? And your name fits so well for a warrior's child."

The low chuckle from Lleia was admonishing. "Nara may not wish to hear that! When not birthing babies, she is still our best female warrior."

Brennus brought Lleia into the cuddle along with his daughter. "Aye! Rightly so, but I do not talk of the next few moons. I mean the new generations at Garrigill who will lead us from the yoke of tyranny."

Garrigill steadily gained in numbers as more babies were born, the hillfort slowly reclaiming its wealth and prosperity since Governor Julius Frontinus had honoured the treaties the Brigante leaders had made with Rome. The northern tribes had been left to a relatively peaceful existence. They had never had the oppressive local Roman *cohort* presence as was experienced around settlements like Witton, though patrols were regularly to be seen conducting discreet surveys.

Small Roman fort-building had gone on north of the line of forts Cerialis had established, and some land areas were monitored more than before, but Garrigill and the neighbouring villages had never been required to pay their toll in human labour. None had been forced to hew wood from the forest, like Brennus had at Witton. Garrigill continued to live and farm as it chose to – accommodating the necessary payments of the harvest, as was required according to the treaties made.

Warlike training of the younger warriors was confined to closed areas behind the wooden ramparts of Garrigill. Though the yoke of Rome was not contested in warlike fashion, Brennus helped with the training of the youngsters, male and female, so that they would be prepared for change, and also because it continued their Celtic tradition. As part of the treaties made, they could never show a display of their prowess outside the fort walls; any large groups carrying weapons would be held under suspicion. That aspect did not change, and was constantly monitored by the Romans in the area.

"It will be a long time before any at Garrigill forcibly breaks the pacts Lorcan and Nara have made with the Roman oppressors." Gabrond spat into the dirt, no lover of the negotiations, though he was practical about the need for the semblance of peace.

As overseer of the equine stock, Gabrond's work had been arduous. After the battles at Stanwick the amount of horses at Garrigill had been low, and it was taking time to increase again. His helpers were young striplings – female and male – but they learned well.

"None of us may break the pacts, yet ill times loom again." Brennus hoisted his daughter onto his shoulders, and set off at a brisk pace beside his brother. The main horse enclosure was within the wall defences of Garrigill, but Gabrond was breaking in some new ponies out in the field area by the old training ground.

"Did you hear more about a change of Governor?"

Gabrond had not been at the meeting with Lorcan and Nara the eve before, and had not heard Brennus' update from his visit to a village situated on the western coast. The tribesmen there often had news of Roman fleet movement before anyone else.

"Aye! But most of the information cannot be substantiated yet. Frontinus and his *Legio II Augusta* still continuously attack the last resistance in the hill country of the Ordovices and the Demetae. Permanent forts, and garrison fortresses, are now at such short distances apart, that the resistance of our Celtic brothers in those southern areas seems over for the present time."

"Will the fort building of the Roman Empire ever come to an end?" Gabrond sounded despairing as he took the reins of one of the broken-in ponies from his handler.

Brennus shook his head, almost dislodging little Kaideigh who gripped his side braids so tight he feared she would pull them straight from his scalp. He let her down to scamper towards the handler, knowing she was safe with the young woman. His daughter loved to ride seated in front of him, and had no fear of any beast – broken or unbroken – and thus had to be closely monitored.

"What they had to tell is inevitable. There has been steady fleet movement on the west coast, but it seems mainly to keep their troops in the west supplied. No main fleet movement appears to go regularly further north than the Deceangli. Their northernmost port of call is the encampment named Deva, though I did hear one rumour that at least one Roman ship had sailed as far the lands of the Novantae, to our neighbours over the high hills."

"Checking the shoreline for habitation?"

"I think that is most likely, and for safe harbours to berth their ships. Though why Frontinus would want to advance north at this time is a mystery. He has not made a heavy advance into northern Brigante territory, and I can not see him capturing north of the lands of the Novantae only from the sea. The Roman fleet supplies manpower and goods, but the Roman foot moving on the land is their prime method of subjugation."

"Could this be a last attempt of Frontinus to settle on more of the Brigantes and Carvetii lands? Frontinus has been governor for a longer term than Cerialis. The Empire must beckon him back to Rome ere long."

It was easy to echo Gabrond's snort of derision. Brennus agreed with his brother's words, and wished them true. He wanted all Romans recalled from Britannia, but that was unlikely.

"Aye! That may be so, Gabrond, to gain the glory first. His successor will be inclined to attack the west, I am sure."

Gabrond threw the reins back to the female handler, and lifted Kaideigh into his arms before striding to an area where some horses were enclosed behind woven hurdled fencing. Brennus tagged behind. He loved watching his daughter being so excited, knowing a horse ride was forthcoming, Gabrond being her well-favoured uncle.

Gabrond settled the child, and steadied her with one huge fist at the back of her tunic before clucking the horse into a walk. "They must have some idea who will replace Frontinus as Governor of Britannia."

"Aye! Gnaeus Iulius Agricola."

"Agricola?" Gabrond halted for a moment, his expression sickened. "Agricola is returning?"

"I would rather not dwell on that rumour. I have had too much experience of Agricola. If he is indeed the replacement, then we must make ready for battle. He will not content himself with subduing what they regard as petty skirmishes of the Ordovices. His sword will be vicious."

Brennus' words came home to roost.

AD 78 After Lughnasadh – Deva, Cornovii Territory

"I come with my skills as healer."

Ensuring efficiency in her voice, Ineda stepped past the young *tironis* posted at the doorway of the *Praefectus Castrorum*. The next statement was not true, but the guard was not to know it. "Tribune Valerius sends me to help."

Gaius had recently returned from the same short visit that the *Praefectus Castrorum* had been on, but she knew she would get no information from Gaius immediately. His lips were always tightly clamped after being out of the fortress, increasingly so since Agricola's reappearance.

The *tironis* slipped inside, returning a few moments later. "The *Praefectus Castrorum* has already been treated, but has heard talk of your healing skills. He bids you enter."

Ineda suppressed the feeling of triumph as she followed the guard. Hermanus, the *Praefectus Castrorum*, had been appointed by Agricola on his return. Over the moons of his tenure, Hermanus had proven to be a tough old veteran, though it had been an unusual decision for the camp commanding officer to journey out with the fort. A decision he may have regretted since he had been injured. Though no weak talker, Ineda had already found ways of extracting the tiniest snippets of information from him. Along with other bits and pieces, she was able to put together some updates for her new contact made via Orchil, a woman whose access in and out of the fort was regular. That was a much better option than making too many visits to the old herbs wife.

"Ineda!" The commander's voice was peremptory when she was ushered in. "I suppose Gaius sent you?"

It was as well he gave no time for her to answer, as she had no wish to lie. The last of his heavy chest plating was removed by his *militis* before he continued.

"I have faith in my own surgeon, but I have also seen your healing skills at work. You may look and tell me if your treatment differs."

Ineda knew how to handle his comment, since Rubrius remained at the camp near Nidd.

"How long is it since Rubrius looked at your wound?" She could see nothing of his fingers, the strapping around his arm having slipped down, well past the tips.

Hermanus held his arm out for inspection. The covering was filthy and bloodstained, and barely held itself together around his forearm. Ineda sidled closer to sniff without making what she attempted obvious. Carefully unrolling the strip of cloth, she watched his facial expression while he was occupied with terse requests for wine and food. Purposely rotating his wrist the tiniest bit as she unravelled, she watched the wince Hermanus tried to conceal. Before she had even fully removed the wrap, she deduced there was a break to the forearm behind the main wound, but what else she needed time to assess.

Dropping the cloth onto the floor, she supported his arm gently at the wrist and inspected his fingers. It had been a while since the blood had properly flowed in them. They were not completely bloodless, but it appeared that the severe swelling at the wrist prevented their full functioning.

"Did Rubrius only bind your arm to stop the bleeding?"

Hermanus gulped down the wine offered him before answering. "Nay! He used wood, but the binding came loose during my journey."

"Did the person who rebound it not set the wood back in place?" Exasperation leeched, for there was no wooden slat to be seen. Rebinding was a simple enough task, even for a useless *tironis*.

The grunt that exploded at her ear gave her an idea of how much pain the man was in. "Ineda. Have you ever tried to replace a splint, rebind an arm with your less dextrous hand while riding hard on a horse?"

She needed no more explanation. What had been a second open gash had already scabbed over. Though the edges of the wound were an angry dark red, they oozed only a little yellow pus. That was not the cause of the problem to his fingers.

"Would you please lie down?"

Gesturing to the nearby couch, she was not sure if he would comply, though to her surprise he did as bid. She needed him to relax, and yet be supported on the padded bed. Kneeling alongside she made some general inquiries as she carefully felt the swollen flesh around the forearm break, before moving down to gently manipulate his severely swollen fingers.

"The splint you lost would have prevented this extra swelling." She knew she was telling the old veteran nothing new, but needed him to talk.

Hermanus closed his eyes and grunted. A frustrated low moan. She was uncertain if it was exhaustion, agony, or just her female touch that caused it. He was an old man, she knew him to be well past forty winters, but she was sure he still functioned well enough when necessary if in the presence of a camp whore.

"I'm going to clean the wounds again before I do anything else. Rubrius has done a fine job of sewing the main one, but your travel has clearly not been without incident." Blackened signs of dampness on the cloth that had originally been light coloured indicated rain had fallen on it, or Hermanus had traversed a deep river ford.

She hoped he might tell her something important as she bustled about ordering some clean warm water from the *militis*. The clay pot she had carried in with her contained an unguent she used regularly for healing of open wounds that showed no major suppuration. She brought it close to the couch before clearing the dried blood away.

"I have little time to waste, Ineda. I must be ready to move again."

"Do your fingers tingle still, or have you no feeling at all?"

Hermanus grunted at her ear. "Oh, they tingle, and sometimes I feel sharp darts of pain." The sigh that followed was chasm deep. "At other times I feel nothing at all."

The risk of losing a sword-wielding hand was something every soldier lived with every day, but the reality for Hermanus was as important as it would have been for any soldier above *militis* rank. Once trained, a soldier needed both hands to be an instrument of fighting. The Brigante in her wanted to chop them off right that very moment with the sharp knife she now concealed about her person. The healer in her wanted him to retain the entire goddess-given parts of his body.

His almost despairing sigh won over her healer's heart. Her grandmother Meaghan had taught her too well.

"You will have full function, but only if you regard my instructions, Hermanus." She knew how the extra pressure could be relieved, had even seen it work before, and began to issue her instructions.

As she renewed the bindings on his arm, her blood surged in horror at the information that spewed out of him, his agitation to be fully mobile winning over caution. Agricola's orders were to give no mercy. Any resistance was now to meet with the sharpest of blades, any attacks on his newly-built forts would incur the severest of reprisals – not just to the actual perpetrators, but to all who dwelt in the surrounding area. That was a devastating escalation of suppression.

Worse still, it was his intention to march over the high hills, with no stop to accommodate the cold weather, which was of utmost importance. Attempting to prattle in an unconcerned way, she asked an occasional general question.

"Will that not be a difficult task? Will it not ride the horses too hard over ground that is frozen and snow-clad?"

"Ineda!" Hermanus' tone altered. It was too late to bite her tongue for asking such a question. "You have seen the animals we use. Our pack mules can withstand much fouler weather conditions than our horses, and can travel for much longer distances before needing rest or fodder."

Pretending some forgetfulness, she forced a laugh to cover any awkwardness. "I had forgotten your use of mules. I have seen them in the animal pens."

"Thanks to the excellent tribunes at this fortress, our mule stocks are high." He went on to name another of the tribunes who dealt with supplies that Gaius rarely needed to oversee.

Rain, snow, sleet or hail, Agricola's troops would march steadily every single day in the near future over the high hills and into the territory of the Selgovae and the Votadini. If they met with any confrontation, the orders were clear. Quash it with ferocious force, establish a monitoring presence, and then continue to move northwards. Not even the inhospitable weather of winter in the high hills was going to halt Agricola's progress.

"Tribune Valerius has made sure our campaign needs are already in place. He is exceptionally good at such tasks..." Hermanus' voice drifted off, a spasm of pain gripping him as she gently inserted his arm into a sling, to keep the arm motionless.

"You must keep your arm thus for good healing." She was sure her words were ignored. In his pain, Hermanus was dwelling more on current events as he divulged more details.

"You believe Governor Agricola will expect you to move out on the morrow?" She kept calm as she gathered her unguents.

Hermanus' laugh was scathing as he lay back down on the couch, drawing in some deep breaths as though to gain control of his feelings. "Who knows what Agricola plans? We are only issued new orders the instant he wishes action to be taken. Preparations for leaving are in place, but it is not beyond our General to choose to attend to some other matter before we head north via the lands of the Setantii."

Ineda now knew the route Agricola was likely to take.

She fretted as she worked out how to get immediate word to her contact. Hermanus' wound was not really likely to become infected, and the swelling would reduce quickly if the arm was kept at rest, but in his present frame of mind he might believe it if she said she required different herbs to treat it.

"I know of a herb which should quickly reduce the swelling, and will make it easier for you to travel. I do not presently have any, but Orchil, the herbs wife, will have it. If I could…"

"Permission to leave the fort, Ineda? Of course you have my permission. My fingers must return to full strength as soon as possible."

It was significant that Gaius was deep in correspondence. Otherwise, she knew she would not have managed to walk out of the gates with only her *tironis* in her wake.

Freedom?

No. Her son was still inside the gates.

Chapter Six

"What did they think to achieve?" Lorcan moved awkwardly around his dwelling, his agitation quite clear to Brennus.

Brennus had just returned from a journey that had been beset by high winds and driving rain, Lughnasadh having passed more than a moon ago, the season changing to fallen leaves earlier than usual. "What does one small tribe ever think to achieve when they attack the forces of Rome, my brother?" He was exhausted and hungry; not a good combination to tolerate any ranting by Lorcan.

"They destroyed an *ala*? The Ordovices had the gall to storm and destroy the fort housing a mounted regiment?" Lorcan's sarcasm was not often seen these days. Anger? Aye! And censure a-plenty, but biting sarcasm was a thing of his past.

Brennus' answer was cool, not rising to Lorcan's taunts. "They have been successful, my brother: burned the defences, set the beasts free, and destroyed the innards of the fort. Why do you not rejoice for them?" He knew the reason perfectly well, but could see that Lorcan needed to vent some frustrated anger that had been simmering for some time.

"It bodes ill for all of us now! Agricola will not sit back. We can expect a relentless retaliation from all the legions he now commands, not just his old *Legio XX*."

It was the truth. Agricola was indeed the new Governor of Britannia, having recently arrived in the far south. All who had knowledge of Agricola's former methods knew he would not tarry in the Romanised Britannia of the southern coast, as his predecessor had done. The Ordovices had thwarted Agricola's plans when he was at Viroconium Cornoviorum as

58

Legate of the *Legio XX*. As Governor, he now had more might at his disposal to annihilate them

Some nights later, Brennus learned that Agricola had indeed marched north and had destroyed the Ordovices. His tone was bleak as he faced his brother and the elders of Garrigill, a gathering having been hastily summoned. "The little petty rebellions by the Ordovices are over for now, and maybe for ever. Agricola's sword was brutal. Men, women and babies live no longer. Agricola has allowed few to carry on the tribe, few to foment another minor revolt."

"Where will his sword fall next?" Lorcan sounded even more depressed by the latest news.

"My new informant in the area sent word that he has arrived at the new fort building at Deva. He will likely remain there over the winter months."

"What of the tribes around there who have not had any dealing yet with the Roman butcher?" Lorcan looked well out of patience now.

"Scortin, and the settlements nearby, prepare now for imminent attack. Though, I very much doubt whether they would aid the Ordovices who made this *ala* assault. They all look to their own winter defences rather than make plans for battle elsewhere. When the warmer moons come, I fear the story may be no different." He broke off from speaking on hearing the noise outside.

Nara bustled in with her young brood in tow, accompanied by his daughter Kaideigh.

"*Athair*! I have missed you, father!"

The little one launched herself onto his lap, though 'little' was not so appropriate really. She had inherited his height, maybe even his strength. A large child for not yet having passed three winters, she was even more fearless than she had been when a babe. He ruffled her braids around her cheeks, tickling her.

"And how fares my frightened little hen?"

"I fear no thing!"

"Oh aye, you do, my little chick."

"No Romans. Nara says my arm is meaty!"

Tired as he was, his laughter roared around the roundhouse, the others joining in. Kaideigh had good speech, but sometimes not quite correct.

"You mean mighty!"

The mulish look on her little face brought forth more laughs. Her repetition of the word fell somewhere in between: clearly Kaideigh did not like being mocked.

Nara intervened. "Your father chides because he loves you and has missed you, little one."

The wobble on the lower lip turned to a weak grin as he hugged her tight. He truly did love his little daughter.

"I missed you." Kaideigh's words muffled into his rank tunic before she squirmed away, and turned her head to fresher air.

He had been riding hard and had slept outdoors for many nights. Rising to his feet, his child still cradled close to him, he addressed his brother. "The other news is urgent enough, but not so bad that it cannot wait till food is in my stomach, and I have cleaned my stinking body."

Kaideigh's pig-like snort and turned-up nose attested to the truth of that as she wriggled her way down to the beaten earth floor of the roundhouse.

"Where is your mother?"

Nara answered since Kaideigh had rushed to the door entrance. "Lleia is over at the quern stones. Our spelt-grinding seems a never-ending task since Lughnasadh."

"Run and tell your mother I am returned, my daughter!" Brennus watched Kaideigh scamper out, needing no more bidding.

Lorcan waved him away, smirking and wafting his nose at his own children, as though agreeing a bathing was essential.

"Do not tarry too long, my brother. We may talk well into the night. I have had other news since you have been away from Garrigill. Our treaties become too impossible to maintain, since Agricola has come to take up office as Governor. He claims these new reforms he insists on implementing immediately will be better for all Brigantes – we are less sure of the benefits."

Brennus did not doubt it. He was only one of Lorcan's eyes and ears for the northern tribes.

Striding off to the stall he shared with Lleia, he knew any more personal welcome from her would have to wait till the night had waned. Plans had to be put in place. Circumstances were changing too quickly.

He used the bowl of warm water, provided by Lleia who had rushed in on hearing of his arrival, to wash off the filth of his travels. He yanked on clean braccae, and a tunic, before he supped the broth she thrust his way. The meal came from the pot hanging over the small central fire, and the chunk of bread that she mutely handed him was fresh from the warming slab at the fireside.

Slurping down the small beer poured for him, he gathered Lleia into a loose embrace whispering at her ear. "Once I have spoken to Lorcan and the elders, we will have more time." His lips lingered a while at her cheek before dropping to lightly cover her mouth.

Lleia's vague smile indicated her understanding. She did not have his love, but she still engendered a good dose of lust, even after a few winters of being together.

AD 78 One Moon Before Samhain – Deva, Cornovii Territory

"Tribune Valerius!"

Gaius acknowledged the sentry while the man warned of his arrival, and then he paced around outside Agricola's door, awaiting entry. The Governor's unexpected arrival back to Deva, a few days previously, had set the whole fortress into a flurry of extra special activity, and had caused some confusion to officers like him. The element of surprise seemed to be a method often employed by Agricola.

As Commander of the Britannic legions, Agricola had already been to Deva during the past cycle of the moon, but had chosen not to advance northwards immediately as had been rumoured, and indeed planned for, even though the winter season approached.

Instead, Agricola had postponed those plans and had gone off east to Eboracum to attend to matters relevant to the judicial and civic Governing of Britannia, for which he was also ultimately responsible.

Word had then come to Deva that Agricola would march northwards with troops from Eboracum. So why he had tramped back west to Deva was unfathomable.

The areas around the fortress of Deva had been mostly under control for a long while. Petty bickering between the troops had been kept to a bare minimum, and the news had been favourable regarding any minor tribal uprisings. Gaius knew, because he had been instrumental in those processes.

"Enter!"

The bellow from inside startled him from his introspection.

His salute made, he faced Agricola and the other senior officers of the *Legio XX*.

"Gaius Livanus Valerius. You have done a fine job of keeping the tempers of our troops suppressed in the local forts, and have done a commendable job as our metal supplies officer. But your time here is now at an end."

The words should have been complimentary, but the fierce expression on Agricola's face denied any admiration. The sudden lump Gaius felt in his throat was hard to swallow. What he had done to deserve censure, was unknown to him. His duties had been fulfilled satisfactorily, as far as he knew. But keeping his feelings hidden was not difficult as he faced his most superior officer. It was his usual bland composure that he summoned as Agricola rattled on.

"My legion continues to move northwards. You have some experience of the northern terrain?"

Knowing he was now expected to speak, he cleared his throat. "I have not covered the spur of the highest hills, between Brigantia and Selgovae and Votadini territory, though I have travelled over the rest, General Agricola."

"Never traversed the high terrain to the territory of the Selgovae?"

A spark of hope blossomed. Was the serious tone nothing to do with his conduct, and all to do with a new assignment of subduing the tribes north of the boundary of high hills? The Selgovae were claimed to be as formidable as the Brigantes had been, though all of Brigantia was now under varying degrees of Roman presence – heavy in some areas, though less intrusive at the most northerly reaches. He was more than ready to march forward with his legion. *Speculatores*, and a few *cohorts* of the *Legio XX,* had already been north of the high hills.

"Not yet. But I would like to, sir."

Agricola ordered him to come closer to the table that was set out with the usual mountain of scrolls: all part of the job for a senior officer of Rome.

"Some of my advance troops have already settled a portion of Votadini territory, as you well know. Not all of it, granted, but enough to secure passage of my main troops to the extreme north. My expeditionary forces have also arrived on western shores, and I am here at Deva to issue further instructions to the fleet in the west. The standards of Rome will march to the furthest reaches of this long island of Britannia ere long, and nothing will prevent that happening. You, Gaius Livanus Valerius, will also ensure that very success with men from *Cohorts* Four and Five of the *Legio XX*. You know those men like no other officer here in Deva."

Gaius briefly bowed his head, his heart hammering, restraining the urge to grin. He was advancing north? To be in the forefront of Agricola's forces was a heady notion. He could not wait to get started, realising that in a way his own choices in accepting advancement had stifled his need for adventure. He did know *Cohorts* Four and Five extremely well. Agricola was most likely correct about that, since no other officer of Rome, at tribune level, had been in post in the area as long as he had – though some of the centurions had served longer terms.

Agricola began to strut about, walking behind his back, to-ing and fro-ing in the chamber. His voice boomed and ebbed as he moved around, an agitated animation emanating from him which seemed to make its way right through every part of Gaius.

"So far, Rome has captured less than one-half of this island of Britannia, but I will march over every part of it before I am done. Its warring tribes will come under the auspices of Rome, or they will die! And you, Gaius Livanus Valerius, will be central to ensuring this new stride forward."

Later that night, Gaius was deeply preoccupied with his orders from Agricola when he entered his own quarters. He still vacillated between elation and disappointment, his insides churning with excitement. His preference would have been to advance northwards, in direct company with Agricola, but it was so gratifying to have his hard-won experience appreciated. His new orders were a thrilling responsibility.

The new status would also mean changes to his arrangements with Ineda. He had never publicly acknowledged Ineda as his concubine, his rank being too high for that and her background far below – though all at the fortress knew her to be his woman. His tight security had ensured she had never strayed from his bed, and he had no intentions of ever changing that. It was no longer because he believed she would attempt to escape – he was hopeful her mind had changed on that – but as his woman she was vulnerable to the small amount of dissenters who still remained at Deva.

The security which followed her was her protection. Anyone who bore a him grudge could take their ire out on Ineda, and he never wanted that to happen. And the safety of his son was vital.

He had no doubts that Dubv carried his blood, and the blood of his forefathers. Ineda had been given leave to give her son a Celtic name for daily use, and she had done it well. Dubv, meaning dark-faced, suited his son admirably since the sun-kissed skin tone matched his own. He also had named his child. Rogatus was his official Latin name, since he wanted all to know his son was a wished-for child – quite different from the earlier reputation he had had of having a dislike of begetting a child.

"Gaius?" Ineda removed the cloak from his shoulders and set it on a hook near the doorway. "Agricola sent for you?"

Even after all the time Ineda had been his woman, he was still not entirely sure of her loyalties – or, in fact, if she could ever love him unreservedly. She did anything he requested of her without failure. She was now fond of him, he was certain of that, time and proximity had nurtured that. Yet he was not sure her regard was as deep for him as his had become for her.

Love? He often asked himself if he loved her. He would publicly not name it such, but his regard definitely came into some realm of love. His son was another matter. Dubv was a very bright little boy whom he doted on.

"Dubv sleeps?"

Ineda's cheery laugh brightened up what had been a trying day. "Gaius. It is late, and darkness settled in a long while ago. You will see him on the morrow. Do you wish for some food?"

He had eaten some time ago with the other tribunes of the *Legio XX*. Shaking his head he reached for her. "I ate enough. Now I need to sleep. And think."

"How can you think while asleep?" Her small hands towed him along to the couch where she stopped in front of it, to remove his belt. He watched her carefully place it on the low table alongside the recliner as he removed his tunic.

"We need to talk, Ineda, but I am exhausted."

Her small smile of sympathy reached into his soul, her silent regard always encouraging. The woman grounded him to the soil of Britannia, kept him on its shores. He knew it, but had no words to tell her of his feelings.

"Dawn will be time enough, Gaius. Rest."

He made no protest when she urged him down onto the bed and followed him after removing her clothing. He made no protest when she snuggled in close and her small hands soothed his body.

Sometimes he wished he could summon the courage to tell her of his feelings, of a love that had its origins at the instance of their first meeting. He had not known at the time, or acknowledged it for what it was, though it was now hard to deny. However, none of that altered the fact that she was his slave, and a woman of inferior origins.

***

Ineda lay fully awake. Something was amiss with Gaius. She did not know what, but knew he would not share it with her till he was ready. But it would not be difficult to find out, because if Gaius was disturbed by something, Pomponius would be gossiping with her on the morrow. She had allowed Pomponius to believe that Gaius shared everything with her, though that was far from the case.

Agricola must have given Gaius some astounding news: he had not been so distracted for a very long while. It could not be Gaius' conduct that Agricola had held in question, since the execution of his duties was exemplary. Gaius was tired, as he had claimed, but she sensed that some other thing both excited and set an anxiety on him.

General Agricola's sudden arrival at the garrison had changed the usual tenor of daily life. Gaius and his fellow officers clamped down on lax behaviour, so any immediate correction of that would not be needed. It was more that a general excitement and anticipation had permeated every action from dawn's light, and had continued all day since his arrival.

"Thank you, Rhianna!" Her words whispered into the cover as she prayed to her goddess. She had managed to send a message about Agricola's re-appearance, but she knew she must worm out even more details from Gaius about the general's purpose. She would let Gaius rest for a while first. That usually worked.

Her eyelids closed. She willed sleep to flee, flickering her eyes open again since she needed to seduce Gaius before long.

"You are setting out for Selgovae territory at dawn?"

She was not sure she managed to keep the fear from her tone, a while later. Unlike their first couplings, now seeming so long ago, Gaius afterwards often lapsed into talk. That was exactly what she had planned for when she began to make love to him, having roused him from his short sleep.

His news was indeed startling.

"I am leaving at dawn, though I am not heading directly to Selgovae lands, Ineda. I must stop at many of our small fortlets along the route to where we will cross the high hills. And after Selgovae territory, I will march wherever Agricola sends me."

Excitement flared in Ineda, and then instantly died. He would leave her at Deva! That was what he had done before. But if he was away from Deva for many seasons, he could not possibly leave her in similar fashion? During his short absences, he had left her under guard. Surely that could not happen, if he went off for long moons?

Her heart was conflicted, and set her into a great confusion. A part of her would miss Gaius, having grown so used to their life together, even though resentment over her captive state still lingered. Dubv! By Rhianna! What about Dubv? Worry for her son was even greater than the worry for herself.

Her skin chilled at her next thought. If Pomponius accompanied Gaius, she did not know who she would get her information from. Other sources could not be trusted. Her mind whirled so much she almost missed Gaius' next words.

"I should leave you and Dubv behind the safety of the fortress walls, but I have no wish to be parted from my son for so long."

By Rhianna! Did he mean to take Dubv with him? And leave her? Making sure her question was casual, she prompted for more details.

"Then you do not expect this to be a short campaign? Not only a few days away from Dubv?"

Anticipation lightened Gaius' features, making him appear almost boyish. "I expect it to be more than one season, and perhaps even many."

Ineda's heart lurched. Fear for Dubv, if Gaius took her son into hostile territory. "You go into great danger, Gaius. The tribes beyond the high hills are a formidable opponent. They were when Brigantes challenged Selgovae, or warriors of the Novantae."

"There will always be danger for the Roman Empire, Ineda, but we have our methods which reduce our losses. You know that well enough by now." His voice softened as he drew her in tighter. "Are you worried for me?"

Her fingers running smoothly over his chest were an expression of her concern. Not for Rome, but for Gaius alone. He was a good father, and he had in many ways been kind to her. The hitch at her throat was real.

"I am."

"Would the worry be less if I tell you that you and Dubv will be with me?" You are his mother, and I will not be parted from my son." Gaius' eyes sparkled in the weak light shed from the tallow candle. His deep kiss assured her that he meant what he said. Snuggling into his neck, she dared another question she found she really did not want an answer to.

"Will you lead your *cohort* into battle, Gaius?"

"Perhaps, if we are attacked, but Agricola gives me a special function."

Silence reigned for a time. She knew the best option was to let it lie before any more conversation, but this situation was not normal. It was Gaius' way to ponder and dwell – without her involvement – but his body alongside her was agitated, as though fit to burst with excitement and anticipation, maybe even a sort of trepidation.

Courage was never a lack with Gaius; she had learned his greatest fear was failure.

More subtle questions would worm out useful information regarding his campaign details, but for now a most important one had to be asked. He had already named another tribune who would be leaving with his *cohort*. "If you are not here to oversee at Deva, who will do the task instead?"

"You have not met him yet. A new tribune has come with Agricola. He replaces the leader of the third *cohort* who was recently recalled to Rome. The new tribune has been at the fortress at Lindum, and will now take over duties here."

Her method of questioning worked well. In the darkness of the night, Gaius gave up more important information. The surge northwards that had been expected a moon ago was now about to happen. Guilt lay heavy on her when she used him in such ways, yet, though she had more information, she did not know how she would pass it on. They were leaving as soon as possible.

She resolved to create a better line of communication, since what had gone before would no longer work. As sleep claimed her, she vowed to find a way. The news was too important for it to be missed.

She also felt, for the first time, that she was betraying her son's father.

Chapter Seven

AD 79 Just Before Samhain – Garrigill, Brigantes Territory

"Lorcan!"

Water dripped from his newly-wet hair as Brennus hurried into the chief's roundhouse at Garrigill. His head-dip into the metal pan of cold water outside the door would have to do till later, and filling his stomach had no priority either. Lorcan needed to be told immediately of his dire news, though it was not quite as alarming as having the Roman Empire at his very heels.

"No time to squander?" Lorcan looked to Nara to remove the children when Brennus erupted in through the entrance tunnel.

"Who will chase me?" An excited flurry, and squeals of laughter, followed Nara as she ran outside ahead of the brood, with Lleia at the rear.

"It's ominous, Lorcan." Brennus did not even wait before speaking, the children's noise covering his words as he placed his spear and other weapons into the metal rack at the side of the doorway. He chose his words with such care, not wanting to convey them at all. His spirit ached to mouth his news while he removed his bratt and draped it over a low beam to dry off. "The death of the Roman Emperor Vespasian has definitely signalled an end to the complacent seasons we have endured."

Lorcan tossed himself down onto a low stool, seemingly unconcerned about any objects that might cause injury, fireside tongs lying scattered around after Nara's hasty retreat. "I know that only too well. The signs have been there for a while, since Agricola's arrival."

70

Brennus regarded his brother settled enough to continue, but held from conveying his worst news as he, too, sat on a stool at the fireside. "Vespasian's death is not the only thing I have heard that has the troops of Rome feeling restless. Scortin was full of a tale of a massive catastrophe that has occurred somewhere near Rome itself. The fury of their gods has descended, and covered thousands with a rain of black fire from the sky. A whole Roman town has been engulfed." To the sound of Lorcan's hearty chuckle he warned, "Laugh, my brother. But you know how superstitious the Roman Army is. If they believe their gods have taken them in ill favour, it will eventually bode ill for us. A fidgety army of Rome will be an even more dangerous foe."

Lorcan sobered enough to answer. "How so, Brennus? Why should that affect us?"

He could tell Lorcan merely tested his reasoning. "In some way, or another, we shall bear the brunt of any panic on the part of the Roman Army. They will descend upon us, as though they are that fire of black from the sky, and swallow us up. If Agricola has instability within his ranks, he will draw their attention elsewhere. To us!"

"Is that a prediction?" Lorcan's expression was a combination of being quizzical, and one of admiration.

"Nay! I left predictions to Meaghan, my old healer, and to Ineda. They truly did have the gift."

Inside, a little bit of him chilled. He could never bring Ineda into a conversation without a direct stab at his gut…or maybe his heart. It was the same ache. As ever, his fingers strayed to the silver ring that still lay against his chest. It was a symbol that all who knew him well understood the significance of, even Lleia.

"We will deal with what they throw at us, Brennus. We have done so in the past. But that is not so ominous. Tell me all."

Astute as ever, Lorcan was correct in sensing that he still had more to update.

Dispirited, and disconsolate, Brennus held his hands out to the low blaze, finding that the words would not come easily.

71

"Rome's armies can fight amongst themselves all they want, so long as it has little effect on us." Lorcan probed gently, though his expression betrayed some agitation.

Lorcan's words sounded confident, but Brennus knew his brother considered well what might happen. The Roman Army in Britannia was a volatile entity of old, and was only predictable in that the Celtic tribes had suffered when any disruption happened amongst the legions.

Loyalty was an ongoing fickle thing amongst the *Legio XX*. Rumour was that it always had been, and he had even heard lately that the *Legio II Adiutrix* had been suffering from similar internal disruption.

Brennus cradled his head in his palms, his voice a whisper. "Rome is such an unpredictable enemy, Lorcan."

Lorcan flexed his arms, his yawn becoming infectious. "Aye! You speak true. But the colder weather is almost upon us again. Agricola will do little till the new thaws after Imbolc."

Brennus had not told his brother all his news, and it was not the best saved till last. His deep sigh held all of his despair as he stared at the bright orange dancing flames in front of him. "Not true."

Lorcan latched on to his meaning immediately, his gaze incredulous. "Agricola really does move further north, although winter is nigh?"

Brennus chucked a log into the fire, creating a dangerous rise of sparks. "Aye. He has already marched through Setantii lands."

"Are you saying Garrigill will be in Agricola's path within days?"

Brennus' throat hurt to speak of such news as he shared Lorcan's anguish. "Aye! That is exactly what I am saying, though I can not say when. The information that came to us during the last moon cycle, when I was told Agricola's full forces were on the move, proved wrong." He watched Lorcan's confirming head-nods. "But that only gave us false security. The latest news tells me that the forces of Rome are definitely advancing."

"But a hard frosting on the grass has already crept over the fields of Garrigill!" Doubt was not only in Lorcan's eyes, his voice cracked on his next words. "Like our Celtic brothers, the Roman Empire remains in winter quarters, and they do no battle till the spring thaws."

Brennus felt his own voice rising, anger leaching. "That may have been so in the past, but the contact from Deva got word to Scortin while I was there. Agricola plans to keep his legions moving through the colder weather, and it is said he will be right there along with them."

Though exhausted, he could not settle on the stool. His pacing was agitated as he strode opposite his brother. "The road Agricola has laid between Deva and the fortress on the west coast – the one he names Luguvallium in Carvetii territory – is expected to be flattened even more ere long, by the feet of his whole *Legio XX*. The Governor of Britannia is also the General of all Britannic Legions, and he is a man who likes to lead his armies, not a soft leader who likes his home comforts provided by those assimilated Celtic tribes in the far south."

Though he still padded around, he exchanged troubled glances with Lorcan.

"If ground can be broken for his temporary camps, then Agricola will move on northwards. I'm informed that this time he intends to strike on over the high hills to the Selgovae and the Votadini, without stopping. The Brigantes are no longer a threat to him, though any resistance by our tribes will be met with ferocious consequences to all within the environs, and not just during any warrior band attack."

"Garrigill cannot withstand assault from a *cohort* of Roman soldiers, far less from a whole legion." Lorcan had risen to pace around as well, thumping one fist against the other in agitation.

"Agricola will have more than that. His plan is to subdue from both the west and from the east, as they did when Venutius was vanquished. The garrison at Eboracum has been mobilised. The *Legio XX* will subdue the Selgovae from the west, while the *Legio IX* will do the same with any reluctant

Votadini as they stride northwards, on the eastern side of Britannia, to their base at Corstopitum."

Lorcan's fingers rifling through the weapon stack at the doorway showed his agitation as nothing else could. His sword located, he held it aloft, inspecting the blade's cut. "Is this new contact reliable? Can there be doubt?"

"All the news from him, so far, has been frighteningly accurate. I have no reason at all to doubt any warnings from him."

"Who is this person?" A few slashes whistled through the air as his brother tested the balance of the blade. As a negotiator and peacemaker Lorcan mainly used his tongue to settle issues, but he was still a formidable sword-wielding warrior.

"The chief at Scortin does not know. The Deva messenger sends word via a chain of couriers in the territory of the Cornovii, a chain that goes all the way north into Setantii country and to Scortin. It will be the death of the man, if his identity becomes known. He has close contact with the top leadership at Deva, and his word has, so far, always been true – apart from the alarm of one moon ago which proved wrong. He hates the Roman scourge as much as we do, but prefers to live in daily mortal danger to get the intelligence to us."

"A brave man indeed. I would like very much to meet him." Seeming happy with his check, Lorcan replaced the sword into its scabbard, but still ambled around.

Brennus would like to meet the brave warrior, too, but presently his task was clear. "Lorcan, you need to endorse a new man to train our young blades."

Lorcan filled wooden beakers with small beer from the container near the doorway, before handing one to him. "Aye! You will need to go farther afield, immediately. Those who dwell well beyond the high hills need fair warning."

"Do you wish me to go to Tarras first, and tell Nara's father?"

Lorcan took a while to answer as he sat down again, clearly despondent at the thought of uprooting his people. "Aye, though I can spare you only two horses. I fear Gabrond's current stock will not be sufficient for the exit of all of my people from Garrigill."

"Two are more than generous, Lorcan, though I can make do with one if need be."

"You will have two of our best." Lorcan was adamant. "Your journeying may last much longer than mine, and you must be swiftly at Tarras to prepare Callan for our arrival."

Brennus knew when to allow Lorcan his say. The fate of Garrigill now rested on the shoulders of Lorcan and Nara.

Lorcan took a long draught of his beer before continuing, his thoughts clearly troubled, the angry glower deepening. "But you will need to go as Bran of Witton to continue your chain of contacts. I will send a trusted warrior immediately to warn Callan of your two identities. He has long agreed that we will all be welcome to dwell there, should the Roman turds continue their northerly sweep." His voice increased in volume to a violent shout. "I will sharpen our long-made preparations, but I will not uproot my people until I am convinced the threat will arrive at my door!"

Brennus winced as Lorcan's drained beaker bounced off a high rafter, his brother's usually calm demeanour well-shattered. His blast of anger over, Lorcan's arm descended from aloft to cradle his knees, his head bowed. The words muffled into the beaten earth of the floor, a harsh despairing whisper.

"I have dreaded this day for many seasons, yet the fate of our tribe is sealed. I can do no other than take what is left of the people of Garrigill to safer climes, or we will die under the *gladius*. Though I have bargained with the Roman Empire for long winters, I will not live with them encamped at my door while they surround my people, and make us into Romans."

Nara's entrance was timely, just perfect to hear Lorcan's last words. "We must go to Tarras?" The sting of tears was in her throat as well as in her expressive eyes.

Lorcan's hand snaked out to pull Nara down beside him before he repeated the latest update. "While Agricola is determined to subdue more territory, then no part of this Celtic land of ours will remain a safe refuge."

"Our Celtic way of life must not die!"

Brennus dreaded that Nara's vehement words had too much of a ring of truth in them. The high hills were a natural barrier which he hoped would halt the influx of thousands of Roman soldiers, but his faith in those rugged slopes was not strong – he had easily crossed them himself with his brothers, back at the time of Lorcan's first meeting with Nara.

A whole Roman legion advancing was a formidable force, and there were more tribes to the north than Nara's Selgovae who would be under attack.

"We will leave as soon as you wish, Brennus." Lleia sounded so firm in her decision when she was given the news, after her return with the children in tow.

"You may be safer here with Lorcan and Nara." He knew the words had a ring of untruth if the Roman might descended upon them, but his task would mean constant travel.

Lleia's usually even tones were laced with accusation. "If you leave without us, it may be the last sight you ever have of your daughter."

Brennus noted she made no mention of herself. He had no intention of fostering Kaideigh with Lorcan or Gabrond, as was the normal Celtic custom, and wanted to keep her by his side, but his path would be fraught with danger. "I think only of your safety, Lleia."

Her small smile was full of a resignation that he understood. "I know you do. We will journey to Tarras with you. And after that, we will come to a new understanding depending on the winter weather, and how that affects our travel."

"We may not find a shelter every night, Lleia, if ill weather prevents us from reaching the next hamlet or village. Are you prepared for that?"

"I cannot say I like the idea of sleeping under the stars, but if needs must, then that is what we will do."

Brennus saw that his chuckle startled her, the conversation not a particularly light-hearted one. "I have an idea about avoiding that. I know exactly what Ineda would have recommended."

The ever-present pang at saying Ineda's name was squelched. He rarely brought her name into conversation, but Lleia understood. Though neither had dwelled on it, they had talked about their lost loves.

"A shelter of leather hides?"

"The Roman army sleeps well under one. We can do likewise, though ours need not be so large."

"So be it. I will have Nara aid me, and we will construct this shelter as you describe. It will not take us long." Her wide smile was rare. It heartened him that she would contemplate the journey he had planned, for the thought of being parted from Kaideigh was not a good one.

Lleia was not quite done. In an uncommon moment of closeness, she nudged him. "The time has also come for me to publicly name you Bran of Witton – though I may occasionally forget, and call you Brennus when we are alone."

"In private, I definitely prefer Brennus." He drew her into a tight embrace.

Chapter Eight

AD 79 Before Samhain – Bremetennacum, Setantii Territory

"Give the order to move on!"

Ineda noted that Gaius' instruction was given after his thorough look all around him. Intense excitement gripped as she looked beyond the open gates of Deva. So many possibilities had gone through her head, since Gaius had revealed his plans.

She had wanted to know more about what he did when he disappeared from Deva, and she was now about to find out. Gaius' new posting as co-ordinating officer for all of the northern bases would mean moving on from place to place, and it seemed he intended her to be with him along with Dubv.

Their initial step was to journey a short distance from Deva to the fort at Bremetennacum. Her knowledge of the smaller auxiliary fort was limited, but she had heard it held an *ala*, a mounted cavalry troop, which regularly patrolled the surrounding area to keep the upper hand. The local Setantii tribe she knew a little more about, since it continuously resisted Roman domination, the small skirmishes and raids created by them something she heard about frequently, via her contacts.

By morning's end, Ineda's initial excitement disappeared, and was quickly replaced by a deep uncertainty that she had not anticipated, and could not quell. Being so far away from the protective walls of Deva was unsettling in ways she found baffling. For many long seasons, she had yearned to be way beyond the fortress, but had only been outside to visit Orchil. The old herbs woman's hamlet lay close by, so close that the palisade was still within sight. Although those quick visits to her Celtic contact were fraught with the danger of possible discovery, there had been great excitement in being temporarily free to find out about the constant skirmishes that took place between the Celts and the Roman Empire. Now that the walls no longer surrounded her, the lack of them produced an unwanted anxiety.

What the future held now preyed on her mind.

"Do you not ride well, Ineda?"

Pomponius' unexpected question startled her. She had not realised her feelings were displayed for all to see, although she could tell from the smirk on the secretary's face that he would relish it if she was a poor rider.

"I am enjoying the ride very well, Pomponius."

The man's horse sidled into hers. It seemed Pomponius was the one who was not in great control of the beast he rode.

"Moving on with Tribune Valerius is something I have been accustomed to," he crowed.

Pomponius' tone was meant to indicate some superiority, but it did nothing to impress Ineda. Doggedly, she answered his idle chatter for as long as he prattled on. It was the horse shying which eventually gave her respite from Pomponius, the man falling back in the line when he sought to control the beast's fretting.

As her horse clopped along the beaten earth road towards Bremetennacum, a growing vulnerability overshadowed the excitement of being out in the open. She had not travelled in a Roman convoy of vehicles before, and had no notion of just how well-guarded they were. She was also aware of the constant state of alert Gaius was in, as were the men under his command.

Her feelings were tattered. Being proud of the local Celts for instilling such unease was hard to suppress, but she also bore a reluctant fear for Gaius' wellbeing. Though she had not known of it, he must have experienced this situation every time he had gone forth from the fortress.

The trek was a slow one, since their three wagons were heavily laden, even though the mules doggedly paced forward and seemed to require less rest than horses. It gave her too much time to mull over her situation, and that was not good, being swamped with ambivalent feelings. As Gaius' woman, her life was not one of hardship. She was still his slave, but she wondered how the new situations might affect that status? It was a worry she could do without, yet apprehensive thoughts rolled around in her head. Her son was loved by many of the soldiers, since he was a bright engaging child. Always eager to learn and of a happy disposition, Dubv was essentially a Roman child. Nothing seemed likely to change that status either.

The idea of escaping from Gaius had troubled her thoughts, though she would never contemplate that unless Dubv went with her. Since her son always rode with Gaius, the opportunity was lacking for her to flee with him. If she did escape, where would she go? Would local tribespeople believe who she was, or would she be considered a traitor in their midst, even if she managed to come face to face with contacts she only knew about, and had never met?

She had been so long away from the life of the Celt, she had almost forgotten what it was like.

She fretted that the contact chain would be broken when they moved on, but could do nothing more at present. A last message to Orchil, about this first part of the route Gaius and his goods were likely to take, had hopefully been sent via a new slave of the cooks.

The man was of the Carvetii, and had been taken prisoner after an unsuccessful attack on one of the forts the tribune had recently visited. Ineda was not sure how to react to the man. He was not inclined to leer, as many men did, but she often intercepted some deep stares. Any tentative overtures on her part to find out where the slave's allegiances lay had not been successful. The man had not divulged who he owed loyalty to – but then neither had she. Even after more than a moon, she was still unsure of his motives, yet leaned heavily towards believing the man would rally to the cause of the Celts, if he had the opportunity to pass on messages. As a last resort whilst still ensuring her own safety, she had had a conversation with the cook before their departure that morning, her voice loud enough for the slave nearby to overhear.

"I would like to have made my farewells to my old friend, Orchil," she had said. "I will miss being able to ask her wise advice and will surely run out of my stocks of healing herbs after we journey beyond Bremetennacum, and then onto Luguvallium."

Conversational enough, but whether the intended destinations would be conveyed to Orchil, she could only hope on.

"Attack!"

The harried call of the forerunner was so startling it almost unseated her. It set everyone around her into motion.

Gaius leapt from his horse and squashed Dubv towards the rear of the first cart which had pulled up short. "Ineda! Protect my son!"

She was already off her horse and squeezing in alongside Dubv, her mount scurrying off in panic as the first Celtic spears landed within range. By the time she had enclosed Dubv within her bratt, and had dropped to the ground in a tight crouch, the dismounted guard who had accompanied them had formed ranks all around the three vehicles, their scuta held up in a protective wall.

The sudden darkness behind the shields was a horror of its own.

The first hail of Celtic spears thudding against the wood was a sickening clamour, yet there seemed no panic at all on the part of the Roman guard, as she took in the back view of them. The soldiers all around her braced themselves, tucking in tight together, their *pila* drawn and ready. As she had noticed during their training, they all held the weapon in the same hand and silently awaited next orders.

The notion of battle had seemed so enticing long ago when she and Bran had discussed it, but the reality of even a small raid was shocking when she and her child were right at the centre of it.

"Let me out!"

Dubv's cries were alarming, muffled against her chest as he struggled to be free, pummelling his little fists against any part of her he could reach.

"I want to see!"

Dubv was not even a bit terrified, his pleas to be freed continuing so that he could watch what was happening. More spears thudded against the shields as she fought to keep him protected, her crouch even closer to the rear of the wagon. Gaius bawled orders, but they seemed distant over the din her son was making.

When the men around her moved away as one, it caused her heart to almost stop. The darkness that had been created by the scuta wall gave way to broken light as the legionaries raised their *pila* and fired. Gaius' next order she heard clearly.

"Leave none alive!"

The next moments were a flurry of movement, the noise of metal hitting metal an unforgettable screech. Screams of outrage and agony were all around, though mostly in the tongue of the Celts. Squirming into a position where she could see, but her son could not, she watched, totally sickened, as the forces of Rome cut down and slaughtered the small number of local Celts who had dared to raid the convoy. It took only a short while before the road around her was a red-sodden mess, a line of broken and bloodied bodies a testament to the fact that Rome gave no quarter to anyone who attacked them.

The legionaries were poking and prodding with their smaller *pugiones*, the daggers ensuring the bodies really were dead, when Gaius appeared at her side. He was not unscathed. Blood smeared all across his breastplate. A steady flow of red ran down his arm and dripped from his fingers, though a nick above his elbow was all she could see. He enclosed her and his son in a fierce grasp, a swift kiss at her brow when she sent him a silent plea. No words of any kind would form, when his furious voice whiffed at her hair.

"I curse every last one of these local tribesmen. When I find out the conspirator who gives out our transport information, I will leave no pieces large enough to be buried!

Stay huddled, Ineda, till we search the area. When I come back, we will move on."

Dubv had ceased to plead for freedom when the Celtic cries had become real and the skirmish had no longer seemed like practice. Gaius peeled back the bratt, just enough to speak to the child, yet still shielding him from the carnage.

"When I return, you will once again ride with me, my son. Till then you must take care of your mother. She looks very afraid and needs you to hold her tight. Do you understand me?"

Dubv's chin wobbling at her chest confirmed, his little arms squeezing tighter.

When Gaius came back, a short while later, he lifted his sleeping son from her arms and set him up in front of him on his horse.

There had been no need to drag the corpses out of sight, though she knew Gaius would have ordered that if necessary. Dubv was being taught Roman ways, but he was still too young to bear witness to such slaughter. Ineda sensed it was some kind of turning point for Gaius, and guessed her little son would be gradually acclimatised to the notion of war and death in a much more realistic way.

The slow death of the informant was also a certainty, if Gaius found that person.

Suspicion might already be at her feet.

Like Gaius, a few of the soldiers had insignificant cuts and nicks, here and there, but no one was sufficiently injured enough to delay them further. Her offer to bind wounds was rebuffed; like their tribune, they had roughly bound their wounds and moved on. The cleaning of them would come later, in the security of the fort. It was more important to reach the shelter of the next fort without delay.

If Gaius had been an unkind master, had beaten or abused her, she would have delighted that he and some of his men had been wounded, even though they were minor wounds. The opposite was so true it made it difficult to hate him, difficult to even dislike him, and impossible to banish the feeling of fear. What she felt for Gaius was not love, but she did reluctantly hold him in great respect. She still had great hatred for the Roman Empire...but not personally for Gaius any more.

The remainder of the journey was torture. She was no longer sure how much of the Celt was left in her; no longer certain she could continue to send messages. She had played the role of slave and almost concubine for so long. Seeing the effects of her information, in the form of attack on a convoy, was too real.

She needed to think a lot about what her future responsibility was. Gaius may have been nicked by a Celtic sword, but as many as fifteen Celtic warriors lay hacked on the ground awash in blood and hacked-off parts.

Because of information she had sent on.

AD 79 Samhain – Tarras, Selgovae Territory

"Bran of Witton comes to visit Callan of the Selgovae."

Brennus' declaration was made at the gates of Tarras, quite different from his memories of his last visit when he had accompanied his brother Lorcan. Suspicion had been rife back then, but it was clear he was expected now.

Callan was little different from how Brennus remembered him, a little greyer but just as irascible when the Selgovae chief gestured him to be seated at the hearth. "I have no time to waste in apologies for past misdeeds. It is the present we must speak of, and what must be done now."

Brennus was amused. He had no intentions of apologising for not marrying Nara, his own story having been relayed to Callan long since, though he had no wish to make an enemy of the man since he needed Callan's help. "For the task I have set myself, I will need a great deal of your assistance."

"I know you will!" Callan's bluster remained, this time making Brennus smile broadly. "These Roman usurpers must be thrust from this land! You will have all the help I can provide."

A few nights later, a more detailed plan was formed between them. Callan already had a network of contacts amongst the Novantae and the Votadini, in addition to those within his own tribe who were alert to Roman movements on the land.

"The Novantae will resist every bloody blade, bloodying their blades even more. The Votadini, I do not always trust. Their High Chief has not the strength of a new-born lamb, and yet he has the cunning of a wolf. I cannot prove it, but believe he knows more of Rome's Empire than he tells me. But your opinion may differ from mine when you meet him!" Callan strode around, though less fit than he used to be when Brennus had last visited Tarras. "No Celtic tribe north of the Selgovae has your experience of living under the Roman whip. You have much that should be shared. In sharing that experience, it is hoped it will prepare them better."

"Our longer string of contacts will warn of the impending arrival of Roman troops, but I cannot stop that from happening."

"Aye. True enough, but you can sound out which of the tribal leaders will be prepared to assume leadership. Who might be prepared to amass all Celts together, and who will lead them into battle."

"Do you already know of such a man or woman?"

Callan's hearty laugh rang free. "The tribes around here are just as it was between the Selgovae and the Brigantes not so long ago. They can never agree on anything, yet something, or someone, must stir them into action."

"Is that already happening?"

Callan guffawed. "If so, I have heard none of it. Like my tribe, our neighbours live to rear their crops and see to their sheep and pigs. They have no idea of what happens in the far south of this land that the Romans name Britannia. Fireside tales are only half-believed. You must make them believe."

"You think I can?"

"One look at your scar will tell them that it was not made by a flat Celtic broadsword. You have had a neat slicing there. From a Roman *gladius*! Use it as evidence! And the tales you have regaled us with these past nights have an entertaining ring. A song can sometimes be more believable than mere words. More memorable, too!"

Callan was as organising as Brennus expected him to be. They had not been there more than a se'nnight when they were ready to move on, with warriors from Tarras to guide their way.

"Living with Callan is too terrifying. I much prefer the thought of constant journeying, than live with that domineering man watching my every move." Lleia was determined to go on the travels with him, even though it may not be comfortable.

Brennus laughed. "Aye! He is quite taken by your beauty, Lleia. You would do better to choose him for your mate. As the woman of the chief of Tarras, even if he is too old to bed you properly, your position in the tribe would be secured."

"How can you even imagine I would willingly go near the man?" Lleia was horrified. "It is not that he is an old man which repels me, more that his leer is too acute."

She would not be dissuaded, even with the promise that sooner or later Nara and Lorcan would lead the people of Garrigill to Tarras. Regardless of the hardship, she was determined to accompany him.

On the morning of their departure, Brennus was once again amused by Callan who stood awaiting them at the horse enclosure, fully ready for travel.

"The winter bite is not harsh just now, and travel will be good. I will accompany you. My warriors Esk and Nith likewise, and having copied the structure of your leather shelter they are well-prepared for a longer journey. They have their own horses and an eager taste for adventure. I trust them with you."

Brennus was not sure what to make of that statement. It could be that Callan did not trust him on his own in Selgovae territory… or it might just be that Callan preferred Lleia to have more men to guard her safety. Either way, having got to know the brothers during the past days, he was content to have the men join his little band. Though younger than he was by a number of summers, they were strong and able men.

They first headed for the settlement of the High Chief of the Selgovae, which lay further west than Tarras. Callan's idea to gain assistance from the High Chief, in the form of guides who would escort them between settlements and villages, and even on across into Novantae territory, was a welcome one. As he thanked Callan, he felt Lleia move closer to his side.

"Our dealings will progress more smoothly, if I conduct your initial request." Callan was so certain of the outcome that Brennus believed him.

Brennus' nod was appropriate as he masked the smirk that wanted to break free. "I am greatly honoured by your gesture."

After staying a few nights at the settlement of the High Chief of the Selgovae, Callan bade them a hearty farewell on what was a gloriously crisp winter dawn, moisture misting the grass and foliage with pretty patterning. Nara's father had done what he had set out to do, and had smoothed the path for Brennus in Selgovae territory.

"If the chain of messengers breaks, it will not be done by me. You will receive messages passed on from me that are intended for Bran of Witton, but will also find some personal ones are for Brennus of Garrigill! See to it that you keep to your word, and relay all movement of the Roman scum. We must all be on our mettle!"

"You have my word on that!"

Callan's handshake was as firm as ever as he got in the last words. "And be sure to look to that woman of yours. I tried to persuade her to stay here with me, but for some reason she prefers to be with a half-lame, half-blind stubborn Brigante! She must love you well enough."

A long time ago Brennus would have taken great offence at Callan's remark about his infirmities, but the smile that softened the barb was enough for him to know there was some genuine concern for Lleia. It was pointless to tell the irascible old man that it was not love that bound them, but loneliness. Lleia played her part by thanking Callan for the hospitality, though he noticed she remained firmly at his side, as though a feared that Callan might still snatch her at any moment.

As expected, Callan had the last words. "Esk and Nith have my permission to continue with you on your travels. They are kin to Nara's mother and are two of my best warriors. They will keep you safe and will help to feed you all along the journey. No villager is going to turn you away, if you can reciprocate their generosity. Esk is the best man I know at killing a bird with his spear, and Nith's sling-shot never misses its mark. They will also help keep communication going in the names of Bran of Witton, and Brennus of Garrigill."

"I will be honoured to have them accompany us, and will greatly welcome all of those skills."

Callan's thumping pats on his shoulder, he imagined, were intended to reassure though he wondered about the sincerity. "Your voice and instruments will entertain the people you meet on your journey, but a bird for their pot, or a small animal for their fire, will never be rejected."

Feeding his family along the way had been a concern that Callan had just resolved.

"Farewell, and may the gods go with you, Bran of Witton!" Callan's loud leave-taking established his identity.

AD 79 After Samhain – Novantae Territory

So the trekking started on a westwards route that never took them far from the coastline. Though the winter season was upon them, the land around the coastal fringe was rarely frosted, and no snow fell. Biting winds and rain were usual, but that did not hold them back from travelling on. Each time Brennus moved to a new Selgovae village, he remained there a short while, and then a new guide escorted his little band along the quickest route to the next, and then across into Novantae territory.

His line of contact as Bran of Witton continued to be established. Brennus was pleased to have the continued support from Esk and Nith, but was not deluded about the fact that his hearth-woman drew some of their admiration, though Lleia looked upon them with the same indifferent kindness she bestowed on him.

The journey was a revelation, each day bringing new learning of some sort. He had never imagined how much of the Novantae coastline faced directly south. It was even more surprising when they rode further west and he was informed it was still possible to walk a long way more or less still hugging the shore.

"You are saying that on a very clear day if I sailed directly south from here I would come to land on the shores of the Ordovices?" The idea was quite startling as Brennus stood with his guide at the cliff edge on a cold and crisp but clear day, the god Taranis having favoured them with a solid blue sky.

His guide guffawed, amused at his ignorance. "Aye indeed! The island you can just discern as a vague shadow is Manannan, island of the sea god. It is a long island and if you sail from its southernmost shores, in a southerly direction, you will reach Mona's Isle."

"The island of our Druid brothers is so close?"

"Not so close, Bran. You would have to sail twice the distance from here to the one you see in front of you to reach Mona's Isle."

The scudding waves lapping up on the shoreline were not gentle. The notion of braving much choppier waters was enough to make Brennus relish being a traveller on the land. He had never been over the waters, and was not sure he wanted to. "Have the locals here seen any sign of the vessels of Rome?"

It was a worried look that greeted him. "Too many of late. Even though it is almost Imbolc. The sightings of Roman vessels have continued over the winter season on calmer days, and they are not all sailing back to their base at Deva. They are plying the waters between the lands of the Carvetii and the island of Manannan."

"Have any of them come right up to here?" Brennus looked to both sides of him where high cliffs were interspersed with lower dunes, leading to long stretches of sandy beaches. Many opportunities lay below for bringing a vessel to shore.

His guide's head was nodding, chin up, chin down. "I have only seen one since last Lughnasadh, but many of my fellow Novantae have seen more. They do not believe it is the same vessel; more likely a number of them which investigate our shorelines."

"More will arrive, then, when the spring flowers appear and the seas are less rough?" Brennus was deep in thought as he surveyed the huge stretch of water in front of him.

"Perhaps. Though it may also be that Agricola still only confirms earlier surveys."

His guide sounded unsure and hesitant. Brennus wished he felt as hesitant, but that was sadly not true. Agricola did not only want to learn the physical ins and outs of the coastline, he was sure the Roman Governor was surveying for as many landing sites as possible.

He looked westwards, using the thumb of his damaged hand to point. "Does the land of the Novantae turn northwards beyond that far cliff?"

The raucous laugh emanating from his guide showed just how ignorant he was of the land. "Aye. This Novantae coastline goes in and out around the huge bay that you see here, but that far-off cliff marks the turn."

"If the vessels of Agricola sail north from there, where will it take them?"

"The stretch of water, between the coast of the Novantae and the huge island of Erainn to the west, is not so wide. If the Roman fleet sail north through those waters, they will pass the Novantae western coastline, and soon they will find themselves on the shores of the Damnonii. The winds from the west in the strait are often ferocious, and vessels are frequently blown onto Damnonii beaches."

"Have the Damnonii seen signs of the Roman fleet?"

His guide's head shook vehemently. "I have no knowledge of that. I have not spoken with any Damnonii. You will have to travel closer to the place where our tribal lands meet, and ask your question."

Brennus' eye flicked across the headland to where Lleia and the others waited, drawn by the sight of a rider approaching. In no time at all Esk approached, his riding casual enough to make it be known the news just arrived was important, but not critical to their present safety.

"Lorcan and the people of Garrigill have arrived at Tarras."

"By Taranis! If that is the case, then Agricola will soon be breaching the high hills."

Cursing under his breath, Brennus vowed to thwart the Roman turd.

Chapter Nine

AD 79 After Samhain – Bremetennacum, Setantii Territory

Their stay at Bremetennacum was short, Gaius working from dawn till dusk. Ineda barely saw him, and mainly kept to his assigned quarters, except for occasional times to take Dubv out when the weather slightly improved. The dampness was creeping, the rain-filled skies constantly murky, but Dubv needed a little respite from being confined indoors to keep him from being cranky and restless.

The soldiers of Gaius' guard were as bland as usual when she encountered any of them, but those from the fort were blatantly hostile. It was horrible to find she was an object of such censure, the glares and actions of many of the men of the fort directly threatening. When she greeted them, they rebuffed her friendly approaches. Some were openly lewd in their loud comments as she passed by, and others tried to accost her in ways that had never happened at Deva. She was sure only the presence of her small son at her side made them desist when she pushed them away.

She had no *tironis* or *militis* alongside her, as she had had at Deva. In Bremetennacum there was no such guard set up. Too late, she realised just how much Gaius had protected her in the huge garrison fortress of Deva.

After arriving at Bremetennacum, Gaius had told her to keep to their quarters as much as possible, and he expected her to obey him without question. The best he seemed to manage was to send his junior aide to check on her welfare a few times a day. When he eventually fell late into bed beside her, he was too exhausted to do more than bid her goodnight. There was none of his gentle lovemaking pre-dawn and no congenial conversation.

She was glad, since it meant no remorse at not continuing to send on information, and she did not have the worry of stopping the process on her conscience, since she had no contact.

Pomponius kept well away from her, and only once did they have any meaningful conversation when she and Dubv were walking about the fort for exercise.

"Tribune Valerius has much to sort out here in a short time. There have been heavy losses within the horse and mule stocks recently during these petty raids the locals will insist on attempting. But, naturally, you would not know he has to find success with replacing the animals at short notice. Moving wagons of iron is much easier than finding quality beasts to restore the numbers. The small Celtic ponies, so favoured hereabouts, are useless for our needs!"

"I had no idea he would have to arrange livestock for the fort." Placating Pomponius in this vicious sort of mood was the only way to deal with the snide secretary.

"It takes time for mules to be sent this far north, since the Celts have less use for them. Breeding mules is a delicate business! A mule is infertile, which means it takes many matings to produce a good-sized herd."

Ineda knew very little about mules except that they were the product of a mating between a male donkey and a female horse. The Celtic places she had lived in had never had mules in the livestock pens. Nor donkeys either, but she had seen both at Viroconium Cornoviorum.

"You would, indeed, have to tell me about that since I know little of mules, except that Tribune Valerius claims they do better as pack animals than horses because their temperament is more predictably even."

Pomponius huffed as he paced along towards the office Gaius had been assigned to. "The temperament of the mules is not the tribune's only concern. It is also the equestrian tempers he has to deal with. The men of a mounted *ala* not only earn far more than a legionary, they believe themselves superior in all ways. It seems they resent everything, and everyone, at this fort."

"But Tribune Valerius has some experience of being with an *ala*. He will know how to deal with all these issues you speak of."

"During that past assignment he did not have a personal whore traipsing after him, nor a half-breed son. This particular fort has no place for an unavailable Celtic prostitute in its midst!"

Pomponius stomped off, clearly unhappy at being at Bremetennacum, and when he was disturbed she always bore the brunt of it. The last words he spat at her ripped her to shreds. Pomponius rarely dared call her whore.

What Gaius was facing had to be bad. Bringing her along as his personal woman was clearly causing many problems.

The lack of women might explain the vile treatment. The small auxiliary fort had constant changes of officers and men, their residence only for a short duration. She could only surmise that the reaction of the men was because Gaius had a long-term woman at his behest, which the men at Bremetennacum did not.

Whatever the reasoning, she was pleased when Gaius announced they were moving on. She sensed his relief, but wondered if her treatment would be similar at all of the stops on the journey Gaius still had to make. He had not shared it with her, but she imagined they would visit quite a few more.

For the beginning of the new journey they had a heavier mounted escort, which relieved some of Ineda's concern. And when that escort wheeled around after a while to bid Gaius farewell, she steeled herself and forced more confidence. She hated feeling vulnerable, and was tired of being feeble. She was not yet certain, but believed she was again with child, and was not sure she was happy about that.

Birthing another child was not the problem; she was certain she could do that without help. What bothered her a lot more was the possibility that Gaius would be unable to take her with him on further journeys, if she was in the later heavy pre-birth stages. Once again, she felt her situation was precarious. The reactions of the soldiers at Bremetennacum had hurt deeply, her natural exuberance flailed in their presence. Physical

94

attack during the journey worried her less: the infantry around her had already protected them, and would do so again.

The following day their route took them near Marske, the village of Ineda's upbringing. The surrounding countryside had been devoid of people as though they were all in hiding; the disgusting weather as inclement as her mood. Her distress was deep, the relentless rain that pelted down making it even deeper when they were forced to raise an early camp not far from the nearby river, the cold and damp conditions making it all seem even worse. The convoy was well-guarded, but there had been no need. There had been no adverse interaction of any kind with the local Brigantes.

"What ails you, Ineda?"

Gaius could be quite perceptive at times. She had tried to hide any distress that she felt, but had clearly failed. "I used to live in a village near here."

Gaius made no answer, and merely set off to organise their tent. After days of constant rain, it was evident that the baggage wagons could not travel on the unpaved road till the sea of mud had subsided. Resigned to a miserable wait, Ineda was surprised in the early evening when Gaius suggested they take a walk, the clouds having rolled away and weak sun having appeared in the sky.

"Does this way lead to your village?"

He had not forgotten. Away from his troops, he hoisted Duby onto his shoulders and took her hand.

"Aye." She lapsed into Brigantian, but Gaius made no remark on it. "If we continue to follow the riverside and then cross that meadow over there, we will come to it beyond those trees. The wood looks deep, but it is deceptive. The walk is not far."

Thoughts of Meaghan, and her father, came to mind as they picked their way through muddy terrain. Tears silently rolled when images of her mother and brothers appeared before her. She had purposely not thought of any of them for a long time. Children she used to play with at Marske also intruded, some of whom had made it to Witton, and others long gone. And with the image of Witton, came Bran. The pain at her heart almost sent her to her knees; the love she had felt for Bran had not diminished with time.

Gaius' hand squeezed, reassuring, but she could not find it as comforting as he clearly intended it to be.

Finding the burned-out remains of her village was not difficult.

"There is no fort here. Where did you live?" Dubv said, as he scampered around the blackened and rotting stumps which had been the posts of the roundhouse walls.

Her son had rarely ever seen any Celtic roundhouses, so it was not surprising he had no idea what the remains had originally been for. When she stopped at the place which had been Meaghan's house, she tried to describe what the dwelling had looked like, but Dubv soon became bored with her explanation.

"Come back here, Dubv!" Gaius sounded stern when his little son scampered off in search of something more interesting.

"But there is nothing to be seen there."

He was correct. Nothing but memories. Ineda sank down onto a quern stone which had sat just inside her grandmother's low entrance. Gaius squeezed her shoulder, and set a tiny peck at her cheek before he went off in pursuit of Dubv who had decided to climb the nearby hillock.

Ineda allowed salty and bitter tears to properly fall, unrestrained. Her last abiding memory of the spot was of leading Bran by the hand, and seeing the Roman auxiliary's flaming brand setting alight the grasses of the roundhouse roof.

Feeling so conflicted was heartrending. Gaius was her lover, but he was not and never would be Bran. Those deeply-loving feelings for Bran of Garrigill would never be experienced again. Her life was now wrapped around her son…and Gaius.

A few days later, her tamped-down sad feelings burst free again as their journey continued. The innocent question Dubv put to Gaius ripped open the tender wound.

"Where are all the fierce Brigante warriors you told me about? I wanted to see them come to fight you, *Pater*."

Dubv was tired from the trek, and petulant. It was unusual for him to annoy and pester with tiresome questions, but Ineda thought he had picked up on her mood. She, too, was irritable and snappy about little niggling things, since her outburst of feelings at Marske.

"Did I not already tell you, my son?" Gaius sounded patient, though she knew he probably was not as he looked down at the head of his son who sat in front of him.

Ineda looked over at Dubv from her own mount, and acknowledged how much her son resembled his father. They shared the same sun-dark skin and deep brown eyes. Dubv's stubborn streak she believed also came from Gaius, though Gaius had often told her that the inheritance of it came from her. Dubv's little chin firmed. He was taking time to answer.

Her son eventually responded breaking the tense silence. "I do not remember. Will you tell me again?"

"The warriors around here are forbidden from attacking the forces of Rome, and they would not dare attack since they know you are travelling in these parts."

Dubv scrunched around to look up at Gaius. "Am I so special that they would do that?"

Gaius lightly cuffed Dubv's chin, a broad smile on his face at the seriousness of the question. "Of course. You are my son."

Dubv would not be pacified so easily. "But warriors did attack the wagons when we were at Bremmetna—"

"They did, and they were all killed for being so rash as to confront our Roman convoy."

"Who is around here that you would have to kill?" Dubv's curiosity was obviously not quenched.

"There is no one left here now, Dubv. The forces of our mighty Roman Empire swept through these parts not long since, and the tribespeople of the hillfort of Garrigill have fled."

"Garrigill?" The single word penetrated Ineda's introspective mood. "It is here?"

Gaius looked amused by her question. "Not far from here. It was the largest hillfort in these parts."

"Garrigill has been abandoned?" Dread sat heavy in her stomach.

"A few of the old and infirm remain. They give no trouble, but my reports tell me that most of the able tribespeople fled over the hills to the lands of the Selgovae."

Ineda was distracted, trying to remember things that Bran had told her about Garrigill. "Nara was of the Selgovae."

Gaius picked up on her hushed whisper. "Then this person called Nara will be long gone."

She had no idea if Gaius meant Nara was dead, or if she had returned to her roots.

"Does that mean we are going to see the warriors over the hills, *Pater*?"

Barely listening to Gaius' conversation, she thought about how much Bran had loved speaking of the hillfort of Tully of Garrigill. And now it had been dealt the same fate as many others. So many Celtic tribespeople dead or displaced, so many lost and maimed and…some who had bowed down to Roman rule. She felt sure if Bran had lived, he would have fled rather than live under the yoke of Rome as they had done at Witton.

Bitter were her thoughts, for she had also bowed down to Roman strictures, though not totally by her own choice.

"We may, Dubv. Which hilltop route we take will depend on what we find at the next fort that we stop at."

Luguvalium.

One more place that the forces of Rome had settled on. Ineda was deep in thought all the way to their destination. Dubv had drifted off to sleep, held securely in Gaius' arms, and there was absolutely no conflict involved with the Carvetii along their route to Luguvalium. Though she had no desire to experience another convoy raid, she was also saddened to see no resistance in the area.

She had lost her contact to resisting Brigantes via Orchil, and had no idea how to restore it, even if she had news to send on.

AD 79 Samhain – Luguvalium, Carvetii Territory

Ineda learned that Luguvalium fortress had already been in use for many summers, initiated by Cerialis. It was well-organised, a sight which pleased Gaius greatly when he found that two well-laden vessels of the fleet were soon to arrive at the estuary a short distance away, and would make immediate transfers to the fort.

He had shared some details of his tasks with her, so she knew that those supplies had been shipped from the south of Britannia. Three ships had safely weathered some autumn storms off the western coast which had lately been quite ferocious; two had put in at Deva for a short halt, and would arrive soon at Luguvalium, the third smaller vessel having already arrived that morning.

"You look pleased with yourself?"

As he often did, Gaius chose not to answer "Our stay here need not be protracted. We will move on as soon as the supplies are ready for transportation."

The news came as a surprise, since Gaius had told her they would likely linger there a while, though she knew he was restless. Gaius really wanted to move on with the expeditionary forces of Agricola which constantly moved further and further north, always ahead of them. But his task was to ensure regular supplies to the new forts, not forge ahead into hostile territory.

"We are heading now for Selgovae lands?" Ineda idly asked the question as her son sparred with one of Gaius' junior assistants, his little wooden sword already an extension of his right hand.

"No. First we will head east along the new road, across Brigante territory. There are coal deposits near a place the locals name Cori. Specialist *agrimensors* have also assessed the ores in the nearby areas. You may not know it, but black smithing coal works effectively in the forge, which will greatly aid creation of our metal stocks, and Agricola has found a perfect spot for me to set up a northern supplies base."

"You will be in charge of a fort?" Ineda was stunned. Gaius was going to be the instigator of a new fort?

"You misunderstand, Ineda. The walls of a fort have just been established, but it will not contain the usual patterns of buildings. This one will be mainly for storage, and will be set out differently from most of the forts you have already seen. I will be ensuring the buildings are set up for those specific needs, and will ensure that supplies are well-stocked."

"Does that mean you will remain there for some time?"

Gaius looked unusually animated, a small eager smile baring white teeth, the fervour in his brown eyes an unusual sight since he mostly kept his feelings well-hidden. "For as long it takes for me to be sure all is in order. Then I will move on. Agricola's new road from Eboracum will link up with the site at Corstopitum, and will then continue to be laid up into the lands of the Votadini, and eventually further north into Caledon territory. I want to be on that road as soon as possible."

They had already travelled on routes which Agricola had earmarked for his major roads, so she could not fathom what was exciting Gaius so much.

"This new fort appeals to you?"

His exasperated tones were tempered by huge smiles and an unusual crushing hug. Displays of tenderness were never public. It lasted only moments, but was clearly important to Gaius. "My task for the transportation of all goods, especially the iron and heavy goods, will be made easier. Once the road system has been established, I will ensure all the provisions will move more effectively, and more safely, to our troops at all the new forts Agricola plans to build."

"He has already built many new forts, Gaius, and set down roads. I cannot see how this news is so exciting to you."

His grin was infectious. In spite of herself, she found she was smiling along with him.

"Agricola has now deployed many troops from the other legions to pave the roads. He cannot spare the amount needed from the *Legio IX*, or the *Legio II Adiutrix,* to get them constructed as quickly as he requires, since he needs them to

100

forge on ahead and quell any native uprisings. Extra deployment from the southern legions will soon arrive here in the west, along with the supplies, and the same situation is mirrored on the eastern coast."

"Agricola will not halt at northern Brigante territory?" She already knew expeditionary forces had gone further north, but so far Gaius had never spoken of it.

"Ineda, Commander Agricola is an ambitious man. He intends to put the Roman mark on the whole of Britannia, and I will be assisting in his domination of the tribes not yet under Roman rule."

Ineda clutched at his arm, her concern for Gaius impinging on her horror about the further expansion of the Roman Empire. "Will you march with Agricola, then?"

Soft dark eyes caressed her. "I may, but I think it unlikely. My task is to ensure that areas Agricola has subdued remain subdued. As before, his advance forces will infiltrate and control the natives. A new fort, or fortlet, will require to be built at regular intervals to monitor that control. And, of course, he will organise new guard towers along the routes. My task will be to ensure that supplies for the new wooden structures arrive efficiently, and that the forts are constructed quickly to over-winter the troops that will be needed to control the areas. Prompt and continued deliveries will be needed from Corstopitum for that to happen. Agricola demands many structures in a very short time."

Ineda now saw the import of the store fort at Corstopitum. "Do you mean that Corstopitum will have many goods stored there, but will have minimal personnel guarding it?"

Gaius' hearty laugh rang out, startling the people close by. "Some of the goods temporarily stored there will be auxiliary soldiers, so I believe that answer is no."

Ineda was puzzled, yet also knew Gaius teased her. It was endearing, but she hated him being playful when she was probing for answers.

"Many troops will be needed to fulfil Agricola's plans, Ineda. Vexillations of troops will have to be moved from the garrison forts of all four legions that are in Britannia, to build new forts, but also to advance northwards. Agricola plans well to ensure his campaign into the lands of the Caledons will be a successful one. Many of those troops will arrive to the north by sea, but they will temporarily be housed at the supplies base at Corstopitum, before being dispatched to the forward line."

AD 80 One Moon Before Beltane – Corstopitum and Votadini Territory

Gaius' enthusiasm bore fruit. They had not even been at Corstopitum for five moons when his situation changed again. The fort walls were in place, the wooden storage buildings had been erected, and supply lines were well-established – though most of the transient troops still continued to inhabit a typical tented camp inside the walls. Ineda knew he was pleased with the constant daily movement of goods in all directions. Some paved roads had now been laid throughout Brigantia, and the road had been planned for southern Votadini territory. Agricola was adamant that all of his new northern routes be fully completed, as soon as possible. And for Gaius, that meant no hitches in forwarding supplies to the workers who made those roads appear.

"Ineda!" Gaius strode into their rooms, his voice barely containing his urgency and enthusiasm.

"Is it Dubv? Where is he?" Immediate concern for their son was her first thought, since she had not laid eyes on him for a while.

"Do not fret. He is with Pomponius, looking over my new commands."

Dubv would be well looked after, since Pomponius doted on him, always praising his bright learning. "Then why are you here?"

"Did you listen to what I just said, Ineda?"

Her eyebrows formed a frown as she recalled what he had just said. Her pregnancy was to blame for everything lately, including (as far as she was concerned) her forgetfulness. After the raid near Bremetennacum she had miscarried one babe, and did not wish to lose another. Anxiety regarding the welfare of the latest child in her womb had made her over-fretful of many things. Had Gaius just mentioned commands?

"You are no longer remaining at Corstopitum?" When she asked Gaius questions, she always asked about his whereabouts rather than their collective ones, even after all the time she had been with him.

Gaius drew her into his arms and danced her around the room. "I have been given a temporary post as *Tribune Militum* of the *Legio IX*."

"*Tribune Militum*? The most senior tribune? But that is…" She had no words for the honour that was being bestowed on him.

"Agricola has singled me out!" Gaius was rarely animated by anything recently, but this was a huge boost to his morale.

Looking up into his face, she felt his repressed excitement when he bent down and gave her a fierce kiss. His need to touch her did not last long, though, because he let her go and strode around, his movements jerky and restless, eager to begin his new task that very moment.

A new task that sent them south to Eboracum, where he helped organise the mobilisation of most of the *Legio IX*, and *cohorts* of the *Legio XX* for the march into Votadini territory.

Ineda was learning many useful pieces of information, but still had no one to convey it to.

Being inside the fort walls at Eboracum, as an almost-concubine of Gaius, was vastly different from the anticipation of achieving entry when she had been trading goods with Bran. Just the mere thought of Bran sent her into a pit of guilt and despair. Bran was gone…but then, so too was the Ineda he knew.

She was certain Bran would hate the Romanised Ineda that she had become.

Chapter Ten

AD 80 One Moon After Beltane – Damnonii Territory

As Brennus made way into the lands of the Damnonii, the news from each new village and hamlet was increasingly disturbing. Evidence of Roman patrols seemed to be everywhere. The settlers who lived in the coastal villages had alarming tales to tell, of many sightings of Roman vessels which had been seen hugging the shoreline.

"Do they beach the ships at any time?" This question of his had been voiced in many places.

The answer seemed to be consistent. "Aye, they do. Small Roman patrols disembark and make small camps, their first stop always to establish a nearby water supply. They terrify the famers and villagers across the territory, but have only engaged in attacking the locals if they are directly threatened."

"Has that happened often?"

The next part was also consistent. "Aye! Those who are left flee. They have no wish to die under a Roman *gladius*, but they have been able to return to their soil fairly soon after. The Roman patrols make their observations, and then leave quickly."

"These ships do not disgorge hundreds of soldiers? They do not build any of their small forts?"

"Nay! Only small numbers of the Roman scum come to shore, but do not linger. They move quickly across the land."

"Where do they go when they leave their first camps?" Brennus had a feeling the answer would not be favourable.

"That I do not know, but I suppose they must go back to their vessels, because they sail off after only a few days."

Brennus nodded; it sounded very much like Roman tactics. "Aye. I can believe that. Once they take on a fresh water supply, and the *venators* bring back some animal kill – that would be time for them to leave."

His guides could not say if the people who dwelled well away from the coast had seen any Roman presence, therefore he deemed it necessary to travel inland. It was high summer, so the travelling was fair. The terrain they traversed was peppered with undulating hills, the population who settled there fairly sparse. Some of the even higher slopes were much like the hills between the Brigantes and Selgovae, the moorland too wild and inhospitable for crop growing. He was not surprised to hear of few dwellings there, and was glad his guide knew how to skirt the highest peaks to find habitation.

At each new hamlet his question rarely varied, and his answers were returned in like fashion.

"We are valley farmers, Bran. We only see our nearest neighbours a few times over the seasons when we celebrate our feast times, but we have certainly not seen these soldiers you describe to us."

At every stop, he pulled out his ocarina and flute and entertained the settlers, Nith and Esk providing some fare for their communal eating. At every stop, he established a strong chain of messengers. And at every stop, he looked for a leader who would rouse the people into action against the Roman Empire – but nowhere did he find that man.

He would not allow himself to become despondent, though it was a trial to carry on at times. The farmers he spoke to would fight for their own land – there was no doubt of that – but there was a great reluctance to fight against an enemy they had only heard talk of around the fireside.

"Our guide awaits us." Esk was at the entryway of the roundhouse Brennus was sharing with Lleia, Kaideigh and the village chief's family. "He would like to move off soon. A messenger has arrived with news of a Roman patrol having been spotted not so far from here. The route we must take will skirt that area."

Their farewells were brief. Brennus quizzed the guide as they moved on yet again, the man confirming that the route they would take would be the quickest to the next village.

Coming down from some foothills and on to a flatter plain in front of him, Brennus turned to his guide. "Will we reach any large Damnonii settlements soon?"

"We have larger villages, but few of those can be named settlements. The hillfort of the Damnonii High Chief is our largest settlement. To get to it, you will have to travel on to the part of Damnonii territory where the land is the shortest walk."

As ever, Kaideigh's ears were alert. "What does that mean?"

Brennus looked to the guide to confirm the answer for his inquisitive child. "You must mean a part of the land that is extremely narrow between the waters of the west, and those of the east?"

"I mean exactly that. The Damnonii High Chief's settlement is on the southern bank of the large sea going river that is up ahead. A trek from his stronghold to that of the Votadini High Chief near the eastern sea is across that shortest stretch of land."

"Is it only a few steps wide?" In her innocent childlike way, Kaideigh asked a very important question.

"Not so narrow. If your father walked very fast, and was able to walk directly from sea-river to sea-river, it might take him only three new dawns, but of course our hilly land does not make the walking so easy as that. Depending on the weather, it may take longer."

"Does it take such a short time to go across the narrowest part?" Brennus was taken by the idea. "I mean, all the way from the west to the east coast?"

"Why does that make you laugh so much, Father?"

He cuddled Kaideigh to his side. "I am just thinking on how long it took us to go westwards from Tarras to the point of Novantae land where it eventually turns north after the headland."

Lleia's worn-out voice drifted down from the horse she was riding. "That was indeed a trek of many long days, but we did not journey directly west. We visited many villages along the route." She looked at their guide. "Are there many high hills across this shortest stretch of land that you have been speaking of?"

"There are some, but none are really high. It is the best and flattest farmland of all the Damnonii territory, though naturally the land undulates, and there are many smaller peaks between the level areas."

Brennus could see the next village was not far off, and was just able to make out the smoke spiralling up from the roundhouses.

"Is that the settlement of the High Chief?" As usual Kaideigh was interested in places of some size which might have some children to play with.

"Nay. You will have to journey on the morrow to reach that one. Dusk will be settling in soon, so we must stop at this village for the night if you want to avoid sleeping under your leather."

The elders of the village confirmed that Roman patrols had been in the area just the day before.

"How many soldiers?" This was important information to send back via his guide.

"Less than twenty men, but our High Chief has spread the word today that many Roman troops have landed near his settlement."

"How is it possible for you to get news like this so quickly?"

The elder laughed. "Our seaways are easily navigated by my fellow Damnonii. The Romans may have landed on our shores, but we have dugouts that regularly ply up and down the firth. They sometimes carry men and goods, but often they are also our quickest whispers."

Brennus was glad to know that the Damnonii villagers had good communication links, even though their villages were quite far apart. It gave him confidence in the links he was establishing.

The following day the guide was a young warrior, full of battle fury, eager about fulfilling his role to lead them to his High Chief. Kaideigh chattered endlessly as they walked through a leafy glade. The sun was high, and warmth had

107

already chased away any early cool. "Are we going to see a great big river?"

The young lad was patient, even encouraged her to talk since it made the journey pass more quickly. "Nay, it is not really so deep, but we will soon come to the riverside where it has not yet reached the open sea. It is very wide there, and in places not at all deep, but a crossing is much quicker by boat because of the fairly fast current."

Kaideigh looked unhappy. "Then we cannot jump over stones like yesterday? When we crossed at the ford?"

Brennus named the ford they had crossed the pervious day.

"I know that one. You cannot cross like that on the river ahead. To do that you would have to journey well into the hills, a very long tramp to the river source."

Brennus was just as inquisitive. "Will we see signs of the river after we pass through these woods?"

"Aye! Though you may not realise it, since it is gradual, we have been steadily climbing. When the last trees open out, the whole of the river valley ahead is visible. And a merry sight it is to see on a clear day like this."

Even Lleia, who rarely commented on anything, was spellbound when they exited the woods. "I think I see the settlement down there." Her finger pointed the direction.

They were engrossed in the sight before them when Brennus tensed and drew a quick breath. "Did you see that?" Sometimes the sight in only one eye made him doubt his vision. He had been looking far in the distance to the high hills on the opposite side of the river. It was the slow movement of his eye which had made him aware of a flashing across the twinkling river, a flare that was well beyond the river edge.

The lights sparkled again.

"I saw it this time." Esk stood stock still and peered, waiting for it to happen again. The flickering did not disappoint. "Only many weapons or shields would do that on a sunny day!"

"Romans! Across the river?" Kaideigh was excited in her childlike way. The others were deeply alarmed, since what they saw could only mean many soldiers.

108

They made haste to the settlement of the Damnonii High Chief.

The chief welcomed them in time-honoured fashion, but Brennus sensed the man's repressed fury. "From the nearby hilltop we watched them land two ships on the north side of the river estuary, a few days ago. Many soldiers, some with horses, disembarked and marched off. I have made contact with the settlers who live near the woods we name Bear's Den. They tell me that only some of those Romans make an encampment nearby. Others have moved on eastwards across the valley."

"How large were these vessels?" After he asked, Brennus realised the chief probably had no notion of how many extra men a Roman vessel could carry.

"I have nothing in my experience of ships to compare with them. Our largest dugouts that are based on the south shore of the estuary can perhaps carry some twenty-five men. But maybe a hundred men disgorged from those two Roman ships, and moved on extremely quickly."

Brennus confirmed that the vessels seen may have been small compared to some of the *Roman Classis Britannica* – those used for transporting the Roman seaborne troops. He told of vessels he had heard of which could convey almost a *cohort* of soldiers, sometimes more than four hundred men.

The chief was horrified. "So many as that?"

Brennus sought to calm the man. "That seems too large a vessel to me for sailing in waters near here, but I have heard tell of them nearer Rome. I think the Roman vessels of the Britannia fleet plying your waters are the ones they name *liburnae*, and those are much smaller."

The next days were fraught. Brennus left Lleia and Kaideigh at the settlement, and went a short distance up-river with some of the Damnonii warriors, Esk and Nith at his side. When the local warriors deemed it the best place, they waded across.

Dripping along the far bank he was thankful the day was warm and sunny. It would not take long to dry off, especially with the brisk pace set by the Damnonii prince.

"We must journey through those woods." The Damnonii chief's son indicated a deep copse over to the west.

"Brennus!" Esk's cry halted their progress.

The sight of some seven or eight mounted soldiers approaching from the east set them to their heels. Brennus cursed his lame leg as he loped after his Damnonii guides when they aimed for the advantage of a natural hillock. It was when he needed speed that his leg always let him down. Having climbed a short way up the slope, the small band readied their weapons.

"Together! Stand with your shields together. Keep them tight together!" He knew his orders would confuse, since the warriors were used to having their own space to do their own battle cries and spear-wielding. Repeating his furious orders, the warriors around him obeyed.

They were all tested young men, but they had never faced the Roman Army. "When I give warning, raise your shields above your heads to deflect their spears. Mounted troops are likely to carry more than one of those javelins. Ready your own spear, and do not miss your target! But hold your weapon back till they have fired a first torrent!"

The Roman in charge of the mounted unit gave cry, and a hail of *pila* flew towards them.

"Shields!" Brennus prayed the warriors around him would comply.

A disorganised huddle of Celtic shields rose above heads, but it was sufficient. The pinging and snapping of Roman *pila* embedding in the wood was a resounding clamour as he bellowed his next order. "Spears!"

The tight clutch separated immediately, to enable them the leverage to hurl their spears.

Brennus was taken aback when the Roman in charge bawled an order for retreat. On his words, the horses wheeled around and sped off back towards where they had come from.

"Cowards! Why do they not stand and fight?" The young warrior alongside him was so enraged, he charged after them. As did many of his companions, squealing and hollering battle cries.

"Stop! Come back!" Brennus shouted. "They have orders which prevent them from killing all the local tribes."

"Why would they do that?"

His words made no sense to the Damnonii, who had had no dealings with the Empire of Rome. "If their orders had been to kill us, they would have done exactly that. The one in charge called them to order, and commanded them to return to their fort."

"Do you understand their language, Bran?"

"Enough to know what he bade them do."

Brennus was heartily glad only one young warrior had been the victim of a Roman *pilum,* which had embedded into the fleshy part of his lower leg. The shaft had split on impact, but they had to spend some time removing the remainder. He was relieved the metal had pierced the bulky part of the warrior's calf, but had not shattered the bone.

Two of the local warriors were tasked with helping the wounded man limp back home. He looked in little danger of losing his leg, but the bleeding was steady.

"Do you still wish to carry on?" asked the Damnonii guide.

Brennus could see the man was not too keen to go on, but it was even more important now. "I need to view the area where the vessels were beached, and find out what they favour as a landing spot. Your father, the High Chief, will need such information, so that he can warn other tribes in the area of where they might need to monitor more thoroughly."

Keeping a wary eye open, they followed the river's edge for some time before turning towards the far hills. Brennus did not need to go far before he could see a large Roman encampment on the flat valley plain. It was a sizeable camp, but he did not think it would hold a whole *cohort.*

The Damnonii chief's son gave them information. "We call that area Bears' Den. They may not wish to camp there for very long, when they discover why the place is so named."

"Where is your nearest Damnonii settlement to here?"

The son of the Damnonii chief pointed. "It lies by that hill: at that large rock where the river spills out into the western sea."

111

"Then perhaps they have fled from the Romans already, since that has to be near to where the Romans have beached their vessels. Perhaps some of your warriors could check their welfare?"

Brennus had seen enough for that day.

The Damnonii High Chief soon had word from his northern reaches. Although ships of the Roman fleet had navigated a way up through the many sea lochs and inlets on the western shore, it appeared that they had not disembarked any sizeable infantry detachments. Their many stops had only been to take on fresh water, and to investigate the terrain nearest to their landing place before setting off again. They had not attempted any kind of confrontation with any of the locals.

Brennus discussed the possibility of his travelling to those tribespeople of the sea lochs, but the chief did not recommend it.

"Much of Damnonii land is not easy to march on. I do not think the forces of Rome will attempt the many mountains and hills they would need to cross over in my coastal territory. Few people dwell there. Your small party could traverse the peaks to visit my tribespeople, but it will take you much longer than travelling on the flat plains around my settlement."

Brennus decided against journeying any further on the western coast. The elders had convinced him.

"I have good contact now with the chief of the Epidii, of the tribes of the west coast islands. He promises to keep me abreast of any landings the Roman fleet may make on his territory. It is mainly rugged and inhospitable, the living there harsh. We do not believe Agricola will settle any of his troops there."

Brennus could not be sure of that. If Agricola had his way, every footstep-worth of Celtic soil would bear the imprint of a Roman iron-nailed sandal. When his host declared that tribesmen of the Epidii would defend their own soil to the death, he believed it. But the facts were clear – the islanders could rely only on themselves, unless they had been warned of invasion well in advance. Brennus wished the islanders a safe future, but knew it was unlikely that they would avoid all bloodshed.

A message also arrived from Tarras which stunned him. Callan had taken ill, had deteriorated quickly, and death had come swiftly. In some ways Brennus considered it a blessing, since the Romans threat was now so close to Tarras. The old man would have died sword in hand, rather than give in to the Roman scum. At least Callan was now past making decisions for his tribe, though that task now fell on the shoulders of Lorcan and Nara, who had been nominated as joint leaders of the tribe. Lorcan was no coward, but Brennus was sure his brother would keep moving north to avoid being under the Roman thumb.

During the following days, more disturbing news arrived – some of it having a ring of truth, but some perhaps exaggerated. The only way Brennus could prove the accuracy was by moving east with his small band, though that sounded hazardous.

Evidence of Agricola's troops was reported all across the narrowest stretch of land between the seas, the Romans never remaining encamped for very long before marching off again. It was also rumoured that some of the Roman troops had headed northwards towards Venicones territory, though others appeared to be making as direct a route as possible to the eastern sea. Hundreds of terrified and harassed Selgovae villagers, who had sufficient warning, were said to be abandoning their homes.

Esk's droll tones rumbled into the silence after that particular update. "We can be sure they will definitely not be running to the south."

Nith's question softened the sarcasm of his brother. "Where would these people aim for, if they go north?"

Their host could only guess. "Some would go to distant relatives in Venicones territory."

Another elder was more certain. "They will escape into the mountains, even if they have no kin to go to. The lower hills and glens will provide them with places to hide that they would not have on the flat valley floors."

That sounded all too credible, though Brennus feared for those tribespeople, come the winter snows.

"We have to go east first, Brennus. It really is the only way to be sure of this information." Esk had put forward his thoughts on where they should next travel.

Brennus always made the final decision, but it had become customary to listen to the views of Esk and Nith. Nith did not always blindly agree with his brother, but on this occasion his opinion concurred.

They left the hillfort of the Damnonii High Chief soon after dawn. For sure, before the sun was high in the sky, evidence of the Roman army was blatant across the landscape. Walled mounds and ditch traces of temporary habitation were a clear sign that the Romans had recently been encamped.

By the time dusk was approaching, Brennus and his band had climbed low hills and walked down into valleys, but had kept clear of the main river. Although he relied on the local guide to take them the safest way to the next village, he had learned enough of Roman troop movements to know where to avoid. So had his companions. He suppressed a grin when a confrontation started between Esk and their present guide.

"The village is not far from here, but it will be quicker to skirt through those woods to get to it." The young warrior guide had been given a task that he wanted to fulfil well, but wanted no deviation from his usual route.

"How can you know the Roman troops are not presently in that forest area, or just beyond? Were you there already this morn?" Esk rounded on the lad. He could be ferocious when riled, and the disagreement had already stopped their progress for a short time.

"You know I was with you at the High Chief's settlement." The lad appeared confused as well as annoyed. His ability to lead them safely was being questioned.

Nith joined the fray. "What will we find beyond that forest? I ask since we have had no way of knowing. We have not been on a hilltop for some time now."

"The forest opens out onto a fairly flat stretch of land where there is a sizeable loch."

Esk's laugh rumbled freely, though it also had a serious tinge to it. "Precisely the kind of area the Roman Army loves to haunt. This loch is not stagnant, it is full of fresh water?"

"Naturally it is fresh water. As I said, it is a large body of water." The boy was now defensive.

Brennus felt it time to intervene and halt the play the brothers were so good at. "You are not to know, lad, but there are a few things that are acutely important to where the Romans make camp. A plentiful supply of fresh drinking water for their men, and for their animals, is always needed. They cut fuel from the forest for cooking, and for heat. And they are used to walking from after dawn till the earliest tinges of dusk, before they halt to make their fortifications for the night. We must be cautious in this wood."

"Do we need to skirt this loch to come the village?" Esk's tone was still serious.

The lad shook his head. "I can lead you along a track that goes only partly through the forest before it veers well south of the loch. You will not even see the water, if we go that way, though it will be longer."

"So be it," Brennus said. The trek had already been long, the hill climbs tiring. Yet, he would much rather avoid any confrontation with the enemy, even if it took more time to reach shelter.

Though Esk had been correct to alert the lad to caution, Brennus was pleased to see no signs of Roman troops on the last stretch to the village. But the news on arrival was not so good. Many Roman soldiers were thought to be encamped on the northern shores of the loch.

Each new place had its own tales of the Roman encampments, though some of it was just hearsay and not genuine experience. Many of the villagers were curious about the large threat to their way of life, never having encountered such a large fighting force, but most were sceptical. Brennus knew that for some, he was just a fine storyteller who exaggerated well. Those people he truly despaired for.

His greatest worry was that the exploratory troops of Agricola had already learned every nook and cranny of

Damnonii land. He remembered how sneaking their infiltration had been long ago, well before the battles at Whorl which partially robbed him of his sight. There were many hills and valleys in the softly undulating land of the mid-Damnonii, but it appeared the exploratory forces of Rome had been spotted almost everywhere.

And all the while Brennus found no man or woman who looked to be a leader who would rally the tribes, and halt the invasion of the empire of Rome. After his warnings, and after his entertainments, no warrior stood up at the fireside and declared that the men of the Damnonii should stand together. And none volunteered another.

One constant he was heartily glad of, on what was becoming a despairing trek, was that Esk and Nith were definitely more skilled at killing an animal or bird than he was. Their loyalty and trust was priceless as they visited every hamlet and habitation, their optimism remaining high. They, too, were desperate to find the man who would be a great leader, and fervently wished to volunteer to be part of that man's resistance forces.

Brennus had no worries about the two brothers continuing with him on his travels, but he worried greatly about Lleia and Kaideigh. Walking into the path of the Roman Empire was no place for them. Whether Lleia liked it or not, he needed to take them back and leave them at Tarras.

"Nay, Brennus! I will not be left at Tarras, even knowing Lorcan and Nara are there. My place is with you. Send Kaideigh if you wish Lorcan to foster her, but my new child and I will journey on with you."

Lleia had been sick of late, though her constitution was normally good. Another child like Kaideigh would please him well, and he rejoiced in that thought, but knew that traipsing on would not be easy for Lleia, the birth expected within three moons. Nonetheless, she would not be persuaded to stay at Tarras, no matter his pleas, and he felt he had no right to force it upon her.

They kept on their slow eastward progress.

Chapter Eleven

AD 80 Lughnasadh –Eboracum, Brigantes Territory

"Agricola has arrived."

Gaius' anticipation was unmistakeable as he strode into his quarters.

"Agricola? So late?" Ineda went towards the low table and poured a beaker of wine.

"The *Legio IX* will move out at daybreak." Excitement flared in his eyes as he began to undo the ties of his breastplate.

"I thought Agricola was at Deva?" She held the cup until his hands were free to take it from her.

Gaius had been disappointed a number of times since arriving at Eboracum. He had believed it would be only a matter of days before Agricola would begin his campaign to enter the lands of the Selgovae and the Votadini, and that he would be marching along with his general. That had not transpired.

On their arrival, Agricola was not even at Eboracum. He had instead decided to inspect the small fort building around the northern Brigante territory himself, and then had chosen to go to Deva where he was organising various fleet movements in the western seas.

Some of that information was interesting to pass on, but Ineda was more cautious than in the past. There could be no possible suspicion falling at her feet, though she had found another slave of one of the senior officers who might possibly be a good contact.

Ever the dedicated tribune, Gaius had launched into his temporary position as *Tribune Militum* and had kept up with many of his previous responsibilities, awaiting orders from his

General. Only his commitment showed by day; but his impatience and frustration came out at night.

The sudden arrival of Agricola had clearly made changes to that.

"He was, but he is now ready to ensure the Votadini High Chief fully capitulates. The man has been hesitating for too many seasons. Making promises he does not keep."

Ineda had no idea what Gaius could mean by that, but it sounded as though the Roman Empire had been dealing with the Votadini for some time.

"Will they go straight into battle?" Thinking about the prospect was easy, yet she feared the answer.

Gaius looked incredulous, his chuckle an indication of what he thought of her words while he drank off the last of the beaker. "You think Agricola will need to engage in battle?"

Ineda knew when to remain silent.

Gaius strode around, his tension and eagerness palpable. "This time more than a legion will march into Votadini lands. We will make many camps around the hillfort of the Votadini High Chief when we reach it. I'm told Dunpendyr sits on a high plateau – a perfect spot for Rome to besiege. The Votadini will be trapped up there, and will not even take up arms when they see how many Roman soldiers are below. Their water supply will be governed by us. Agricola will shed little Roman blood. The chief will capitulate ere long. Starvation does that." Choppy words reflected his animated thoughts.

Ineda shivered at the idea of fellow-Celts starving. Gaius sounded so matter-of-fact about hundreds of Celtic tribespeople facing a lingering death, or succumbing to the diseases which tended to accompany ill health at such times of entrapment. She remembered being at Witton, where the crops were so readily commandeered by the usurping forces in the area, and could not restrain her sarcasm.

"The early harvest is almost upon us. Would it not have been better for Agricola to be in place before then?"

"Agricola has been busy as usual. He has many duties, Ineda, and leading his army is only one of them. He has been

118

to the south to monitor the progress of the many civic reforms that are being put in place."

Only part of what Gaius had said made sense to her. "I have heard this word civic, though I do not fully understand it."

"Agricola wishes to make things fairer for the people of Britannia. He pushes through many reforms which will make life more comfortable, and more stable, for the tribespeople of this huge island."

"You mean he will Romanise the Celts?" Scorn was hard to suppress.

"Our ways of living provide much comfort, Ineda. You have seen the evidence of that in our buildings at Deva. And Agricola's reforms have greatly improved security for the tribes. They no longer make regular and constant war on their neighbours."

She could not deny that the buildings of the Romans had more comfort than Celtic roundhouses. Or that the bathhouses were surprisingly comfortable. But the security he spoke of so proudly was only achieved through the subjection of her Celtic peoples.

"Will you also leave at dawn?"

Gaius threw off the last of his clothing and strode over to the bowl of water. His words muffled into the splashes he made. "I need to be ready long before that. But we will all leave at dawn. See that Dubv is prepared in time."

"Will you sleep a while?" she asked, but was fairly certain of his answer. He was too restless to sleep, though she knew a way to calm his agitation.

"Agricola will sleep little, so why should I?" Gaius' words were low as he reached for her and drew her into a tight embrace, his lips at her neck and chin as he released the belt around her waist. "I can think of something much better to celebrate this news."

After a furious coupling Gaius immediately fell asleep, although she knew his slumber would not last for long.

Her life on the move had made it impossible to make contact with the rebellious Celts, but she needed to get word

119

of Agricola's intentions to someone. Though how? They were leaving so soon. She feared the guilt of not passing on such vital information would eat at her gut for many moons to come.

The Gaius who lay beside her was not the man who had taken her prisoner. Since being more in contact with Agricola, he had been infused with such zeal that he was almost a different person. The bland-faced Gaius she had initially met now seemed to be constantly battling to suppress an excess of enthusiasm for subordinating every Celt he came into contact with. He spent less time with her, but when in her company he reached for her more often to assuage his lust. She could not be sure if any love was in his gestures, and was not certain how she felt about that. Where before she would have scorned the fact that he could love his slave, now she feared she looked for what had perhaps had once been, but was now gone.

Vulnerability sat on her shoulder every day.

AD 80 After Lughnasadh – Dunpendyr, Votadini Territory

"Are there larger settlements in Votadini territory?"

Brennus' expectations were much as when he had asked the same question in Damnonii territory. He was pleased to discover there were indeed a few large Votadini settlements, hillforts built on high plateaux.

At the huge settlement of the Votadini High Chief, he and Lleia came to a compromise of sorts. To his amazement, she found the settlement of Dunpendyr to her liking, and agreed that she and Kaideigh would remain there till the birth of her child, while he learned all parts of Votadini territory, and kept abreast of the constant movements of Roman troops across the narrow stretch between the east and west seas. His opinion of the Votadini High Chief was similar to what Callan's had been: the man was a weak leader. But Lleia was not in the man's company day by day. The roundhouse she was staying in was hospitable, and the woman of the hearth not related to the chief.

Signs of the Roman army were to be found near the shoreline, but when he was led inland evidence was rarer. After a moon of trekking around, he made sure to speak to Esk in private. "Do you think the Roman scouts have avoided these mid-Votadini lands?"

Esk looked around to ensure privacy before answering. "I have had no proof to speak of this with you, but it seems to me that we are being led only where Dunpendyr wants us to see."

Brennus feared the same. Contriving a reason to send Esk back to Dunpendyr was easy enough. He had been away from Lleia for more than a whole moon, and was keen to know how she fared. Esk was set to return to Dunpendyr by the most direct route, as far as his other companions were concerned. Esk was, of course, going to do a bit of scouting on his own.

"You do not have to do this if you feel it is too hazardous." Brennus wanted his friend safe, and did not want him to feel compelled to strike out on his own.

Esk's uncomplicated laugh and wrist-grasp sealed the bargain. "You know caution sits on my shoulder. I will return soon enough."

True to his word, it was less than a se'nnight later when Esk caught up with him.

"Not only encampments, Brennus. I saw at least one fortlet that had been set up not so long ago, but is now abandoned."

"Why would Agricola have abandoned it?" The notion seemed so strange since the location Esk described sounded as if it was on an important northwards route up through Votadini territory.

Esk's head shakes refuted his question. "Not Agricola. The wood has been deteriorating for some seasons. My guess is it may have been built by the forces of Cerialis, or perhaps Frontinus."

The very idea that Roman presence had been north of the Brigantes some time ago was alarming, but Brennus had witnessed what the *Roman Classis* was capable of. If Cerialis had sent expeditionary forces to Votadini lands by sea, the Brigantes would only have known of it if informed by the Votadini themselves.

121

It sounded as though the Votadini High Chief was more than just a man who wavered in his decision making: he was rapidly looking to be a long-time secret ally of the Roman Empire.

Sending word of this new development to Lorcan was not yet prudent. He and Esk kept their suspicions to themselves, though he did ensure that his messages were getting through properly to his brother by requesting answers that only Lorcan could know. A result of his suspicions of the Votadini High Chief was a delightful boost – he found that his messenger chain was actually strengthened, and that word was sent on more quickly and more effectively than before.

After more than two moons of visiting Votadini hamlets, villages and even the two large settlements of minor chiefs, he despaired that nobody was prepared to take up mass arms. Though small uprisings were happening, and some Celtic deaths the result, not one chief would commit to amassing his fellow Celts to battle alongside each other against the usurping Roman Empire.

It made him rant. It often made him extremely sad, and though it was regrettable, he had to conclude that no Votadini would willingly go to war against Rome.

It looked as though Callan had definitely been correct. Though Roman presence was on the northern Votadini boundary, and the Roman fleet had been seen landing at many of its beaches for some time, the High Chief made no show of resistance, claiming he did not believe the Roman Empire would settle on his lands.

Some of the Votadini villages were quite large, yet they had no interest in fighting anyone, preferring to till their land, the presence of Roman exploratory forces seeming to have little impact on them. During early summer, Brennus was at another of the larger settlements – one which was at the Votadini northern estuary border with the eastern sea – when his contact rushed in.

"Agricola's main legions are flooding the southern lands of the Selgovae and Votadini. They have marched over the hills from both the west and the east."

"Did the contact say what their route might be?"

"Only that it was likely the *Legio XX* would be taking a west to east route into Votadini lands, and that the *Legio IX* would continue on their northwards path from Eboracum, and up through Corstopitum."

Brennus knew that meant they could easily be at Dunpendyr within days. He was a day's walk away, but would not see his family trapped on one of the high hillforts favoured by the Votadini.

As he scurried back with Esk, Nith having been at Dunpendyr with Lleia and Kaideigh for some time, he fretted about the escalation of danger. If the main legionary forces of Agricola were already into Votadini territory, he wondered what kind of advance instructions had been given to the expeditionary forces which plagued the areas all around him.

He needed to move on to the tribes even further north, beyond the Black River estuary, to still seek someone who would make a large stand against Rome.

AD 80 Two Moons After Lughnasadh – Easg, Votadini Territory

Gaius was furious, the urge to lash out with his fists immense. A fight with Agricola would go a long way to improve his temper as he barged into his tented quarters.

"We are breaking off from the main legion."

Ineda gaped at him, curiosity rising in her gaze as he stripped off his breastplate and let it slip with a noisy clank to the ground – not his usual practice, since he was extremely careful of his armour. Shrugging and wriggling his shoulders to free them from the weight of the metal, he strutted around the small space inside the tent while he yanked off his tunic, the smell of his own sweat strong at his nostrils.

The day had been long and difficult, his tension at odds the whole time. He balled the garment in his hands. Dropping it would be too easy, so instead he sent it sailing onto the leather door flap where it made contact with a resounding smack, before slithering to the ground. He wanted to rant, but knew

123

that as a poor choice since it would awaken Dubv whose small cot was behind a low partition, at the side of the tent.

Ineda went to the small bed and tucked the blanket around Dubv. She did not even attempt to lift his discarded uniform, and only looked a tiny bit wary as he strutted around the restricted interior. She knew well how avoid confrontation with him; though he guessed she was probably itching to know what was angering him so much. She always wanted to know everything. Her eventual words were soft into the heavy silence, treading as warily as her eyes.

"Breaking off?"

"New orders."

It was rare that he felt so angry he could not speak. Agricola had often made changes to plans which had disappointed and annoyed him, but they had never made him livid like those he had just received.

"You are returning to Eboracum?"

"No, Ineda. Not Eboracum. Agricola has decided that I need to remain at the old fortress near Easg, when the column arrives there on the morrow."

Easg. Not even proper Latin. The very name annoyed him. There had been fort-building in Votadini lands some summers ago by expeditionary forces of Cerialis, the tiny fort of Easg one of them. Easg was on the route Agricola planned to use to take his legions north, but the fortlet was now too worn for their current needs. Gaius had just been given the task of overseer of the stability of the area while the fort was rebuilt. While improvements were made to the rough-laid roads, Agricola had decided it was in a crucial position to ensure the steady flow north and south, of men and goods.

Gaius thought of what the task would entail while he continued to strut around.

"Easg? Easg?"

Ineda let the name roll over her tongue, stopping his agitated prowl. The act drew his eyes to her expressive little face; to those lips he rarely had time and vigour to lay his own on. He had barely been in her proximity for many long days, far less enjoyed her body.

"I do not think I have heard you mention this fort."

Her words continued soft, and seductive. It still amazed and annoyed him that he always found her to be so alluring. He set to pacing again, to quell the lust she always generated with a mere look. Even more perplexing was the fact that many of those looks often held barely-suppressed disdain.

He watched her bend to pick up his armour before he crushed it, placing it carefully on the stand, a task he usually did himself. Again, her tilted body halted his roam. He felt the anger drain from him as he answered her, replaced by a strong physical reaction after she retrieved his tunic. When she began to shake and stroke it free of dust and dirt, he could watch her no longer.

He turned away from her and summoned the restraint necessary to refrain from taking her in such an angered state. He was so angry he might unintentionally harm her, her being so slight. Words dripped out while he sought to calm his blood.

"I have known of the fort at Easg for a long time, but have given it little thought since it was disused some time past. Our recent focus has been at other places. Now, there will be new walls and inner buildings erected at Easg during the coming moons."

He felt the cup at his elbow before her single word flowed over him.

"Drink!"

She had no need to tell him it would calm him. He glugged it down and held it out for a refill, even though it was the vinegary wine. "Agricola wishes me to ensure the nearby road is free of attack, while the locals are put to work breaking and laying the gravel for it."

"You are to be doing the work of an *agrimensor*?"

Laughter bubbled from him at her statement, and even more at her puzzlement. "No, Ineda." He knew his words had been ill-thought–out, and could hardly blame her for the confusion. "It will be engineers who will properly lay the road that runs north from Eboracum, the track we have already used to get us here. And naturally, engineers will construct the

125

fort but, as always, I need to ensure that all the equipment necessary for that is travelling freely – as well as, it seems, for every other need that goes north on this campaign."

"Is that not an honour, Gaius? Does Agricola not acknowledge your expertise?"

Gaius flung himself heavily onto the low cot, knowing she was correct. "Yes."

"But you are angry because you wanted to march north with him, along with the legions on this momentous campaign?"

As usual Ineda could express the heart of a matter very well. He needed to guard his tongue, since she absorbed everything he said. Her memory was acute, and some of the information he had just gleaned from Agricola was not yet shared with the legion; indeed, some of it was particulars that would not please many of those on the campaign.

Agricola was the most ambitious man he had ever encountered, a man whose personality and work ethic was so strong it ensured his plans were fulfilled.

Gaius pulled Ineda down to him on the cot, knowing one thing about his new orders which would please her well. She would not have to be in the encampment surrounding Dunpendyr when Agricola set up a siege and starved the Votadini High Chief's settlement. His new posting would spare her that offensive experience.

Though he had made Ineda accept many of his Roman ways, in his gut he knew she was still a Celt at heart. He had no intentions of ever seeing her hurt, and had taken many measures to prevent it at the garrisons he had been stationed in, even though he doubted she was aware of the depth of resentment she caused. He was not sure that her Celtic pride could ever be beaten out of her, and it was that very pride which was recognised by all who envied him.

He pulled her under him and began to make love to her. As he stripped off the last of his clothing, and hers, another thought occurred. Agricola was not likely to witness the Votadini capitulation either.

Agricola would have moved on to somewhere else.

He gave up harping thoughts about his commander, and sank into Ineda's body. She always gave him solace like no other could.

Chapter Twelve

AD 80 Before Samhain – Venicones Territory

"When you come to the next great river, the Tatha, you must journey along the northern bank."

Brennus nodded that he was following Earn's directions as the man continued to instruct.

"The river widens out quickly, and seems to be out to sea before you know it. But do not be deceived by the sight of the magnificent water spread before you, because that is not yet the sea. You will remember that?"

Brennus was polite. He really was able to hold directions without them being repeated, but the man was trying his best. "I will not forget."

"You must continue your trek along the northern shore to where the distance between the banks narrows again. By then you will easily see Trune's hillfort up high on the hill." Earn's hearty laugh rang around the horse enclosure as Brennus prepared the horses for their next trek. "You cannot miss it!"

They had just spent a few nights at the roundhouse settlement of Earn, one of the minor Venicones chieftains. From Earn, Brennus had discovered that the lands of the Venicones stretched for many long days, skirting the high mountains of their neighbours to the west – the Caledons. The Venicones territory was mostly the fertile plains between high mountains and the eastern sea coast. He now knew he would not be able to trek due north in Venicones lands, but would need to journey in a north-easterly direction before he would reach the stronghold of Trune, the Venicones High Chief. The directions had seemed clear enough.

"That does not sound difficult to find." He handed over a pack to Esk, who was clambering onto one of their two horses.

"Nay! It should be easy enough. You should not be troubled by Roman patrols on the shoreline, but you will find they have many signal posts, and small encampments, on the mountain side of our flatlands. In many places, your problem will be to avoid detection from these high towers."

An elder of the tribe added further information. "The landscape is sparse of woodlands, and in parts extremely flat. You will need to stray from the easiest paths, and use the small hillocks for cover. Even a small band of people will be seen from afar."

More helpful suggestions were made for their safety.

"You will find those hamlets just mentioned, but no large villages. Each one will direct you forward to the next, till you reach Trune's hillfort."

Esk had a question that for some reason had not been properly asked. "Have there been any skirmishes between Trune and the exploratory Roman patrols? Has he put up any resistance?"

"Aye, but they took place some moons ago. A good number of Venicones warriors went to the otherworld as a result, and Trune has made no large confrontation since then."

"Do the Romans infiltrate his hillfort?" Nith sounded eager to meet the Roman invaders face to face.

"Nay. We do not understand it, but since Trune gave up his attack they leave his people alone. They are more concerned about preventing the Caledons from flooding the valley from their mountain passes on the western side of the flatlands."

Brennus was having difficulty envisaging the strategies that the Romans were adopting, their *exploratores* having investigated the terrain and all its tribespeople.

"Once you crest the long gradual incline I spoke of, you will understand about the lie of the land. Seeing the Venicones lands in the far distance will make it clear to you what the Roman scum are doing. It should also be clear to you to see what Trune does not do, and why."

"Will we find any villages along the shoreline of the river?" Esk was looking towards Lleia who fussed with the baby to hush its weak cries, barely having the sustenance to

129

breathe herself, she looked so ill now. Her skin bore the flushed look of high fever, and she coughed a lot making the baby bound to her front rouse with feeble wails.

Brennus had suggested they wait a few more days till her harsh throat declined, but she would have none of it, insisting she would have time to recover at the High Chief's settlement. The Roman army always seemed to be not far behind them, and she wanted them all to be in a less vulnerable place than a small village.

"None. There are only hamlets of a few roundhouses. The farmers of our valleys work just a little of the land, and few people live across the stretches you will walk on. The farmers do not till the marshlands."

"Do you have someone who will guide us?" Brennus asked, as he checked the strapping of the packs on the horse, though he knew that going into potentially dangerous territory might not be a good prospect for Earn's warriors.

"You will need none after you crest the long incline. All will be seen before you. Keep the eastern sea in view, and all will be well."

"How long will we stay at the new place?" Kaideigh was exhausted as she trudged alongside the old horse, a poor beast that had done its turn and was now really too worn to be carrying Lleia, the new baby, and packs of goods dangling around its flanks. Their other horse was now being ridden by Nith.

Brennus had no real answer for his daughter.

"I believe about the same time as we have spent at other places. Why do you ask?"

The wan smile belied the anticipation in Kaideigh's gaze.

"I would like a new friend."

Kaideigh still loved meeting new children, though sadly that was not always reciprocated. Some of the children she had tried to befriend had rebuffed her attempts. She was always the stranger in their midst.

Silence walked alongside them for a while, till Kaideigh picked up the thread of the conversation again. "My best friend, ever, was Seaonaigh."

"I know she was, but you will meet others who may be her match."

"I wish that Seaonaigh had come with us on our adventures."

When Kaideigh quietened, Nith filled the gap.

"What did you understand of Earn's claim that the Votadini have known for a long while that the exploratory forces of Agricola have been in the lands of the Venicones?"

Brennus' answer was wry. "I prefer to believe what Earn has just told me than the Votadini High Chief. I suspect there is much more that the Votadini have kept close to their chests."

Esk intervened. "I am inclined to believe the same, Brennus. Yet, if that is so, the *exploratores* units have covered more ground than we have expected, and must be well ahead of us right now, perhaps even in the lands of the Taexali. They are so adept at marching long distances by day and then bedding down for the darkest hours behind those ditches. It takes them no time at all to dig the sods of earth and bank them high before they rest behind their turf walls. And the smallest patrols find other shelter without a need for the obvious defences we find littering our lands."

Nith had asked many thoughtful questions about the Roman movements in Brigantia when Brennus had lived there, but it seemed there was always another matter to be answered.

"Did your fellow Brigantes ever challenge any of these small exploratory patrols before the battles at Whorl?"

"Aye, indeed they did, and some Romans were successfully routed or killed. At other times it was impossible to come upon them in surprise, because the stakes they plant prevent an easy climb over the ditch."

Kaideigh had been only half-listening to the talk. "What stakes?"

He patted her head to encourage her to keep moving, since she was flagging, her breathing uneven. "The Roman auxiliary soldier walks with many things packed and dangling around his back. His shield lies close to his bones, but to the front of that is a crossbar with many things dangling from it. Are you seeing this, Kaideigh?"

"I am!" She had been told many times what a typical auxiliary might look like, in order to flee from the sight.

"One of those items is a pick to break up reluctant soil. Another is a shovel to dig out the earth."

Her little voice grew in strength since she knew of this part. "They use the shovel to remove the turf?" When he nodded back, she continued, "And then they scoop the soil and form a wall?"

"Aye, daughter they do. And when they are done with the ditch digging, they place the turf back on top of the mounded soil, and that is when they remove the stake from their pack and ram it into the top of the wall, making a palisade."

"The stakes are all neatly spaced?" Kaideigh was quick to learn things.

"Aye! Very even. The soldiers have perfected this."

Esk added the next bit. "And what do they do come the morn, Kaideigh?"

She looked puzzled, but only for a moment. "The man has his stake tied to his sack every day?"

He nodded. "Aye, he does."

"Then each man must pull up his stake and tie it back on?"

Brennus patted her head and gave her a shoulder hug. He was so proud of his little daughter's ability to reason so well.

"Exactly!"

"But they do not flatten the earth, and put it to rights before they leave?"

"Nay!" The laughter of the adults rang around. "They spend no time on that. They pack up and move on to the next place. The ditches and ramparts tell us where they have been."

"How do they know where to go?" Kaideigh so loved to know things.

"Some of them are mounted, and they scout well ahead of those who march. They are also incredibly good at reading the landscape."

In the way of a small child, her next question was a good one. "What are they looking for?"

Nith answered first. "They look for settlers living in the area to fight or chase away, and then they look for the best places to build their signal towers and forts."

"Aye! And some of the Romans know how to describe the landscape to others. They make plans, and write on wax tablets and on paper rolls. I have explained about these to you before."

Her little smile showed she remembered what he had told her of his life as a trader to the forts. "Are the Romans making their camps on the way to the hillfort of the Venicones High Chief?"

"We hope not, Kaideigh, but the main forces who were down at the Black River, those all around Dunpendyr, have been building where we were less than a se'nnight ago. That is why we needed to leave Dunpendyr quickly. You heard the messenger tell us that in Earn's roundhouse. They are not far behind us." Nith was so patient with her, but his next question was for Brennus.

"If exploratory Roman scouts have been hereabouts many seasons ago, why did Cerialis, or Frontinus, not conquer the tribes north of the Brigantes?"

"I have no answer, Nith. It may have been a question of needing the legions' soldiers elsewhere in Britannia. The shorelines of the Selgovae neighbours are extensive. The Roman fleet could easily have landed many ships and disgorged thousand of troops."

"Could that be what they have done in Venicones lands?"

"Perhaps. You also heard Earn say that the Venicones have a long coastline which could be breached by *Classis* vessels in many places."

Nith's question set him to pondering about the rumour they had recently heard about Roman troops in Venicones territory It sounded as though they had not all tramped up there by a land route. He dreaded learning that so many soldiers had arrived from the sea, yet feared it must be so.

It was a while later when Kaideigh repeated her earlier statement. "I would have liked Seaonaigh to be your foster-child."

His answer was as soft as he could manage. "Seaonaigh may not have liked that idea as well as you do. Do you not think that she would have missed her mother and her little sisters?"

"Will I have a little sister soon, father?"

Brennus looked at the hunched, drooping figure of Lleia. After his son had come into the world he had vowed never to touch Lleia again in such a way as would beget another child. She had done well by him, but he had done ill by her. Lleia had given him all of her strength in birthing his son. The horse carried an almost empty shell; Lleia had said little during the whole ride. If it had not been for her harsh and hard-won breathing, he would not be sure she was even with them. Yet to give an unhelpful answer to his innocent daughter would pain her very much.

"The gods will decide what brothers and sisters you will have. You have already been taught that, Kaideigh. You have a little brother, now."

Kaideigh's sigh went deep into the soil, her head bent. "I know, but he is really sick, is he not?"

His fingers trailed over her braids. "Aye. And your mother too."

"Then I pray the goddess Brigantia lets me stay at our new place for a long while, enough for me to help them to get better, and maybe even longer after that."

"Why would you want to stay for longer, instead of learning new countryside and meeting new children?"

"I liked being on the high hill of Dunpendyr. Did you not? Seaonaigh showed me so many places to hide from the Romans. Did you know that?"

His laughter hid a deep concern. "Nay! I do not believe you ever showed me any of these places, my well-prepared daughter. Tell me of these spots to make the journey shorter."

Dunpendyr was the largest hillfort he had ever seen: much larger than Garrigill, and was seated so prominently on a high saddleback hill. It could be seen from far in the distance, from all directions, as it towered above the wide flatlands which lay vast around it.

134

Before Brennus had left Dunpendyr, the Votadini High Chief still clung to the idea it would be impregnable. Brennus had emphasised that the warfare methods of the Roman Empire differed from those of the Celts, but his information made no difference to the chief's attitude. By the time he had left the *oppidum*, the High Chief of Dunpendyr had already made plans to strengthen the defensive walls around the high hill. But the settlement covered a wide area and housed hundreds of roundhouses. Full new defences would take many seasons to install, and Brennus knew that time for the chief to accomplish that was not likely. He also could not trust that the Dunpendyr chief would actually do anything at all.

The knowledge that the Romans would settle down on the plains below, and would not do much fighting, was not welcomed by the chief, who blustered that his warriors would rally around him and chase off the invading scum. Brennus knew enough of Agricola's brutal methods. He would shed no unnecessary Roman blood. If Agricola's legions encircled the hill of the Votadini, the sheer numbers would have the hill-dwellers trapped. The Votadini would be unable to access their farms and food stocks, but more importantly the Romans would control the main water supply. Brennus feared for their survival, and guessed they would capitulate quickly. But his task was not to starve alongside a foolish leader. He had to push on northwards, to find the one who would lead the Celts to victory.

Kaideigh's little voice piped up after a short pause, as if she had eventually decided to reveal a large secret.

"There is a special, little, tiny cave in the rock on the hillock near Seaonaigh's roundhouse. Only one person can hide in it, but it is a good place."

"Would I be able to hide there?" He was sure he would not, but loved to tease her.

Her childish scoff was good to hear, her exhaustion banished for a moment. "Nay! Your bottom and legs would stick out for all to see. You are far too big a man for hiding anywhere. I think you must be nearly as big as our sky god Taranis!"

"Would I be able to conceal myself in any of the other wonderful places?"

Viewed from the plain below, Dunpendyr had looked completely flat on top, but that was not so. Nature had created many low hillocks inside the fort.

His question had Kaideigh deep in thought, her little face filled by a puckered expression.

"Seaonaigh showed me the old grain pits that are not used any more. They are big holes where we could hide for a long time."

Old Meaghan, who so long ago had kept him alive, had successfully done exactly that. It was one place that Seaonaigh might have some success in hiding, though he doubted it. Dunpendyr was not like the tiny village of Marske, and little Seaonaigh did not have his old nurse's experience and cunning.

Thinking of Meaghan led to thinking of Ineda. His gut twisted in the way it always did when thoughts of her intruded. And they intruded more than he wanted them to, even more as time marched on. He had loved her, and had not known her love for what it could have been. No other person in all his travels and meetings had ever made him feel as much as Ineda had. In the now habitual way, when his thoughts turned to Ineda, he fingered the ring beneath his tunic.

"Is the next chief going to live up on a high hill like at Dunpendyr? I can tell him all about finding a little cave to hide in from the Romans. He would like that. Would he not?"

"Do you not remember what we were told?" He knew she had been listening to Earn's instructions.

A huge sigh escaped. "Nay. I have forgotten."

"We have to look for a hillfort on a small hill, near the shores of the next river estuary."

For a moment her expression perked up. "How much longer before we reach the sands?"

His heart went out to her. Kaideigh asked questions, but never complained or whined about having to walk. Practicality was already ingrained in her, because Lleia and his sickly son needed the ride. Over time, their mounts had diminished to only the two. Lleia had to have one all the time, and they took turns to ride the other. His little son, Moran, was living up to his name too well, his name meaning 'white as the sea'. Lleia had given him it when he had been birthed early, bloodless and limp. The babe still struggled with a weak hold on life.

On the day of his birth, two Roman ships had battled the winds in the estuary, and were unable to put to shore. The sight should have given Brennus pleasure, and it would have if he had been confident the ships would flounder. Yet he knew they wouldn't. At that point, the ships had been well up the river estuary.

They, too, had been well up the estuary. They still tramped the south bank, having roughly followed the water's edge for four long days after leaving Dunpendyr. They had not yet come to a fordable part of the river, the river mouth being extremely long. Nith had spotted a mounted Roman *ala* well in the distance, across the fairly flat valley floor. The horsemen were riding west, and most likely had not seen them, but cover around his little band was limited. Sparse copses of trees were dotted around, and some low scrubby bushes were bent here and there in the prevailing winds, but the area had no natural woodlands where they could take cover.

It had been his urging Lleia to move faster that had brought the birth on too early, and he now bitterly regretted hurrying her along. There had been no roundhouses to be seen, the land too boggy and inhospitable for farming, or as grazing for animals when Lleia's eventual cries had forced them to halt.

The best he could provide for her was some scrubby bushes as dusk fell. His son's first feeble cries came well into the dark. Lleia had birthed the babe with Kaideigh holding one of her hands, while he held the other. He did not dare light a fire; the weak moonlight was the best he had to follow Lleia's instructions. The only good thing about that night had been the high summer warmth, the winds of the day having died down to a warm breeze.

The morning had brought no respite for Lleia, or the babe. They had to trek on further to find the first village, after they

137

eventually forded the river. Though Lleia had claimed the birthing had not been too arduous, he feared she had bled too much.

Now, moons later, she was still losing blood, and he could do nothing about it. Lleia had again refused to stay at any of the Venicones hamlets, claiming she would rather face her future by his side as he made his way to the settlement of the High Chief.

Kaideigh's voice interrupted his gloomy thoughts.

"I liked those people of the wolf. They were very welcoming. Did you like them?"

"I did."

His impression of the Venicones was that they were a peaceful people who just wanted to get on with their farming, and daily living, free from threats from Celtic neighbours or from Roman invaders. Again, they were people who would not plan a huge battle against the Romans. Their land was fertile and prosperous, and he could not fault them for that.

Nor could he impress upon them that the Roman presence would change all that. Abject failure to rouse the tribes to action made him so disappointed – both in himself, and in them.

Kaideigh's little face scrunched up, her eyebrows almost meeting in the middle of her forehead, in that endearing way when she was confused. "Votadini and Venicones sound much alike."

His laugh startled Lleia from her dozing slumber. "Then call them the people of the wolf, if it is easier."

"Will we stay at our next place for a long time?"

Kaideigh probably knew the answer, and most likely dreaded it, though she had asked anyway. He could see her tripping gait meant she was maintaining the talk to keep herself from drifting into slumber.

"I will not know how long we will stay till I am there, little one. Though, you may make even more friends with the Vacomagi, if we move all the way north east into their territory, since they are the people of the strong bond."

"What does that mean?"

"I have heard tell the Vacomagi are a helpful and friendly people who will always help a stranger in their midst."

Kaideigh stopped short, almost tripping herself up. "Votadini, Venicones and now Vacomagi. Does every tribe around here sound the same?"

This time his raucous laugh startled Moran into wailing. Lleia's weak voice shushed and pacified his son, making him feel remorseful for disturbing them.

"Taexali. There is also a tribe called the Taexali. That is different enough."

"Will we find a roundhouse soon? I am really tired of walking now."

He knew that Kaideigh was not really complaining, it was more of a statement of fact.

Dragging off his bratt, he wrapped it around Kaideigh before deftly swinging her up onto his shoulders. She knew the drill of how to arrange it so that it covered them both, yet still allowed him to see.

"Soon. We will reach the next village in no time at all. I believe it will be after we get to the top of that hill that we are about to climb." There was a Celtic beacon fort just visible near the top: too far to see details, but a welcome sign.

"I like climbing hills, but I like running down even more."

He could already feel her little body curl in around his neck, her weight on his head. He could not carry her asleep in the position for long, but before then he would pass her over to Nith who rode their second horse. He could not stop to let any of his family rest. The forces of Rome were not far behind him, though not Agricola himself, if the last contact spoke truly. Agricola was said to be still in Brigantia, busy with measures to Romanise the people, the ones who had not fled Roman tyranny.

As he journeyed on, his hopes grew. If the High Chief of the Venicones was not the leader needed to rally the Celts of the far north, he would keep journeying on into Taexali lands. He was not so certain of climbing the mountains, but the concept of meeting the Caledons was also appealing.

The footsteps of the Roman army had to be halted.

Chapter Thirteen

"Would you like some fresh fish?"

Ineda studied the expression of the man who had come to the encampment, and who had called to her as she walked past his basket, near the periphery of the tented camp. Fresh fish was less plentiful on the plain near the Celtic hillfort of Dunpendyr, and Gaius was quite partial to fish of any kind, fresh or salted. Any haggling with the man would no doubt be well worth it. In her usual friendly fashion, she learned small details when she engaged local people in such a way. It was also extremely good to be able to leave off the Roman tongue, and converse in the language of the Celts.

"And what would you call fresh?" Ineda's question was not lightly made.

"This fish has been caught locally and brought here along the newly-laid route that leads to the camp gates. Is it not wonderful that the road comes north all the way from the place they name Eboracum?" The trader gibbered on, a wide smile encouraging her to answer as he set her more little questions.

"I am sure people will take it from you here at the camp, but if not, the people up in Dunpendyr will also appreciate your catch."

She had been disheartened during the last Samhain to hear that the Votadini High Chief at Dunpendyr had capitulated to the huge Roman presence around his hillfort. But she had also rejoiced that little Celtic blood had been shed, and that none of the people of Dunpendyr had needed to starve. The small death toll had only arisen during small, localised skirmishes as Agricola and his legions had advanced northwards in Votadini lands, late in the previous summer season. Now the Roman encampment around Dunpendyr was smaller, many *cohorts* of the legion already marching northwards, even though the winter bite still descended with a vengeance well after Imbolc.

"It is more difficult to catch the fish in freezing weather, lady, but it also means it stays fresh." The fisherman's smile was influencing.

The news of Votadini capitulation had reached Gaius less than a season after they had settled in at Easg. And, since Gaius always set to with a will, by then the fort at Easg was well repaired, its troops more than ready to fulfil the task of overseeing the safety on Agricola's main route in Votadini lands, both to the south and the north of the fort.

Some local Celtic warriors had already been assigned to break the stone rubble necessary to pave it, the treaties made with the High Chief necessitating physical labour from the tribesmen.

And always alert to the possibility of someone being a contact, she openly declared her relationship with Gaius. Drawing Dubv to her side, she stroked his dark hair as she smiled at the trader.

"My son's father, Tribune Gaius Livanus Valerius, is fond of this fish." She pointed to the smaller of the two types of fish on offer. "But before I buy, I would know where the fish was caught, and how far it has travelled to reach here?"

The man's voice dropped to the merest whisper, his gaze penetrating. An exchange of words ensued which made her more certain of who he was. Nonetheless, caution always ruled.

"Will you be selling similar fish come the morrow?"

The man sounded hesitant. "Aye. If I have caught more of it."

"Who else would buy your fish?"

A small smile broke free from the trader, his eyes understanding. "Only you, and the slave Aeonghus, will be buying."

Ineda had heard enough. Aeonghus was now a trusted contact, another slave in the camp who worked for the main cooks to the officers. It had been a great shock after such a long time to discover he sent out messages, though she had been reluctant to restart transferring information till she had some proof of his trustworthiness. That had been soon after their arrival at Dunpendyr. When she was sure of Aeonghus' allegiances, she had begun to feed him less important, but still useful, details.

Now, a waxed moon later, so much was happening during this advancing campaign of Agricola into the lands of the Votadini, and their neighbours, that she was desperate to send word to her fellow Celts.

Nonetheless, she would first speak with Aeonghus before parting with any information to the fish trader.

"Aye! That is the contact." The following day Aeonghus whispered the words as he bustled past her going the opposite direction, making sure no one saw them talking, the trader in the same place as the previous day.

"Dubv?" She gained her son's attention. Her little boy had seen someone to talk to and had become distracted. Children were not plentiful in the camp, and times for play rare. "Would you like to go over for a moment?"

A pat to his head sent him across the area of stalls. She never liked him near her when messages were actually exchanged; he was far too bright not to notice something was amiss with his mother. Though she was determined to maintain her role of messenger, she wanted no danger for her precious son.

The trader held out a fish for her inspection. "The fisherman who caught this one awaits news of how tasty you will find it. He tells me he journeys far to hear of the very best catch."

Equally quiet as the trader, she pretended to smell the fish for freshness as she bent down over it. "Use this information with caution. What I lately overheard is more like a long-term plan than for the short term, and Agricola is a man who often makes delays to oversee other important actions in Britannia."

The man eyes flickered his agreement. "Tell me what you can. I have already heard the Governor of Britannia has to change plans often if insurgencies arise elsewhere, or if something thwarts the progress of his arrangements."

Ineda was glad the man had an idea of what Agricola was like, and pressed on. "The Fourth *Cohort* will move north in two days. They expect to be at the ford to cross the Uisge For, the Black River, three days hence, at a place which faces some high hills named Monadh Ochail. I am told there already is a well-established Roman fort some half day's march south of this crossing place, though they will not wheel around that way to visit that camp."

The trader confirmed. "I know of where you speak."

Ineda spoke hurriedly, eager to tell all she knew, even though her information may seem to be a bit mixed-up. She could take no time to organise her thoughts, and had a lot to convey. "After crossing the river, the Fourth *Cohort* will head up through the pass near the western end of those hills. They will march past the northern reaches of Damnonii territory, and on into southern Venicones lands. They will establish bases at short distances apart, subduing the natives, and taking as much time as they need to create a stable situation."

"Will they remain there?"

Ineda dare not even shake her head in case she was watched. She instead pointed to another trader, as though making general inquiries. "There was some discussion of this. I heard that if winter snows arrive early, they will remain encamped in the territory of the southern Venicones, but if the winter bite is not too harsh then they are very likely to march further north. That might perhaps be even on to the north banks of the next river which flows out to the sea. I believe that to be named the River Tatha, which may border the lands of the Taexali."

The man's smile beamed as he nodded at someone passing nearby, his words barely heard from the side of his mouth. "Aye. You speak of the Tatha."

Ineda pretended to watch Dubv who played a game of 'Knucklebones' with his little friend. "The advance troops who have already gone to these places have routed out local opposition already, I believe?"

The man's nod was minimal, but sufficient to clarify what she had been told. "Aye, though only to some extent. There have only been small skirmishes. Nothing large enough to make the High Chief capitulate yet."

"When the tribune's two *cohorts* of the *Legio IX* arrive later on, they will halt at this place in southern Venicones territory, and they are expected to remain there during the winter moons.

They will build wooden forts for overwintering: perhaps more than one of good size. The longer-term plan is to strike northwards, into Taexali lands, during the next seasons. The *cohorts* will split up, and will make their usual terrorising raids on the tribespeople who live near the foothills of the mountains, where glens open onto the plain. Once they establish their supremacy, the normal Roman pattern of subduing will prevail. New fortlets will be built at all of these crucial glen mouths to hold back any Caledon attack from the mountains. Agricola will send sufficient troops northwards for this when the time is right, but, as before, Tribune Valerius' main role will be to ensure supplies to these new structures."

"This news is good." The trader kept his voice low. "Any further update?"

Ineda nodded. "Only that the *cohorts* will split up on the flat plains, but all of the units will co-ordinate with the arrival of the fleet at some later time."

"Agricola will send many vessels of the fleet?"

"I do not know this for sure. Agricola already has ambitious plans for the fleet off the west coast of Britannia. If most of the vessels are used to help pacify the Novantae and the Epidii of the islands, then he will have fewer mariners to land on the shores of the Venicones and Taexali."

"Agricola is a determined general."

Ineda's head nodded before she realised what she did. A hasty look to where her son played followed the imprudent move. "What I heard was that once the troops are disembarked, and barracked in some place in from the shoreline, a large subduing attack will be mounted – though I do not believe that will happen till many seasons have come and gone. The troops from the fleet will burn from the shoreline, and will prevent escape in that direction."

Ineda scanned around to make sure no-one was near. "I have no knowledge of how soon any of this will happen, but the troops under Tribune Valerius' command will run a large fort on a flat plateau near the river, close to where the Tatha River emerges from the hills. The fort will be built to house a legion and more. Many Roman troops will be dispatched from elsewhere to this place. It will be the vexillations soon to arrive who will go on the offensive across the plains, and who will block off all the mountain passes to keep the Caledons at bay."

"Then our Celtic forces must attack this structure, or prevent it from being built!"

Ineda was now unsure that anything at all would hamper the development of Roman domination. "Perhaps a raid will halt progress temporarily, but it will take many Celts to halt them forever."

Her answer was the best she could give. She was likely to be at that fort soon, if Gaius' planning was sound. Her own safety was not a concern, but she fretted all the time for her son and for her soon-to-be-born child.

"Ineda?"

She froze on hearing the call from behind. Pomponius had sneaked up on her, so intent had she been on delivering her message. Surely he had not been close enough to have heard her low words? A deep dread filled her. Confidence about the future sent a shiver down her spine.

"Ineda? Why is Dubv wandering so far from your side? I do not like him talking to that boy over there; he is the offspring of a camp follower!"

Turning to the officious secretary, she pasted on a smile willing her heart to cease its thumping. Though Pomponius had a great love for her son, his hatred of her seemed to grow every day. His finding more to complain about her was not only tiresome, but worrying. Being only tolerated because she was Gaius' woman was a precarious position.

Being found out to be a traitor would be a disaster.

145

"He is not so far from my sight, Pomponius."

AD 81 Samhain – High Chief Trune's Hillfort, Venicones Territory

"Brennus, you must send Kaideigh to Lorcan and Nara. Vow to me that you will?"

Lleia's plea tugged at his feelings as she lay fevered on a cot in the roundhouse of Trune, the Venicones High Chief. They had reached the hillfort a mere three days past. Moran had ceased to live around dawn, the local herb woman having told Brennus that it was the tainting from his mother's milk that had been slowly killing the baby. Lleia was now also losing her own tenuous hold on life, though she had battled hard.

Moons after the birth she should have been free of the lack of vitality. A high fever was now upon her, which the herb wife could not control. The birth sickness within Lleia was now hastening her death.

"I will do everything I can to ensure she is safe, Lleia. You have my word." Brennus gently squeezed the frail fingers in his grip, his focus on the ashen features before him.

It was not an empty promise to his dying hearth-wife, even though they had never actually shared a hearth in a roundhouse of their own. His daughter was the light of his existence, and he would protect her with his own life.

"You slept through the last messenger visit, Lleia."

Her feeble smile was as interested as she could summon. "What news then?"

"Nara, Lorcan and most of their people have quit Tarras. They are already making their way directly to this place."

"But the Roman Army follow our footsteps, Brennus. It will be more dangerous for the children..." Her voice broke off into harsh coughing.

"Fear not, Lleia. Lorcan will find a way to keep them safe. He will arrive soon, and Nara will look to Kaideigh. You know that will be no hardship to her, for she loves our little daughter as much as her own."

Lleia's sweet smile was heartbreaking. The news seemed pleasing to her. "I am so glad, Brennus. She is so precious…" Sleep was claiming her again, but so was the fever that beaded even more around her temples. The herb wife gently pushed him to the side and wiped yet more moisture from Lleia's face. He had thought Lleia asleep; her eyes were closed, but her voice drifted up. "I am glad Nara and Lorcan did not remain at Tarras under the *gladius* control of Agricola. I pray the goddess keeps them safe. It will be good to see them… again."

Brennus feared they would be too late to say farewell to Lleia.

"I will also be pleased to see my brother, Lleia, though I expect he will be exhausted. His fitness for such fast travel is now in question."

Lleia's filmy eyes opened and stared at him, so cloudy he wondered if her sight was as hazy as his blind eye could see. Her fingers reached out to him. Squeezing them very gently, he waited for her to draw a deep breath before being able to speak again.

"You must not wait for him, Brennus, and wait no longer for my passing. I heard Esk and Nith talking earlier with Trune's warriors. You must find this leader they now speak of. They are desperate to prove their worth in battle against the Roman scourge. Go, and find this man." Her grip slid away as she drifted into another troubled sleep. Slowly detaching his fingers from her clammy palm, he took up the cloth and wiped the moisture away from her burning cheeks, as he had seen the herb wife do.

Although he agreed with Lleia about the need for haste to find the great leader, he found that could not leave her bedside.

"Brennus?" Nith's voice was close to his ear. He had dozed off. "Come outside for a moment?"

He knew it must be important, though he did not wish to miss Lleia's last breath, which he knew must come soon. She was so weakened. Squeezing her hand with the gentlest of touches he whispered, "I will only be away a few moments."

147

Warriors he had never seen before stood in a cluster around Trune, the High Chief. When prompted, one of the warriors spoke up.

"Agricola's army already floods the foothills between the Caledon mountains and our southern borders with the Damnonii. He has blocked off the first three mountain passes. His troops are so numerous, and they move across our flat valley floor quickly."

Another newcomer added, "We do not understand it. For strangers, they seem to know exactly where to go without hesitation."

Brennus paced around the small group. "That is exactly it. They do know where to tread. Their scouts will have been across the land some time ago, and will have sent back their information to Agricola and his senior officers. Those *exploratores* know well how to conceal themselves when necessary."

"Why do they set up at the mountain passes, and yet have not come to confront me again at my hillfort? Though I am loath to mouth it, the pathway to my settlement is much easier." Trune seemed as baffled as the other Venicones gathered in the huddle.

Esk's answer rattled out, before Brennus could give any reassurance. "The *Roman Classis* will do that task from the water, have no doubt on that."

"What is this *Classis*? Where can we intercept them?" One of the warriors from the foothills was exasperated, as though tired of learning about more of the Roman Army, yet desperate to act immediately against the interfering presence of the Roman scourge.

Esk looked to Trune. "The *Classis* is the Roman Empire's sea-going vessels. You have sighted the ships already, have you not?"

Trune nodded, resigned to his answer. "Aye, we have. More than once they have been seen near our shores, and they have sailed far up into the river estuary. Do you believe that is how the forces of Agricola will attempt to confront my hillfort?"

Brennus hated having to be more alarming, but Trune needed to be prepared for an attack from the sea, or the land. "Perhaps, but the man also rules a huge fighting force on foot. He has split his legions on the land before now, and may do so again. That way he suppresses more land in the shortest time – especially if there is little or no resistance to him. When a chief surrenders, and pledges their allegiance, he swiftly moves on."

Trune looked devastated. Brennus did not envy the man. The chief would have major decisions to make ere long, if the Roman Army was encamped across the valley floor. He turned back to the warriors who had come from the foothills.

"Is there any resistance from the people who dwell at these mountain passes?" Brennus feared for their safety, but in his heart hoped there had been a show of defiance.

"Aye! But to no avail. Already a number of the villagers have been slain by the Roman *gladius*. Other warriors have fled into the hills where there is talk of a Caledon gathering some show of strength. I do not yet know this man's name, but he has claimed he will not acquiesce quietly. He will allow no Roman on his lands without fighting them first."

That news was the best Brennus had heard for many a long day.

However, the Roman legions having already terrorised the local tribespeople who dwelt near the southern mountain passes was disturbing news to Brennus. Agricola's forces were so close behind him. If not prevented, the Romans would turn the encampments into permanent forts before the winter snows, to ensure the soldiers had better overwintering conditions.

Kaideigh surprised him the following day, after the ceremony of cremation for Lleia and his son. His little daughter had seen death before in many of the places they had lived for a short time, but he had thought the deaths of her mother and brother would have had a more devastating impact on her.

"They have not been properly well for a long time, *Athair*. I prayed and prayed to my goddess Brigantia, but they only got more and more sick. I wanted my mother to have no more pain."

Brennus cuddled his too-wise little girl, thankful she had robust health. As he mourned Lleia and his son, he thought Lleia could have done better than taking him as her only man, yet he could never regret their liaison. Lleia had given him Kaideigh.

During the following days, fresh news was reaching Trune's hillfort. The only good part was that an un-named Caledon leader was indeed gathering warriors together, though had not yet attacked any of the Roman forces who now blocked the southern glen mouths.

Brennus needed to find out if this famed Caledon's fervour was true. He greatly wanted to meet the leader who had vowed not to sit back and wait for Agricola to infest the area where the river Tatha emerged from the mountains, a glen mouth to the north of where Agricola's forces already sat tight. The mountain pass where the Tatha came forth was a strategically important pass, the fresh water supply a hugely important feature.

Brennus had long learned there were crucial requirements to where forts were placed. A source of fresh water that would continue to supply hundreds of soldiers at any given time was essential, as was a plentiful stock of suitable wood from nearby forests. The Romans needed the hewn wood for their fort building, but also needed a constant supply of firewood for cooking, and sometimes heating purposes when the weather was inclement. Nearby hillocks were also sought for placing their sentry and signal posts.

"Aye! It is as you say," Trune confirmed. "The glen mouth where my Tatha emerges meets all those requirements you have just mentioned."

Before Trune could make any decision about increasing the amount of Venicones at that glen opening, a message arrived for Brennus.

Agricola intended a whole legion to be based on the Tatha?

The messenger was thoroughly quizzed. "A whole legion? You are certain those are the words you have to pass on to me?" The man could not confirm who had passed on the message; he only knew that the news had come through at least three contacts, or possibly four, before he had received it, and that it had taken some time to arrive to his ears.

From the rest of the information given, Brennus could only surmise that the message came from someone who was not with Agricola's main forces, but was still somewhere south.

Though Trune was stunned at the idea of some five thousand soldiers setting up a permanent residence across his valley floor, Brennus thought it likely, since conditions there were very much in the Roman favour.

Better news was that the talked-of Caledon leader continued to rally troops alongside him, making Brennus sure he must be the one leader he had been seeking for a long time. He itched to ride forth into the mountains and find the man!

The quandary of what to do with Kaideigh was resolved when Lorcan and Nara arrived the following day with their four children. They were bedraggled and exhausted from the continuous journey, because Lorcan had made no stops like Brennus had at Dumnonii and Venicones villages.

"Gabrond is not with you?" Brennus was overjoyed to see Lorcan, though worried about his other sibling and family.

"Never fear." Lorcan sought to dispel his alarm. "They are journeying northward, but at a slower pace. The group is large, and they have few horses to share amongst them. They must also be even more circumspect in evading the many Roman patrols along the route."

"Then let us pray that Taranis will guide them well. Slow is good, if it keeps them safe."

"The Roman dung is cutting a swathe across Selgovae and Votadini lands," Lorcan told the High Chief of the Venicones as they sat around the fireside. "After we departed Tarras, word came to me that the High Chief of the Selgovae had capitulated – though much of his clan's blood has been shed. In despair, to save his remaining people, he has given his allegiance to Rome. I am told the Roman presence around here is sporadic, but when two or three *cohorts* descend upon hillfort surroundings the result is much different."

Trune looked around his fireside. "I could not easily summon similar numbers to repel a few *cohorts*, Lorcan. You already know that we are farming people, and rarely congregate in large numbers."

Later, Brennus walked with his brother around the perimeter of the hillfort. They looked out across the wide expanse of river that was visible as it opened out to the eastern sea. The hillfort's defences were of a single ditch, and would not repel even a *century* of determined Roman legionaries.

"Trune told me two vessels of the Roman fleet were seen well up the river, around the time of the last Lughnasadh." Brennus pointed inland to where the ships had been berthed.

"These Venicones people are welcoming, Brennus, but they just wish to be left in peace. They will negotiate with the Roman Governor of Britannia, rather than have mass bloodshed at these gates." Lorcan was despondent.

Brennus was of the same mind. "It is what I have encountered at every village, hillfort and settlement so far. None of them wish to be dominated by the Roman Empire, but no one is prepared to stand up and lead the local tribespeople against Rome."

"Brennus!" Nith's voice broke up the conversation as he strode towards him, a stripling Venicones warrior at his heels.

"Coram here has some information you will want to hear."

The lad had more news of the Caledon leader who had made attacks on the new Roman forts and signal towers at the glen mouths.

"This man is the chief of a mountain tribe?"

The young lad laughed. "Nay! He is not a mountain man, but comes from the foothills. The Caledons have many roundhouses near the places the Roman Army are already encamped on."

Lorcan intervened. "If he is not a chief, then this man has no power to summon men to this cause, yet you say he persists in doing so?"

Brennus thought it both a courageous and foolhardy notion.

The young lad hastened to explain. "What I heard is that he is the son of a Caledon chief. He gathered a band of some fifty men to accompany him on the raids he has recently conducted."

Nith prompted the boy to finish his information. "Tell Brennus the other information you told me."

The lad's smile beamed. "Fifteen of us are leaving on the morrow, to go and find this man."

"His name?" Brennus felt the most eager he had been for long moons.

"He goes by the name of Feargus Dubv."

Brennus knew he had to be along with the group when it left on the coming dawn. Lorcan would not be dissuaded from accompanying him, though Nara remained at Trune's hillfort to ensure the safety of all of their children.

Chapter Fourteen

"Another fortlet?"

Lorcan was astounded. They had arrived at the village of Kilmahog, one of the minor Caledon chiefs, just the day before.

"Aye! At least a half-*cohort* have arrived and have begun to lift the turf." Brennus was out of breath, furious and frustrated. He flopped down onto the hearthside of Kilmahog and groaned. "Where is Agricola getting all these troops, Lorcan?" He looked to his brother for an answer, even though there was no possibility that Lorcan could know.

Lorcan tried anyway. "He must have the Emperor Domitian's permission to redeploy the troops from the far south of Britannia. As well as soldiers from the *Legio XX*, *Legio IX* and the *Legio II Adiutrix,* he may even now have newly-created vexillations, new detachments that have perhaps come from the *Legio II Augusta.*"

"Can he somehow have acquired more auxiliaries into the *Legio II Adiutrix*?" Esk's question sounded so plausible.

"I believe you may have the answer, Esk. The legions of the Roman Empire are of a generally fixed number, and they are scattered around the Empire. It would take huge reorganisation to send troops from places like Germania, or Hispania, to control more territory in Britannia.

An easier way would be to increase the number of men assigned to a *cohort*, or to create a brand new vexillation detachment that is only intended for subduing the lands around here. That is perhaps what Agricola and the Emperor are doing. That would account for the many troops who are now encamped all over the lands of the Damnonii and the

154

Venicones." Lorcan brooded as he stared into the crackling fire.

Kilmahog, a wizened old chief, passed over a cup of small beer. "You say this small fort they are building is on the Rusky water? So close to here?"

"So close that if you climb your Ben Dearg you will see them build their turf ramparts." Esk sounded disheartened by the news they had to convey.

Roman encampments, Roman forts and Roman signal towers were now all across the lands between the Venicones High Chief's settlement at the mouth of the Tatha River and Kilmahog's village well in the foothills. The amount of Roman soldiers sent to the area by Agricola had been staggering.

"Is it not just one of their temporary camps, and then they will move on to another place?" The aging elder's voice was hushed, and hopeful.

Brennus had no encouraging answer for him. "The depth of the ditch in a temporary camp is not usually as deep as the ones dug for a small fort. At Rusky they are digging deep."

"Your area around here is a strategic one to gain control of, as you know already, Kilmahog. Your forebears would not have settled here otherwise." With a small nod, Lorcan accepted the bannock from a serving woman.

"Aye! My clan have guarded this land for many generations, and will continue to guard it." Kilmahog's pride was evident in his declaration, but Brennus knew the actions the man could take against the forces of Rome were limited. The chief's guttural voice echoed around his small roundhouse, angry and strident. "What will it take to clear our lands of this scourge?"

Lorcan, ever the diplomat, attempted to encourage. "It will take a very strong chief to band together many more Celts than the amount of Roman soldiers who plague our land like the midges at your loch side. The bite of your tiny flies is fierce, but the Roman bite lasts much longer."

Kilmahog turned to Brennus. "I wish I could be that man, but I am too old and worn. I can summon maybe a hundred men from my clan around the lochs, but they will not be sufficient to stop this insidious enemy."

"Like my father before me, I will say to you: it takes only one stone to start a cairn. We may need to call on your hundred warriors soon to rid this island of the Roman usurpers." Brennus seethed inside as he looked at the warriors congregated around the fireside.

Another three seasons had passed by, and that elusive leader was still not found. Along with Lorcan, Esk, Nith and Trune's warriors, they had visited every small settlement of Caledon territory to the west of the Venicones border. No one, not even the one named Feargus Dubv when they located him, was prepared to name a place to gather many Celtic brothers to fight against the Romans, although Feargus Dubv was continuing to organise small raiding sorties on the newest Roman fortlets.

Esk spat into the fire to rid himself of a bone that annoyed his mouth. "I will that day to come soon, Kilmahog, but even if it is seasons from now, will we still have your support when battle calls ring out across the land?"

"Aye, indeed you will. Just like you have the support of my western Caledon brothers."

Brennus stared into the fire. They had spent the last three moons climbing hills and sleeping out of doors in mountain passes. The Caledons of the west were fierce warriors, but the clans were small and scattered around the inhospitable mountainous landscape.

Nonetheless, it was good that they had pledged support, since the Caledon leaders knew fine well that their lands were not the terrain to assemble the thousands needed to fight against the Roman Empire. For that, a wide terrain around the foothills of a high hill was crucial. Negotiating mountain passes and glens was not the terrain for a large-scale confrontation.

"I am most concerned at how the Roman *agrimensors*, and *exploratores*, are continuing to identify the strategic glen mouths to the north," Lorcan said into a lull, as the warriors around the fireside chewed their roasted pig ribs.

"They seem to be far too skilled at that," Kilmahog replied. "They also seem so adept at making their encampments so close to our Caledon settlements by the loch sides."

Brennus was sad to agree. "Fresh water is a need they cannot do without. It plays a large part in where they set up camp."

Kilmahog belched loudly before stretching, a weak grin spreading across his sunken cheeks. "If they are encamped now at the Rusky water, then at least they will not dig up my village here at Venachar."

"I would not be too certain of that." As usual, Esk was his taciturn self.

A flurry of movement at the roundhouse door heralded a newcomer. "Kilmahog. I have a message for Bran of Witton, and the same for Brennus of Garrigill."

"Well give it, lad." Kilmahog beckoned the young warrior towards the fireside. "This warrior here is Bran of Witton, though you may also hear him named Brennus of Garrigill."

Brennus had found that the wearing of his two names had become impossible. Keeping the identities separate had been a problem, and in truth it was not so necessary amongst the Venicones and those Celts of the north. He answered easily to both names. The messages which were passed on now tended to come in both of his names.

"The villagers at Drumvaich say that the Roman fort nearby is all a-flurry. An important Roman tribune has arrived, and is preparing to march troops further north."

"I already feel snow in my nose, boy!" Kilmahog was scathing. "Why would they do that when winter already bites deep?"

"Agricola." Lorcan's one word explained all.

Brennus had no difficulty agreeing. "That sounds exactly like the Roman Governor of Britannia, and the General of all of the Roman armies."

Nith rose to his feet and paced around. "Are they certain it was a tribune, and not Agricola himself?"

The boy's head shook. "I can only say that the message I was to pass on said 'an important tribune'."

"Does that mean that the fort will have fewer soldiers to protect it?" asked one of the elders.

"Nay. This tribune arrived along with many soldiers. I believe the message perhaps means that some who have been there already will be replaced by the ones who have just arrived."

"Aye. That sounds like the strategies the Romans use." Lorcan was sure of that, as he too got up and stretched himself. "I think we need to move on as soon as we can."

Brennus agreed with his brother. He had not yet encountered that elusive leader of leaders, but the messaging system, instilled as a necessity at every place he had visited, was working admirably.

AD 82 Samhain – Glen of the Eagles, Venicones Territory

The shrill whistle of a distressed kingfisher rent the air. Brennus hand-signalled his band to scatter through the forest fringe, knowing Esk's alarm meant Roman troops were close by. The strident version Esk could produce was piercing, yet so realistic.

Taking cover behind a large boulder outcrop, he sidled along to allow Lorcan space.

"They must be very near. Your Esk is the best scout I have ever encountered. We must give great thanks to Callan for recognising his worth." Lorcan's whisper tickled his ear.

Rather than speak, he nodded as Esk mimicked another bird, this time the Red Grouse, as though the bird had been startled into an upwards flurry from the heather: the signal that it was only a small group of Romans. Their use of bird calls and animal noises had been perfected, and had helped keep the band alive more than a time or two.

Pulling his bratt over his light-coloured hair, Brennus slowly peered around the side of the rock. They had been forced to traverse the lower foothills almost the whole journey to avoid detection, and he was weary of the need to slink past the Roman scum. Along with his brother, and his small band of followers, they had agreed that a confrontation every time they encountered the forces of Rome would do them no favours. The otherworld was too likely a result for some of them, since they had come across so many patrols. However, that did not mean they would not fight if an opportunity arose where they were likely to be the victors, and come out of a skirmish unscathed.

An animal noise was just discernable, the soft repetitive scratching of a red squirrel clawing at tree bark. Nith. He was much better at animal noises.

Brennus could see no sign of any Romans, but pulled back to mouth at his brother. "Only around ten of them."

A grin broke free. He had no present notion of exactly where his companions were except Lorcan, but Esk and Nith's alarm calls meant they were nearby. The others wouldn't have gone far either.

Lorcan's dunt at his elbow drew his gaze to the other side of the outcrop. "Over there."

His older brother's whisper was drowned out by the sound of tramping feet. The Roman patrol was walking alongside the burn at the hill foot. There was too much exposed ground for Brennus and his men to attack them in their current location, but if the patrol continued their present direction they would soon enter the copse that lay ahead of them. It was likely that they would, since Brennus knew the far side of the copse led to the pathway which opened out at the glen of the eagles. There had already been a temporary camp there when he had set out seasons ago to seek out the Caledon leaders. If the Romans continued their usual methods, then a permanent camp was probably somewhere near, since it lay on the strategic north-east route up through the territory of the Venicones to the River Tatha.

Peering out Lorcan's end of the outcrop, he caught sight of Esk's spear tip just above the rock where he was sheltering, though the man's body remained invisible. Giving a soft hoot Brennus waited for Esk's head to peek out. After making a silent hand signal to remain above the patrol and negotiate a path that would lead to the copse below, he expected his men to follow when he and Lorcan silently set off, maintaining their cover.

It took only a short time for Brennus' band to be in place, ahead of the Roman patrol.

"Now!" His alarm cry sent his companions out from their hiding places.

The ring of metal on metal was almost instantly all around, the surprised cries of the Roman auxiliaries a sound that was most welcome. Brennus had managed the element of surprise, the small group of Romans unable to form any kind of defensive shield. They were doomed. Nith had been correct. Only twelve Romans, and his group outnumbered them by seven.

Lorcan's battle cries deafened his ears, his brother's long sword crushing the *lorica hamata* of the nearest soldier of Rome. Not enough to sever the links of the chain mail, the blow was still strong enough to send the smaller man to his knees, one of Trune's men at the ready to whack the Roman's neck.

Brennus' spear slammed into the upper leg of an escaping Roman, Esk moving in to finish off beheading the screeching soldier. Similar engagement was all around the area, blood and flesh spattering around till all noise was extinguished.

Brennus bent down to retrieve his spear from the auxiliary's leg. The half-rent head lay in a pool of dark red blood, the eyes surprised by the speed of the attack. It was just a young lad, Brennus guessed not much more than sixteen winters and someone who had probably lied about his age.

He beckoned his brother over to the carnage at his feet. "Agricola's troops seem younger and younger."

"Aye! And he looks no different from our own young warriors, wherever he has come from."

"Is anyone hurt?" Brennus called around to check on his band.

Nith replied, kneeling at the side of one young warrior. "Only two wounds, but neither is a serious one. A binding will suffice for now."

Chapter Fifteen

"Tribune Gaius Livanus Valerius comes!"

Ineda rode her horse in the file behind Gaius as he halted on approach to the fort gates. They waited while the *signifer* raised the standard, and called a further greeting to the guard post.

She had seen the effects of similar announcements many times. Since leaving Dunpendyr, they had stopped at various encampments as they headed north. There had been almost no signs of local tribespeople, and there had been little resistance to Gaius' *cohort* as it had tramped up through the lands of the Damnonii.

Gaius had warned her that their stay at each fort would be short on leaving Dunpendyr, and he had been correct; his visits were only to ensure the needs of each fort were being met in term of supplies.

All the Celts who dwelt on the land they had traversed had seemed subdued, but she could not be sure of that, since she had seen so very few. Only tribespeople who had been assigned to cut trees had been visible, though she had been told some were working at other tasks like hewing stone. Of course it was early winter, so no heavy farming was being done, and many tasks were only being undertaken when the weather was fair.

Though a rough swathe had been cleared across the landscape for a basic road, she could see no other signs of Agricola's road-builders at work. It had been a cold, damp and exhausting ride from the last fort on the flatlands near the mouth of the Black River. The recent pelting rains had clearly halted the creation of any kind of better road structure.

161

Their arrival at the fort on the Allan Water was different from the previous ones.

As soon as the gates were opened, Gaius was apprised of the latest developments, the fort commander jabbering his news as he welcomed them in.

"When did this attack occur?" Gaius was livid.

"The evening before last."

Ineda suspected it was anxiety that made the commander flinch.

She slid from her horse and drew Dubv away from the heated conversation. She could not stride off, since she had no idea where she would be housed, but her son had no need to hear the curses so close by. The design of the fort was much as usual: familiar enough that she knew where to go that would be out of earshot, yet not too far.

"Come with me, Dubv. We will stretch our legs along the *intervallum*."

Dubv did not want to miss anything of interest, and tugged at the hand she held in a tight grip. "I want to find out what has happened."

Dubv had a tendency towards petulance when overtired. Towing her protesting son along, she scanned the area. Guards manned the watchtowers as normal, but to the inside of the fort gates, more soldiers than normal were at the ready.

"You lost fifteen of your men in this skirmish?" Gaius' voice echoed all around the empty *intervallum*. "I will talk to the survivors."

Ineda did not need to hear the centurion state there were none; it was easy to guess from the man's gestures when she sneaked a look backwards.

"Ineda! Bring my son back, and stay well away from the walls."

She noted that the guard was doubled that night at the gates when she took a slow stroll around the torch-lit walkways, once Dubv was fast asleep. In a strange way, she felt excitement that the local Celts were retaliating successfully, albeit in small raids, yet she was also in an extremely vulnerable situation. Gaius and the fort commander were still deep in talk, and it was well into the deep of night when she became aware of him sliding onto the cot beside her.

"Do you need anything?" She rubbed some sleep from her eyes and turned around to him.

"I ate a while ago, and wish for no more wine tonight. I must be clear-headed come dawn. Agricola is due to arrive from the site that's on the southern fringes of the high mountains, a half-day's march from here. The local tribes around there were subdued before your festival of Beltane, but it seems some other Caledon leader has been inciting them to take up arms again."

He flopped onto his back, making the thin mattress bounce.

"Agricola will not have that area disturbed. It is crucial to maintain and properly defend all of these glen defences, so that none of the marauding mountain Caledon men can upset Agricola's campaign of claiming this northern Britannia for Rome. These glen head forts must hold back any challenging Caledons."

"Then Agricola will not be pleased to lose men from this fort?" It was a question that needed no answer.

Gaius punched at the round pillow behind his head. "Not in the least. He is never pleased at hearing we have lost some of the newest recruits he has had trouble acquiring."

Tension rose from Gaius in waves. Reaching for him, she pulled him close and stroked his back. "You have only just arrived, Gaius. He cannot possibly blame you for the loss of men at this fort."

"When Agricola loses men, we are all to blame, Ineda. I am presently the temporary *Tribune Militum* of the *Legio IX*, and these recruits were from the *Legio IX*. I have been in regular correspondence with the commander of this fort. That patrol should never have been in any vulnerable position that could be ambushed."

Gaius' usual method of ridding himself of tension was employed. He took her body quickly, with little love in his embrace, using her more to vent his frustration. It was something which was happening too often of late, and which reawakened Ineda's deep resentment.

163

More soft snowflakes began to drift down as Brennus and his band approached Trune's hillfort.

It had taken them much longer than planned to return there, and not because of the bad weather. While he and his band had spent seasons in the western Caledon villages, the Romans had built more watchtowers and encampments along the north-east route. The plains between mountain and sea were awash with Roman presence which had to be avoided.

A band of some twenty men did not go unnoticed on open flat ground, and they had had to scatter a number of times to avoid small Roman patrols who scoured the land around their encampments.

"Kaideigh!" Brennus hoisted his daughter high into the air with a hug that almost crushed her. "You have grown so tall." He had missed her so much. Over her head, he caught sight of another loved one he had not seen for such a long time. Giving Kaideigh a last squeeze, he relinquished her to reach forward.

"Gabrond! I am so glad to see you." Firm claps around the shoulders brought him into a hug with his brother. The teary grins from Gabrond's wife Fionnah and their children made it hard to swallow.

"I arrived here to find both of you had gone a-wandering without me!" Gabrond admonished. "You have been on your travels for a long time, my brothers!"

"We have much to tell you of our visits to the Caledons. Aye indeed," Lorcan answered, "but first, some dry clothes and food."

Beathan, at ten winters, was a tall young warrior who was already itching to take up arms against the Roman army. "I do not want to be left behind the next time you go off to make contact with the Caledons, Father. I want to be there when you wipe the Roman scourge from our lands."

Beathan sounded so fierce as Brennus watched Lorcan draw his son into his chest, his shoulder slaps strong and encouraging.

"Well said, my son," said Lorcan. "But no journeys will be made by anyone till the weather turns to spring. Not even Agricola is moving across this deep winter landscape."

Brennus knew his men required some rest, and time to plan. Trune had received many communications that required much thought, and a half-moon's worth of relaxation sounded exactly what they all needed.

After the festival of Imbolc, a large group were ready to go north, the winter having been colder and wetter than usual (according to the locals). Brennus had found it much damper and colder than winters at Garrigill, and said so as they began their trudge north.

Lorcan heartily agreed. "The mountain men of the Caledon areas are hardy men indeed, for what they experienced is much worse than the lighter snow that falls near the sea coast."

"Where are we heading this time?" Kaideigh had forgotten already, even though their trek had barely started. Having left at daybreak, only half of the time had passed till the sun would be directly overhead.

Nara clapped her niece around the shoulders and drew her into a hug. The band of twenty-three had only six horses, so most of them walked. "Lunan Lochs. That is where we are going."

"Lorcan said we would meet some fierce Caledon men. Is that true?" Kaideigh's questions were relentless.

Brennus answered. "We have already met men of the Caledons, and they like being called fierce, yet they are really no fiercer than those around you right now."

The decision had been made to strike out together as a family unit, to forge more bonds with Caledon clans. Lorcan was of the same mind as he was: it would do none of them any good to settle around Trune's hillfort. Though the hillfort had not yet been surrounded by Roman troops, they believed that would happen ere long, especially if the fleet disgorged men down on the shoreline when the spring thaws came.

"We will protect you, Kaideigh." Though still young, Beathan sounded so sure of their prowess.

It amused Brennus that the lad thought himself a fine young warrior, because he had not learned total caution.

"Beathan!" Lorcan admonished, though not too loudly. "Although we can see no signs of Roman presence near us, that does not mean we can make so much noise. Guard your laughter, and save it till you are in a safe place. "We will be within sight of the line of Roman forts and watchtowers soon. We must be on our mettle and keep a sharp look-out."

Though Lorcan reminded all of them in such a way, Brennus knew his brother intended the command to be for the younger children.

Brennus added, "Aye! That goes for you too, Kaideigh. Save your breath for walking. We have come through the pass between the hills we spoke of earlier, and are well past the old Celtic hillfort near Shien Hill. The flatlands ahead of us are our greatest challenge. We will have to pass between two of the new Roman forts which were started after the last Samhain. We know of only one watchtower on the *dubv* hill north of these forts, but there may be others that have been set up recently. Soon we must split up as we discussed. We cannot be seen to be gathered in such numbers. Do you remember that?"

The adults had all tried to ensure the little girls knew what would happen. Kaideigh was more familiar with evading Roman patrols than Lorcan's two daughters were, and Nara's young son was still too young to understand. Gabrond's sons and daughters were older than Beathan, and well able to understand.

Esk's bird call alerted them, sending them scattering into small groups and scurrying into the copse nearby.

AD 83 Before Beltane – Lunan Lochs Caledon Territory

"We have to carry on with our normal rites, Lorcan." Nara was angered.

The congregated crowd around the small fireside was unsure. They had based themselves at the Mause, on the small River Ericht, for some moons. The local villagers were not

166

numerous enough to have a large Beltane festival, but they did purify their animals and conduct the usual rites.

"I agree with Nara."

Brennus was unwilling to forgo any of his traditions, even though the Romans had begun to build a large fort on the north bank of the Tatha, not so far away. This latest one looked to be even larger than the other recent ones, and it was in a really strategic position to oversee the movement of the Caledon men when they came over the hills, and down into the valleys. "You will be able to double the guard, and make the fires just large enough for your needs. Will you not, Duncalden?"

Duncalden, the clan chief, nodded. "We have always used the one place for our Beltane rites, it being the only long stretch of flat land hereabouts, but it would be easily visible from the hill towers they have built at the Inchtuthil. Though our Beltane fires need not blaze for too long."

Esk was to the point as usual. "They know we are here anyway, so why the need for secrecy?"

It was true. Over the last seasons, the Roman Army had subdued all the tribespeople between the Lunan Lochs and the coastline of the eastern sea. Word had come from Trune, the High Chief of the Venicones. Trune had come to an accommodation with the Romans on his soil. He had not totally capitulated, but some agreements had been made.

"My Caledon High Chief has not yet surrendered to the *Ceigean Ròmanach*! The Roman scum find our mountains repel them." Duncalden sneered, as though it would never happen.

Brennus hoped Duncalden's confidence in the mountains being a barrier would prove to be true, though he doubted any land features would stop determined Roman advances.

Lorcan's smile was consoling. "It is good that your Caledon hill country is not so easily traversed, but it is more important that your land holds little of value to the Roman coffers. If these mountains held important ores that could be easily excavated, then the Roman Empire would not be leaving the Caledons alone. They have traversed much higher

167

mountains in Germania to subdue all of the people in order to take their tin, lead and even more precious metals from them."

"We do have precious ores in the mountains."

Duncalden's peeved expression made Brennus laugh. "Aye! You do. But are they easy to get at?"

AD 83 Beltane – Bertha, Venicones Territory

"It cannot be done, Pomponius!"

Gaius threw aside the correspondence, and drew forward yet another scroll, even though the answer he needed was not scribed upon it. He had pored over the recent communications, again and again.

"You wish me to inform General Agricola of exactly those words, Tribune Valerius?"

Pomponius still managed to annoy him, even though they had worked tirelessly together for so many summers. Just sometimes, the man's droll humour could not be resisted. A weak grin slipped free.

"That would definitely send you back to Rome, but not in a manner you would wish!"

Gauis knew that Pomponius' desire for advancement back in Rome had never waned. Being reminded of it regularly no longer bothered him, but just sometimes lately he wondered if his secretary could be correct about life being much easier as a tribune of the forces stationed in Rome, as opposed to anywhere around the vast empire. Pomponius had been even worse since he had reverted back to being only a tribune of the *Legio XX*, his temporary position having ceased when the injured tribune had returned to duties.

He accepted the scroll that Pomponius had unearthed, knowing it would not have been tendered if there was not something significant on it. Unrolling it, he half-listened as Pomponius outlined a possible plan.

"Divert the supplies from the lead mines on the highest peaks in the lands of the mid Selgovae." Pomponius pointed to a particular reference on the scroll. "The lead coming from there is being sent to Corstopitum, and then it goes south via the road to Eboracum. It is the most reasonable supply you can commandeer for this new fortress that is planned. If Agricola as Governor of Britannia wants the new site to have those comforts so quickly, then the builders cannot wait for it to be shipped from southern Britannia."

Gaius stared at the references. If he were not so tired, he might have worked it out for himself. It seemed he was relying on Pomponius more and more as the demands of Agricola's fort building grew and grew.

"What is your solution to generating a supply of lead and of iron, up here in the lands of the Venicones?"

Pomponius' cackle took off the strain behind the question. "That might depend on what Agricola can provide from the Caledon Mountains. I am told there are untapped sources everywhere in Caledon territory."

Gaius' deft flick of the re-rolled scroll was easily caught by Pomponius, and passed on to his junior secretary who hovered by the doorway.

"See to it that the first of the supplies reach here within seven days." That was all the instructing necessary. Pomponius would do the task admirably. "Now, I must somehow replace the wagon and the supplies that were ambushed near Ardoch. I swear by the goddess Etain, I will find these Caledon rebels, and skewer the life out of them one by one."

He had not been long at the fort of Bertha, sited not far from where the river Tatha flowed out into the estuary and out to the eastern sea, its placement strategically important. Soon Agricola's fleet would be landing supplies and men. Gaius was not responsible for the movement of the vexillations of men going north on Agricola's northern campaign, but ere long, he needed to have the supplies flowing to the fort Agricola was naming Pinnata Castra. It truly was on the wing, but he would ensure that given time it would excel Corstopitum.

A huge supplies base was sorely needed in these northerly climes, to ensure Agricola's plans of advancing and building forts all the way to the northern coast were successful.

Gaius' work never ceased.

AD 83 A Half-Moon After Beltane – Pinnata Castra, Venicones Territory

Ineda hoisted her younger son higher into her arms.

"Gaius?"

Gaius was never pleased when she interrupted him. He was always busy, and invariably short-tempered about everything now. Not even his sons were getting much attention.

"Gaius?" Her tone demanded his notice from the inevitable scrolls that littered his desk. "I do not interrupt for trivia. Your second son has barely seen you these past days. He is already more than two moons old, and you have yet to see his eye colour." The latter was not entirely true, but she felt it made her point.

Exasperation warred with some regret in Gaius' expression when he looked up. "I know this, Ineda, but at present I see no way to improve that situation. Agricola demands much of me, and every single instruction needs to be enacted immediately. He aims to build so many forts on this northern campaign in a very short time and all of that takes me hours of preparation and planning."

Ineda had not seen the Commander of the Armies around the encampment for days, though that was normal, since his visits were fleeting. He descended upon them, ranted for a while, and then left, but she did know the toll he exacted on Gaius. Agricola marched his forces relentlessly onwards, and was often to be seen at the head of the column, but to do that meant fit and healthy men must be well-supplied with all resources, supplied by overtired officers like Gaius.

"I thought all was progressing well here at Pinnata Castra." Ineda could not believe otherwise, since close by the temporary tented encampment the walls of the huge new fort had been completed.

"It is because all is going well that I am so busy, Ineda." Gaius' smile was weak. Exhaustion had been pushed off for many long days, and he looked grim.

170

"This fort is not the same, is it?" It was an awkward question, but the layout she had seen in past visits to Roman forts, small and large, was not being repeated at Pinnata Castra. She wanted to know why, for reasons of natural curiosity…and for others.

"This will be a strategic base in the north-east. It will be a much more critical one than the one at Corstopitum and will fulfil many functions beyond a normal legionary base."

Gaius had already told her that larger workrooms than were usual would be installed, since Agricola wanted to ensure that his troops on his most northerly campaign lacked no necessary tools, weapons or supplies. And that the problem of overwintering under wood, rather than leather, was addressed during the proper seasons.

"I thought that the smiths already functioned in their new quarters?" She was sure they were, since she had heard the constant ring-ting as she had passed along the fort pathways close to those newly-erected buildings. The fabrication areas were huge, and many men were already hard at work.

"They are working so well that my supplies constantly need to be renewed, Ineda. As soon as batches of nails are forged, they are dispatched to be used to reinforce all the small forts at the glen mouths, which are constantly beset by annoying raids."

The smile told her that Gaius felt his exhaustion well-rewarded.

"You arrange everything so well, Gaius. I am sure that you must have that problem solved?" She knew he was a competent organiser.

His stare was serious. "I may organise well, but I cannot ever be sure that all of my requisitions will reach Pinnata Castra. Another convoy of base metals was attacked two days ago. Those marauding Venicones, and southern Taexali, are too adept at foiling my deliveries. By Jupiter! I do not know how they can be so successful at interception. I do not know yet who their informant is, but I am determined to find out. And I tell you now, that I am closer to that discovery than ever before."

171

Heat creeping into her cheeks had to be suppressed as she gathered her baby son closer to her face, his keening cry hopefully disguising her dismay. Trying to appear normal, she focused on why she had interrupted Gaius.

"You need to rest some time soon, but till then, eat the food brought for you."

Slinking away, she resolved to be more cautious for a while.

Over the next days, the workload that Gaius undertook only got more extensive, the problems of transporting the supplies hampered by some of the barely-laid-down roads becoming quagmires. The weather was poor, though fewer raids had happened to the convoys. However, Agricola's ambitions remained constant. He was determined to push his troops further and further north, though he himself was presently back in Eboracum till the spring thaws. No new forts on the north-eastern line were being established during the winter weather, but Gaius' supplies base had to continue to run efficiently, and manufacture the necessary tools and equipment for the campaign restart come Imbolc.

Ineda had to be so careful passing on any information since their arrival at Pinnata Castra. Gaius seemed to have become wary of everyone, and spent most of his days away from her presence. Only Dubv, who was still his pride and joy, got some of his attention, the child often playing around Gaius' command tent. Saying he worked elsewhere to avoid the cries of the new baby was an excuse. Gaius was avoiding her.

The time had long passed after little Uallas' birth for her to be an active lover again, but Gaius had not made any advances to her, though he still shared his tented quarters with her. It was highly unlikely any other woman had captured his attention, since there were few of them around the fort. She fretted that he might somehow have found out about her being a messenger, yet that was dubious, since her contact had not made an appearance for many moons. That also meant she had sent no word of anything for a long time.

Her general situation had worsened too. It was easily noted by those close by that Gaius paid her little note, and

Pomponius had no time for her at all. If Gaius wanted her apprised of anything, Pomponius sent one of his underlings to convey the message. The soldiers and traders she regularly dealt with on Gaius' behalf were often openly leering, the taunting comments about them becoming her lover she ignored.

There was no one she could trust at all at Pinnata Castra.

It seemed quite appropriate that she had named her second son Uallas – meaning foreigner. He was definitely a foreign entity to his father.

Chapter Sixteen

AD 83 A Half-moon After Beltane –
Great Sea Loch, Taexali Territory

"This is definitely the one!" Esk tossed his spear into the rack at the doorway and bounded towards the fireside.

"We have heard those words so many times, Esk, what makes you so sure?" Brennus loved Esk's zeal, but there had been so many disappointments.

Nith was a few steps behind his brother. "More than one hamlet has word of a Caledon who is calling for Celts of the north to rally together, and take a stand against Rome."

"And where will this Caledon be found?"

Lorcan sounded as sceptical as Brennus felt, though if the information proved true then he would lead a rousing celebration. It had been difficult of late to make his songs and music joyful and encouraging. He had searched in vain for so long, for this elusive man Tuathal had predicted would take a stand against Rome.

Esk ripped off a piece of bannock from Nara, his voice muffled. "We will need to travel for some days to reach him. Nith and I have heard this man named as the swordsman in three different places we have visited. "

Creigh, the host and chieftain of the small roundhouse village on the shores of the great sea loch by the eastern sea, beckoned the lad forward who stood guard at the door. "Is there someone to give us more information?"

Esk pulled the beaker from his lips. "Aye! A lad waits outside. He has further news."

Reaching into the neck of his tunic, Brennus pulled forth his wooden ocarina and began to play a soft melody. It was a tune of hope and promise, a pleasant entertainment designed to put joy into the hearts of those clustered around the small fireside, as they waited for the lad to be seated.

The news was promising, the most promising for a long while. The man called the swordsman was a Caledon leader at some distance from the fireside Brennus presently sat around, but the tale was that he had already gathered many men to halt the influx of Roman soldiers in nearby territory.

"This man is a Caledon and not of the Taexali? Are you certain of this?" Creigh's snapped question made the lad squirm.

"He is not Taexali. I heard that his own hillfort is about four days trek from here, but his territory would not be suitable for a battleground. He names a rallying point near the hilltop of the mother's peak."

"Why would he name this place, and not somewhere else?"

"The mother's peak already has an old Celtic hillfort on it, and the peak is easily visible when coming from any direction." The boy was clearly repeating what he had been told, his speech hesitant.

"Why would that be important?" Brennus had an idea of the man's intent, but wanted to hear what the boy had to say.

"When the Romans hear the Caledons are mustering, they will march up from the south, from around these parts."

"Well done, lad. You have remembered your information very well. Who instructed you like this?" Lorcan wanted to know.

"The warrior came from Feugh."

Brennus turned to Creigh. "Is Feugh of the Taexali, or the Caledons?"

His host's smile was broad. "Taexali, but he is a border chieftain. His lands are near the pass of Ganachy. If anyone would know about the dealings of the Caledons, then he would. His word is good."

Another visitor entered. More news. Brennus' chain of communication was still working well. Warriors of the southern Caledons were involved in more raids on Roman convoys. It did not do much to expel the flood of Roman soldiers from the lands of the Venicones, but it showed there was still resistance against Roman domination. Good news which made the evening a merrier one.

Two dawns later, they were on the move once more. The journey was again not going to be easy. To reach the place named as the gathering of the swordsman's followers, they would have to traverse another line of signal towers that Agricola had recently built in Taexali lands.

It was only a short while later, as they were cresting a hill, when Kaideigh called out to them. A few paces ahead, her keen sight had noted something way down on the flat valley. "The walls of a fort are built already!"

"Will Agricola never stop?" Nara gathered her children around her.

AD 83 Two Moons After Beltane – Pinnata Castra, Venicones Territory

"Dubv. I am only going to ride out a little distance and meet up with the next convoy of wagons."

Gaius had not spent much time at all with his elder son in recent days, being always too busy. He had barely talked to Ineda either, his mind constantly preoccupied with all the details he needed to sort out. He could not afford any further mistakes, not after the humiliation at An Dun where so many legionaries had been slaughtered.

"I have not ridden with you for a long time." Dubv's plea was a cross between petulance and wistfulness.

"Dubv can ride with me," Pomponius said, reaching for the boy's shoulder.

Pomponius was always at the ready to accommodate Dubv, had spent much more time lately with the boy at his heels than Gaius had. A fine father he was, ignoring his son when others took up all the reins. Looking down the crestfallen little face, Gaius supposed he could take Dubv with him, since he was only going a short ride away.

"You may come with me but you will have to be very well behaved when I am busy, Dubv. Will you be able to manage that?"

The smile on his son's face made him both squirm and be highly proud to be his father. He clearly did not delight his son often enough, for he rarely saw such adoration from Dubv.

The day was fine and warm. A light breeze blew across the open ground, whipping up the seeds from grass and dandelion flowers, as he rode on with Dubv in front. The guard he had with him numbered a *contubernium* of mounted men, some in front and some behind.

Riding downhill to the river crossing was a pleasant change. He had not been outside the fort walls for quite a while, too occupied with his never-ending duties. In truth, he did not really need to go and meet the convoy, but he needed some exercise and loved a fast ride.

"Hold on tight to the mane now, Dubv. We are going to ride quickly."

The riders in front picked up speed. Gaius urged his horse onwards, a dust cloud rising up around the horse's flanks. A roadway had been cleared, but since it was only beaten earth, the dry weather had made it a powdered surface. A pleasant change, certainly, from the muddy quagmire it often was. He was happy to put up with a little dust.

They galloped hard across the flat valley floor where the river meandered, the water twinkling and sparkling in the sun before seeming to disappear when it curved behind the woods. The road cut a swathe through the woodland before coming out again at the riverside. If the message he had had was correct, the convoy was likely to be close to the far end of the woods, if it had left the nearest fort soon after day break as was planned.

"I love being with you, *Pater!*" Dubv's squeaky little voice giggled back to him as they slowed down to canter through the swathe cut between the trees.

The whirl of the first spear hitting the exposed leg of the rider in front was the first sign of danger.

"Attack!"

The second was the hail of spears that followed, all of them finding a mark on either a soldier, or horse, as a large band of Celtic warriors burst out from the trees alongside the road.

"Aieee!!" Pomponius' cry at his side was ear-piercing before the man slumped forward, a second tip having gone right through his secretary's throat.

Even more Celtic warriors erupted from the woods.

"Get Dubv to safety!" Gaius managed to shout to one of his guards, before a spear propelled both him and Dubv off the horse, the rein yanking through his limp fingers.

"Dubv!" Gaius' cry was cut short when he thumped face down on the ground.

***

"What is happening?"

Ineda's cry rang out over the general clamour that rang around the fort. Soldiers rushed hither and thither, responding to the calls from centurion and decurion alike. She had never seen this kind of flurry before. No one stopped to answer her. Something unexpected was happening that set the soldiers close by into such a whirl of activity.

"Dubv!"

Her son was nowhere to be seen.

"Tell me what is going on?"

A soldier speeding past called an answer. "The signal post has given warning. Local warriors have attacked nearby."

No Celtic tribes had ever attempted an assault so near the fortress since they had arrived. Ineda had never been in such a situation before, and had absolutely no idea what to do. Gaius had left early that morning to ride south, his intention to meet and escort a shipment of crucial supplies coming up from the fort at Bertha.

Clutching her younger son tight to her body, she ran in the direction of the western tower. She had no intention of leaving the safety of the walls, but the guard post might give the answers she needed.

"Where does the enemy approach from?" The words stuck in her throat. The enemy as she had just named them were Celts as she was, but Gaius, the father of her sons, was out there and in danger.

The guard on the tower barely spared her a glance before answering, his gaze trained to the west. "I see no sign of them yet, but the signal came from the glen west of here."

Rushing back to the *principia*, she called out constantly for Dubv. Her son loved to be around the soldiers; he was generally watched over by Pomponius, if not with Gaius.

She changed her plea as she approached Gaius' office. "Pomponius? Where are you?"

A junior assistant erupted from the room, his explanation hurried as he pushed past her at the doorway. "Pomponius went forth with Tribune Valerius earlier this morning."

"My son?" Ineda was frantic. Pomponius had earlier said he would make sure Dubv was well-occupied.

The assistant looked askance before he answered. "I am certain your son went with Tribune Valerius and Pomponius."

A trumpeted alarm call sent the man scurrying away.

Ineda drew huge breaths, and tried to focus her mind on what to do. The Roman garrisons and forts she had inhabited had never been under attack before, but they had never been so undermanned either.

Agricola's insistence in driving forward during his northern campaign had come at a price. The troops who manned the series of small fortlets around Pinnata Castra were worn thin, and the fort itself was seriously short-handed.

"Take care!"

She needed no urging, as she ran from the corner post holding tight to her baby. There was a rush of movement, auxiliaries forming together in tight rows and clusters. Some were still checking their breastplate strapping was secure, or their helmets, or other equipment whilst on the run to their mustering place – mainly those who had not been on duty.

The *intervallum*, which was usually deserted, became a heaving mass as a fully-armed half-*cohort* assembled. Warnings rang out from those who manned the corner towers. The gates opened, and the first wave of soldiers passed through the entrance and poured out onto the plain outside.

While Ineda ran to Gaius' quarters, she realised the auxiliaries were not defending Pinnata Castra, as more and more lines marched out to engage with the enemy. Were they going out to attack? But that did not make sense when she was being urged to take cover. She still called for Dubv, but no one answered. No one she passed by had seen him.

The sun was well set when the sound of a *cornu* was heard at the gates. Heralding the arrival of Roman troops, the doors of the fort opened.

"Gaius?"

Ineda ran from the wall she had been propped against when she heard the creaking of the wooden doors, having sat there for ages – waiting.

At the head of the column which entered was a figure she had not expected to see. She had thought Agricola to be further north with his advance forces. He glanced her way from atop his horse, his expression furious, and then he blatantly ignored her. Riding in after Agricola were the most senior officers who accompanied him on campaign.

Gaius was not amongst them.

Frantically watching for Gaius and her son to appear, serried lines of still relatively tidy soldiers were followed by bedraggled, bloodied ones. And following them were corpses, which were being carted inside. A small bloodied arm dangled from one of the wagons.

"Dubv?" Ineda's wail was only surpassed by the noise of Uallas when the baby picked up on her distress. As she rushed towards the cart, the decoration on the breastplate of one of the other corpses brought forth another keening howl.

Gaius could not be dead as well! That was not possible. Frantically willing it not to be so, she ran alongside the wagons till they came to a halt in the *intervallum*, in a place which would allow even more soldiers to enter the fortress.

The hands tugging at her elbow she tried to fend off, before she realised it was Gaius' junior assistant. "Come, Ineda. You can do nothing for them now."

"I want to hold my son!"

The young man took Uallas from her, realising she would not be dissuaded. Another clerk from Gaius' office held her back by the elbows while the dead were lifted from the wagons, and laid down in rows, according to rank. The number slain seemed to be a huge number.

"Gaius!"

His body was taken to prime position in the ranking. Dubv was then placed in Gaius' arms.

Blinding tears dripped as Ineda cradled her son and her lover, the father of her children. The talk around her barely impinged on her grief as more troops entered the fort than had left. At first she vaguely heard the assistant's questions, barely absorbed the answers, while she shuddered her grief on her lost ones, till one answer drew her attention.

"Tribune Valerius and his men were ambushed between the signal posts. They were seriously outnumbered, and the supplies we have been desperately waiting for have been pillaged and removed."

Ineda railed at the man in disgust. "The supplies concern you more than the dead who lie scattered at my feet? Your tribune and his son have been almost hacked to pieces, and you mention precious supplies?"

Three days later Ineda had no inkling of what she should do. Even though torrential rain had fallen incessantly for hour after hour, Gaius had been burned and feasted to the otherworld as befitted a soldier of his rank. She had managed to get help to bury Dubv separately, since she would not have him cremated in Roman style, though no-one had even attempted to suggest that the son of Tribune Valerius be added to the pyre with Gaius. The relationship between Gaius and Dubv was not officially acknowledged by anyone around her; least of all by Agricola. She had had to stand at the back of the rows when Gaius' funeral pyre had been lit, since no invitation had come for her to attend the ceremony.

Her reason for being in Pinnata Castra no longer existed. She had heard that Agricola bemoaned the fact that Gaius was lost to Rome, though the man did not deign to send words of condolences to her. In his eyes, she was no more than Gaius' slave.

181

Gaius' junior assistant, one of the few who spoke to her during those difficult days, told her that Gaius had fought valiantly to the end and that Dubv had been one of the first to die, the spear attack so swift that her son had had no warning. That was not really all that much of a solace as she mourned their passing.

Many Caledons had converged on Gaius' *contubernium*, the attack on them a successful one. The Celtic war band had then gone on to attack the convoy which Gaius had ridden out to meet. Having escaped with the goods, the Caledon warriors in turn were attacked by Agricola's forces, he having had sufficient advance notice to deploy enough soldiers to ensure a Celtic massacre. Gaius had not known that Agricola had been heading towards Ardoch; the message to tell him had arrived after he had ridden out that fateful morning.

That Gaius' presence would be missed Ineda did not doubt, though Agricola would find a replacement with ease. It was the way of the Roman war machine. There was always a trained one to step into the shoes of someone newly-dead, or if sent back to Rome.

The death of Pomponius caused barely a blink of an eye.

Though Ineda had not really liked the man, he had been an invaluable aide to Gaius. His passing should have been fêted as well, but as an underling, it was not.

"I look forward to assisting Tribune Crassus. He is an ambitious soldier." The man speaking had been a junior aide to Gaius. "He will be arriving from An Dun sometime in the next few days."

Only a mere three days, and Gaius was all but forgotten. The Roman way was to pick up the threads of the work tasks, and move on.

Gaius' quarters would no longer be available to her; the new tribune would take up residence on his arrival. She had been Gaius's slave, but she had no intentions of waiting around to find out if she had been awarded any manumission. And she would die rather than be forced into being the slave woman of any other Roman soldier.

It was as well that there was a good deal of traffic through the fort doors, since Agricola being in residence meant a lot of to-ing and fro-ing. She could take little with her, but her baby had priority. Blessing the goddess Brigantia that she had managed to keep up a good store of herbs, she prepared a draught that would keep Uallas quiet.

Chapter Seventeen

*AD 83 Two Moons After Beltane –
Near Pinnata Castra, Venicones Territory*

"Halt!"

Awakening with a sickening dread of being discovered, Ineda's body came to rest with a resounding thump on the side board. The cart, having lurched violently, had sent her on a swift slide under the cloth coverings that lay loose on the flatbed of the vehicle. She bit down on her tongue to keep silent as she flinched away the agony at her shoulder and neck, squashed as she now was in an awkward position, since there had been nothing on the wooden-planked flat bed to stop her progress.

She thanked her goddess Brigantia that Uallas was still sound asleep, but that must also mean the soldiers could not have travelled very far. She had tried to remain awake after clearing the fort gates, but the trundling of the cart, the whole sleepless terror of what to do after Gaius' death, and the grief she felt for her loss, had taken a toll on her. Though she felt she could not have dozed for long.

"The front wheel is stuck fast in this infernal red muck!" Curses came next, almost right at her ear, the soldier now so close he must surely hear her terrified breathing. Willing herself to calm, she worked out what to do if they should need to unhitch the mule and cart, to make a repair.

"Back up the beast! That will perhaps get it out of this soggy rut."

The sounds of clicking teeth and the flicking of a leather whip came next. Unable to see from under the cover, Ineda's hearing seemed frighteningly acute. She dare not lift the edge even a little, because the soldier who cursed violently was

184

walking around the cart, the squelching of his sandal-shod feet making sucking noises in the muck.

She had been unable to see how many soldiers accompanied the cart, but suspected it would only be a few, if the usual routine applied. Her contact, a slave of the cooks who prepared the meals for the garrison officers, had told her that the cart would be journeying at dawn to go to a nearby roundhouse village. Another vexillation of auxiliary soldiers was due to arrive at Pinnata Castra. More soldiers meant more oats were needed for the common soldier's fare of porridge, and stocks were being requisitioned from the local farmers.

Reminded of how it had been when she had been living at Witton, she feared for the local tribespeople during the coming winter. Many supplies had been removed from the local Taexali after the harvest festival of Lughnasadh, and now even more was being acquired from them. It mattered not a whit to the Romans if the local populace starved – if the Roman Empire needed some item, they took it. The good thing for her was that a cart had to leave the fort to go and fetch the grain. The worst thing had been to hide herself on the cart during the night dark, terrified that she would be discovered.

The jingling of the harness indicated the men were unhitching the mule. A near-silent wriggle got her body straight, her arms aching from holding her baby so close. Next she would try to roll, so that if needed she could be on her knees quickly.

The whoosh of a hurtling spear was followed by an agonised cry as the weapon cracked against flesh and bone.

"Aieee!"

Germanic curses deafened before a second cry gurgled from someone. From the jostling and thump of a body slumping against the cart, she guessed it had to be the one walking around the cart and not the one who seemed to still be riding it. Other sounds of scuffling, of spears hitting their mark and more frantic sounds signalled the panic of the seated Roman. The cart swayed wildly, Ineda imagining the man's fear as he jumped off, his scuttling feet pelting away from near her head. The terrified mule harrumphed and thrashed in its traces, sending Ineda on a second slide, though the impact was not enough to upend the flat-bedded vehicle, nor to free the wheel from the rut.

"*Marbhaich gun duine dhiubh a chaomhnadh!*"

Ineda understood the fierce Celtic cry. 'Kill down to the last man' seemed to be exactly what was happening, the clamour around the cart indicating a relentless attack.

More noise told her all of the soldiers had to be dead, the whooping and hollering seeming to come from a number of local warriors.

The whipping away of the covers saved her the anguish of wondering how to reveal herself, though her appearance was clearly not what the warrior expected to see under the mound that was her curled-up body. Uallas held tight in at her chest, she peered up into the brightness of the day, her eyes unable at first to make out the man's features.

"Colm! You should take a little look here." The warrior continued to stare at her, unmoving. Not threatening, but not friendly either.

Warriors clustered around the wagon as she scrambled to her knees. The five she could see were a fierce-looking band. Not all of them resembled the huge the red-haired warriors that Gaius had mentioned when referring to the Caledons, but at least two of them were as tall and powerful as Bran had been, their hair more of a mahogany red hue.

One of them eventually spoke. "Who are you?" He spoke slowly, as though not expecting her to understand his tongue.

"I am Ineda. I have been slave to Tribune Gaius Livanus Valerius of the *Legio XX*. Your people killed him a few days ago during the raid south of Pinnata Castra. I hoped to escape the clutches of the Roman Empire, but did not plan for it to be this way." Though scared, Ineda wanted there to be no confusion over who she was.

Her Brigante Celtic language, not so different from the local one, flowed over the men as she explained how long she had been slave to Gaius and where she had originally come from. They listened to her, though many of them stared at the Celt who lay prostrate on the ground.

186

"Standing looking at that will not help your fellow-warrior!" she admonished.

Ineda could barely credit how ten men, all well–grown, could just stand and stare at a bent *pilum*, one of the warriors not having fared as well as his companions during the ambush. The man lay face-down but was still conscious, rough swearing and low moans coming from gritted teeth. A Roman spear had pierced his upper back, the shaft having bent on impact. Celtic spears were not designed to bend; therefore it was clearly a novelty to view.

"Let me get closer to him," she ordered, while she carefully unwrapped a top layer of cloth from around her son. Once the material was free, she flapped it in the air with one hand. "His wound needs to be bound."

The warriors were sceptical of her talents, but then she was a complete stranger.

"Use this, if you will not allow me to tend to him!" She thrust her cloth at the man who appeared to lead the band.

The silence that greeted her gesture was telling. They had clearly not expected her to aid the wounded man. Or perhaps it was because she was taking charge of the situation.

"You believe you can help him?" The leader still sounded wary.

"I am well qualified as a healer, and can do much more than bind a simple wound." There was some blood flowing free down the warrior's tunic, but not enough to indicate a really deep cut.

"If you will allow me to help him, I will trust my son to you!"

She thrust a still-sleeping Uallas at one of the young warriors, who accepted the baby without thinking or complaining.

She pointed her finger at two of the warriors who stood the closest to the man lying prone on the ground. "Hold his shoulders tight against the grass!"

It took little effort to remove the spear head, and stop the bleeding with the folded pad of cloth. Urging the man to sit up, she used her bratt to wrap the pad tightly in place. It was a

187

temporary binding, but would get the warrior home, and had been done with more diligence, she believed, than any of his companions would have managed.

"This will need proper cleaning when the warrior returns to where you have come from, but the damage is only minor," she instructed as she retrieved Uallas from the soldier who had been cradling him.

A nod from the one who seemed to be the leader acknowledged her suggestion before he began more questioning.

"Nay. I am not from anywhere near here. If you have heard of the lands of the Brigantes, well south of the Selgovae, then that is where I come from."

Doubt was a common expression. It was right that they should be suspicious of her, and she expected no less.

"Why were you attempting to escape from the Roman fort?"

"That tale is a long one, but I would rather be at a greater distance from Roman eyes when I tell you."

Though she could see no obvious signs of them, the Romans at the nearest signal post would be monitoring the area. The attack had taken place in a sheltered copse, but the wagon would have been tracked on open land earlier. If the mule and wagon were not seen soon, an alarm would be raised, the countryside being generally flat for long stretches.

"Where were you heading?"

Ineda's curt laugh made her son stir, a feeble cry indicating his displeasure and discomfort. "I have no answer, except to say I had to leave the fort or risk being killed, or worse than that, used as a whore. I have never been a whore, and will die rather than become one."

Her vehemence made a few eyes blink, including the one who next spoke. "You do not know this part of Venicones territory?"

Again her sarcasm broke free, as did some measure of relief. These warriors could easily kill her, yet their curiosity seemed to indicate that would not happen. "The only Venicones territory I know of are those tiny bits where the

188

Roman scum have planted their forts. I was not brought into the Venicones territory at my behest. I have been the hearth slave of a Roman tribune for many, many seasons, and have had no say at all over what I did with my life."

"Put her on my horse!"

The command came from the warrior who seemed to be in charge.

The ride to their small settlement did not take long, the warriors knowing good ways to ride to avoid being seen by the Roman look-out posts up on the small hills, and hillocks, that dotted the land between sea and the glen mouths of the Caledon Mountains.

Her welcome was hesitant, suspicion still being rife, and when her tale was told she waited for a verdict to be placed upon her. She had left out nothing, but whether she would be believed was another matter entirely.

The chief had listened, only interrupting occasionally for more clarification.

"How can you prove your tale?"

Ineda had thought about that question, but could only say that she had had no outside contact save the slave of the cooks.

"Who is this slave's contact on the outside?"

She did not know. "It would have been death for the man if he had become known. I only passed on messages to my own contact. The message then went down the chain, possibly passed through a number of mouths."

Till her words could be proved, or disproved, she was sheltered in the roundhouse of an older woman. Still a prisoner, but a happier one.

Come the morning's dawn, the village was rife with rumours and panic. Her own plight became secondary to what was likely to occur to the people around her. Retaliation for the attack on the convoy was brutal – ordered by Agricola. It did not matter to the Romans that the nearest village to Pinnata Castra was not responsible. The *gladius* had flashed, and the village had been destroyed. Anger surged around her, every warrior irate at the gall of the Roman army, but there was also fear. A great deal of fear. No nearby hamlet, or village, was safe.

"I am heading north to the settlement of my sister." The woman who had given shelter to Ineda was wrapping up some meagre supplies in a spare old bratt, her children doing likewise in other spare cloth, as she pointed hither and thither. Ineda had already learned the evening before that the woman had no hearth-husband to rely on. Even if he had been alive, most of the villagers were desperate to flee the area as soon as possible, most heading into the mountains. "Come with me if you wish. My sister will give us all safe harbour."

"How far will you travel?" Ineda's question was not an idle one. She knew well how far Roman troops marched in one day. Pinnata Castra was the main base hereabouts, but it would be routine for the *Praefectus Castrorum* to order centuries of infantry to maraud in all directions in retaliation. Wherever she went, she wanted to be as far from Pinnata Castra as possible.

"It is a long day's walk, but if we have to avoid Roman patrols it may take longer." The poor woman looked terrified.

Their night out in the open was an uncomfortable one, but at least it was summer, and the warmth of the day lingered long enough to keep her baby warm at her breast.

AD 83 Almost Samhain – Balbithan, Taexali Territory

"I see it!"

"That has to be the mother's tip! It must be." Beathan was as excited as Kaideigh who jumped up and down alongside him, pointing and squealing.

When Brennus crested the rise of the hill, a few paces behind the children, he could see it well in the distance, proud against the skyline. Halting at the top of what had been a long gradual incline, he took in the view spread before him. There was little doubt that what lay ahead was the place they had come to find.

Below him was a gently-rolling valley floor, very low hills blocking what lay behind, but with many flatter areas below the gradual slopes. In the distance was a hill range, the highest peak quite distinctive with a darker ring visible around the summit. Beinn na Ciche. It did resemble a mother's breast, the nipple jutting high into the sky.

The day was a beautiful one, even though it was well past the harvest season with only a few days to go to before the feast of Samhain. It was nipping cold, but there was no wind to bother them, and a clear blue sky blazed above them.

"We need to keep the hilltop in view as we go down through the valley." Lorcan reminded them of the last instructions they had been given at the hillfort near the Obar Dheathain, where two rivers ran close to each other before flowing out to sea.

"Aye. It is still a fair step away, but we may reach the meeting place in two days." Brennus was hopeful it would not be any longer than that.

There was no hurry. There had been no sign of Roman presence since well south of Obar Dheathain.

His plan was to head first for the hillfort of Balbithan.

Beathan gathered up the little ones like a shepherd tending his flock, and steered them eastwards along the spine of the rise where they stood admiring the view. The boy was dependable, just like his father, Lorcan. Once told, Beathan did not easily forget an instruction.

"We'll be at the river soon Kaideigh, if we go this way." Beathan's voice rang firm and confident. "You might even find that we can do some stone-stepping across the water. They told us back at Obar Dheathain that the river is narrow and shallow in parts."

"We have been told to keep to the southern bank, Beathan," Nara mildly chastised.

"I know, but the little ones can play a while in the water, if we keep up well."

"My son knows what he is doing." Lorcan's laughter was picked up by the adults.

Brennus shared a smile with his brother. "Aye. He is good with his little sisters and Kaideigh. He is a caring and mindful lad."

Before they got anywhere near the hillfort of Balbithan, they were stopped at a bend in the river. It was clear from the ten-strong warrior band who confronted them that the chief, Balbithan, was alert to movement on his territory.

"Nay! The Romans have not encamped on my lands, but patrols have been seen not so far hence." Balbithan growled across the fire from where Brennus was seated. The welcome they had received had been fine, even if the man was gruff in sound and expression. Balbithan's dismay at housing such a large group was quelled easily when Brennus explained they could use their leather shelters.

"Nay! Nay!" Balbithan blustered. "Your families will need to split up to share our roundhouses, but we will get you all under a roof."

"It seemed to me that you had been warned of our arrival." Brennus' words were polite, but he wanted to know just how effective passing of messages was between the tribespeople of the Taexali.

The loud snort and continued cackle from the chief was answer enough. "I have my men at all the main passes. They intercepted a messenger from Obar Dheathain who was on my land well before you were. It seems you follow instructions well, Brennus. The messenger, however, knows of many shorter routes to Balbithan. What he failed to say was that there were so many of you."

They celebrated the festival of Samhain with Balbithan's tribespeople, Brennus helping to entertain, and then they remained another half-moon after that, the time well spent in learning the countryside around them. Lorcan had been surprised to learn that the eastern coast was only a day's walk away – on a summer day, though, and not always on a winter one.

"We are taking Beathan with us, Nara, though Gabrond has agreed to remain here." Lorcan accepted the drink from Balbithan's hearth-wife.

Balbithan gulped from his cup, and then belched before he spoke. "My best scout will accompany you, although any of my warriors could take you to the shores."

Nara cuddled her youngest son but looked at her daughters and Kaideigh. "You like it here, do you not Kaideigh?"

Brennus felt his daughter launch herself at his side, taking him aback. She was never a needy child. Her words, as usual, surprised him. "I have made three new friends already. Do I have to go with you? Even though I do love to play on the sand." The last words were more reflective than the earlier ones.

"Nay. You do not have to come with us. We will only be gone a few days."

Nara looked just a little wistful, as though she would like to journey with them. "You are heading directly to the sandy shores?"

He watched Lorcan slip his arm around her shoulders. "We will cut across country by the most direct route to the nearest shoreline, but it will do no harm for us to journey along the sands. Balbithan tells us the white sands stretch south to Obar Dheathain, and northwards for a walk of many days."

"We need to see for ourselves how easy it would be for the Roman fleet to come to shore." Brennus was not confident that the fleet had not already landed, but no word had reached Balbithan, even though his contact with Taexali neighbours was good.

The following day, the sight of the sea stretching before him was overwhelming. Brennus looked all around him, turning full round. He was on the last hillock a short walk from the sea. The weather was crisp and biting cold, but the sky was blue, clear to the farthest extent of the glistening, rippling water.

Beathan was astounded. "Such empty water and no land in sight..."

Lorcan was less impressed by the prospect. "So many landing places. Brennus. The Roman fleet could land anywhere along that coastline."

Their guide chuckled. "It seems that way from here, but it is not so. In some of the areas the water is rarely still and would be a hazard. From here the beach looks like a narrow strip, but that deceives; the water can be a good walk from the tilled land. The marram grasses and sand dunes may be very deep in between."

Brennus felt the chill from more than the biting cold at his nose. "The Roman fleet are skilled on the water, Lorcan. They could land those huge ships which can hold an auxiliary *cohort* on those stretches of sand."

Mheadhain, the chief of the village at Baile Mheadhain, had disturbing news. "Aye. We have had sightings of small vessels close to shore since Samhain. The last time they did not beach the boats, but turned and went south again. They made good observations, perhaps for a choice of landing place to be made later."

"That is assuredly how Agricola works." He wished he could console the chief that the Roman fleet had made their survey, and would not return.

"They must have come from some shelter that was not too far afield, since the last sighting was late in the day, well after the sun was high in the sky. The darkness would have fallen too soon for a long row, because the day was almost windless." Mheadhain could tell them no more about the ships, his knowledge of the Roman fleet limited. "I suppose a smaller vessel could come close enough to shore to disgorge its crew and perhaps some cargo, but it might not be so easy to offload the horses you speak of. My guess would be that they would be disembarked near Obar Dheathain, or much further north at the place where the Ythan river meanders into the sea."

Brennus was inclined to disagree. "The *liburnae*, the smaller vessels that are favoured by Agricola, are flat-bottomed and are designed to beach easily. They are very resourceful boats used for ferrying men, goods and beasts. Someone told me they are the most commonly-used ships for transporting their mounted *cohorts* around our shores."

Lorcan's head nodded in his usual pondering fashion. "Balbithan heard that the walls of a new fort were being built at a place less than three days' walk to the south of Obar Dheathain. Could vessels of the Roman fleet already be berthed somewhere near that fort, on the nearby coast?"

194

The chief paused before he answered. "The coastline south of Obar Dheathain is not sandy for a long way like you see here. High cliffs and bluffs make access difficult, but there are some bays where they could land their vessels. There are some steep cliffs in places and low hills near the coastline. I doubt the Romans would consider the land close to the shore suitable for fort-building, though the hills would be good places for a signal tower. I would think that any fort would need to be built in the long valley, near fresh water, but a few of those beaches would only take a walk of a half-winter day."

"Are there many rivers going down to the sea at this coastline you speak of?"

The chief shook his head and pursed his lips. "Not a large flow like at Obar Dheathain. I do not know them all, but I have one woman here who comes from a clan nearby."

While they waited for the woman to come, Brennus learned all the knowledge that the chief had of Roman *exploratores* patrols in the area. That news was not good, but it did not surprise either. On fair days, Agricola's scouts were out scouring the countryside, adhering to his aim to continue to move northwards, regardless of the season. Mheadhain confirmed the patrols had not been near his area of the coastline, but he had been told they made many forays around the forest of Durris, south west of Obar Dheathain.

"There is talk of the Roman infiltrators at all the local firesides. Exactly what is true, I cannot say."

Lorcan grumbled across the fireside. "We will accept it as true, Mheadhain. If the Roman scouts are not there yet, then it is likely they will be soon."

Brennus tested the strength of Mheadhain's feelings. "If the Roman fleet landed on your shores, would you make a stand against them?"

The chief hid his fear well. "We would, but I can summon no more than fifty warriors to my cause, Brennus. Though we dwell near the sea, it is our farming skills which keep us fed. There are not so many of us to confront the hundreds of Romans you speak of."

195

"Would you rally to the swordsman's aid, if he names a meeting place?"

"All of my able warriors, myself included, would hie to his side." Mheadhain was adamant on that. The door flap being slipped aside warned of a new arrival. "Mhariidh! Come. We have some questions for you."

Brennus was pleased to see that the woman was eager to help with her answers. She confirmed that someone of her kin had warned of a new fort being built in the area she had come from, south of Obar Dheathain, and described the area for them.

"There is one large river that spills out into the sea near the huge sea loch."

Beathan could not remain silent. "I have never seen a sea loch. Can you explain this to me?"

Her smile was apologetic. "We name it thus, though the water is not fully contained by land. There is a narrow passage which leads out to the wide sea. We call it a sea loch since the water is salt like the sea."

"And this river which leads into the sea loch is a wide one?"

"In places it is wide on the flatter valley floor, but mostly it is a narrow river and easily fordable in many places."

Brennus turned to the chief. "The Roman Army chooses well where to place a fort, because they must have water for thousands of men, and animals. A whole legion numbers close to five thousand, and that is a lot of water. Though some of the forts we saw on our journey would only hold a few thousand men, when all are behind the palisade."

Lorcan thanked the woman. "Your information has been helpful. It seems to me that some vessels of the Roman fleet may be overwintering at this sea loch, or if not there, not much further south. A fleet berthed off the shores of the Brigantes could not travel anything like as far north as here in winter days. Agricola would not want his men to perish in the squally storms that winter brings."

Chapter Eighteen

AD 83 After Samhain – Tullos, Taexali Territory

"You entertained us well, Brennus. You will all be very welcome again." Balbithan clapped him heartily across the shoulders.

"Can the swordsman count on your support?" Lorcan was confirming the Taexali leader's loyalty.

Brennus knew his brother was not as convinced of it as he was.

"He can," Balbithan confirmed. "On that you have my word. And if any Roman should set foot on my territory, you will hear about it as soon as my own people do. I will not forget where to send the message."

Once again they set off, this time following the river upstream. At times, the drumlin of hills named Beinn na Cìche and The Mither Tap itself loomed closer, at others they disappeared behind small hillocks as the river meandered. It was not long before they came to the confluence of two rivers where they took the larger of the two, the Dheathain, still following the main river towards The Mither Tap. Wide sweeping curves were followed. And similarly to what happened previously, near Balbithan, a large group of armed warriors came into sight, forming a long barrier across the untilled flatland.

"You must be Brennus of Garrigill, a man of many stories?" The call rang out loud and clear.

"That I am!"

"What took you so long? We expected you all long ago."

Following the warrior line, they rounded the copse and trudged after them.

"I see the roundhouses!"

Kaideigh's shout was heartening. It had not been such a long trek since leaving Balbithan, but the daylight was already waning, the days short after Samhain.

Kaideigh was correct about seeing roundhouses, their smoke streaming into the air, but there were not so many of them. What lay in front of them was a large village rather than a settlement.

Tullos, the local chief, came out to greet them. Brennus felt his heart plummet. The warrior was old. Could this be the man he sought who would rally many Celts? He could not believe this was the man he had been relentlessly looking for, when the old voice bid them welcome.

More disappointment was to come.

The swordsman had been and gone.

"Calgach has had the pledge of all us around here, though we are Taexali and not Caledon. When the cloak of winter has been well shed, he will give word of our gathering place." Though old, Tullos' conviction seemed very strong.

"How can I find this man named Calgach? I wish to speak with him before this mustering you speak of."

"I can have guides take you to his hillfort, but I suspect he will not winter there. His intention is to travel the mountain areas to rally all to him when he stands against Rome. For that to happen, he must prepare them during the winter season."

Lorcan interrupted. "Will this man return here after the festival of Imbolc?"

The old chief laughed heartily. "Nay! I can see you have not experienced enough of our long winters. It is more likely to be after Beltane before we have word of him, or see him, but that will depend on what kind of spring thaws that we experience. We have many moons to winter before then, and Agricola will remain in his southern winter quarters as well."

Brennus disliked the idea of another long wait before confronting the Roman foe, yet knew that winter was not the time for clashing swords.

Tullos beckoned to the group. "Come. Your group will have to squeeze into many small spaces, but we will find shelter for you. The coming night will be a cold one, my nose

198

tell me so! We will all do well to be before a warm fire by then."

A frosted ground was of no use to anyone, yet Brennus felt he had to impress upon the chief that Agricola may not wait for the spring thaws before marching further north. "Only the very worst of weather will halt the progress of the Roman Army, Tullos. They will march even in snow. These men are extremely hardy: all they need is to get that first spade-worth of soil excavated."

"Tell me more of these soldiers which I have yet to set eyes on." Tullos led them to his own roundhouse dwelling.

Long talks went on over the ensuing days with Tullos, and a few of the other nearby Taexali chiefs who came at his behest.

Brennus was walking around the horse enclosure with Lorcan a se'nnight later.

"Do you want to spend the winter here, or go on into the mountains, even if we do not find Calgach at his hillfort?" he asked. Lorcan's old foot injury had been troublesome of late, and Brennus worried about his brother's fitness.

The morning had dawned to display a deep hoar frost on the bushes and trees. It was very crisp and beautifully white, but not good conditions for travel, and definitely not for being outside at night. The days were at their shortest, the winter solstice not long to come. Brennus itched to meet Calgach, but did not wish to drag his whole family with him. "If you would look after Kaideigh, I propose to take Esk and Nith with me to at least try to locate the swordsman, and find out if this really is the man who will lead the Celtic tribes. We have had our hopes raised and then have been disappointed before now."

"Aye! That you have. I, too, would like the man's dedication confirmed. Gabrond and I can remain to look after Kaideigh and the others, but you should also take Beathan. The boy needs to be toughened up even more before battle rings around this flatland."

A firm shoulder clasp confirmed their pledge, and the love the brothers bore for each other. "You can be assured that I will look after your son!"

Lorcan clapped him again, a deep rumble of laughter lightening the seriousness of the moment. "Let it not be that my son looks after you, but that you all look out for each other."

Brennus' answering grin sealed the pledge. "That we will."

Lorcan looked around him at the space within the fortifications of the village, and pointed to a vacant space. "Depending on how long you travel, we should have a home for you to properly shelter under when you return. Tullos gives us that space to build a roundhouse, or two."

Brennus contemplated the area as well. "Aye! He told me so, as well. The old man is a generous spirit."

Again Lorcan's snort of laughter lightened the parting. "More like that the old man likes the look of my wife."

Brennus remembered how it had been with Callan and Lleia, and told his brother the full story, Lorcan seemingly appreciating it well, having known the irascible old Callan.

"Callan was ever a wily old goat! Nonetheless, my brother, I feel it in my bones that it will be good to settle here. " Lorcan's grin continued to be encouraging. "Nara can easily handle Tullos, I have no fear of that. It also fares well that Tullos has promised men to help build for our group, as soon as the weather makes it possible."

AD 84 After Imbolc – Balbithan, Taexali Territory

"Will we see Balbithan soon?" Ineda's question broke the silence.

She trudged up the long gradual incline, near the head of the snaking group of people. With five others like herself, all displaced people, she journeyed north – three of them adults and two older children. The day was bitter cold, a light wind at the summit whipping up the edges of her bratt, the cool draught of air seeping into her backbone and sending chills all the way through her. It did little to encourage her to keep moving, but she had been told they would reach the settlement of Balbithan within a half-day. The days were lengthening, though daylight hours were still limited, it being only a se'nnight after the festival of Imbolc. It had been well after daybreak when they had left the last village, and she feared they would not reach the shelter they sought before the darkness fell.

The guide answered when he stopped at the crest of the hill. "Stand alongside and follow where I point."

Ineda slid next to the lad. Though extremely cold, the sky was a clear blue well into the distance. Taranis was favouring them.

Beautiful.

It was a fine sight to behold the valley that spread below. Gentle undulations broke up the landscape, the view clear all the way to a rise of hilltops straight ahead. To her left, far in the distance, were much higher white peaks, the snow cover extensive.

The lad pointed to those far hills first. "The mountains of the Caledons lie there, but they are many days' walk away in winter."

Ineda looked to the peaks ahead. "And there?"

"That is Beinn na Ciche. The Mither Tap is the most prominent peak."

Ineda suppressed a groan but had to ask. "Is that where we are heading?"

"Nay!" The lad's laughter gurgled. "Balbithan is not nearly so far."

"Oh, look! I can see smoke rising way over there." One of the children almost jumped with glee, as she pointed to the thin column of smoke rising above a deep clutch of trees, not too far to Ineda's left.

"Balbithan!" The other child joined in the shout.

"Nay!" Her guide corrected the assumption. "That is only a hamlet over by Skene water."

Ineda's gaze followed as his arm swung to the right in an eastwards direction, till it settled, pointing to a heavily-forested area.

"Beyond that wood lies Balbithan. You cannot see it from here, but the river from Obar Dheathain runs through those trees."

There were some columns of smoke rising from there as well, and though it would still take a while, it was cheering to see their destination.

She slid into motion behind the guide as he started down the hill. "Have you heard of these Brigantes who are said to dwell at Balbithan?"

"Aye! Most folk hereabouts have heard tell of the one who sings and plays so well. I was not at our settlement when he visited, but he proved very entertaining, or so the tale goes."

Singing and playing? Ineda could not help but think of Bran. It had been some time since she had thought of the man she had given her love to so long ago. Bran had been such a fine entertainer. He had been so fine in many other ways too, but she could not let herself dwell on that. Why she felt the need to find the Brigantes made her pause for thought. She decided it must just be a yearning for her origins, yet something more seemed to drive her onwards.

Uallas' whimpers broke the spell. Adjusting him in the sling she wore around her body, she guided his mouth to her nipple. He now needed more than just her mother's milk, but it would have to do till they took rest.

Since her escape from Pinnata Castra she had walked and walked, and had then walked some more. She was always moving north to put herself at a greater distance from the Roman Empire's soldiers who seemed to dog her footsteps, though she was only one of many Celts who were fleeing. Agricola was definitely intent on placing his foot on all of Britannia's soil.

She had spent time at many different villages and hamlets on her journey north from the Pinnata Castra area. The first village she had headed to after her escape had not been a good choice, since the Roman *Classis* had landed at the shoreline nearby, though Rhona, the woman she had accompanied, had no way of knowing that when they had set out.

The woman had been distraught to learn that her sister's village had been abandoned, the people having fled northwards to escape the Roman ire. A simple woman, Rhona had no idea what to do. Ineda had had to work extremely hard

202

to persuade her new companion to keep moving on northwards to safety.

During those moons before Samhain, they had changed direction across the countryside numerous times. They had encountered many fleeing people; most of whom declared they were heading for the mountains when more Roman signal towers had appeared all the way up the long flattish valley floor.

Only in the mountains, the fleeing tribespeople claimed, would they be safe from the hundreds of Roman soldiers who were flooding the flatlands between the mountains and the eastern sea.

Most had run, rather than confront the Romans sword–on–sword.

It was when she had been at Obar Dheathain that she had learned of a band of Brigantes who had travelled northwards. People from her homeland also so far from their origins? Not for the first time, she regretted what had happened to her. If she had not been taken captive by Gaius, then perhaps she would also have fled Brigantia when all hope of defeating the Roman Empire was lost.

The first winter snows had fallen at Obar Dheathain, making it impossible for her to travel. She had had to bide her time, but was desperate to find her fellow tribespeople, even though she was always given hospitality at the villages which still had people dwelling in them.

She gave thanks to the goddess Rhianna, and to her grandmother, many times during those moons of flight. It was her healing skills which made her a valuable temporary guest. In many of the places she had stopped at, there was no herb wife or healer. They had gone to the mountains with some of their kinfolk.

Her quest was now to find these Brigantes she had heard about.

AD 84 Beltane – Creag An Eunan, West of Beinn Na Ciche, Caledon Territory

"There are many possible peaks with suitable foothills around these parts for engaging in battle, Brennus, but any past combat that I have been involved in has not needed the amount of space we will require for an engagement with our Roman enemy."

Brennus had no difficulty agreeing with the swordsman. His time at Whorl was relived all too easily, especially so as he had shared the details of it with Calgach, and the other Caledon chiefs who had congregated.

"You do not deem this peak, Creag An Eunan, which we stand on just now, as a suitable battleground?" Brennus looked down hill to the view below. It was not one he would have chosen. There were too many undulating hills for him to feel confident that a battle waged there would be successful.

"Nay. The forests are too thick behind us, and these hillsides too steep. We need more space all around the foot of the hill for our chariots, horsemen and spearmen. Though fear not. That is not why I brought you here. Look at that hill to the south. It has suitable lower slopes and flat plains at the foot, almost the full way around it."

Something was recognisable about the mountain cap, but Brennus could not be sure. Nonetheless, he risked a rebuke for his lack of knowledge of the surroundings. "It has a look of Beinn na Cìche about it, yet it looks different."

Raucous laughter rang around. "The Mither Tap it is. Her milk comes from a different sightline than from the village of Tullos."

"Then Mither Tap is definitely where your warriors will congregate?"

Calgach's head nodded avidly, the fervour in his gaze pronounced. "It is. Come high summer, the foothills will be speckled with encampments of warring Caledons and Taexali, and many of the Vacomagi. They have also pledged to stand alongside my men in battle, as have many fleeing tribespeople from southern tribes who have sought safety in our mountains. They, too, vow to stand against Rome."

"Has this place on the foothills of Beinn na Cìche, the Mither Tap, been in your thoughts for some time?"

Calgach's expression was cynical. "Not so long. This kind of decision does not happen overnight. I have had to discuss long and hard with many of the tribal leaders of the north, since word of Agricola's legions reaching Damnonii and Venicones lands. Many chiefs have put forward possible places for the battle, from the first glen openings on southern Caledon territory. For varied reasons, we rejected the other sites, especially since the forces of Agricola march northwards so swiftly; more speedily than anyone anticipated. What point is there in mustering for battle on land they have already overrun? When they settle on land, little except total annihilation will remove their presence. We have to meet them at a place they are newly arrived to."

Brennus could empathise with that; he knew too well how swift the Roman foot was over Celtic soil. Calgach continued to speak, making it unnecessary for him to work out how to answer without seeming pessimistic.

"More importantly, our place of battle has to be able to be reached by all warriors within days, and that can not be in our Caledon Mountains. The battlegrounds must be closer to the flat plains between mountain and sea. We could plan to be in a place that would confront any new seaborne troops, but that would not solve the problem of the thousands already on the land."

The campfire was a place of introspection that dark evening, Brennus' songs and music playing low and wistful. Just before they bedded down for sleep, news arrived from the coast. Agricola's fleet had landed in many places just south of Obar Dheathain, and soldiers were terrorising the few tribespeople who had remained in their villages and hamlets. Sightings of more ships sailing northwards had been detected. The couriers did not yet know where they would land, but Brennus had a good idea, having visited the coastal villages. The morrow would no doubt bring news of new atrocities near the coast.

It was time to return to Tullos' dwellings and to his family. The time for battle was not yet ripe, but the latest news brought the confrontation closer.

AD 84 Two Moons After Beltane – Balbithan, Taexali Territory

"Bring him in here and lay him down carefully!"

Ineda's cry alerted the older woman who had been her host since arriving at Balbithan. Uallas had fallen sick soon after her arrival at the roundhouse hillfort, and had lain for days in deep fever which set Ineda into a dreadful panic. She had feared her skills would not be great enough to save her own baby, but along with old Marsali's help, they had pulled him through.

It had been a major disappointment that the Brigantes she sought were long gone, but with Uallas so ill, she would have been unable to follow them anyway.

"Is he much hurt?" Marsali freed a space on the cot by lifting the napping Uallas into her arms. Taking the child nearer the fire, she placed him down on a pile of furs.

"It could have been much worse," said one of the young warriors who carried the unconscious man. "We were only just within spear range of the Roman patrol."

Marsali fetched a bowl of warm water from the fireside hot stone. "How many of our Balbithan warriors are wounded?"

"Not so many. Perhaps five men who need more tending, but they are at their own hearthsides. This warrior has no family here at Balbithan, and is one of the recent arrivals from the south."

"Hold his shoulders," Ineda instructed the warriors, having inspected the wound. The bent *pilum* had been partially removed, though part of the spear tip was still embedded in the young man's upper chest.

While Ineda removed the metal and cleansed the wound, she learned of the confrontation.

"A large group, perhaps almost a hundred, of Roman soldiers were near the loch of Skene. We were mounted, had been patrolling the surrounding area, and had just cleared the nearby woods when one of our youngest warriors gave a cry of surprise. A first sight of the forces of Agricola is an

206

alarming prospect. Their arms were raised almost immediately, and a hail of spears came at us."

The other man who had helped carry the injured warrior added some detail. "We numbered only ten. How were we to win against such a huge number?"

Ineda sympathised with their plight. "They are a formidable fighting force. You did the correct thing in returning to Balbithan. He needed to know the Roman Army is now so close." She had no real idea of where the Skene loch lay, but had learned how vigilant Balbithan was. His warriors combed the countryside every day, always alert for such events.

Later that evening, Balbithan gathered his tribespeople outside his roundhouse so that all could join in - young and old. "We can wait to see where this Roman scourge will encamp next. Alternatively, we can leave this hillfort and join the numbers who plan to gather below Beinn na Cìche, at The Mither Tap. I know what I want to do, my people, but what I want and what I do must be prudent for our future."

Grumbles and moans circled around the gathering. It seemed that none of them wanted to leave their homes.

"What will happen if we do remain here and the Roman Army encamps nearby?"

Balbithan turned to Ineda. "You have the most experience of these Romans. What do you think they will do, Ineda of the Brigantes?"

Ineda had already shared most of her knowledge with Balbithan, but not all with his whole tribe. He looked to have her alert his people to the life of the yoke that would befall them. She chose her words carefully, but put all of her heart into her warning.

"The Roman way is to arrive at your roundhouses in their huge numbers, fully-armoured and menacing. Force will be used till you capitulate to their dictates, or you will perish under the brutally-sharp *gladius*. They will break your will, and will demand their share of your food stocks. They will commandeer your animals for their own use. They will make you toil in your own fields, and extract the yield for their own

207

use after the harvesting. Your choices will be yours no longer – the Roman Empire will make them for you!"

A clamour grew around Balbithan, since the prospect was horrific, but Ineda knew that the people needed to be aware of how limited their choice really was. After a while he calmed the gathering, and drew the questions to a close. "I have no wish to leave my home. I have no wish to turn tail and run. Equally, I have no wish to engage in battle with this whole Roman legion on my own."

Someone at the rear of the circle called out, "But we can muster more than a hundred warriors!"

"Well said." Balbithan was wise enough not to scorn. "I am certain I could rally as many as a couple of hundred male and female warriors from the surrounding area. Do you believe that would be sufficient, Ineda?"

Again Ineda acknowledged just how Balbithan was using her to placate his people. "Nay! It would not be. What was seen today would have been only a *century* of Romans. They will be forward scouts, laying the best road for the legion which will follow behind them. Those seen today will have been clearing a pathway wide enough for Agricola's troops to follow. Pack animals and baggage wagons need space – the flatter the path the better. Those advance troops fell trees and shrubs when necessary, to ensure the most effective pathway is created across the landscape."

She knew that Balbithan had been warned by the Brigantes who had visited, and others who had arrived from the south (those fleeing from Roman domination). Her information was not entirely new; she merely reinforced what had gone before.

"Balbithan!" The warrior's horse had been ridden hard, evident in the lathering across its flanks as the rider hauled it to a stop, not far from the chief at their outside gathering.

"What news?" Balbithan was beside the warrior immediately.

"Thousands of them have now passed the Skene water and are heading this way."

Ineda shouted over the hubble-bubble of panic. "Before nightfall, Agricola's forces will have set up camp. By then, they will have constructed their overnight ditch defences. They will choose a place where there is plenty of wood." She looked down the hill to the opposite side of the river where there were plenty of small woods. "They also need a lot of water for four thousand men."

It seemed all eyes swivelled to view the river Dheathain below the hillfort walls. Ineda had no personal allegiance to Balbithan, save that he had been a generous host to her and her little son, but she was loathe to remain if Rome descended on the hillfort come the morrow. Old Marsali had also been welcoming, and she would not leave her to a Roman fate, either.

Horror ensued. The clamour of terrified voices rang around the area.

Balbithan's cries were rousing, despite the horrendous situation his people were in. "What say you, people of Balbithan? Do we stay and confront this Roman legion of more than four thousand skilled soldiers? Or do you wish that we leave now, to congregate with the other tribespeople at The Mither Tap, where we can fight this scourge along with thousands of other Celts?"

"Leave now!" Many voices shouted the same thing.

Terrified people were bawling it out as they ran off to collect whatever belongings they could manage to take with them.

The sun was already well past its hottest time of the day, though dusk would not happen for a long time, it being close to the Summer Solstice when daylight was longest. There was plenty of time for the people of Balbithan to walk to The Mither Tap – provided they did not tarry.

Few chose to remain at Balbithan's hillfort, most wanting to fight the Roman scourge, though not alone.

Chapter Nineteen

AD 84 One Moon Before Lughnasad –
Tullos, Taexali Territory

"You have two to choose from, brother!" Lorcan greeted Brennus home with a hearty back-slap before his arm extended to point to the newly-constructed roundhouses.

"Tullos has done you proud." Brennus walked around the new dwellings, appreciating their construction.

"Ay, indeed. He is a generous chief. We have been enjoying a real welcome here, my brother. As you will receive, too, if you linger for long enough."

"*Athair*!" Kaideigh launched herself into his arms, having been told of his arrival. Her greeting was followed by those of Nara and the rest of the Garrigill clan.

"How quickly you grow, my little chicken!" Brennus declared as he hugged his daughter. General laughter and comments followed his teasing. He had never grown tired of naming her thus, though her protests were less as she grew older.

"Come, inside," Nara urged. "We need your update immediately."

"Tullos must know first, Nara." Brennus softened his words with a still slightly lopsided smile.

Nara looked abashed. "Forgive my presumption, Brennus. You are so correct. I sometimes forget who is in charge."

Brennus could see living under the auspices of another had not come easily for Nara and Lorcan, so used had they been to making the decisions.

Tullos had his own sources of information, as was expected, but was pleased with Brennus' news. "My small settlement will not accommodate all the warriors who will congregate in these parts, but we will do our best. Not only do you return, Brennus, but I have just been informed that people flee from the settlement of Balbithan. The tribespeople are dispersing themselves amongst the hillforts, hereabouts. I expect some to arrive before nightfall."

"This news I have not yet heard. Does this mean the Roman threat comes nearer?"

Lorcan's face distorted. "Agricola's whole legion is expected to encamp somewhere near Balbithan. They were a striking distance away at high sun today, and you know their methods. Balbithan has a fine water source from the Dheathain River, and he has woods a-plenty around his settlement."

Having given all of his news, Brennus allowed himself to be dragged back to the new roundhouses, Kaideigh tugging on his hand. "I sleep in the dwelling of Nara and Lorcan, but I have also been invited to stay by Gabrond. Please will you share Nara's home with me?"

"Will I be invited, my daughter?" Brennus knew the answer, but asked anyway.

Kaideigh looked shocked that it could be anything but so.

Nara took pity on his little daughter. "Show your father the stall we have already allotted to him, Kaideigh. The one you chose yourself for him, when the building of the roundhouse was underway."

Again, the tugging on his hand prompted him to move. "So, I was expected?"

Lorcan's laugh was good to hear. "Oh, aye indeed. Wait till you see where you will sleep, my brother. Your daughter is so admiring of your erstwhile champion status, and deemed it must be you to guard the dwelling!"

"What? Kaideigh? Am I given a stall outside the roundhouse?"

"Nay!" Her laughter was bright. "You have been given the very best place by the entryway. Lorcan says it has to be the biggest and strongest warrior who sleeps there. Only the largest will guard it, and fill the doorway first if attack happens."

Kaideigh now excelled at repeating what an adult had said, her words delivered with such belief.

"It could be that, my chicken. Or mayhap it is the most unwise who sleeps there!"

Later that evening, Tullos sent warning of the arrival of the fleeing people from Balbithan.

***

"Marsali? That smoke from beyond the wood must be coming from Tullos' roundhouses." Ineda really did not know, but since they had seen no other signs of habitation, she guessed it must be so.

Marsali's head rose from her preoccupation with where to place her feet. The going was not rough; it was merely that the old woman could manage little more than a shuffle. "I have never been here before, but surely the location must be near. Would it matter to you if this is another roundhouse settlement?"

Ineda had not the heart to disappoint her old friend, for such had Marsali become in a short time. She would prefer to have reached the place where she heard the Brigantes had headed for after leaving Balbithan some moons ago, but for the coming night any hearth would be a welcome place. Uallas was not really a heavy baby, but trekking with him strapped to her body was so wearying.

Some Balbithan tribespeople had passed them a while ago, but they were intending to head further north, claiming that following the Urie River was their preferred location. They had pointed Ineda in the direction of Tullos' hillfort, and she had prayed to the goddess Rhianna that she had listened well enough. Dusk was already well fallen, and seeing any pitfalls was becoming a trial.

"Any place to rest our bones will be well received by me, Marsali."

The sight of the spirals of smoke spurred Marsali on. Well before the settlement, they were intercepted by guards and led on to the roundhouse of the chief.

"Your tramp towards my hillfort has been monitored for some time, but now that you have reached me you are most welcome to my hearth." Tullos' friendly greeting was a balm to Ineda's tired spirit.

Ineda introduced herself, as did Marsali, who had distant kin in common with some of Tullos' people. Bidden to sit at the hearth, food was quickly produced to revive them while Tullos told them that he had expected their arrival.

"Some of the Balbithan people are already given shelter in our roundhouses, but since the darkness has already descended we do not expect any more this night."

After some general questions about other Balbithan refugees, Tullos remarked on Ineda's speech being slightly different from the local one. On being apprised that she had come from afar, and was of the Brigante tribe, Tullos' old laughter rang around the roundhouse. "My fame must be spreading well. You are not the only Brigantes to gain succour here. I already have three Brigante families who have sought refuge."

Though exhausted, Ineda found she was desperate to hear about people of her own tribe.

"Times have been extremely hard for Lorcan and Nara and their family, but I believe they are happy to settle here." Tullos' grey-haired head nodded.

Lorcan and Nara? The two names used together had to be of significance! Ineda's tiredness vanished. "Lorcan and Nara from the hillfort of Garrigill?"

"Aye!" Tullos' chuckle was heartening...and showed a large degree of surprise. "Do you know these people?"

Ineda shook her head. Her blood was pumping a fierce rate, since these people would be bound to have known Bran. "Nay, I do not know them but I used to know someone who grew up at the hillfort of Garrigill. His name was Bran."

Disappointment flushed through her when Tullos' lips pursed and his head shook. "There is nobody named Bran, but I am certain they will be pleased to talk to a fellow Brigante come the morrow. We have had no gathering planned for this evening, as many of my warriors need a long night's rest –

that is those I have not sent to guard us. We have no intention of being set upon unawares by the *Ceigean Ròmanach*. My warriors are spending whole days patrolling my lands, scouting for Roman presence. It is not a time for festivities, but if it had been you might have heard the fine singing voice of one of the Brigantes. He is a large warrior, well used to injuries of battle, but he can play his flute like the finest finch and he chants a fine story."

A fine voice? Bran had such a fine voice, and the mention of battle scars set her to dwelling on the past. Memories of Bran filled her tired thoughts.

"Go now with Insch. He will take you to a hearth that will accommodate you, but Marsali must remain here for now."

Marsali had slumped on her low stool and was already fast asleep, a chunk of bread still gripped in her curled fist.

Sleep came almost immediately to Ineda after she was shown a hearth space, and a makeshift straw bed made for Uallas. It was unfortunate that it did not last long. Her son's cries of distress woke her as a faint pre-dawn's dark-blue filtered through the entryway of the roundhouse. Lifting her son up before he awoke her hosts, she stumbled outside. Shushing Uallas to sleep again, she wandered around, barely acknowledging the sentries posted all around the small hillfort, yet glad to know they were alert at their posts.

Near the entrance gates, she stopped to rearrange the bratt in which her son lay close to her chest.

"Unable to sleep?"

The guard up on the sentry platform alongside the entrance gates was barely discernible, the darkness deepened by the wooden walls. All she could tell was that he was tall, since he towered over the fort palisade, his upper torso backlit by the low rising sun. If an attack was imminent, he was of a height that would need to crouch if on patrol.

Ineda almost laughed aloud at the wrongness of the man's question. "After the slow trek from Balbithan yesterday, I could sleep for a very long time. But my baby has other ideas."

"You were Tullos' latest arrival?"

214

She moved closer, just under the voice before she answered. "Aye! Well after dusk had fallen, but my companion from Balbithan is wearied. Her old bones could not trail any faster, so we were well behind the others."

The warrior moved slightly and stared down at her.

Her heart lurched. She had to be seeing things. The sight of the figure above made her sway on her feet. It could not be Bran, yet the warrior above her resembled him so much, at least what she remembered of him. Tears filled her eyes as confusion flooded. As she stared, the warrior leapt down from the platform and landed unevenly in front of her.

"Ineda? Am I dreaming you again?"

"It is you!"

Brennus reached forward to envelop her in a hug, but leapt back when he remembered the sleeping baby.

Ineda's lovely eyes were tear-filled; the trickling down her cheeks a twinkle in the faint light around them. "Bran? Tullos told me that none of the Garrigill people went by the name of Bran. I do not understand."

Instead of answering, Brennus called softly to the nearest guard. "I need to be relieved from duty. Can you summon another to take my place for a while?"

Brennus listened as the message passed along from guard to guard. While he waited for a replacement, he drew Ineda by the elbow to a place where the faint moonlight shone a little brighter.

"I never thought to see you again, Ineda. It has been such an age since you were set upon." Though the dimness still veiled much of her detail, she looked well and …just as beautiful as he remembered her.

Ineda just stared.

Had he changed so much since she had last seen him? It took a good few moments before the smile that he used to love wreathed her face, her lips still quivering.

"I may not understand why you are here, but I am glad, so glad to see you alive." Her lovely voice had not changed much either.

Brennus felt the inner peace wash over him, the feeling of great contentment that Ineda always brought to him. He had not appreciated it for what it was all those seasons ago.

"Is there a problem, Brennus?" asked the guard who joined them at the gates.

"Nay!" Brennus felt the laughter bubble up inside him. "This is a really old friend of mine, newly-arrived late last night. We have not talked for a long time. I need a few moments to speak with her, then I will return to my sentry tasks."

A brief nod was all that was necessary, and the young guard leapt up on to the platform.

He watched the question flare in Ineda's expressive eyes, her smile almost as mischievous as it ever was. "You now name yourself Brennus. That is why Tullos told me no Bran of the Brigantes was living here."

Taking Ineda's elbow, he towed her out of earshot of the other guards at the wall. "I am Brennus. I have always been Brennus."

Ineda's eyebrows furrowed. Her lips puckered in that irresistible way he remembered, her head-shakes denying his words. "You were Bran of Garrigill."

A faint cry as the baby stirred made him remember her child. A sudden lurch inside his chest was unsettling, his blood raced. Was his god Taranis playing unfair with him again? Was he to be reunited to Ineda, to find that she had a loved hearth-husband she had given a baby to? He needed answers, but not presently.

"Ineda? We need to talk, but it will have to wait till my guard duty is over."

Arranging to meet later, he made his farewell and then sprang back up onto the platform to free his young replacement. He was set to guard till the sun was well in the sky, but that would give him plenty of time to mull over his instant reaction to seeing Ineda again – time to think and praise his god, if no Roman patrols were spotted. She still engendered that excited feeling inside, that feeling he had, many moons ago, belatedly called love.

216

Guard duty was generally a time which he had no hesitation over, but irritability and impatience settled upon him. He could not wait to see Ineda again, and discover all the things that had happened to her, since they had last been on that cart together.

"Lorcan!"

He bent to gain entry into the roundhouse, almost tripping in his haste.

"Brennus? What ails you?" Nara came forward her concern evident. "Are the Romans within sight?"

He sought to still her flight towards the doorway, realising that Kaideigh and Nara's brood must be outside, yet felt the excitement rise in him. "Nay! No Romans, but news I have difficulty believing. Ineda is alive. I saw her here early this morning."

Nara halted and gently touched his arm. A different concern was now showing on her expressive face. "I met her briefly, too."

He did not like her dull, worried tone. Could she not see it was a momentous time for him being re-united with Ineda? "Can you not be glad for me?"

Nara's eyes filled with silent tears. "She carries a Roman baby around in her arms, Brennus."

Dread replaced excitement.

"Roman?"

He did not want to contemplate the implications of that.

Nara steered him to the doorway, then seemed to think more on that since she turned him back again and propelled him down onto a low stool. "Ineda is now at Tullos' roundhouse, along with Lorcan and other elders. They are worried she may have been sent here by the very Romans who threaten us now. They are questioning her loyalties; to work out if she has been sent to gather information."

He sprang up and strode around, the idea making anger boil into heavy pacing. "Ineda is no infiltrator. She would never send information back to the Roman Empire. I am sure of it. She was so set on doing the opposite, working for the cause of Venutius and our fellow-Celts."

"That was some time ago, Brennus. You have no idea what has gone on in between."

"No. I do not, but I aim to find out now. Ineda will not lie to me!"

Chapter Twenty

"There was force involved in the first coupling?" Tullos' question was softened by a flicker of sympathy in his old eyes.

Ineda answered as truthfully as she could. "I was given no choice, but Gaius Livanus Valerius ensured he did not hurt me." Ashamed, Ineda could not look the chief in the eye. Looking towards the doorway she realised who had just entered, having heard the footsteps. A cold flush washed over her.

Bran! He had just heard of her shameful past, yet there was more to come.

Confusion flooded her insides. She had no idea who the man really was. She knew him as Bran, but others around her named him Brennus.

"And afterwards?"

Drawing her focus back to Tullos, she concentrated on his next questions. "Nay."

"You were his slave to do as he bid in all things?"

"I was."

An elder who sat alongside Tullos put his question to her, though this man showed none of Tullos' sympathy. "Did this Roman beat you?"

"Nay! In all the seasons I was his slave woman, he never beat me, though I know that certainly was done to others."

More queries rattled out at her. Why did the Roman scum capture her?

She was so conscious of the man she called Bran as he stepped closer to the fireside. "I can answer that one for you," he said.

219

His declaration was so certain, he drew the interest of the whole company.

"Brennus? You can personally relate this story? You know this woman?" Tullos was a man whose expressions were open and, at present, he was all amazement.

"I was with Ineda, travelling to the Roman fort at Nidd, when the *contubernium* of Romans attacked us. Ineda is the woman I have already mentioned to you. It was her grandmother, Meaghan, who healed me after the battles at Whorl. Ineda is the woman who sought out information alongside me to send to King Venutius of the Brigantes. Together, we set up trade with the Roman forts to glean useful information. Ineda had her own contacts she sent information to, as did I."

Nods of assent bobbed around the hearthside.

"You did tell us some of this information, Brennus, but not the full account of the attack." Tullos continued. "Tell us now what happened."

Ineda felt Bran's one-eyed gaze fall upon her. There was a twinkle of memory there for her alone before he spoke: a memory that came rushing back to give her a flush of embarrassment. Bran's first ever kiss! And the only proper one she had had from him.

"Ineda and I were unaware the patrol was on the other side of the hedge. I had slowed the horse down to…discuss… something with her, when the soldiers erupted through a gap. They dragged Ineda from our cart, and clubbed me from behind. I fell upon the horse and then blacked out for a time. The Roman scum had tied my hands behind my back, and were beating me when I heard Ineda's screams. I could not save her."

"What happened then, Ineda?" Tullos again sounded sympathetic.

"Gaius Livanus Valerius stopped his men before they raped me. They had beaten me, but not violated me."

Lorcan, who had been sitting silently, seemed stern as his question came next. "This Roman was the one who violated you, instead of his men?"

Ineda shook her head. "Nay. Not immediately."

Bran's angry shout echoed around. "Was this Roman you name Gaius the tribune who arrived to find out what was amiss? I saw the anger on his face when he heard your screams. Was he angry that his men were attempting what he should have had first?"

Ineda had to swallow hard before she could speak. The mood inside the roundhouse was angry now, and she could not detect if they were livid with her. "Nay! Tribune Valerius was the one who stopped his men. He took me back to his tented camp where his *militis* – his junior soldier – tended to my wounds and bruises."

Tullos' look quelled the angry mood. "This tribune did not violate you on the day of the attack, but he did later?"

Ineda nodded. "Yes, but not till after more than a whole moon had passed. Though I must be honest with you all. It was not a violation. I did not welcome it, but neither did he rape me." She could not face Bran as heat flooded her cheeks.

"So this tribune was kind to you?" Lorcan's interest was difficult to interpret. His probing may possibly have been laced with concern, but he was so serious she could not tell.

It was hard to keep derision from her voice when memories of that time surfaced. "For more than a moon I was his prisoner – at first in his tent, and then in a small room at the fort of Viroconium Cornoviorum. He never beat me, but he did force me to eat. He would not allow me to starve myself to death."

Tullos was extremely concerned. "You tried to bring death upon yourself?"

Ineda was unsure of what to answer. "At times, I was really despondent. I missed Bran so much. I was alone. I wanted my freedom so desperately, but could not escape" Daring a glance in Bran's direction, she was warmed through and through by his intent stare.

"You attempted this?" Lorcan, again, was grave in his questioning.

"Aye! My attempts were unsuccessful. With four thousand Roman soldiers around you, escape is not a simple matter."

221

More searching questions followed, where she divulged details of her life as Gaius' woman slave. She then told them about making contact with the Celts outside the fortresses she had been kept in.

Lorcan was impressed. "You managed to send details of Tribune Valerius' movement during the Roman campaign in northern Brigante territory?"

"What I could, whenever I could, but it was not a simple matter. Establishing the chain of messengers was much more difficult than when I was at Witton with Bran."

Bran's smile had more than just admiration in it when she looked towards him. It was not the best time to ask his feelings on the matters of her abduction, but she would make a point of asking later.

Bran was now the questioner. "You were the one who sent along messages from the fortress of Deva?" Having asked his question, he added more information for the assembled crowd. "We knew the information came from one who was connected very closely with the highest authorities at Deva, but we did not know who the person was."

She nodded to Bran and then explained to Tullos, "Deva was where I established my message link. It was after my son was born I made contact though Orchil, the herbs wife who lived outside the fortress walls."

Lorcan appeared confused. "Your son is only a few moons old, Ineda."

"I had another first-born son but…he was killed." Preventing some silent tears from dripping was not possible.

It took a while to relate her whole tale, by which time her insides had been turned out.

"So you were my contact at Deva?" Bran's admiration shone as he praised her efforts to the whole company. His continual focus on her was penetrating, and yet embarrassing at the same time. Intensity in his gaze warmed her all the way through, so much she could barely wait till they were alone.

Tullos brought the questions to a close. "Your life as a Roman has not been all bad, Ineda, but neither has it been good to be separated so long from your culture. Soon, we will hear more from you that I am sure will be of use to us, but for now, you must understand that until we establish your true allegiances, we must ask you to quit the roundhouse. Those assembled need to discuss the latest news from Calgach, but without your presence."

"Leave now, Ineda. We will speak again later." Lorcan of Garrigill was so stern.

Ineda swallowed her pride and made her way from the hearth. She knew a discussion after the questioning was the usual practice if anyone was under any suspicion, but she feared the result. Afraid that they might think she should have done better at escaping, her legs were weak as she stumbled out through the entrance tunnel. Fear that they would not harbour someone who had lived so long with Romans gnawed at her gut. Nausea bubbled and threatened to erupt as she made her way to the two roundhouses of the Brigante settlers. Before the meeting Uallas had been taken there, to be tended to along with all of the other Brigante children.

Now, she had to know he was safe.

"Uallas has been such a good baby," Gabrond's wife, Fionnah, said as she handed him back to her.

"My thanks to you. I could not have been questioned by Tullos and the elders in such a thorough way, if I had had Uallas fretting alongside me."

Secretly she wondered if the enquiry would have been less traumatic if she had refused to relinquish her son into the care of another, and had had him by her side. Making her farewells, she returned to Tullos' dwelling.

Ineda waited outside for Bran to emerge. She had not the courage to delay any new reunion with him. He had listened to all she had divulged, and now knew she had been the woman of a prominent Roman tribune. The silent scrutiny of her did not seem to indicate any revulsion of her, or any anger at her conduct, yet it could easily be hiding his true feelings. If there needed to be a confrontation, then she needed it to be over.

It had only taken one look, and the knowledge that he still lived, to know he was still the only man she had truly loved, though she fretted that his feelings might be entirely different.

She worried even more that he might already have a woman at his hearth who had gained his love.

Pacing around the area, she pacified Uallas in her arms.

"Ineda!"

She wheeled around at Bran's shout and watched as he approached, having just exited the chief's roundhouse.

"We need a quieter place to talk."

She did not think Bran angry, especially when his arm cradled her shoulder and propelled her between the roundhouses and out towards the animal pens. The contact set a flush to her middle; the gentle squeeze of his fingers was reassuring, though his pace was not. Was he so keen to get the talk between them over, so that he could then forget about their former partnership? Clutching Uallas tighter to her chest, the love she bore her young son was the only reliable thing in her present existence.

When Bran drew to a halt beside the horse pen, she braced herself for his rejection. Doubts were all she could think of. He could not possibly want to associate with someone who had been so close to a Roman? She could never forget that Uallas was a Roman child, but he was her much-loved baby. If Bran rejected her child, then she could never be friends with him ever again.

To be merely a friend was too tame a concept. She wanted Bran's wholehearted love and acceptance.

He turned her face on, his hands bracketing her shoulders and his full one-eyed gaze upon her.

"I am sure Tullos and his elders believe your tale, Ineda, but I need more information from you. Will you tell me the truth?"

He looked agitated, as though her answer might disappoint too much. She wanted to tell him something that would console his anxiety, but would not conceal anything. It was impossible to erase her past. Urging her nerves to be calm, she answered, "I could never lie to you, Bran. Surely you of all people know that?"

"Did you come to love this Roman tribune?"

The truth?

224

She did not quite know what the certainty of that question was. "I came to admire many of his good qualities, even though he was a Roman. After a long time, I came to like very well the man who was kind to me, and who, perhaps in his own way, loved me. But I did not love him."

"You say he kept you as his own woman, but did not allow you any other man? Did you hate him for that?"

Such a question! "I hated him for many things, for a long time, Bran. But I admired him for keeping me for him alone. It was not uncommon for an abducted female Celt to become the garrison whore. Those women did not survive long; I can assure you of that. Gaius Livanus Valerius flew in face of envy by keeping me as his private woman. There was much resentment by the men he was in daily communication with. They could not understand his motives, but he always disregarded their jealousy and admonition."

"What did you hate him for?"

"I hated that he had taken me prisoner, and that he removed all choice from me."

Bran paced around her. "Were you kept locked up all that time?"

"It is as I told Tullos and the gathering. Once he began to bed me, I had a little more choice – though never freedom."

Ignoring the baby in her arms, Bran crushed her in close. As though unable to help himself, he bent down to her and groaned into a breath-robbing kiss. It lasted only brief moments, but it was done with such fervour she could not think him angered at her. She searched his eyes for the truth in his heart.

"I can tell you more of my life with Tribune Valerius, but I cannot prove any of it."

Bran started to pace around again. His lips curled in the lopsided smile she had missed so much. "But I am sure that I can prove some of it!"

He sounded joyous, and so convinced she wanted to hug him back, but it was not yet time for such an act. She could never resurrect their joy in each other if he still harboured any doubts at all. "I do not see how you can do any more than you

225

have already done in Tullos' presence? What makes you so sure?"

"Patience. It will take time, and we must endure till proof comes to me. Some of those gathered in Tullos' dwelling still hold you under suspicion, though my gut tells me I do not. I do not know the woman you are now, though I did know the woman you used to be. Nevertheless, know this, Ineda. When we traded with the fortress at Nidd, I waited far too long to tell you of my feelings, believing you too young for me, and I wasted many nights denying that you were more than a foster-sister. I will not wait so long this time around, but first I must prove your innocence. Till then, you and I both must have faith!"

Having heard him deliver such a fervent speech, Ineda was astounded when he kissed her fiercely and then walked away, leaving her standing near the horse pens.

Any meetings with Bran during next the half-moon were bitter-sweet, since they were always in company. He ensured they never met alone, but the looks of longing that passed between them were suffused with frustration and need. It was as well that everyone was busy preparing for the arrival of yet more warriors to the area, as the numbers rallying to Calgach were huge. The warriors trained all day long and made many plans. Ineda was not made party to any of the sensitive information that caused them to declare an immediate gathering, and neither was she invited.

A sense of despair was setting in. She feared that she had re-united with Bran, yet rejection by him would be the result, and there was nothing she could do to alter the situation.

Chapter Twenty One

"Some five thousand warriors are now encamped hereabouts," Tullos declared to the huge gathering that encircled an open fire, outside the temporary encampment of Calgach.

Row upon row of warriors sat listening to the latest battle plans, the campfire set at a short distance away from crude shelters made from tree-trunk frames and bent sapling twigs which had been covered with all sorts of materials – thatch, leather, hides, and woollen bratts.

"Many more have yet to rally, even though Lughnasadh has already been celebrated," another chieftain added, having explained to the assembly that he had journeyed from the northern sea coast to join the throng. "The northern Taexali will send many more able warriors to repel Agricola. They have no wish to see his infantry forces meet up with the soldiers on the ships that have already been sighted in the estuary of *An Cuan Moireach*. Though, as far as I know, none of those soldiers on board have yet set foot on the soil of the nearby Vacomagi."

"They will ere long." Lorcan's voice rang out over the heads of those seated. "Many of Agricola's ships have already spewed out mariners who are presently terrifying all the villagers who dwell near the Taexali coastline. They focus on the areas nearest the beaches before meeting up with those who have marched northwards over the land route."

Brennus was impressed by Calgach's quelling of the tumult of questions before it got too heated. "You heard the rumours last evening that at least two legions worth of Agricola's forces were encamped near the hillfort of Balbithan, on the

227

River Dheathain. My envoys now tell me that four *cohorts* from that encampment have just established a new camp to the east of Beinn na Cìche. They have this night built their fortifications for a very large camp, a camp that will hold many fists."

"Then *Moran Dhuirn*, the camp of many fists, is what we should name it!"

A fearsome cry went up full of enthusiasm and heartfelt eagerness. Again Calgach stilled the gathering, his hand held aloft and palm open. "The time is almost here, my brothers. I have sent my couriers to rally all here within the next se'nnight. Agricola will feel the mighty force of many thousand Celtic warriors – something he has not yet encountered in our part of northern Britannia!"

The whooping and merry calling was deafening, so fired up were the assembled warriors.

One of the other chiefs, whom Brennus had briefly met, drew the attention of the throng back to listening to battle plans, his particular focus being an update on the mounted Celtic warriors and the charioteers who were currently mustering on the western side of Beinn na Cìche. Assessing such numbers was not simple.

Brennus listened to more of the planning, glad to have something more definite to occupy his mind, thoughts of Ineda tending to be all-consuming at times.

When the gathering broke up, he made his way back to Tullos' hillfort along with his brothers. Almost at Lorcan's dwelling, he heard someone call out.

"I seek Brennus of Garrigill, also known as Bran of Witton. Can someone give me his direction?"

Two mounted warriors were waiting near the entryway to the roundhouse. Still mounted was unusual, but the fact that they had gained entry to the hillfort had to be for a good reason.

Before Brennus could name himself, Lorcan intervened. "Why would you seek this man?"

"I bear news about Ineda of the Brigantes, a resident of Witton, and formerly of Marske."

Brennus rushed forward. "You have news for me? I am Brennus of Garrigill, the man you seek."

It was clear the men had been travelling for many days, the stench of horse and sweat quite overpowering. Brennus had no care of any of those details, but needed the information the men brought to him. "Tell me what you know."

Lorcan, ever the diplomat, held his sleeve as he all but dragged the men into Lorcan's roundhouse. "My brother, let us not forget our hospitality. At least allow the men something to ease their parched throats, before you tear the information from them."

In his eagerness, he almost missed Lorcan's tease.

Formalities of welcome exchanged, the couriers were given time to bathe before returning to the hearthside, where Nara extended her hospitality to them in the form of a hearty broth which had been simmering in a pot, on a hot stone at the side of the blaze.

"I can do better than that," said Arun, one of the newcomers, in answer to the inquiry about Ineda having sent messages to Venutius. "Although we never formally met, Ineda of Witton was pointed out to me. I am sure I would recognise her again, for she was such a comely female."

Brennus felt a glow spread all around his insides. Every question Lorcan, Gabrond, or he himself put to Arun and his companion, Dermatt, indicated that Ineda had indeed been the person who had sent messages from Deva, and who had established that link. The man's testimony praised her allegiance to the Celtic cause.

"Tullos must know of this information, Lorcan." Brennus did not really need to prompt his brother, since it seemed Lorcan was heading towards the door entrance anyway, his pacing having gravitated him to that area. Knowing Lorcan so well, it was typical that his brother would not make any kind of move towards Tullos till he was convinced the facts spoke truly.

A little file of people made their way to Tullos' roundhouse, where space was made for them at the hearthside, and proper introductions made.

"Naturally, I know of your arrival and your intent. Tell all now that we are all assembled." Tullos' old eyes sparkled. Brennus had learned enough of the old man to notice his keen interest.

A little while into the conversation, Arun went on to describe an attack that went wrong. "We made many attacks on convoys of metal supplies as a result of her information, she being close to the tribune who organised such things."

Brennus stopped the man, horrified at what he was hearing. "You attacked the convoy that Ineda was travelling with? Even though you knew she could be killed?"

Arun seemed only a little discomfited, his reply also snarled. "Save your venomous aggression for another, Brennus of Garrigill. I was not present at that attack. I had passed on Ineda's information about the convoy being set to pass on the road to Bremetennacum. The updated information came too late that Ineda would be accompanying the tribune. She had never travelled with him before that time. As it happened, our warriors were inept in their ambush. They were the ones who were mown down. The tribune had trebled his guard since Ineda and their son travelled with him."

Lorcan looked as though some piece of information now made sense. "Was Ineda's young son killed during this raid?"

Arun was aghast. "Not as far as I heard."

His companion, Dermatt, piped up. "No. The first son of Tribune Valerius was killed in a raid on Venicones territory. She was not with the tribune during that raid."

Brennus needed more details. "How can you be so sure of this information?"

Dermatt's voice was grave. "Ineda had no knowledge of this, since it was often a long time between her messages, but we always tracked her movements."

Arun intervened, "Well, it was not exactly Ineda's movements, you must understand, it was more that the travels of the tribune were tracked. Someone was always alert to where he journeyed to, and thus we knew where our contact, Ineda, was. At each fortress, or small fort, Ineda was often inside the walls when Tribune Valerius travelled forth."

Dermatt was quick to add more. "We, perhaps, did not know all of the man's journeying, but I would say we knew most of them. Tribune Valerius played a key role in the support of Agricola's troops during the campaigns so there was always someone who could tell us where the tribune was moving on to."

Lorcan's words were sharp. "How did you extract that information?"

Dermatt's sarcastic laugh rang out. "Agricola may have given the tribune a really high profile task to do, but he was sparing in giving the tribune skilled soldiers to work with."

"Aye! It was not so difficult to worm out information from captured *tironis* or *militis*. Tribune Valerius lost one or two of those during his journeying northwards."

Brennus was not sure if that was a comfort or not; he had already been told that Ineda had been constantly guarded by soldiers of this first and second recruit level.

"And what can you tell us of Ineda's dealings when she was in the fortresses of the Votadini, and the Venicones?"

Brennus had always been aware of Lorcan's ability to question thoroughly, but almost wished his brother would just accept what had been already confirmed regarding Ineda.

Dermatt sounded dismissive. "She managed to make contact with us a number of times when she was in Votadini territory, but the intelligence she gave us was not really news."

Arun cut in. "Not until she sent word of Agricola's plans to build the forts at the glen mouths. That was extremely important. That forewarning gave the local Venicones, and Caledon Tribes, sufficient time to organise many raids."

Brennus had heard enough, and was losing patience. "Do you now believe Ineda had been a traitor to the Celtic cause during all these seasons in captivity?"

Tullos' hand halted his tirade. "Brennus of Garrigill! Hold back your harsh words. The evidence given by these two men provides us with much to make decisions upon. I will now put it to my elders to give their opinion. Your personal feelings for this woman shine through, but you are aware of how we make decisions. Bid your tongue to remain still, now!"

Brennus felt as though his blood would burst out and spatter the roundhouse. No decision had ever seemed so important to be resolved. Local tribespeople put forward their opinions, a few asking more questions of Arun and Dermatt. Brennus blocked them out and visualised Ineda.

"Send for Ineda!" Tullos' declaration brought Brennus out of his daydream.

He could barely watch as Ineda entered the roundhouse, her insecurity evident in the hesitant smile she gave Tullos.

"Ineda. Sit by me." Tullos was once again the affable old man who welcomed strangers.

Brennus watched him gesture for Arun and Dermatt to rise to their feet. "What say you, Arun?"

Arun beam was wide, as though pleased to answer positively. "Aye, Tullos. This is definitely the same woman who was named to me as Ineda of the Brigantes, of Witton and formerly of Marske. Her beauty is not much changed since I last set eyes on her, the hues of her hair very distinctive, as is her short little chin."

Brennus watched Ineda's brows knit as she processed the man's words before turning to Tullos. "I do not know what trick this man seeks to play, but I am certain I have never met this man."

Tullos' smile accompanied a gentle pat at Ineda's arm. "Your response is as it should be. Listen now to what this man has to say."

Brennus paced the distance between the chief's dwelling and Lorcan's roundhouse, unable to remain still. The elders had declared Ineda to be no Roman spy, and then Tullos had requested all to quit his roundhouse leaving him to speak privately with Ineda. What could the old man be asking her, now? They had established her credibility, and the threat of her death as a spy was past. He wanted to barge in and haul her out of Tullos' dwelling, wanted to rush her to the first available quiet spot, and make her truly his own woman.

What was taking them so long?

Lorcan popped his head out of the roundhouse low entrance, and called to him when he strode close by.

232

"Brennus, there is no point in fretting a deeper pathway to Tullos' door entrance. Come inside, now. Your impatience is more than your daughter Kaideigh's, and I mean when she is at her very worst."

Brennus stared at his brother's expression. "You may well find this amusing, Lorcan, but you were never in this position of being clawingly-desperate for a future long denied you."

He allowed Lorcan to usher him inside, bending his head first to avoid the low entrance roof.

Once clear of the doorway, Lorcan's finger-point to an empty stool, and his exasperated expression, were so blatant that the chatter inside immediately hushed. As though a silent signal had been given – and in many ways it clearly had – Brennus watched the expressions of the children in the roundhouse, as they scampered out, probably believing that he was in trouble.

Nara's laugh rang free. "Do I need to leave to avoid your wrath, as well, Lorcan?"

Her answer was obvious to Brennus when Lorcan caught her hand, and tugged her down beside him at the fireside.

Brennus sourly noted that their hands remained clasped. And that Nara sat snugly on Lorcan's lap.

After a lingering, and loving, look exchanged with Nara, Lorcan eventually answered the question Brennus had asked outside.

"Nay, Brennus, I was not denied my desired future for as long as you have been, but I do remember what it was like to dread that Nara was soon to be hand-fasted, to another man."

Brennus plonked himself down on the stool next to them. In spite of his agitation, a grin was spreading. "Ha! You were so well-favoured when I did the honourable thing, and let you be Nara's Beltane lover."

"And for that, I have always been immensely grateful. You know that, Brennus. I have no idea what Tullos still needs to ask Ineda, but you must think positively."

A rustle at the doorway had Brennus leaping back up to his feet. Ineda rushed inside and launched herself at him. Her arms wrapped around his neck, her grin infectious. "One day,

Bran. We need only to wait one more day, for our hand-fasting ceremony."

"Thanks be to Taranis!" He dropped a swift kiss on her wide smile, then pulled back to look deep into her eyes. "I will happily be hand-fasted to you come the morn, Ineda, but I refuse to wait that long to make love to you."

Lost in a lingering kiss, Brennus was only vaguely aware of Nara's comments.

"Lorcan, I believe Uallas is in need of some fresh air. There are things he is probably just too young to witness, in this roundhouse, right now. Do you think we should all go and visit Gabrond and Fionnah? Will they welcome our company? Or ignore us, like some of our relatives are doing right now?"

"Stop teasing them, Nara." Lorcan's laugh was hearty. "We will look after your sleeping son, Ineda. All night long."

Without breaking the kiss, Brennus flapped them away with one hand.

Ineda eventually pulled back from him, to draw breath, and look around her. "They have all gone. Did I hear properly?"

"Mmm…" He was back to devouring her. "They can do what they like, but I know exactly what I am going to do with you."

He heard an echo of Ineda's giggles, and they sounded as though they were just outside the roundhouse.

***

The following day, Ineda sat patiently while Nara combed out every single strand of her tuggy hair.

"Why did Tullos keep you alone in his roundhouse for so long yesterday, Ineda?"

Ineda grinned. She knew that they were all wondering. Some days she loved to tease, and this was one of them. She was so brimming-happy that she needed everyone else to be the same.

"Well, he wanted to be sure that I understood why he had to be so strict about keeping me under suspicion, till my innocence had been proved." She laughed at Nara's sceptical

234

look and Fionnah's derisive snort. "And it was to make me aware that it would take some time to hunt, to provide a ceremonial feast, since his stocks had already been shared so thinly, and that a hand-fasting might need to be a moon hence."

Nara peered around to look at her. "I am thinking that you must have changed Tullos' mind quickly about that?"

"Aye," Ineda nodded. "I told him that I did not expect a feast at all, and that it is not appropriate anyway, when war is looming."

"Did Tullos suggest having the ceremony this morning, or did you?" Fionnah asked.

Ineda laughed. "That was me. Since I seemed so desperate, he needed to confirm that any hand-fasting with Bran was my choice. I think his message was that although Brennus – as he calls him – is a great warrior, I should not feel obliged to hand-fast with him."

Fionnah held up the clean dress, that one of the village women had delivered for Ineda to wear at the ceremony, her expression questioning. "Did Tullos doubt that Brennus truly loves you?"

"Nay, he knows that. It was my feelings he was making sure of. He offered me a place to live, even if I did not become hearth-wife to Bran."

Nara stopped combing and began to create side-plaits. "Was that wily old chief asking you to become a second wife to him?"

"Nay." The banter continued while Fionnah and Nara got Ineda dressed and ready to leave for the clearing in the nearby woods, the place where Tullos' ceremonies were normally conducted.

Standing next to Bran just a short while later, Ineda had never been happier. There was no druid to conduct the simple hand-fasting ceremony, but Nara did it as well as any she had ever heard before.

When it was time for her vows, her small hands lay engulfed in Bran's large ones, his part-fingers warmly curved around hers. Across from him, she looked up into his loving gaze and spoke unrehearsed words, but ones which came forth from deep inside.

"Bran.
I give you my body, that we will always be one,
My spirit is yours, till our lives be done.
While we both wish it, our lives are entwined,
May the joys of living, both of us find.

Bran, let go of her hands, to slip one inside the neck of his tunic. Drawing free a leather thong, he pulled it over his head, and untied the knot. As she watched his movements, her heart sang, even more. The previous night, Bran had tried to give her the arm ring that had belonged to Meaghan, her grandmother, but she had asked him to wait and give it to her during the ceremony.

She felt the slight tremble of his fingers, as he slipped the ring over her wrist, all the while maintaining her full attention. He clasped both of her hands again, and when he eventually spoke his vows, his voice was loud and clear.

"Ineda.
May your sunshine warm my every day.
Your music will be the best that ever I play.
You will have the first bite from my plate
And the cup we will share.
May our children roam free across our lands
And a happy hearth always be below our hands.
Be sure to know you hold my heart
And only in death, sent by the gods, will we ever part.

Dropping her hands again, he slid his fingers in under the arm ring, binding them together. "This ring should have been yours, long moons ago, Ineda. But, let all who see it now, know that it, and you, have always been close to my heart."

Dipping his head, he dropped the lightest of kisses on her quivering lips. His next whispered-words, she realised, were not meant to be publicly shared.

236

"Till later, Ineda. You and I have a lot of time to make up in the marriage bed."

***

Ineda walked across to Tullos' dwelling, a meeting having been called. Treading close to her destination, she had to suppress the almost permanent smile which creased her cheeks. Such happiness had never been in her grasp before. She had relished every single moment of the three days since the hand-fasting, with Bran.

She named her new hearth-husband Brennus when appropriate, but he was still her Bran of Witton in her mind and heart.

The only cloud that made her smile slip was the escalation of battle plans. As she slid into the back row of those assembled outside Tullos' dwelling, Gabrond's voice rang clear.

"Our horsemen and charioteers are now assembled on the plains at the back of Beinn na Ciche." More details were given of the strength of the mounted forces that had come from far and wide.

"Good to hear, Gabrond. Keep us informed." Tullos turned to Lorcan and one of his own elders who had been monitoring the movements of the Roman army. "What of the Romans at Deer's Den, on Balbithan territory?"

"Around four *cohorts* have now marched to join those at *Moran Dhuirn*. It would appear Agricola is playing some sort of waiting game. He is choosing to only move a few thousand infantry at this time."

"Do you have any opinion on why he does not move all of the men from Deer's Den?"

Brennus cut in before his brother could speak. "At this moment, Agricola has mounted cavalry arriving at *Moran Dhuirn*. Two ships of the *Classis* have disgorged them near Mheadhain's territory."

Ineda knew of the specific tasks which had been doled out amongst the Brigante settlers. Bran's was to monitor Roman movement near the coast. Since their hand-fasting, he had had to disappear for a few days at a time, to gather information, and to establish daily links with Mheadhain. Agricola's fleet was now harassing the tribespeople who dwelt near the sea much more than before.

"It would appear that Agricola is close to a confrontation?" Ineda did not think Tullos' question was put to anyone in particular.

Brennus answered. "He now has more than enough mounted troops assembled at *Moran Dhuirn*. More than one legion of legionary troops is already encamped there. Mheadhain's recent message states he suspects that the auxiliaries, who now make their way to *Moran Dhuirn,* are vexillations drawn from some other part of the Empire."

Ineda did not know whether the excitement she felt was good or bad. Battle was not far off. Whatever time she had before then with Bran was not going to be wasted. Catching his gaze across the seated throng, she was sure his focus on her meant he felt exactly the same.

A few evenings later, Beathan erupted into Lorcan's roundhouse where Ineda sat at the hearthside with Bran and his brother. Nara was by the low cots of the younger children, near the back walls.

"Agricola has arrived at *Moran Dhuirn*, along with those soldiers who were left at the Deer's Den camp in Balbithan's territory."

"Who told you?" Nara asked as she sat beside Ineda for the news.

"I was near Tullos' dwelling with my friend when Tullos popped his head out and told me to fetch you!"

"You mean you knew a messenger had just arrived and the two of you were lurking around Tullos' door?" Lorcan playfully cuffed his son's shoulder as he and Bran headed for the door, the laughter in his words tempered by the sober expression which followed.

"Who is requested?" Nara's question was reasonable. Ineda had become used to different groups being gathered depending on Tullos' planning.

Ineda felt for the lad when colour rose in Beathan's cheeks. She had long since learned how conscientious the boy was, and saw him as a great credit to Nara and Lorcan. It was at times like these that she wondered if Dubv, had he lived, would also have grown to be so responsible. The pain of never knowing was always with her. He had been a Roman child, as was Uallas, but she missed her first-born son every day.

"Tullos requests only Father, Brennus and Ineda."

Ineda wondered if she was being put to the test yet again as she made her way across the hillfort, Bran's hand curled around her fingers. When the question was put to her, she dreaded the reality of it.

"Aye. I would know Agricola, even though he never ever deigned to talk to me directly."

Tullos was reassuring. "We do not believe that will ever be necessary, though we had to know if you would recognise him."

The thought of being so close to Agricola and his senior officers churned her stomach. Now that she was back in the bosom of a Celtic tribe, she never ever wanted to be surrounded by Romans again, though the land around was again saturated with the *Diùbhadh*. She hated the scum so much.

"Where will you be, Lorcan?" Ineda sensed the anxiety in Nara's question as they all sat around the hearth in Lorcan's dwelling a few evenings later.

She was not surprised when it was Bran who answered. "We do not know as yet where Calgach would have us go, Nara. What we can tell you is that we will not be with the warriors in the front wave. We are too worn, and not fast enough for that, but speaking for myself I will not be far behind them."

Ineda's stomach felt hollow. She had no idea of what it was like to be one of the warriors who rushed with Celtic fury towards the enemy, no idea of how it felt to sense your fellow-warriors clash with the foe, or see that first wave mown down. It was already decided by Tullos that she and Gabrond's wife Fionnah would have an allotted place where they would tend to the wounded, along with others who would not be taking up the sword. Along with other healers, they had been preparing for the inevitable casualties.

Two day later, she no longer had to imagine.

Ineda looked across the flat expanse of the valley floor which spread out in front of her. Presently, the mounted cavalry and charioteers of Calgach's assembled troops rode their way into place at the edge of the foothills of Beinn na Ciche. She and Fionnah had climbed The Mither Tap, knowing battle would take some time to commence, though they could easily see that the warriors below were speeding their way into place.

Across from them, on the other side of the valley, the Roman army was doing exactly the same thing, the metal of helmets and weapons glinting in the sunlight. A fearsome amount of soldiers, judging from the massed flashes and sparkles.

"Agricola has thousands at his command." Fionnah's voice was hushed, fear lacing every individual sound. "They stand so perfectly in formation."

It was true. What Ineda could see were faultless blocks of soldiers arranged on the foothills straddling the low waters of the River Urie. From such a distance she could see no actual men or features; rather it was the blocks of colour they displayed.

Tullos had told her that the river was easily fordable at many points across the valley, and at no place was it very wide or very deep. Horses could easily jump the water, and men could make the crossing easily by placing planks across the flow. That had no doubt already been done. And even if they had to wade across, it was no deeper than a man's chest, according to Tullos.

The water was necessary for the Roman camp at *Moran Dhuirn,* but crossing it at the battle site would not hamper Roman plans.

Ineda was sure that the main blood-letting would not be on the side of the Roman encampment that lay further up the hill

240

on a natural plateau. She had lived with them long enough to have gleaned those kinds of details.

"Did you ever see them assembled like this, Ineda?" Fionnah's question whispered off in the light breeze.

"Never. I saw full *cohorts* assembled in the garrison fortresses at special times, but never more than a legion battle-ready like this."

The throng across from her was an awesome sight. Getting ready for a confrontation that had been coming for far too long.

"Where will Lorcan and his brothers be?"

Fionnah, who usually seemed a strong enough woman, looked fretful as she reached out to grasp Ineda's arm. They had grown close enough during the short time Ineda and Uallas had shared her roundhouse, before her hand-fasting with Bran.

Ineda softly squeezed Fionnah's fingers, which should have been warm in the sunshine, but were freezing cold. "Bran told me they would be on the southern flank. In the second wave."

She had made her brave farewells with him before dawn, as had many of the women who were not warrior-women. Those who wielded a sword alongside their men were already down below on the foothills, or were making their way to the upper layers of the battle site. Though she wanted to be with Bran, she knew her skills did not lie with the sword. Never warrior-trained either, Fionnah had been assigned to help with any wounded, and it seemed she had also accepted her task.

Chapter Twenty Two

AD 84 Just Before Samhain –
Beinn na Ciche, Taexali Territory

The day truly had come.

Calgach's thousands of warriors stood ready to demonstrate their strength. Adorned for battle, their tribal insignias displayed their Celtic allegiances; their spears held poised and shields in place showed their fearsome antipathy to the Roman pestilence on their soil.

And Brennus was just as prepared as his fellow-warriors – his infirmities almost forgotten.

He sat alongside his brothers in prime position at the inner edge of the cavalry right flank, anticipation crippling, his heart thumping a merry beat under his metal-studded leather armour. This time he was atop a horse, not below it, and that was the way he intended to remain.

Though the battlefield was not silent, no warrior around him spoke – all remaining alert for the next developments. As far as he could see, every single Celt looked to be in position, with nothing left to organise, or halt the proceedings, since Calgach had been ranging his foot warriors on the hillside long before dawn's pink hues crept over the valley. He focused on the figure of Calgach way in the distance.

The Celtic leader stood well-balanced on his chariot bed, higher than most of those around him. His presence so commanding, he was easily discernible in the Celtic battle-lines which stretched far along the valley floor. It was a hugely impressive gathering, many thousands more Celts than Romans, the sight of which made Brennus' heart sing. Pride was not always a good thing, but it humbled him to know he had played a part in getting this vast congregation of Celts together, tribespeople who refused to meekly accept the oppression of Rome.

In the front line, ranged alongside Calgach, were the Celtic war chariots, their agitated horses neighing and harrumphing, forelegs stamping, and raring to be let fly across the flat valley floor to meet their foe.

"By Taranis! I wish I was there beside Calgach!"

Gabrond's low heartfelt mutter impinged, but did not break Brennus' concentration. He knew, too well, how his older brother felt. Gabrond, the best charioteer of Garrigill, was no longer fit to be in that front line of warriors. The standing position necessary to drive, or even as the spearman, was not something he was able to sustain any more.

"You will play your part, Gabrond. You are still a fine enough horseman," he whispered, his words breaking up in a throat that was hoarse and clogged by mucus. An inevitable amount of dust floated around, coating his mouth, but at present it was nothing to what it would be like once the charioteers surged into battle. The weather had lately been fine, only light rain had watered the ground during the last se'nnight. Good battle weather in that the soil would not become slippery, or bogged down too quickly, but the dust clouds would become almost as fierce a foe as the Romans would.

His horse shied around, restless and filled with the fear and anticipation of its fellow-beasts. Brennus counted himself so favoured that Tullos had insisted on mounting him and his brothers from the finest of his horse stock. What was indisputable, in Tullos' eyes, was that the Garrigill brothers were the only ones who had ever engaged the Romans in real battle. They had come to Tullos as strangers who sought a place to lay their heads, but the old man was resolute in acknowledging their former seniority as sons of a clan chief.

The glints of Roman metal, catching the glare of the sun on the flat land opposite, were as numerous and impressive as Brennus expected them to be. Perfectly disciplined, the Roman auxiliary *cohorts* who faced the Celtic chariots were distinctive in their rigid blocks of colour, the standards of their legion flying high alongside. Difficult to determine exactly, but Brennus thought it looked as if Agricola had amassed around eight thousand infantry, if each group marked a whole *cohort*, though they appeared to be spread thinly across the flat lands rather than in blocks of deeper rows. Flanking those auxiliaries to right and left were some three thousand cavalry. On slightly higher ground, and behind the trickling River Urie, were what Brennus thought looked like two infantry legions, equally spaced across the low rise behind the auxiliary infantry. To right and left of the legions were more mounted soldiers.

"Why are the cavalry split up like that?" Gabrond's question broke Brennus' concentration on counting numbers. He looked to see what his brother meant, but Lorcan intervened first.

"I would say Agricola has an auxiliary *ala* on his front right and left flanks, and it is his legionary cavalry who await on that gradual slope behind."

Brennus agreed with Lorcan. The pattern seemed to fit with information given from Ineda about Agricola's previous preferences in battle plans. She had recounted to the assembled leaders, even in Calgach's presence, all the knowledge she had gleaned though her questions put to Gaius, and more particularly Pomponius, who had loved to talk about all things Roman.

Gabrond's curses were vehement; low but violent. "Is the Roman turd so confident he would keep his best troops in reserve? Or, are they too terrified of our fearsome show of strength?"

Scanning the volume of Celts amassed around him, it was difficult for Brennus to believe Agricola could be so blatantly arrogant, yet what he had heard of the man's character – from Ineda, and in his own experience – it all pointed to Agricola being the most assured and egotistical General of the Roman Army he could ever imagine.

On the opposite side of the valley, the Empire's troops also appeared to be silent, awaiting Agricola's direction, although he could see no sign of the Roman Governor. Being at a distance from the centre did not make it easy for him to see, dependent as he was on his one eye, but there appeared to be no movement yet. No small group of Romans coming forward to negotiate, or to precipitate the engagement.

Of course, the centre of a battlefield was not the usual place for a quill-using governor, but it was the ideal place for Agricola, who was first and foremost a soldier and a general.

"What takes the man so long? By all the gods, what must he still discuss with his troop leaders? They have been assembled as long as we have!"

Though Brennus listened to Lorcan's frustrated jibe, which seeped into his every word, he dared not move his head now. He must not fail Calgach, or even old Tullos by missing any signal.

Tullos' charioteers were somewhere in the throng, but he could not pick any of them out. It had not been his place to organise them, though he knew Gabrond had been party to the instructions given by Calgach and those other Caledon, Vacomagi and Taexali chiefs who finalised the battle planning.

"Do you see Tullos' chariots?" He kept his voice to a mere whisper.

Gabrond answered, likewise as hushed as him. "Aye, though barely, so. They cannot be seen easily from here. They are in the block to Calgach's right, near the back and closer to the foot-warriors."

A quick glimpse of Gabrond's face was enough to see the envy it held, and the sadness. None of the warriors of Garrigill who were present were in their prime, save perhaps Beathan, who was a mighty young warrior, though as yet untried. At almost thirteen winters, he was tall and strong but had never seen battle with Celt or Roman. Beathan was presently amongst the foot soldiers, well up the hillside and alongside Nara and Gabrond's oldest son and daughter.

Much as Lorcan had protested, Nara could not be dissuaded from taking up arms. Calgach needed every possible warrior, young and old, male and female. Brennus did not need to glance at Lorcan's face to know of his brother's fears, but was glad that the Garrigill youngsters and Nara were not down the hill and closer to Calgach.

As a warrior-princess of the Selgovae, Nara could have protested her ranking amongst the tribal leaders who took prime positions near the front of the battle-lines. She could have accepted the offer of a mount from Tullos, as Lorcan had, but she had refused. She had never seen true battle against the Romans either, any combat having only been Celt on Celt in small skirmishes against the Selgovae, and a small confrontation with a handful of Roman soldiers well after the battle of Whorl when she had gone to search for Lorcan. That she had insisted on taking part this day, Brennus believed, was mainly to ply her blade alongside her too-eager son and keep him and his cousins safe. It was to her credit though, that she had requested that her distant kin Esk and Nith should take her place at the front, where they were desperate to be.

"I can just make out some of Tullos' warriors behind the chariots: Nith, too. Esk must surely be alongside his brother, though I do not see him yet. They are all more than ready. Look at their fearsome expressions!"

Gabrond's admiration shone through in his words and in his eager grin when he looked beyond his brother's profile to see for himself.

The youngest and fittest warriors of Tullos, including Esk and Nith from Tarras, stood with the central core of the infantry, the usual place for those with the highest battle-lust and fastest reactions. Brennus remembered that position so well as memories of Whorl flooded back – the heat; the smells of blood and excrement; the pungent stench of entrails and the heightening aroma of battle-frenzy. The battle at Beinn na Ciche had not even started, yet the memories crowded in. But he had to control those memories and convert them into current fervour, and especially not allow them to break his concentration. Yet, he was so far away from Calgach, he worried that he may not even see the first signal. Sheer anxiety ate at his gut at not being closer, although he knew his brothers were both as primed as he was and would not let him fail.

Lorcan seemed to be aware of his every thought, his words attempting to soothe. "We will not miss anything, Brennus. Have no fear."

The urge to be down there with Calgach to confront and engage the enemy directly was so strong. In his memories, he was still that undefeated tribal champion of time past, though his frustration at being unable to engage from closer confines dissipated the longer he stood and waited. All his travels had been for exactly this confrontation, so why were his insides telling him it was his place to be beside the one to declare war on the usurping Roman turds?

While he scanned the Roman hordes, Tuathal's words slammed into his head. He was never set to be the one leading this battle, but he was to be one of those instrumental in making it happen. Other things Tuathal had said made him grin, a wry grin, but it lightened the infernal waiting tension that he expected every single warrior felt, just as he did. He fingered the thong at his neck, his fingers sliding into place around the object given to him a long time ago, by the druid, Tuathal.

Lorcan's low whispering continued, though Brennus knew that like him his brother's focus was fixed on Calgach. "This is not like the battle at Whorl, Brennus. We engaged in that battle with no idea of where each of us was. Indeed, we did not even know if we were all there."

Gabrond took up where Lorcan faltered, "Aye, Lorcan. Our father would be well happy to know we ride out together against this Roman oppressor."

Lorcan rode on his right side, his blind side. Knowledge that his eldest living brother would watch over his weak side was heartening – Lorcan would defend him to the death. Of that there was no doubt. Equally, he would defend Gabrond who sat astride the horse to his left. Gabrond's weak side was then covered by his stronger one. As a trio they would look out for one another.

"I can have no better warriors flanking me. I know it, and soon Agricola will know it, too!" His vow was echoed by both of his brothers.

They had practiced hard together, and had produced the best defence strategies for allowing them to wield their long Celtic swords, and yet allow them to use their shields and their bodies in a tighter defensive knot if they became under too great a threat to operate alone. What they had perfected was much more like the tight cluster of the Roman army – even though they were mounted.

Tullos had been surprised by Brennus' urging the warriors of the hillfort to practise such techniques, but they had capitulated fairly easily and had eventually seen some sense to it. The grumbles over the awkwardness in using the longer Celtic swords in a smaller space, Brennus had laughed off. If they wanted to survive against the Roman *pila*, then he urged that only in unity was there strength. It had been the same when he had suggested as many as possible of Tullos' warriors don some kind of chest armour, or cover. Not usual, it was difficult to persuade the warrior band to relinquish their normal bare-breasted status and wear some sort of protective cover. He was sad that only a few of them had complied. Having been in bloody battle already, he did not believe it less warrior-like to cover his vulnerable chest, and neither did his brothers. They knew up close just how efficient Roman chest armour was.

The noise around him was a restless one, the right flank of mounted warriors having to control their agitated beasts, and keep them at a standstill till the signal was given.

"I see movement." Lorcan's eyesight had always been the keenest, and he was generally the first to give warning.

Brennus flickered his eyelids to clear them of the infernal mucus, the strength of sun's rays directly shining on them not helping one bit. One eye blinded was bad, but he could not allow the vision in his good eye to be impaired.

"A small band of Romans have come forward, and are now in front of the auxiliary foot soldiers." Gabrond's excitement was infectious.

He could see the group of moving figures. There were only a few of them, riding extremely slowly towards Calgach, though remaining well behind the distance for spear-throwing.

The one in the centre was armoured so heavily, he gleamed like the sun itself.

Agricola.

Though everyone was hushed, it was far too far away for him to hear the exchanges between Agricola and Calgach. The talk lasted only moments before Calgach turned his back and bawled at the Celts before him, his urging to battle immediately taken up by the blood-lusted warriors who faced him.

Brennus was aware of the immediate retreat of the small group of Romans, but his focus had to be on Calgach.

A short rousing clamour followed, the battle chants taken up by the frontline troops before Calgach whirled around again to face the enemy. His spear rose to jab high up towards the sky. One…two… three…

The whistling sounds of Roman *ballistae* rent the air as the missiles flew high over the space between the opposing armies.

It was the moment Brennus had been waiting for!

He blew his ocarina; three practised notes which rent the air in a much higher tone than the lugubrious sound of the Celtic carnyces, one long hoot of the huge horns echoing around the valley.

He blew for Tuathal; for his king Venutius of the Brigantes; for every Celt he had known who had been injured, or had died under a Roman *gladius*. He also blew to avenge Ineda's incarceration by the Roman tribune. Blew for the woman he would now gladly die for, but hoped that he would live to share more incredible love with her. The instrument dropped back to his chest – its clarion call over as he readied his spear.

A black hail of them flew from the poised fists of the spearmen on the now charging Celtic war chariots, and from the cavalry around him. Brennus watched the toppling of the front rows of Roman auxiliaries, the sheer volume of Celtic weapons successfully hitting many of their marks. A fierce pride raged through his blood. His fellow Celts were repelling the Roman scum who dared to claim Celtic lands. The forces of Calgach were going to stain the ground red. Agricola and his Roman usurpers would be routed.

Brennus had waited so long for this day!

The war chariots of the Celts stormed across the plain towards the Roman enemy, the infantry masses surging after, their thicker rain of spears fired high into the air. Brennus kicked his heels into the flanks of the fine beast he was riding; kept pace with his brothers; and with other shield-raised horsemen of the right flank. The field of battle was very wide across the plain, the whole area ringing with warrior cries, and snorting and panting horses.

Return volleys of Roman *pila* pinged towards him, though the javelin count was not so numerous. Celtic broadswords and shields rose up to intercept and deflect the deadly points, many of his fellow warriors successfully evading the first throws, as he did.

The Celtic front line continued to surge forwards. More Celtic spears felled the foot-soldiers of Agricola. More and more toppled as stray *pila* were picked up and fired back at the original owners. Screams and cries were all around, some of the squeals those of terrified animals. Opposing armies came head to head, the sheer mass of Celts flattening the metal-clad Roman auxiliaries before they even had time to group with their defensive shield formations.

Brennus sought out the mounted Roman cavalry to engage with, but they were few amongst the foot soldiers of Agricola who rushed towards him. He abhorred the advantage he had atop his horse when he came up against the auxiliaries, but this was war – and each man of the opposition was calling the Roman tune. There would be time later to wonder where the mounted Roman cavalry were, but at that moment, all he focused on was ridding the area around him of living and breathing Romans. Mail-clad soldiers fell under his broadsword swipes, their vulnerable necks more open to his blade. Soon the ground was littered with them.

He constantly fought to control his mount which was terrified by everything it came into contact with: rushing blades, bumping stunned bodies, the flanks and rears ends of other horses and careering chariots. Avoiding his own fellow-Celts became almost impossible, the *melée* of both armies so thick and confused. The only thing he was sure of was that the Celts around him had the upper hand, according to the amount of bodies strewn beneath the hooves of his horse.

Utter satisfaction flooded him until he recognised the bawling of his brother, Gabrond, who was nearby but not as close as they had envisaged staying. "More! Agricola sends in more. Look to your left hand!"

From his vantage point on his horse, he could see Gabrond's pointing sword. "Batavians! Agricola brings forward Batavians!" He knew the colour they wore and the standard they carried. *Cohorts* of them were flocking forward to boost the numbers lost in Agricola's fallen infantry. "And cavalry!"

Over battle field noise, he heard Gabrond's cries. "Agricola has more surging forward on that other flank. Who are they?"

Lorcan's shout was just discernible over the thundering hooves. "Tungrians! Two *cohorts* of Tungrians! But the Roman turd still keeps his legionaries uphill."

He could hear the thunder of hooves, on the far edge of the long lines of battle, over the other horrendous battle sounds. Many hooves on Roman horses.

The warm reek of blood; the stench of horse manure; dripping red entrails… in no time the horror of Whorl returned – but Brennus remained mounted as the fray became even more muddled.

Celtic war-chariots lost their spearmen, many drivers slumped from the vehicles under the onslaught of Batavian and Tungrian spears. With no human direction, the horses drawing empty chariots ran wild amongst the Celtic warriors on foot. More *pila* flew from Roman fists, and rider-less Celtic horses caused chaos amongst the fray, dislodging Celts and Romans alike in their absolute panic.

The central battleground became a complete frenzy as Roman and Celt engaged hand to hand. Spears – Roman and Celtic – were retrieved and raised by the Roman auxiliaries, many easily finding a soft chest. Others were swooped up and fired by now-circling Celtic tribesmen. Cries of rage, frustration, terror and sheer agony filled the air as Celtic broadsword and Roman *gladius* flashed and parried. Tungrian and Batavian tunics swelled the Roman numbers even further, and began to push back the Celtic infantry.

The main area to Calgach's left, which had been held by Celtic warriors, found itself ringed by the new mounted Romans, the charge of beasts Brennus had recently heard swinging right behind the forces of Calgach.

In no time at all, the supremacy held by Celtic troops was diminished. As Brennus fought off a clutch of Tungrians determined to hack either his legs off, or kill his mount, he was acutely aware of those around him fighting hard to maintain the ground covered, yet they were being steadily pushed back up the hill behind him. So, too, was he being pushed back.

Each time he wheeled around and steadied his horse for another attack, he ended up facing his enemies from further up the slope.

As he fought back Roman after Roman auxiliary from high atop his horse, Brennus' elation turned to dread fear. The combat between Roman and Celtic cavalry should have been a balanced affair, but that was not what was happening. The mounted forces were mingled amongst the foot-soldiers of both armies; the dust he had known would appear now clouded the air as though a fine haar had descended. Seeing beyond the immediate misty area was now a thing of the past.

"Fall back! Fall back and we will regroup!"

The call came at Brennus through the powdery mist. Horses whirled around constantly, Brennus' too. He had long since lost direction, but knew his brothers remained close.

"This way!" At Lorcan's command, he wheeled and followed.

"Gabrond's mount is fallen!"

Brennus was too far off to collect up his brother.

"By Taranis!" Gabrond bellowed as he swung up to mount behind Lorcan when the horse momentarily halted alongside. "What is our cavalry doing?"

Brennus had no real idea, as he watched the mounted Celts around him gallop uphill towards the forest edge, after the warrior who was in charge of the right flank, Roman horses galloping hard on their tails. Whirling around they regrouped before the trees, the enemy galloping uphill, a wedge of mail-clad cavalry coming towards them.

"Lorcan! The carnage!"

There was sufficient height to see the battlefield below. Chaos and devastation lay there. Broken chariots were strewn all around. Some lay on their side with one wheel still spinning, though many were merely piles of shattered wood and wattling. Bodies lay everywhere – some were Roman, though many more were Celts. Roman auxiliaries picked their way forwards over the debris of limbs and writhing bodies, the glint of the *gladius* finishing off what another blade had started till no twitches were visible. To his right, Celtic infantry were fleeing into the forest like ants surging up the hill, though many more brave warriors were sacrificing themselves for their fellow tribespeople, making a last foray and refusing to give up arms, remaining steadfast with their shields and blades. Those courageous warriors were doomed. Too few Celts down there now and too many Tungrians.

And still Agricola's legions stood in serried rows up the hill towards the place named *Moran Dhuirn*.

Exhaustion had long settled upon him as he fought off Romans in the forest, having been forced right into the trees. Wave after wave of Romans mounted, and on foot, following. The Celtic carnyces were sounding again – a retreat this time, but he would not be blowing his ocarina.

Along with his brothers, Brennus made a weary and dispirited escape. All three alive, thankfully only minor wounds bloodying their braccae and arms. Gabrond had snagged a fleeing horse so all three were once again on their own mounts.

How could a defeat have happened?

It hardly seemed credible.

Chapter Twenty Three

AD 84 Before Samhain –
Beinn na Ciche, Taexali Territory

"The noise is less fierce, now. I am going to see what is happening!" Ineda fretted about Bran as she clambered around the wounded bodies strewn on the ground around her, and headed towards the edge of the battlefield.

With the tribeswomen who had been designated as healers, she was just around the south side of The Mither Tap, unable to see the battle properly, apart from the fringes nearer to her – though even that combat was still too far off to discern the actual warriors involved in the fray.

She had already aided some twenty or so casualties who now lay in various states of low moaning, or in near silence as they bit off the pain of their wounds, their blood having spattered the soil around. Others who had been lifted from the field, and brought to her, were past her skills. Those bodies had been laid aside by a couple of the women, awaiting the identification which would bring great distress and sorrow to some family – an outcome that many of the women present feared.

"Ineda! You cannot go there!" Fionnah's cries were desperate.

Ineda could hear the far distant clamour of battle, see the clouds of dust still rising, but could not tell what was happening, though it seemed the disturbance across the land was much less than it had been earlier, the battle having raged for some time. At first, she had been able to make out the Celtic cavalry on the right flank closest to her, the mounted warriors edging the swarms of chariots. She had seen the surge towards the Roman front lines after the carnyx call to battle, all before the sight became a muddle of warriors, and chariots, and screeching horses.

It had not been long before casualties had begun to limp towards the women. Some warriors had been tended to, their wounds quickly dressed before they went back around the hillside and back to the fighting, so determined to clash alongside their fellow-Celts to defeat the forces of Agricola. Some others, badly wounded themselves, had helped fellow-warriors away from the battle. Many of them were too exhausted to return, the women still attempting to bind the huge rents in their flesh gained from a *gladius* thrust or from a Roman *pilum*. A couple of handfuls were still alive; their wounds potentially fatal, the men oblivious to all around them.

"I have to see where the cavalry went. They are no longer in sight. I need to know where Bran is!"

Her progress across the uneven ground was halted by the screams of a small lad who rushed towards her. "Agricola has pushed back our warriors. They have scattered into the trees above the burn gulley on Beinn na Ciche. The Roman army is on their heels, and the fighting still continues. Many of our people flee for their lives now, since Agricola has sent in fresh replacements. They are killing all they lay hands on."

"Do the Romans take prisoners from the field?" Ineda held the lad to prevent him from collapsing.

The boy's head shook violently. "Nay!"

That was alarming news. Ineda knew the Roman way was usually to take live prisoners to swell their slave numbers, or to use them in post-battle negotiations with subjected and defeated peoples. What could this mean, if Agricola was being so thorough in bringing death to all Celts who opposed him?

The lad crouched, hands on knees, as he regained his breath. "At first, they looked to be removing captured front-line Celtic warriors. Taking them back to their flanks... but then it got so confusing. The Romans began to kill all who still lived, so that they could get to the warriors who stood firm and did not retreat." Tears leaked from both eyelids as the boy re-lived what he had just witnessed. Anguish poured from him, his words marred by trembling lips. "Though they were far down the hill from me, those tribesmen all but threw themselves at the Roman scourge. None of them can possibly live now."

Ineda took the boy by the shoulders to console him. "Can you be sure of this?"

More tears fell as the lad gulped and nodded, his nose dripping as much as his eyes. "Agricola sent down more reinforcements from the hillside. They swept down on our warriors like a cloud of midges near a rank burn. There were too many of them to flee."

"What happened after that?"

"The Tungrians, I heard someone name them so, had the greater strength since they were fresh. Our left flank, chariots too, were surrounded from their rear and all annihilated. Then the Romans pushed back those of our warriors who were still fighting into the woods. There is no field of battle any more. Even our cavalry do battle in the woods. I heard the carnyx call as I ran back to you. The battle is lost. Everyone must flee. Tullos must be told!"

One of the women panicked. "We must run back to the hill-fort, now! Our healing skills will not give us any immunity from the Roman *gladius* if they come round this way and find us."

Ineda knew what the woman claimed was true. With battle-lust in their blood, their killing would be a slow and painful one, the *gladius* only used when the men had had their fill.

"Wait! We cannot leave these men lying here!" Her shout halted the woman's flight. She, too, wanted to flee, but could not.

Those warriors who had had some time to rest struggled to their feet, weaving around as though too much of the honeyed drink had been consumed. The women, and those warriors who had strength enough to hold onto a pair of heels of the most wounded, made their ragged way back to Tullos' village, avoiding the fringes of the wood which lay on the foothills of the eastern slope of Beinn na Ciche.

Closer to their destination, Ineda could see they were too late.

Fionnah's wail rent the air. "Tullos' roundhouses burn!"

Smoke billowed up; the smell of burning wood filled the air, the flames still burning brightly as homes blazed. Bodies of some old and some extremely young tribespeople littered the ground just outside the palisade. At the wide open gates lay Tullos. The old chief had defended his hillfort, his sword still in his grip, his face ripped open by a bitingly sharp *gladius*.

There was nothing any healer could do for him.

Fionnah's head-shaking indicated none of the Brigante children were among the slain as she went from corpse to corpse; the other women doing likewise after the wounded men were laid down, the focus now on seeking the fate of their families.

"Be quiet!" Her warning came in harsh whisper.

Stopping their progress, Ineda urged the others to caution, her finger at her lips warning them to silence. The Roman blades might still be inside, though she doubted it from the lack of noise around them, apart from the crackling and spitting of blazing wood and thatch.

Fionnah's soft wail came from behind Ineda. "The children? Where are our children?"

All of the women helping Ineda had left their offspring at the hillfort, in the care of the older children and elders of the tribe. Picking her way around the burning buildings, Ineda encountered no mail-clad Romans. It was impossible to enter the flaming dwellings, or even get very close, but signs of fleeing tribespeople lay all around. A bratt here and a metal pan there. Overturned leather buckets and wooden utensils, hacked at with angry swords, were evidence of a hurried Roman attack. She doubted that many, if any, spoils had been lifted by the attacking Romans.

Destruction was their intent.

Back at the entrance, Fionnah's agitated cries caught her attention. "The scuffled earth here shows that many small feet fled through the gates. The trail goes north."

"Then we must follow it. In any case, we cannot stay here." Tullos' village was far too close to the field of battle. "The

Roman soldiers who ransacked here must have swooped down through the trees."

"Maybe some of our men had returned?"

"Followed by the Tungrians?"

Both suggestions were possible. Ineda had experience of Tungrian *cohorts*, knew exactly how good those men were at hand-to-hand combat, but also that they were woodsmen at heart. Fighting a pathway through trees and bushes would have been no hindrance to them.

A couple of the older women refused to flee, preferring to await the return of their menfolk – they would tend the wounded.

Ineda tried to impress upon them their precarious position. Tried to warn that Agricola's forces would give them no quarter, but they were resolute. There was no time to waste.

A great despair descended. Fleeing from marauding Roman troops had been a part of her life for too long. The quiet peaceful existence she sought with Bran was again slipping away from her. Swallowing her fears, she encouraged those who intended to flee to collect up anything useful which could be used for cover, and any food stocks that lay around, as she hurried out of the hillfort. Fionnah followed her; meek as a newborn lamb, as though she had no will of her own, her tears dripping from her sodden chin.

A little way along the track to the north, Ineda halted. She had absolutely no idea where she was going, and neither did Fionnah. One of the less-wounded, though hobbling, warriors followed behind. He assisted another one, arms across shoulders linking them as one, their progress quick considering their now leaking wounds.

"Where does this pathway lead to?"

Panting, one of the men answered, "Across the plains to the River Dheathain."

"Will we have enough bush cover, if we go this way?" Ineda was confused about the River Dheathain being ahead of her, though had heard it was a greatly meandering river.

"Not so much on some parts. As you can see the ground hereabouts is flat, but there are many hills and dips which obscure the view. Roman soldiers coming behind may see us from afar, but we will also be lost to them, at times, until they are really close."

"Is the river easily fordable?"

"Easy enough. This track leads to the ford, though I know of ways we can travel the ground without using this walkway."

The trek was slow, the line gradually spreading out behind the fittest. Keeping together hardly seemed to matter. Ineda knew if the Roman Army caught up with them, confronting them as a group would make no difference to how the *gladius* would slice.

In the distance, figures began to appear, the group having been obscured by the undulating landscape.

"Ineda! Do you see? Up on the hilltop." Fionnah's weak voice held some hope.

Some were tall, though many figures were smaller. It was a large group of people who straggled around and did not have the neat appearance of a *contubernium* , or two, of Roman soldiers. The sight gave them the boost needed to increase the walking pace – just a little.

Her heart thudded. Uallas and the other children had to be in that group. They had passed no roundhouse villages, and had seen no signs of Roman soldiers.

The man who had earlier spoken called to her. "Over the next rise lies the hillfort of Monymusk, near the river. We must bide there awhile."

Ineda was not sure about biding anywhere within Roman striking distance, but dusk was falling. In all of her dealings with the Roman Army she knew they, too, were likely to bed down for the night after building new defences, or they would have returned to already-built encampments. Perhaps that was why they had seen no signs of them?

As they approached the bottom of the hill, the pounding of hooves to her right, coming from the edges of the nearby wood, was terrifying. They had absolutely no cover to hide behind – no bushes, no trees. Wide-open coarse scrubland gave her little band no shelter at all.

"Celtic warriors!" One of the women screamed, the relief in her screech mirrored by the nervous smiles all around her as a band of some twenty warriors erupted from the nearby woods.

Ineda was not so cheered. The men were riding the horses extremely hard.

The first of the warriors yanked his horse to an abrupt stop in front of her. "Romans come behind us. Clamber up as best you can, though our beasts are as exhausted as we are."

Scurrying bodies flung themselves up behind and clung hard, the wounded warriors of her party aided by those already mounted. So heavily weighed down, the horses managed no more than a canter up the gradual incline to the summit. Though not a high hill, there was enough height to see the mounted Tungrian auxiliaries exit the woods. At the call of their *ala* captain, the troop hauled their horses to a halt before turning away to ride off in the direction Ineda had come from.

"Why do they do that?" Amazement filled the woman asking the question.

It was deep relief and gratitude which filled Ineda. "Dusk is already falling. They will have time to ride back to their camp. The Roman Army likes to have their horses behind the walls of their encampment before dark."

Riding down the other side of the hill to the settlement of Monymusk was a slower progress. The Roman threat had passed for the time being, though the morrow would bring a new dawn and new threat. She knew too much about how the Romans operated after a battle.

"Maeldun?" Fionnah's shout drew her gaze to the boy who ran towards the riders.

Ineda's heart thumped, sheer relief flooding her. If Gabrond and Fionnah's second son was at Monymusk, then surely the other children were there too?

Some time later, Ineda was reluctant to lay down her fast-asleep son. She was seated around the hearthside of Monymusk, as were all the fleeing tribespeople who had reached his settlement. Creidne, Fionnah's second daughter, related the terror when warning had come to Tullos' village

260

that the Romans were pushing the Celts up the Beinn na Ciche foothills and into the forest.

"I knew what I had to do, mother." The young lass addressed Fionnah directly. "You had told me well to gather up all the children quickly, and to make my way out of the roundhouses to some shelter outside the hillfort walls."

Another little voice piped up. Ineda had already grown to love Bran's little daughter Kaideigh. "We ran out even before old chief Tullos told us to. We did not stop to collect any things, though we wanted to. I helped Creidne to wrap Uallas into her bratt, since he is the smallest of all of us."

Creidne smiled at all of the Garrigill brood. "They all did a very good job at fleeing, mother. We were well along the pathway when we heard the Roman horses pounding in through the gates at Tullos."

Kaideigh's little voice stuttered, her eyes filling quickly. Drenched with tears her words muffled. "We could not save old Tullos, and I really liked him. My father liked him, too. Where is he now? All of them?"

They all knew she spoke of Bran, and the other Garrigill warriors. And Nara. Nara's youngest son began to sob, his sniffles catching as the other children joined in. Ineda slipped Uallas onto the bratt at her feet, and scooped Kaideigh into a hug as the other brothers and sisters huddled together. "Listen to me Kaideigh. I love your father. I have always loved your father and will always love him. In my heart, I feel his is beating too. I am certain he still lives."

She felt Kaideigh burrow into her chest, so much that the silver arm-ring that hung between her breasts nudged the girl's cheek, enough to make her lean away again.

"What is that?"

Ineda's tear filled smile was hard to maintain. "This is the ring your father wore for me for many long winters when we were apart, but we will share the wearing of it when he returns to me… to us, Kaideigh, to all of us."

Her fervent speech was not a lie. Bran did still live. She was convinced.

Chapter Twenty Four

AD 84 Samhain – Monymusk, Taexali Territory

Brennus came out of the darkened woods. Lorcan sat tight at his back sharing his horse, Gabrond's mount plodding behind them. They were reduced to two horses, yet again, since Lorcan's horse had stumbled in the growing dusk during the hurried descent of one of the many low hills they had covered. Gabrond had had to put the poor squealing beast out of its misery, its broken leg not something that would heal if the animal was let loose. It was as well that the Romans who had earlier pursued them had turned back towards Durno.

"Do not let go, brother, or we will both topple," Lorcan urged from behind him, his voice slurred with exhaustion.

Brennus felt his older brother slump even closer, and tightened the reins one more time around his left hand. He knew Gabrond followed, the steady clump of the horse telling him that much though he could not see around to know what condition Gabrond was in. Of the three of them, Gabrond was now the worst-wounded.

They all had minor slashes to their arms and chests, but none bled as much as the wound on Gabrond's lower leg. Only after they had been sure of being free of Roman pursuit had they stopped to bind Gabrond up with strips torn from his leather armour. It was all he had, and would need to suffice.

Their flight through the woods on the foothills of Beinn na Ciche had forced them to the north of the range of hills – the opposite direction to Tullos' hillfort. Brennus was not entirely sure where they were, but believed they were now circling back towards the snaking River Dheathain which meandered to the south of The Mither Tap. The clear, darkened blue sky was sufficiently moonlit to see the bumpy nipple-like outline of the summit.

They had passed many groups of weary foot-warriors making their way to the mountains, but none were known to them. Nara, Beathan, and Gabrond's eldest son and daughter not among them. Brennus knew his brothers were worn out, but their hearts were even wearier, as was his.

The slow plod allowed too much time to think about Ineda. She had wanted to ply a sword with Nara and the young warriors, but she had eventually been dissuaded by all of those around her. There were other healers at Tullos' hillfort, but battle with Agricola needed more than could be made available. He was certain Ineda had not realised that being at the side of the field of battle was almost as hazardous as being in the thick of it.

He forced his head upwards to look at the star-studded sky. And prayed to his god, Taranis. In his heart he was sure Ineda had survived, but he had had a traumatic separation from her in the past. Yet a prayer to Taranis surely would not go amiss this time.

The darkness of the night was well gone by the time they approached the settlement of Monymusk, the destination they had guessed would be the most natural for anyone fleeing from Tullos' settlement.

As soon as the dark outlines of the roundhouse rooftops were discernible, he began to make soft calls.

"Shelter. We seek shelter, Monymusk."

The guard posted by Monymusk intercepted them before long.

"Aye, indeed we do. We have a number of little ones and some older villagers from Tullos." The guard confirmed as they approached Monymusk's gates.

Ineda and Kaideigh just had to be among them. They had to be!

Monymusk's greeting was a tired one, woken from a light sleep. "You are the Garrigill warriors lately living with Tullos? I have heard tell of you."

Lorcan helped Gabrond down from the horse.

263

"We are," Brennus said. "We need the skills of a healer for my brother. He has needed tending long since."

Gabrond was helped down onto the low cot which Monymusk had just vacated as a woman entered the chief's dwelling. She was a woman well into her middle age and gruff. Brennus was not sure if it was her usual manner, or the perilous situation they all found themselves in as she shushed them away to bend down in front of Gabrond.

"I need more light!"

The one brand held aloft by Monymusk was quickly added to. Brennus grasped one of the torches from the entryway that was thrust into his hand, as did Lorcan. Fighting against exhaustion they held them high as the woman peeled away the rough binding around Gabrond's leg.

Rapid orders were given, and someone near Monymusk scurried off to do her bidding.

"It could be worse. The leg has already had severe wounding and is still attached. He will not lose it this time either."

The woman sounded so sure Brennus believed her.

Monymusk came closer, his voice less rough. "The women from Garrigill have been summoned."

Brennus felt his heart lurch. "Women? From Garrigill?" If so named, they could not be Ineda, but that meant that Fionnah and Nara were safe. Relief warred with jealousy. He loved his brothers' wives well enough, and wished them safe from Roman blades, but the woman he wanted to hear about was Ineda.

The door-hanging rustled as someone entered the roundhouse in a flurry. "Bran? By the grace of Rhianna! Are you here?"

He turned around as Ineda flew into his arms. For such a small woman, her crush was tight enough to almost topple him, his tiredness so profound. The fiery brand in his hand wavered above her hair till someone removed it from his grasp. He never wanted to let her go as he gathered her even closer, and rested his chin on her head for a few moments before he lost himself completely in her frantic kiss.

The people around were important, but none mattered to him as much as she did – save perhaps Kaideigh.

Fionnah's cries brought reality back. "Gabrond? How seriously wounded is he?" Her demands were made to Brennus and Lorcan, but it was Monymusk's healer who answered.

"He will recover, as he has done before. The wound is deep, but he will surely rise to limp again. It is the blood loss which sends him into such a stupor."

Brennus pushed Ineda a little away to see her eyes as best he could. She would not lie to him, but he needed to know about his precious daughter. "Kaideigh?"

The twinkle in her eyes told its own good story. "Our children are all well, due to the good care given by Creidne. She hurried them all out from the village of Tullos, and away from the Roman attack."

Lorcan cursed loudly enough to awaken the whole settlement. "How fares old Tullos?"

Fionnah's head-shakes and utter distress gave him answer, her voice a hushed whisper. "They torched the village and killed those who strayed into their path."

"Tullos dead?"

"Aye, and many children."

The old healer intervened. "This warrior needs sleep now." She had been busy cleaning and rebinding Gabrond's wound, and her work was done.

Lorcan stepped away from the cot and grasped Ineda's elbow. "Nara and the boys? Are they here?"

Ineda eyes filled with silent tears, her face showing deep distress. "We arrived so late, well after dusk. Nothing had been heard of them, when I inquired."

Lorcan paced around the small space. "They could be anywhere just now."

No one wanted to voice the worst possibility.

Brennus felt Ineda squeeze his hand as she reached to console Lorcan. "You arrived here still on a mount?"

It was a reasonable assumption to make. Lorcan's nod was brief.

265

"Think how long it will take the others to walk. If they had to run up through the forest at the foothills of Beinn na Ciche, they may have had to climb much more of the hill to evade the Roman infantry. They may still be somewhere in the forest."

Brennus knew that was very possible. "We came out of the forest on the north side and had to circle back around to reach here."

Monymusk had been silent and listening to the exchange. "There are other places they could be, if they have survived, but for now we must all rest. Come dawn it may be that we, too, will need to flee if Agricola comes demanding our allegiance."

"He will!" Brennus heard the panic in Ineda's cry, and knew it to be true.

AD 84 After Samhain – Ceann Druimin, Caledon Territory

Three days later, they were well into the mountain areas. They had followed the River Dheathain's meanders till it turned sharply south. Asking, always asking, for news of Nara and the other young ones. Of Nith and Esk, they had heard nothing either.

"We cannot go any further, Lorcan. There is little here to feed the local people, far less this influx of people who have arrived upon their hearths. It will be worse in the more remote mountain areas."

Brennus hoped they had evaded the *gladius* of Agricola. It would take a foolhardy leader of an army to undertake any confrontation in the inner Caledon regions, the highest glens too easy to be trapped in, if the terrain was unfamiliar. Rome had learned much of Britannia. He was not duped, though – the mountains of the Caledons were not impossible for Agricola to breach, yet neither were they an easy conquest. The terrain was so different from the high hills between the Brigantes and the Selgovae, which the Romans had easily marched over.

Now, well-surrounded by peak after peak, he was sure his fellow-Celts would have some respite from the flood of

Roman auxiliaries who still roved around the lands of Monymusk, according to new arrivals at Ceann Druimin. It seemed that their exit from Monymusk had been very timely.

"Aye! We will tighten our belts here as well as anywhere."

Lorcan's dispirited tones hurt him as much as the lack of news about Nara and her brood. Brennus deferred to his older brother only in an attempt to rouse Lorcan from his despair.

He had heard tales of many thousands of Celts who had fled the Roman legions at Beinn na Ciche: flocks of them who had escaped into the woods and then had gone back to their Caledon and Vacomagi homes. Those who were Taexali, and still resisted Rome, had not gone home. They were mainly the displaced ones that he had encountered during the long trek of the last days. People like the Balbithans, and those from Tullos, were just as homeless as his Brigante family.

On the fourth day of their settling at Ceann Druimin, four warriors limped their exhausted way into the settlement. One of the four was Nith; the others were warriors of Tullos. Brennus learned that Nith had not fared so well, yet it had been better than Esk, who had been killed on the battlefield.

Ineda flocked to him, to tend to his wounds. Extensive cuts to his arms, shoulders and chest had leaked much blood, though none were deep enough to kill. As she tended him, Nith related what he knew. His chest wounds were deep, but she knew some of the leaking from his eyes to be tears for his brother.

"We were a handful of rows back from Calgach when the carnyx sounded. The spears flew and we rushed forwards behind our war-chariots. Roman *pila* came at us, but we deflected them well with our broadswords and shields. We rejoiced in our success as we fended off the Roman javelins and sent them flying back. Those mail-clad auxiliaries were toppling in front of our eyes, but then we heard the rush of more Roman troops."

Brennus nodded. "Batavians and Tungrians. We saw them flock down the hill opposite us."

Nith continued, "Esk and I stayed with the warriors around Calgach, even when the battlefield became dusty and clouded.

Then the riderless horses and out-of-control chariots caused havoc amongst us. We had to avoid them as much as fight with our Roman enemy. After a long time of heavy combat, we heard the carnyx call. I did not want to believe we were running from the field. I heard my brother's shout from somewhere alongside."

Unable to speak anymore, Nith's head bowed down into his lap.

"He was urging you to flee?" Brennus' heart was heavy. The brothers had become his own family.

"Nay!" Nith found some strength in the tears that freely flowed. "The opposite. His shouts were to kill the Roman scum. The last I saw of him, he had rushed forward to meet the Batavians who had become the new Roman front line. I saw him fall, but I was fighting for my own life."

Brennus knew from personal experience it was too easy to assume a fallen one was really dead. "He could still live, Nith."

Head shakes denied, but Nith was too overcome to speak. Another of Tullos' warriors continued the tale. "We were all close by each other. We were forced up into the forest and later on, even further up towards the ruined hillfort on The Mither Tap. I am not sure what made our Roman pursuers halt, but when we got to the heather belt near the ancient fortifications, they turned back down into the trees. I believe they feared the ancient ones who might lie beneath the soil up there. We remained behind the old fortress walls and tended our wounds as best we could, and slept there till pre-dawn."

A different Tullos warrior finished. "Those of us who were able crept down to the field of battle, to remove our dead. The Roman scum had already lifted off their corpses – I am sure many fewer than ours. In the pre-dawn light, other Celts were doing the same as us, unchallenged by Roman presence." The man pointed to Nith. "We removed his brother."

Nith spoke as though entranced. "We found a chariot bed which still had wheels attached, and set Esk upon it. The warriors of Tullos found some of their fallen, and added them to it as well."

"We made haste to Tullos, but found the old chief already burning, off to the otherworld with others of my kinsfolk. We added our dead to the pyre."

"Esk will know you did what you could." Brennus was sure of that as he consoled Nith. A shoulder-clap was not possible, not with so many wounds, but the strength of his voice and firm hand-clasp declared his sympathy.

Nith looked at him, a question in his gaze. "Before coming here, we heard some people of Garrigill were at Meiklehaugh, but they were gone by the time we reached there. Was that you?"

Some hope flared in Brennus' breast. He knew they had passed close by the place just named, but he had not even rested there. It had to be Nara and the youngsters.

"Nay! We did not stop there, but Nara and our young warriors have not yet been located."

Lorcan got up and paced around.

"They have to be somewhere near!"

He halted Lorcan's agitation. "We will find them. We will set out again, as we have done these past days, and will search again."

The thought of trekking around was as exhausting as his tired body felt, but he would accompany Lorcan in the search. Gabrond was not fit for travel, but he was.

***

By the next day's end, the search had once again been fruitless. The only glimmer of hope was that two people had been seen in the area who claimed to have come from Garrigill.

A very bedraggled Nara, and Gabrond's daughter Enya, slumped their way into the settlement the following morning.

Ineda rushed out of the makeshift shelter when she heard the cries. "Nara has been found?"

"I am here." Nara's words muffled into Lorcan's chest.

Ineda could see his embrace was tight enough to snap her bones, so glad was he to have his woman safely returned to him.

There was no point in asking Nara any questions, not yet, since her lips were far too occupied in returning Lorcan's frantic kisses, tears dripping from both chins. It was hard to tell, but Ineda suspected many were Lorcan's.

She searched for any obvious wounds that Enya might have, but could see none. The poor girl was distracted. The cheery expression which normally wreathed her face was replaced with a hollow horror. Taking the girl by the arm, she urged her to sit down at the slow-burning fire. Ineda fretted that the girl was so sorely disturbed by a personal attack.

"Do you have hurts I cannot see, Enya?" She ensured her voice was calm.

No words came from Enya's lips – only soft head-shakes.

Ineda knew it was not the time to pry for a lot of information. The girl had seen too much of war, and had not yet got over the terror of it, though she had to ask some questions since Nara was now sobbing so deeply that intelligible answers would not come from her for a while. "Enya, do you have any idea where Beathan and Ruoridh are?"

More head-shakes, but this time the softest words were heard. Ineda was surprised when Enya snagged her gaze, the intense sadness that lurked there so heartbreaking. Enya inhaled deeply before the words whispered out. "Nara ensured she remained beside us till we had to flee uphill. Beathan and Ruoridh were right there along with us when we reached the tree line. I know they were, but then they fell back when a lone auxiliary sped through the trees to challenge us. Nara dragged me onwards through the fringes of the woods. We could hear the clashing of swords and expected the boys to follow. After skirting around the southern slope of the hillside, we stopped. There were only fleeing tribespeople, no Romans, but Beathan and Ruoridh did not come."

Ineda patted the girl's arm and cuddled her close. "You are doing well. Continue if you can. Or, take some time. We understand." She had seen that everyone around was listening intently, with the exception of Nara and Lorcan who had stepped a little way away.

Enya's lips trembled, and tears fell freely. "We had to move on with the others when a cry went up of approaching Romans. We ran and ran. Not knowing where we were, except that we were somewhere behind The Mither Tap. Our direction did not matter, since there were others fleeing alongside us who did know where to run. A Roman *contubernium* pursued us till we came to a place where we were able to gain help. The patrol was ambushed by our warriors. They hacked down those Roman auxiliaries so much so that even the crows would have had nothing left to feed on!"

Ineda realised it was the awful desecration of living bodies that had traumatised the girl, much worse in many ways than any single combat that Enya had faced. Gabrond and Fionnah had ensured that Enya had as much warrior training as her brother had. She was a competent warrior and had grown tall and strong, one good reason why Enya wielded her sword much better than Ineda ever could.

That said, the realities of battle also demanded different strengths. And those were of the spirit, as well as of the skilled body.

Ineda encouraged Enya to continue her heartrending tale.

During the ensuing days, she and Nara had sought out the two boys, but there had seemed to be no trace of them anywhere. Not alive, nor dead.

When Nara recovered sufficiently to talk, she added, "A few days after the battle, we were able to creep back to the area where we had last seen the boys. We had often to avoid the wide-ranging Roman patrols, but found neither of them. It was that circling back on The Mither Tap which took up so much of our time. We had to forage for food, and sleep under the skies but no-one we met had word of our kin."

Lorcan was vehement. "Then they must still live! They will return to us."

Ineda felt Brennus' arm sneak around her shoulders before he turned her in his arms. She looked up into the face she loved so well – even though only one eye could see her properly as he spoke.

"We must build anew. Permanence around here must be our future. Are you prepared to raise more family here with me, Ineda?"

There was no question about it. She fumbled into the neck of her dress and withdrew Meaghan's arm ring. Sliding it onto her small wrist, she wriggled it over the two good fingers on her Bran's right hand, binding them together. Nothing but death would part them now, this man whose loving brought such joy to her.

Her kiss said everything that even simple words could not convey to him.

***

The stories of the Garrigill clan continue in Book 4 of the Celtic Fervour Series **Agricola's Bane,** *where we learn more of the fates of those involved at the Battle of Beinn na Ciche, specifically Enya, Nith and Ruoridh. Other clan members also appear, as does General Gnaeus Iulius Agricola who is a main player.*

Gaelic used in After Whorl: Donning Double Cloaks

CeigeanRòmanach! Roman turds!

"Atha math dhut!" Good day to you.

Diùdhah! Scum

Athair! –father!

Marbhaich gun duine dhiubh a chaomhnadh!" Kill down to the last man!

Latin and Roman Army terms used in After Whorl: Donning Double Cloaks

A – agrimensor (engineer/land surveyor); ala mounted force [s] (approx 32 cavalry); auxiliary (soldier with no Roman status)

C – contubernium (group of 8); centurion (in charge of 80+men); century (80+ men); cohort (480+ soldiers)

G – gladius (sword)

I – IX (Ninth legion); II Adiutrix (new auxiliary legion given to Cerialis in Britannia); Intervallum (vacant ground behind fort walls set to the maximum distance within which a missile could land)

L – Legio (legion); legionary (soldier of Roman status); Legate (Commander of legion)

M – militis (level above tironis, 2nd from bottom)

P – pila [pl] pilum [s] (javelin/ spear); principia (central marshalling area in fort); Praefectus Castrorum (camp commandant 3rd in charge of legion); pugio[s] (dagger); pugiones [pl]

S – secutore (secretary/scribe); scribe (office assistant)

T – tribune (officer -one of 5 to a legion); tironis (raw recruit-served 6mths at the stage)

V – vexillationes (additional detachment/temporary task force), venator (hunter);

X – XX (Twentieth legion/ Agricola)

Dating terms:
Time mainly in moons before or after…
Imbolc – Feb 1st
Beltane – May1st
Lughnasadh – Aug 1st
Samhain – 31st Oct
Summer Solstice - 21st June
Winter Solstice - 21st December

Reader Appreciation of After Whorl: Donning Double Cloaks

"…the entire series is set firmly among the very best of early Romano British novels." Discovering Diamond Reviews.

"The author has painted a clear picture of the life of the early Celts under Roman domination - domination being an unfamiliar and bitter pill for them to swallow.

" …gave an insight into how people lived in the time of the Roman occupation of Britain. The book's characters were well-developed and I wanted to find out what happened to them as they journeyed through Britain."

"The third, and best so far, novel in the Celtic series. More of action in this book, but still makes the characters real and alive. The action shifts up to the Garioch area for the decisive battle at Bennachie and the sad aftermath (obviously from a Celtic rather than Roman perspective). I can't wait for the next episode in this fantastic series."

Historical Context

After Whorl: Donning Double Cloaks begins in AD 74, in Brigantia. By this date, the Roman Empire had systematically invaded, and was largely in control of, most of what is currently known as England, though exactly when the northernmost areas (Brigantia, Carvetii and Parisi territories) were totally subdued is still uncertain. Since no records exist with precise dates for incursions into the north, many aspects of what happened can only be estimated and are imprecise.

By AD 73/74, the new Governor of Britannia, Sextus Julius Frontinus, found that his main source of rebellion was in Wales, the Silures tribe being constantly troublesome. Records indicate Frontinus spent much of his tenure in constant confrontations with the tribes of the west. During his governorship, between AD 73/74 and AD77/78, some fort/ fortlet and watchtower building seems to have continued across Brigantia, indicating more areas coming under Roman control, or possibly needing firmer control. Current archaeological evidence also points to the renewing of timbers during this period across Brigantia, indicating that the installations involved had been built during the tenure of previous governors. It's now also thought that some Roman advances may have been made into southern Scotland during this time.

Major change came in AD 77/78 when General Gnaeus Iulius Agricola became Governor of Britannia. His first aggressive offensive was aimed at the tribes of the west (Silures and Ordovices) who were all but annihilated by Agricola's amassed legions. He was no stranger to Britannia, since much of his early career had been spent there – including time spent with the *Legio XX* under Cerialis' governorship. Agricola then set out on a series of campaigns to infiltrate, subdue and control the northernmost areas of Britannia during the next approximately seven years, as Governor of Britannia, and Commander of the armies of Rome stationed in Britannia.

Agricola swept up through Brigantia, and then systematically campaigned around southern and central Scotland during the following few summers. His movements are a little vague, but archaeological evidence points towards more Flavian wooden installations having been built in the southern and central Scotland areas at this time, and repairs made to existing older ones. By approximately AD 83, a series of Flavian Roman forts, fortlets and towers had been built to control the territories between modern day Perth and Stracathro to the north of Dundee. (Gask Ridge and the Glen Mouth installations)

According to the writing of Cornelius Tacitus, Agricola engaged in only one major confrontation with the northernmost Caledon and allied tribes in a battle whose name has come down to us through the centuries as *Mons Graupius*. The battle site for *Mons Graupius* has never been identified, though many possible locations have been suggested. The date is also imprecise, but most scholars lean towards it happening (if it actually did) in the autumn of AD 84. There is archaeological evidence for Agricolan temporary camps having been established from north of Stracathro all the way to the Moray Coast.

According to Tacitus, Agricola conquered 'Scotland', and then almost immediately let it go. Agricola was recalled to Rome in what is believed to be late AD 84, or early AD 85. He had been Governor of Britannia for almost twice as long as any previous governor, a reasonable reason for being recalled to Rome, yet he seems to have fallen foul of Emperor Domitian. Agricola did not take up any new high ranking position on his return, and was dead by AD 93, having retired to his family estates in Narbonensis. (Frejus, Southern France)

The story of *After Whorl: Donning Double Cloaks* spans from AD 74 – AD 84 and is loosely based on the campaigns of Agricola as he tramps his way all around Scotland. My Garrigill warriors, however, are one step ahead of him!

Author's Note

I've learned much more about Roman Scotland during the writing of this third book of my *Celtic Fervour Series,* and doubt I will ever tire of reading new material about the Roman infiltrations of Britannia. It's very exciting that there's still so much more for archaeologists to uncover, and its happening often as I write this. Each new excavation for a building project across the UK can mean possible new discoveries of our past. The dearth of hard written facts for my chosen era, in some ways, makes the study of this late first century AD (CE) so very attractive, because it means other factors, like archaeological interpretations, must be taken into consideration. And it's amazing how many varying interpretations there can be!

I've used many sources for research during the writing of this book but feel that writing a bibliography would be a mistake, because I would be bound to realise, too late, that I had left off a really important book, or a useful academic paper. As a 'hobby' historian, I'm delighted that the internet makes it so much easier to gain access to academic sources that don't appear in mainstream published books.

As before, in Books 1 and 2 of my *Celtic Fervour Series,* in Book 3 I've tried extremely hard to create believable people, in credible settings using knowledge gained through my research. I've loosely followed the campaign trails of General Agricola (as documented by Cornelius Tacitus) for movements of my Garrigill characters, and for those of my Roman tribune, Gaius Livanus Valerius.

I've continued to broadly name the people of the north Celts, and that decision has been made with great deliberation. 'Who Were the Celts?' is an ongoing question. Were the Late Iron Age tribes from across the whole of Britannia, culturally and ethnically similar to Late Iron Age tribes of Gaul, or Germania? I don't know, yet, but there is some evidence that some cultural tendencies of tribes in Gaul were broadly

v

similar to those of north-east Scotland. I've avoided arguments with authors who would rather I had named all of my indigenous Late Iron Age tribes of Scotland as Britons, in the same way that they name those tribes who dwelt in the southern areas of England. There are indications, and theories, that in late first century AD (CE) there was a common language, perhaps with minor regional variations, that was spoken and understood throughout the whole island, so I don't discount that the term Briton may also be accurate for my tribes.

And that brings me to a little language problem and credibility!

My use of a smattering of Scottish Gaelic words is an attempt to give the reader a sense of what was being heard, and spoken, by my Garrigill characters. However, after making that choice some years ago, I now realise I have created complications. The descendants of my Garrigill warriors (fictitious), who settled in north east Scotland, would, most likely, have been called Picts only a few centuries later. I'm aware that across the UK and Europe the current forms of Celtic languages come from two main derivations. The easiest way to explain is to name them P and Q forms. The current Scots Gaelic is, I believe, of the Q form and Welsh more of the P form. The Pictish language is thought to have been of the P derivation, but was supplanted by the Q form some hundreds of years later, after the invasion of the Scots to the west coast. If you've managed to follow that, please excuse that my inclusion in Book 3 is of the modern day (Q form). If I had known this about Celtic languages in 2011, I would have approached a Welsh speaker to give me some translations of my phrases which might have been more authentic for my characters!

There being no evidence of what the tribes of northern Britain called themselves, I've continued to use the tribal names that came down to us via the mapmaker Claudius Ptolemaeus, even though he was making his maps around fifty years after the events in this novel. These tribal names, and Latin names for locations of forts in Book 3, are intended to give the reader a sense of where my fictitious events occur.

The specific naming of characters has continued in this third book of my *Celtic Fervour Series*. I love searching for names that reflect a character trait, or something about their appearance. If the reader is interested in this aspect of my writing they can find more information on this on my blog. (https://nancyjardine.blogspot.com)

I really love writing about my Garrigill Warriors and hope you enjoy reading about them. The series continues in Book 4 *Agricola's Bane*, and yes, this time Agricola is one of my main characters.

You can buy the next books in the *Celtic Fervour Series* in ebook, or in paperback versions, from suppliers like Amazon (https://www.amazon.co.uk/Nancy-Jardine/e/B005IDBIYG/) and other websites across the internet. Or, buy paperback versions directly from the author, and locally at various venues across Aberdeenshire, Scotland – mainly at FOCUS Craft Fair Events.

Other novels by Nancy Jardine
Ancestral/ family tree based mystery/thrillers:
Monogamy Twist
Topaz Eyes
Romantic comedy Mystery
Take Me Now
Time Travel Historical Adventure
The Taexali Game –suitable for ages 10+ to adult.

Email: nan_jar@btinternet.com
Website: www.nancyjardineauthor.com
Blog: https://nancyjardine.blogspot.com

Ocelot Press

Thank you for reading this Ocelot Press book. If you enjoyed it, we'd greatly appreciate it if you could take a moment to write a short review on the website where you bought the book (e.g. Amazon), and/or on Goodreads, or recommend it to a friend. Sharing your thoughts helps other readers to choose good books, and authors to keep writing.

You might like to try books by other Ocelot Press authors. We cover a range of genres, with a focus on historical fiction (including historical mystery and paranormal), romance and fantasy. To find out more, please don't hesitate to connect with us on:

Email: ocelotpress@gmail.com
Twitter: @OcelotPress
Facebook: https://www.facebook.com/OcelotPress/

Other novels by Nancy Jardine

Ancestral/ family tree based mystery/thrillers:
Monogamy Twist
Topaz Eyes

Romantic comedy Mystery
Take Me Now

Time Travel Historical Adventure
The Taexali Game –suitable for ages 10+ to adult.

Email: nan_jar@btinternet.com
Website: www.nancyjardineauthor.com
Blog: https://nancyjardine.blogspot.com

The story of my Garrigill warriors continues in Book 4
Agricola's Bane. (The following excerpt is unedited)

Moran Dhuirn (Durno – temporary Roman Camp)

"On your feet!"

Only the last word was properly heard when the shrill command jolted Beathan out of a fragile sleep. Straight into the horror of his surroundings, he was unable to prevent the uncontrollable shivers that overwhelmed him. Squeezing his arms tighter to his chest, to hold his cloak in place, the yanking of the chain at each aching wrist told him well enough what the rest of the instructions that he had missed might mean.

The clutching fingers at his elbows could no longer keep in any of the mean heat when they were prised away in opposite directions, the length of chain tethering each man to the next only a short stretch. Warriors to either side of him uncurled their legs, and forced their protesting bodies to a standing position leaving him no option but to do likewise. Swivelling onto his knees, he looked around to work out what was amiss, since the Roman guards had left him, and his wretched companions, sitting on the freezing mud for the last long while, the first rays of a pinkish hue sent by the god Lugh having lightened the gloom some time ago.

"Hurry! Get up now." The commands issued came from someone out of uniform, maybe not even a soldier.

Beathan looked closely at the man, as he struggled from knees to standing, his legs stiff and awkward from the cold ground, his neighbour almost dragging him back down again when the chain on the other end pulled sideward. The person who strode past him and continued along the row looked just like his own kind. The tunic, cloak and braccae not much different from his father's, the whiskers at his top lip the mark of a tribesman.

Beathan bent his head, his drained question not really meant to be answered. "A native scout?"

His neighbour had good hearing. "Aye, I think so. Or, perhaps he is the other kind who pretends to be our friend." His words were soft: the snort at the end loud.

The swift return of the scout shut Beathan's lips tight, the man's threat truly menacing. Heavy brows glowered over malevolent dark eyes, which only twitched after a very long ogling of his neighbour. The man's fist curling around the handgrip of the long sword was not really necessary, since Beathan was already terrified.

"Not a sound from anyone."

Beathan gulped. The teeth were predatory as well when the scout paced along a few more captives.

"Do you hear?"

The line had already learned to only nod at such times. Beathan stared ahead biting down his fear when the scout returned to halt in front him, his intent look a long and penetrating one, before the man strode off again. He had only time to decide that perhaps the warrior was one of the infiltrators, rather than just a normal scout, when the next worry began.

The clanking of different metals and distant voices were drowned out by the incomprehensible growled malice spouting from the *centurion* who strode up towards him, his wooden rod whipping forward at every opportunity. Auxiliary soldiers under the *centurion's* command paced alongside, urging him and his fellow captives to stand free of the next tribesman, some of them unable to get to their feet without support.

For once, he almost wished his Uncle Brennus had not taught him about the ranks of the Roman army. Compelled to fulfil orders coming from a lowly soldier was bad enough, but the brown horsehair crest from ear to ear on the shining metal helmet that stopped in front of him meant centurion status, the glittering metal decorations adorning the man's armour an indication, to Beathan, that the soldier had been long in post in the Roman Army.

*